Eric Gardner

Copyright (c) 2016: INTREPID PUBLICATIONS
1st Print 2016

INTREPIDPUBLICATIONS38@GMAIL.COM
INTREPID PUBLICATIONS LLC.
P.O. Box 573
Glendale, MD 20769

ISBN- 13:978-1530893713
ISBN- 10:1530893712

Cover Design: Crystell Publications
Book Productions: Crystell Publications
We Help You Self Publish Your Book

Printed in the U.S.A.

1

Acknowledgements

First and foremost, I have to thank the **Almighty**, for nothing is possible without him. Thank you for blessing me with the gift of writing.

Many people curse God for placing them in different situations. I feel this is wrong on our part because I believe that God does not place us in any situation that we cannot handle. Had I never came to jail I might have never discovered that I had the ability to pick up a pen.

I would have never obtained my GED. Now I sit here 33 years old, the author of two novels. When I die, my books will last forever.

The last time that I did acknowledgments there was many people that felt like I left them out. It was not intentional. This is the biggest accomplishment of my life so you have to understand that I would have a lot of family and other very important people who help make my first novel *MIDNIGHT IN PARIS* the success that it was. Those are the people that I really want to thank.

Floyd Jackson
You're my heart slim. Without your leg's none of this is possible. Thank you for believing in me.

Mary Gardner
Thank you mommy. I call you mommy because no matter how old I get I am always going to be your baby boy. I love you mommy and thank you as well for believing in me. Your initial started all of this. Thank you for allowing me to make you proud. You are my Queen always. Love always, your baby boy Ricky.

Robyn Jackson
To my big sis, Robyn. I love you Bobby.
Thank you for being here for me in this drastic time of my life. You have always been there for me. Thank you for being my sister. In return, I will never desert you.

Janiah Jackson
To my niecey, the faith that you have in me is unwavering. Thank
you for believing in your uncle. I love you, Miss Thang!

Last but not least,

Crystal Carter of the
CRYSTELL PUBLICATIONS FAMILY
I'm still trying to find your wings, because you have to be an
angel. Much love Crystal. You taught me dame near all that I
know about the game. Thank you, Mrs. Lady.

Special Acknowledgements

"Goobs"

I never thought I would look up to a dude 10 years younger than
me. You're a special breed slim. I can't wait to see the man your
sone turns out to be. Never Change, Moe.
Become greater than you are.
The sky's the limit, Slim.

A Letter to an Angel

<u>Macisha,</u>

First, I would like to say that I love you more than words could ever express. Within my life, you were like a shining light in the corrupt state I once lived in when I was on the street. You gave me hope when all was lost. You made me want to strive to be a better person that you could look up to. As much as I tried to teach you, I was learning rom you in the same respect.

I left you when you were three years old and have been incarcerated now for 16 years. I only had 3 years of experience in being a parent. Once I was incarcerated, I was forced to be a parent through the phone and an occasional visit. Not an easy task, but I was up for the challenge. Although kids view their parents as superheroes, I was not. I was a man fighting to raise and understand his child from behind a wall. But I tried my best at all times to show you love and understanding. Yet even still I'm not perfect nor free of mistake.

My mistake was I tried to use your love for me as a weapon and gave you an ultimatum I shouldn't have and didn't mean. I wanted so bad for you to concede to my wishes that I didn't consider how you would feel being given such an ultimatum. I'm not perfect angel and regret it every day. I am so sorry and pray you could forgive me.

I've called you angel your entire life because I feel you were a gift from God, and still do. It's not easy being a parent but I will never stop striving to be the best parent I can be. I love you more than I love myself and would give my life for you in the blink of an eye. I'll continue to pray you'll forgive me and know that I will never take your love for granted ever again.

Always for you,
Daddy

THE KEY TO IT ALL

The answer reveals the biggest twist of the story.

With my eyes closed spinning unconscious thoughts, in a land where nothing is impossible - a time and place where if you die, you're still alive. Clocks don't exist and time isn't counted.   Dates are irrelevant. What am I?

Can you solve this riddle??

CHAPTER ONE 1984
OLIVIA

In some religions it is believed that every human's life is already written to his or her death. It's sad because if this is true, then some people's lives are documented to endure hardships that may get passed on from generation to generation. This was one of those times. My name is Olivia Clemons, and this is my story of a life filled with hardships.

I was born in Washington D.C. at Greater Southeast Hospital, on February 2, 1972. When most kids are born, they get held by their mothers. Well, that was them. That wasn't the case with me and my mother. My mother took one look at me and told the doctor to take me to the nursery. Sad reality for me, because some people *grow* to hate other people, I was hated from birth. When we left the hospital, we went to a house located on Park Rd. in Northwest Washington. In my eyes, this was the epitome of hell on earth.

Now, let me tell you about Ms. Rita. I would call her my mother, but you have to act the part to earn the title. So, I always called her Ms. Rita. Anyway, in Ms. Rita's eyes she felt she had more severe problems to worry about then taking care of a needy child. It seemed that those problems always revolved around her getting high. Ms. Rita was a true junkie, so if I couldn't get her high, then any hope I had at getting a hot meal was gone.

Next, we have the man that started it all. I call him Donny, because just like Ms. Rita he needed to carry out some sort of fatherly duties to earn the title. Donny's behavior was not even close to that of a father. His entire existence spoke no form of the word DADDY, or FATHER for that matter. Donny was a total disgrace to the male race. When someone would say, "Oh that's Rita and Donny's little girl," I was often ashamed. All I could think to myself was, *I just know they said that shit cause they have to be feeling sorry for me since those two are my parents.*

Like his wife, Donny too had a drug problem. His thing was heroin. He had been using drugs for so long that it took him at least an hour just to find a vein to shoot up in. Abscesses owned his body. His 285lbs frame was 75% covered with puss-filled sores. Donny looked so bad that even his wife wouldn't touch him, nor could he pay any prostitute any amount of money to perform any type of sexual acts. Donny did what he thought was the next best thing. He fulfilled all his sexual desires through ME! I was only twelve years old. Though home is supposed to be a safe haven, sadly, mine was my nightmare. The only place that I felt safe was at school.

I attended McFarland Junior High School. I loved school, but with so much negativity in my life, my heart was cold. I even thought about killing myself to stop all the mental pain I endured. People always talked about GOD this and GOD that. FUCK GOD! If there was a GOD, I wouldn't be going through this shit. GOD could kiss my ass.

Other than school there was only one other thing that kept me going. There was a person who actually held a spot in my heart; a boy named Derrick Brown. He was fourteen years old. Derrick lived in my building, and also attended the same school as I. I loved Derrick with all my heart and I could really say that he loved me the same. We were like paper and glue, and nothing could separate us.

Derrick was a bad boy who sold heroin for his Uncle Drew. He was the darkest boy I'd ever seen. His skin had an extremely dark pigmentation that complimented his black wavy hair. He had all the flyest clothes, and could have had a pick of any girl he wanted, but he chose ME. I mean, why wouldn't he? I mean, I was far from ugly with my creamy red complexion and pitch-black curly hair, not to mention my ice grey eyes that have made some grown men lick their lips.

But anyway, I loved being Derrick's girlfriend. It truly had its advantages. For example, I didn't have name brand clothes, and Derrick wasn't having that, so he took some money out of his stash, and we skipped school so he could take me shopping. He bought me Gucci, MCM, and a little Prada. Although those names weren't as big as they are today, I didn't care. I couldn't remember the last time I had a new anything. Once the shopping spree was over, I had one problem. I had to sneak the clothes into my house, because on sight Rita and Donny would have sold my shit before I even pulled it out of the bag. Luckily, when I came home, they were nowhere around. I leaned my back on my room door and breathed a big sigh of relief.

After hiding my things, I got on the phone to call the love of my life. Rita may have been a bad mother and a junkie, but she sold enough pussy and sexual favors to pay the bills. I guess she didn't sell enough to get me a hot meal, or some new clothes. The phone rang about six times, and I was getting impatient. Finally, someone answered.

"Hello," Derrick answered.

"What took you so long? The phone rang a lot," I whined, lying back on my sheetless bed to gaze around my room.

My room only held the bare necessities; a box spring and mattress a top each other, a dresser, and two dingy blankets.

"I was at the door trying to get in. I ran to the phone Kitten," Derrick replied.

Kitten was his nickname for me because of my eyes. Every time he said it to me, I fell in love all over again.

"Are you going to walk to school with me tomorrow?" I asked, hoping that he would say yes.

"Of course, I am. Did you get your bags in okay?" Derrick asked with a concerned voice.

"Yeah. And when I came in, there was no one here." *Thank God,* I thought to myself.

"Hey Kitten, can I tell you something and you not laugh at me?"

"Go ahead, I won't laugh.".

"I think that I love you," Derrick paused for my reaction.

"I love you too Derrick Brown." I laughed.

Then just when I thought that I was having the perfect day, the devil's voice sounded off.

"OLIVIA! WHERE YOU AT!" Yep, it was the Boogeyman of my life - *Donny.*

"Derrick, my dad is home. I'll call you back." I quickly hung up the phone truly scared for my life.

"Hold on Kitten! What's wrong?" Derrick asked, but since I was already hanging up the phone, the dial tone was the answer he got. There was no way that I was going to let Donny catch me talking on the phone with a boy. The last time that happened he acted like I was actually his wife who had been caught cheating. By the time I hung up the phone and turned around Donny was standing in my doorway shirtless with his belly protruding over a pair of dingy brown slacks.

"Who was you on the phone with Olivia?" Before I could even answer, he was rubbing my breast through my shirt.
"My, my friend from school. Please Donny, don't make me do it to you. Please don't." I always cried, hoping he would feel some type of compassion for me and not touch me anymore, but it never worked and I was always the victim.

"Come on Baby, it won't take long," Donny spoke with glossy eyes, and a wicked smile while slowly stroking himself through his slacks. Out of nowhere this fat motherfucker grabbed a hand full of my hair and shoved his long nasty white tongue down my throat. Suddenly, I could feel my lunch trying to ease up my esophagus.

"I saw you with that nappy headed nigga today. You giving him daddy's goods? Huh Olivia? You giving away daddy's kitty kat?"

You could see the fear that he instilled in me. I couldn't speak a word. Then this sick bastard with his nasty ass white tongue licked my ear lobe. Then he picked me up and tossed me on the bed. In one last attempt to keep my womanhood for that night, my voice came back.

"No Donny I swear. Please don't Donny, I swear that I didn't." Once again it was to no avail.
"I don't believe you. I guess I got to check for myself."

And that was it. My own father snatched my pants off as well as his slacks, quickly revealing his semi-hard abscess covered penis. I laid there as he mounted my small body. It was always the worst when he was high on heroin, because it would always be two hours before he would cum and stop pounding on me. I remember when I tried to tell Ms. Rita what was happing, but all she would say was 'Better you then me. I don't want that sick bastard to ever touch me.'
After hearing that, I ran to my room and cried into my

pillow 'til I fell asleep.

DERRICK

It's amazing how life can throw you some of the most wicked curve balls. The curve balls that I experienced always came when everything was going good. I remember the old saying, *with every good comes the bad*. That stuck with me like a cheap suit in the summertime. My name is Derrick Brown. I'll start off by telling you a little bit about myself. I was pretty much spoiled growing up. My mom was a paralegal for a law firm called Piscal and Palent. My dad joined the Army. And subsequently, he was stationed at an overseas military base. In Washington, it was just me, Moms, and my Uncle Drew. He was my father's brother, and basically my father figure.

Uncle Drew was into a little bit of everything - drugs, pimping and numbers, but his main income was loan sharking. Uncle Drew would loan shark everything from money, to bricks of raw heroin and cocaine. He was a go-getter and I wanted to be just like him, so I watched his every move.

I was only 14 but I considered myself a man whether my age said so or not. Unbeknownst to my mom, I was selling heroin 90 going north and was stacking my money. My connection was none other than my Uncle Drew. You see, Uncle Drew always had an ear to the streets, so when I jumped off the porch and started selling nickel bags of weed, it immediately got back to him. He refused to have me pushing for someone who didn't give a fuck about me. He also knew that he couldn't make me stop, so he did the next best thing - he put me on his team and taught me the ropes. I hadn't looked back since.

Uncle Drew didn't have any kids that he knew about, so with me being his only nephew, he treated me like his son. My dad left for the military when I was eight, so to me my Uncle Drew was my dad. It was a match made by blood and business.

And although I sold drugs, I still attended school every day. That's where I met Olivia. She was my heart, and because of the way she hung up the phone the night before, I had been on edge all night. I knew something wasn't right in her house. I knew that she didn't have much and her parents were junkies, but inside I felt like it was something that went deeper than that. The next morning when Olivia opened her door ready to go to school, I was right there. All business.

"Why didn't you call me back last night Kitten?" I was hoping by my tone that she knew I wanted the truth. Instead, she looked off towards the floor as if she was ashamed.

"I'm sorry Derrick, I fell asleep." I knew she was lying.

"Don't lie to me Kitten. Is your dad touching you?" I felt I had no choice but to ask her like that. If not, she might have just kept lying to me about it. Olivia was caught off guard by my statement. Once she comprehended what I said, she slumped her shoulders and cried.

"Come on, come with me, we're going to my house. We're not going to school." I knew it, that fat motherfucker gonna get his! I swear on my momma. I was heated just thinking about that dope fiend touching Olivia. Olivia was crying so hard that I was damn near pulling her to my house. Luckily, my mom had already gone to work.

"It's just me, and you here Olivia. Now are you going to tell me about your dad?" I stared into her eyes. As if on cue she started crying harder. I didn't rush her anymore, instead I placed my arm around her trying to be there for her as much as possible. After she cried for about five minutes, she finally began to speak.

"Derrick he makes me do it to him. His thing has so many sores on it. I cry and beg him not to, but he never listens. He saw me with you yesterday and swore that I did it to you. Derrick, I hate him so much." Olivia continued to cry while I held her close to my chest. I was truly hurt by Olivia's words. It hurt me so much, I felt like I had to do something about it.

"Are you sure that you hate him Kitten?" I pushed her chin up so she could look me in the eyes.

"Yeah, I'm more sure than anything in this world." Olivia replied, looking me dead in the eyes. I guess that's what gave me the strength to proceed with the thoughts that were running through my mind.

"Where is he right now?" I asked while Olivia's head was on my chest.

"He's still in the house sleeping. Derrick I don't want you to go over there." Olivia sat up and grabbed my arm.

"Wait right here. Give me your house keys." I held my hand out and Olivia complied.

I had a trick for this needle pushing motherfucker. He's already dying slowly from that needle. I'm just going to speed up the process. I went to the closet in my room and retrieved my snub nose 32 revolver. I planned to make that his last time ever touching Olivia, or anyone else for that matter.

I crept inside the house and quickly moved towards the back room. When I stepped inside the room there laid a naked sore covered mound of flesh atop the covers. The sight of him made my blood boil. I walked up to the side of the bed and took aim. I slowly cocked the hammer back and mustered up all the strength I could.

"This is for you Kitten."

"BOOM" "BOOM" "BOOM."

I shot that motherfucker three times in the head. When the bullets smacked his flesh, the impact caused blood to splash back on my shirt. I left that sick motherfucker lying in a pool of his own blood. When I walked through the door Olivia was still sitting right where I left her. I thought that once Olivia saw the blood on my shirt, she would start screaming but instead she ran and hugged me. I guess she finally was being shown that love that she never got at home. I kissed her forehead and wrapped my arms around her.

"I'll never leave you Kitten," I whispered in her ear. I meant every word too.

That day Mrs. Rita mourned for her husband, but the next day was just like any other day. She moved on with her life like Donny was never there. It was also the day Olivia and I engaged in our first sexual contact. I'd like girls since I was nine years old, but I'd never had sex. Olivia on the other hand had lost her virginity at the rough age of ten. Through the gruesome encounters she had with Donny, she knew enough to guide me along, so we managed. After that, we were truly inseparable. The only time I wasn't with her was when I was with my Uncle Drew.

Although Mrs. Rita didn't mourn long over Donny, she thought that her husband died behind his addiction, and she refused to suffer the same fate. Therefore, after that incident, she made up her mind that she would stop using drugs and get her life together.

CHAPTER TWO
OLIVIA

It had been a few weeks since Donny was murdered. Although I had no love for Mrs. Rita whatsoever, I was happy to see her get off drugs. She even stopped selling her body. She now worked as a U.S. mail clerk. It wasn't a lot of money, but she was clean, and I got a hot meal more often than before. As they say *with the good always comes the bad*. Mrs. Rita still showed me the utmost hatred for reasons that only she knew.

Through it all I still stayed focused. I didn't do any drugs and was a straight A student. I even still gave Mrs. Rita her respect. Beside my hatred for Rita, I was on top of the world. Thanks to Derrick the kids never laughed at my clothes anymore. You name it I had it, in fact, I was pretty much the best dressed at school.

I was 14 years old, and a full-blown Diva. My body was thicker, and my once 34b breast was now 36d. Even though I was a star now, I still remained loyal to Derrick. Just as before *the good brings the bad*, and my life was about to be turned upside down. My period was late

DERRICK

I can't believe this shit. Last night my mom was robbed and carjacked. Somehow she got in touch with my dad all the way in Germany. Since they were married, all it took was a signature and my mom and I would be on an all-expense paid plane ride to Germany to live on base with him. I was pissed. There was no way that I wanted to leave Olivia, and I knew she felt the same way.

The next morning, like usual, I was outside of her door when she opened it ready to go to school. When she came out and she saw me, she was all smiles.

"I like your outfit Puppydog." Olivia hugged me. Puppydog was her nickname she'd given me since I always called her Kitten.

"Thanks Kitten. I got something that I need to tell you." I spoke in a somber tone.

"What is it? Why are you looking like that, it can't be that bad." I could already hear the worry in her voice. I then took a deep breath and let it go.

"Kitten my dad's moving me and my mom to Germany to live on base with him." After I got it out, I looked at her to wait for hurricane Olivia. Yet, when I looked into her eyes, I could almost literally see her heart shatter.

"No, No! You can't leave me Derrick. I love you and you promised." I was too hurt. I always hated to see Olivia cry, and now was no different.

"We're leaving in two days Kitten. I tried everything I could to stay." I explained to somewhat calm her down, but Olivia wasn't trying to hear it at all.

"Tell her that you want to stay with your Uncle Drew. You can't leave." Olivia continued to pout and cry.

"I tried that already. My parents got the clamps on me."

"I hate you." Olivia's word cut like a razor blade. She then turned and ran inside her house, slamming the door in my face. I was so hurt that I even dropped a tear myself. I then tried to pray about it because as I saw it, I was hit and on my way to

17

Germany.

OLIVIA

I couldn't believe this. My life was over. I can't believe that he would do this to me. My heart was truly broken. Now I had to deal with Mrs. Rita.

"You little bitch, why you around here slamming doors?" Mrs. Rita yelled from the hallway in route to my room. "Rita you can kiss my ass right about now" was what I wanted to say, but instead, I just chose to ignore her and cry into my pillow. In seconds I saw that it wouldn't be that easy. "You hear me you little bitch?" she yelled again, now standing at my door.

I was heated and hurt and wasn't in the mood for her bullshit. The moment she put her hand on my shoulder trying to turn me over, I popped up and smacked the shit out of her. I then grabbed her hair and kneed her in the chest and head area. Once I felt satisfied, I threw her out of my room and locked the door.

"I'm tired of your shit Rita. Leave me the fuck alone!" I screamed at the closed door of my room.

Once I calmed down, I couldn't believe what I'd just done. I just fell onto my bed and cried away the void that Derrick was leaving in my life. I stayed in my room that whole day. The next morning surely didn't feel like the day before. I felt empty inside. I was sluggish even as I got ready for school. But like normal, when I opened my door, Derrick was right there. Just the sight of him made me want to cry. I tried to close the door, but his foot was a tad bit faster.

"Stop acting like that Kitten. I don't have a choice," Derrick implored with his foot to keep the door ajar.
"You promised me that you would never leave me," I cried.

Derrick scooped me up into his arms, giving me a bear hug. I tried to get away, but he held me tight. I loved him so much. I eventually melted in his arms, crying my love into his sweater.

"Come on Kitten I want you to come with me to my house." Derrick demanded.

At that point I would have followed him into the fires of hell. When we reached his house we walked straight to his room. He removed my jacket and kissed me softly. My panties were screaming for him. This time felt so real and different than any time before. This time I could actually feel us making love to one another. Every ounce of the word flowing freely between us. Derrick had my mind, heart, and my soul, and I didn't mind him having it one bit. After we made love, he held me close and tight. We both lay quietly without a word for a long while before he finally leaned down and kissed my forehead.

"I promise I'll find a way back Kitten. If it's the last thing that I do on this Earth. I promise I'll find a way back."

I truly believed that he would make good on his promise. It was hard for me to realize that Derrick was only 16 and still under complete control of his parents, but I eventually had to and did so. The day he left, he also promised that he'd write me as soon as he got there. I would impatiently wait for that day to come. Derrick and his mom hopped in the airport shuttle and that was it. Derrick was gone.

2 WEEKS LATER
OLIVIA

Once again I'm sitting here crying my eyes out over another broken promise, and a re-broken heart. It was all due to the fact that I had yet to receive a letter from Derrick. Because of this, I made sure that every day I woke up and looked into the mirror - I reminded myself of how much I hated him. Although that was a big issue with me, I soon learned that it was the least of my worries, or problems for that matter. I'd missed my period. I decided that I had to confront my suspicions head on, so I walked to People's Drug Store and stole a pregnancy test. It felt like every step I took on my way home was a step closer to me confronting myself with the truth.

When I arrived home to an empty house, I breathed a sigh of relief. I took a deep breath and headed to the bathroom to pee on a stick. At first I was so nervous that my bladder wouldn't move, so I turned on the sink and made it happen. Per the instructions on the box, I had to wait five minutes for the results to come back. Those five minutes proved to be the longest five minutes of my life. When the time was up, the stick showed one line, meaning I was indeed pregnant. I sat on the toilet and cried my eyes out. I was scared, pissed, and heartbroken all at once. With all my might I threw the test in the trash and ran to my room.

After I took a nap it hit me, I now had to tell Mrs. Rita without Derrick or anyone there to support me. In just 45 days my whole world was turned upside down. The bad part was that it just kept getting worse. It was now 6:00 A.M. in the morning. Like I'd been doing for the last few weeks, I jumped up and ran straight to the bathroom to see my dinner. With all the heaving and gagging, when I gained some of my composer I looked up and saw Rita fully dressed and standing at the door with the test in her hand.

"I dreamed of a fish three days ago! I knew your little hot ass was pregnant. You won't have to worry about it though. I'll beat that little motherfucker out of you."

Rita threw the test at me, hitting me in the face.

Because I was already on the floor kneeling at the toilet, Rita saw that she clearly had the advantage. That bitch ran up and kicked me straight in the stomach.

"You little hot ass bitch, you not bringing no baby into my house!" Rita yelled, continuing to slap and beat me around the bathroom.

Within a matter of minutes, I had sustained a black eye, broken nose, and a busted lip. The word pain was an understatement when it came to the actual pain I was going through. To be honest, in a way I wanted to lose the baby just out of my resentment for Derrick.

"And you better not leave this house till I get back." Rita slammed the door and was off to her doctor's appointment.

I just laid there on the cold bathroom floor fuming as I thought of the burden that Derrick left on me. Even though I didn't believe in God, I still prayed that day for a better life. I just hoped that he could hear me. With all the pain that I was going through, I could barely move. An hour after getting the hell beat out of me, I was finally able to gather enough strength to make it to my room. I cried, thinking that I'm only 14 years old, and I couldn't take this SHIT. Soon after, Rita had returned home with the worse news of her life. She'd just been diagnosed with the man-made deadly virus HIV. When she came in the house, her mind immediately refocused on me. She beat me up again, and I could do nothing but ball up in the fetal position and take everything she gave.

"You take that bastard baby, and get the fuck out of my house, you dumb hoe! If you come back, I swear I'll beat your ass again," Rita warned.

With that, I gathered up all of my strength and as fast as I could hauled ass to the front door. Just as I reached it, Rita slung the cordless phone, catching me in the back of my head. I kept it moving, trying to flee as far as possible from this earthly hell I once called home.

Hitting the entrance to the building, I ran directly into the mail man knocking all his mail out of his hand. I still kept on trucking. The mailman, frustrated, disregarded me and began to pick up his mail. Ironically, the first piece of mail that he picked up was addressed to none other than ME, Olivia Clemons, from none other than my former Puppydog, Derrick Brown.

EIGHT MONTHS LATER - OLIVA

I eventually ended up in a shelter for all girls called "Babies First Step." The program was for teenage girls who had no means to support themselves. The program helped me a lot. Finally the day arrived when I ended up giving birth to a beautiful baby girl weighing 9.1 lbs. I named her Paris Lynell Clemons. When the baby came and the doctors cleaned her, I smiled at my bundle of joy. Then I held her in my arms for the first time, and was completely disgusted. It was the literal essence of Donny.

Paris had my ice grey eyes and my black curly hair. She had my complexion, but she looked just like Donny, who was the center of my hatred. My hatred for Donny ran so deep that I didn't care if it meant treating Paris just as Rita treated me. Because every time I stared at my daughter, I would see Donny's face which made me despise Paris even more.

CHAPTER THREE
17 YEARS LATER "2003"

PARIS

Hi, my name is Paris Lynell Clemons. I'm 17 years old and in my last year at Benjamin Banneker High School. If my mother were a complimenting mom, she would say that I grew up to be quite a young lady, but compliments and encouraging words were nonexistent in my household. Besides the little-to-no relationship with my mom, the first 17 years of my life were pretty easy. I didn't experience any hardships that I could see. In fact, the only thing that really made me cry was my non-existing relationship with my mom.

I don't know why, but as far back as I can remember, Olivia has always acted as if she hated me. At times, it was as if she literally held back her tears when she looked at me. Although not having a loving mother was big to me, I was still determined to make something of myself. Long ago I had plans and goals through my dreams to be a Respiratory Therapist. I planned to make that happen by any means necessary. I remember when I tried to share my dreams with Olivia, but she clearly showed her lack of concern for anything that I wanted to be a part of. I even asked her for college money. I'll never forget her answer.

"Why don't you go sell that hot ass pussy of yours and pay for it your damn self. Don't ask me for shit." Those words hurt me to my core, but gave me the strength to succeed and I would do just that.

I strongly resented my mother for the way she treated me. I made a promise to myself that once I moved I would forget about her. She was so sorry that she wouldn't even tell me about my grandparents, or my dad. Constantly, I prayed and asked God to shed some light on my life, because I never did anything to Olivia but try to love her rotten ass.

About ten years ago my mom met a guy named Ron. Then about three years ago she married him. I hated him with a passion. Why? Well mainly because he wasn't my daddy, but mainly because while I was growing up, he would occasionally give me nasty looks. It made my skin crawl. I knew his glare was inappropriate, yet I was too young to realize it. To this day I hated the smell of him, and his entire presence disgusted me.

Coming up in school, I experienced a lot of jealousy from females. I think it was because of my natural beauty. And I only say that because I got into many fights from females hatin on me. I would always say that those girls were just insecure about themselves. There was one girl in particular though that thought she was the shit and that no one could touch her. On top of that, she could care less about how I looked. She saw me for the good person that I was. Her name was Kayla.

Kayla and I grew to be the best of friends and stuck together like paper and glue. Now we are both prospering adults, both in need of college money, so we applied for jobs at the BET Soundstage, which was located in northeast D.C. After a few days, they called both of us as potential employees and we were excited as hell.

"Girl, I can't believe they called us for an interview. I hope we see some rappers or something. God knows that I would love to wrap my lips around some Nelly or Jaheim," Kayla boldly spoke. That was Kayla though; she didn't bite her tongue for anybody.

"Kayla you are such a hoe." I laughed at Kayla being Kayla.

"By nature, but you Ms. Virgin need to get some dick before your pussy dries up and is useless. You gotta want more on your clit then some plastic and some AA batteries. I mean, come on Paris, there's nothing like getting stabbed by some flesh," Kayla reasoned in her usual untamed tongue as we rode the train to Rhode Island Station.

"If your hot ass gets stabbed anymore you're going to bleed to death," I laughed again.

"The only thing I'm going to bleed is someone's cum dripping out of my kitty kat." Kayla patted her pussy. Other patrons on the bus look on as if she were crazy.

"You are so nasty. So have you decided what college you're going to?" I asked, changing the subject before Kayla got real x-rated.

"I was thinking about either Spellman or Howard. They both have good medical programs." Kayla handed me a pamphlet from Howard University.

"Medical program?" I was shocked to hear that. "I thought you wanted to major in Science Tech?" I asked.

"Naw, I changed my mind. I'd rather be a doctor. It takes less time to get your Master's and pays the same as the other." I handed her the pamphlet back.

"Your hoe-ish ass probably wants to be a gynecologist so you can play with people's stuff. I know I'm not coming to you," I teased, and Kayla fed right in.

"You ain't know! While I'm at it, I might sex me up a couple of doctors on the examining table!"

"You're the biggest hoe I know Kayla." My girl didn't have any cut cards.

"And you're the biggest undercover hoe I know. So we're twins."

We both laughed at that. Kayla always knew how to keep the mood moving in a good direction. We continued to ride the train with Kayla being as boisterous as she always was. We would have to catch the D4 Ivy City bus to get to the job site. Kayla and I had a lot in common. We were both an only child, so we treated each other like sisters and were almost inseparable. Then in some other ways we were complete opposites. Kayla was a sex fiend who smoked weed and loved to go to clubs. I was a virgin, and my idea Saturday night consisted of studying even when I didn't have a test. Kayla was my girl though and I loved her no matter what.

Once we arrived at the job site, we were both nervous, but dressed to impress. I had on a white linen skirt by Donna Karen and a matching pair of Jimmy Choo sandals. Kayla wore some white slacks by Donna Karen and white Prada boots. Both of our outfits were compliments of one of Kayla's many admirers that she acquired on a daily basis. Kayla pimped men like she was a female Goldie. However, men from my point of view were not high on my things-to-do list. I was too focused on my future.

Upon entering the building, we gave our names to the receptionist who looked like she was a true hoodrat. Over the years I'd learned how to tell when someone didn't like me for whatever reason. I was now getting that vibe from the female. She eventually told us to have a seat in the waiting area, and that we would be called shortly. I could sense the envy coming from her, but I just brushed her off. I had something bigger on my plate. Kayla on the other hand, wasn't as nice about it.

"You need to show some respect and lose that attitude, Bitch!" Kayla fussed, rolling her neck as she pointed her finger. The young girl just rolled her eyes and answered the phone.

"Would you bring your ghetto ass on!" I stated, pulling Kayla towards the waiting area. I knew that if I didn't, Kayla was going to *Rocky* her ass.

"I can't stand them snotty ass bitches like her. She lucky you pulled me away. Bitch might have made the news," said Kayla, pulling out a box cutter. Kayla was definitely a hand full.

"Girl! Put that up before we lose the interview. You always trying to cut somebody. You ain't no doctor yet," I teased, trying to make her laugh to calm her down.

"If I'm not, and she keeps popping slick, I'm going to learn real quick on her."

I leaned back, *I don't know what I'm going to do with her* I thought to myself. At that point a BET representative stepped out and called Kayla's name first. She stayed in there for about thirty minutes. When she came out, I was called. Then when it was all said and done, we both received jobs as Administrative Assistants.

"I can't believe we got jobs paying this kind of money. I'll pay for college in no time. Forget my mother." I was elated. Ten dollars an hour wasn't much, but it was a lot toward my goal.

"Girl I'm going to miss you when you go to college," said Kayla so sincere.

"You know you're still gonna be my girl; even if we are 10,000 miles apart." I gave Kayla a big hug. Looking over her shoulder, I noticed the snotty receptionist with her nose curled up as if to say "EWW" I just shook my head. "She still hatin for no reason," I said as my words caused Kayla to turn around.

"BITCH!" Kayla blew her a kiss before we exited the building laughing her out. When we reached outside, we went over to the McDonald's next door and decided to grab a bite to eat. As usual we received envious looks from females in the restaurant. Just as we made it to the front of the line, my attention was drawn to the entrance in which a sexy ass brown skinned guy was walking in. Just the sight of him made my virgin panties wet. He was about 6'2 with a goatee and wrist that looked like it would melt in the summer. I was so gone that Kayla had to tap me to bring me back to reality.

"For someone to be a virgin, you sure look dick hungry right now." I couldn't believe Kayla had just said that out loud. I popped her on the forehead and hoped that he didn't hear what she'd said.

"May I take your order please?" The cashier asked with an impatient tone.

"I'll take a McChicken, McSalad, and an orange soda." I ordered my food, but this dude had me curious. I was mesmerized and tried everything in my power not to show it. If I did Kayla wouldn't let me hear the last of it.

"That will be $3.33," the cashier replied. Then my attempt failed as he made his presence known.

"Put your money up Babygirl. I got you."

I looked at the knot he was holding. This nigga was so sexy and even had a toothpick in his mouth. No man had ever had this effect on me before, so all this was new to me. This nigga had me blushing and some more shit.

Kayla then whispered in my ear.

"Super freak, super freak," she teased, singing a Rick James song.

"What's your name Reds?" *Damn his voice deep.*

"First off it's Paris and not Reds, so get it straight and try again." I knew I had to play my hand right. Plus, I refused to be acting like some groupie.

"Damn! I'm sorry I didn't mean to offend you. I like your name though. They call me Trey," he stated, extending his hand. So, I politely shook it.

"Well, it's nice to meet you Mr. Trey, and thanks for the food." I grabbed my food, Kayla's hand, and pulled her out of the store. Surprisingly, Trey didn't follow. Instead, he ordered a Big Mac and laughed at my scared ass. When we got outside

Kayla let me have it.

"Let me explain something to you Paris. You got four types of hoes. First, you got the PENIS HOE, she just want the dick anyway she can get it, and will say fuck her kids. Then you got the MONEY HOE. She don't really care about the dick, especially if a hundred dollar bill isn't hanging off of it. Next, there's the PREMEDITATING HOE- she'll have a nigga paying her car note, rent, and laced in all designer shit with money in her pockets at all times, and he's never even had a chance to smell her kitty kat. Last but not least, you have the DUMB HOE, she'll let an opportunity run right passed her. You Ms. Paris are the best dumb hoe I've ever seen. Ain't no way he was supposed to get out of your grasp. He was smelling all up your pussy, and you brushed him off. His wrist alone spoke a thousand words," Kayla philosophized, as they reached the bus stop.

"That could have been fake! You don't know if it was real." I tried to defend my actions, but Kayla saw right through me. To add more fuel to what Kayla was saying, there was a burgundy M5 BMW that pulled up with Trey in the driver seat, sporting a cocky ass smile.

Kayla then leaned over into my ear and whispered. "I told you it was real dumb hoe."

"Shut up Kayla." I hit her on the arm, and she laughed at how green I was. Trey stopped in front of us and let down his window.

"You gonna let me take ya'll home or ya'll gonna ride that raggedy ass bus?" Trey asked, hanging out his car window.

"My mother told me not to talk to strangers." I folded my arms across my chest.

"Very funny. You got your girl with you. I don't bite, plus I promise we'll go straight to your house, and I won't touch you at all." Trey held up two fingers as if to say scouts honor. But, I won't lie; Trey intimidated the hell out of me. I guess that was the reason I was telling myself to deny his ass.

"How you know that I want you to know where I live?"

"Look I'm not in to all of this begging shit. Here's my number, if you want to holla at me, my phone is available 24 hours a day." Trey handed me his number and sped off up the street.

Kayla and I both looked at his license plate that read GET-MNY. Then she looked at me.

"DUMB HOE."

****

I was really digging Trey to the fullest. It was just, that I was scared to get my heart broken or my hymen for the matter. I've always wanted to wait till I got married to lose my virginity. Every time I was feeling someone, I would brush them off and go into a shell. It wasn't the man that I was worried about, it was me, myself, and I, and I felt like my hormones were getting stronger by the day.

I got home about 1:30 in the morning, and Olivia was working late that night, so the only person home was me and Ron. That never sat well with me, because I knew Ron had hidden tendencies, which I could tell by the constant stares of lust he gave me. Being alone in the house with him was something that I'd never get used to. Even as a little girl I'd find myself scared and always uneasy around him. Hopefully, I'd be able to get straight to my room without having to run into him. That wouldn't be the case though, because as soon as I walked into the house, Ron was right in my face.

"Paris! Why you coming in the house so damn late?" Ron slurred. *No this fat motherfucker didn't just curse at me,* I thought to myself.

"First off, you ain't my father so you can keep that hostile shit to yourself."

SMACK! Ron slapped the hell out of me, knocking me to the floor. I was shocked at first, and then I smelled alcohol coming from his pores. It was on now, and I was pissed.

"Motherfuckers are you crazy? You wanna hit me? I got something for your ass." I tried to get up and run to the kitchen, but I was stopped in my tracks. He grabbed a handful of my hair and slammed me to the couch.

"You don't know how bad I want to take that little cherry of yours. Suck the blood right out of your tender little ass," Ron heavily slurred. Listening to that sick bastard and that sick shit coming out of his mouth caused me to kick him straight in the nuts. And due to the rage, I was feeling from him assaulting me, I grabbed a vase and broke it across his head. Just as it shattered, Olivia walked into the house.

"Paris, get off of him! What the fuck are you doing? Go to your room till I get there." Olivia yelled, trying to revive Ron. *Can you believe this shit? I almost get raped, and I get yelled at.* "Ron, are you okay Baby?" Olivia consoled her husband who was bleeding from the left eye.

"That little bitch tried to come on to me. When I told her no, she turned violent? I think she on drugs," Ron slurred the lies straight threw his teeth.

"Wait here. I've got something for her hot ass." Olivia burst through my room door.

"You little backstabbing bitch!" Olivia tried to overpower me, but in seconds I proved she was no match for me any longer. I slammed her by her hair and slapped her as hard as I could. I couldn't believe her.

"You come in here and try to jump on me when your husband just tried to rape me. Olivia, I hate your ass! I hate you with a passion!"

I grabbed my jacket and the cordless phone and ran to the bathroom. I called Kayla and told her that I was on my way downstairs. She welcomed me with open arms just like I knew she would. Within ten minutes after making that call, I packed an overnight bag and was ready to leave. When I walked out of my room, Olivia was in the kitchen. I didn't say one word to her, nor did I look her way. Once I got to the front door, Ron looked at me and smiled as he held an ice pack to his face.

"I'm going to get that little kitty kat next time. I promise."

"You're one sick motherfucker," I replied and slammed the door behind me.

****

Good thing Kayla lived in the same building that I did. I would have hated having to walk to her house in the middle of the night. When I got to the terrace level of the building, Kayla was already standing in her doorway waiting for me to get there. Soon as I reached Kayla, I broke down.

"Paris tell me what happened?" Kayla said as she examined my face. Kayla wrapped her arms around me and escorted me into the house. As we headed to Kayla's room, Ms. Alice, Kayla's mom was standing in the kitchen with a blue robe on and pink hair rollers.

"Baby are you and that crazy mother of yours at it again?" I said nothing, instead I just looked to the ground as if I were completely ashamed.

"You can stay here the night and go to school from here in the morning." Ms. Alice hugged me with that motherly embrace that seemed so foreign to me. I melted in her arms as if she was my mother and softly cried.

"Thank you, Ms. Alice," I broke our embrace.

"Not a problem Sweetheart. Just make sure that you make it to college and make something of yourself. Paris, you gotta make it out of this hell hole." I could hear the sincerity in her words, so I let those words help motivate me.

"I will Ms. Alice. If it's the last thing I do on this Earth - I will." I returned that same sincerity, and Kayla and I retreated to her room for the night.

Once we got in the room, I told her the story and she became upset about it.

"I can't believe he tried to rape you like that. You need a box cutter," Kayla insisted, holding hers up.

"I gotta get out of that house. The first chance I get I'm gone." I plopped down on Kayla's bed now actually gripping the box cutter.

"Did you call Trey yet? He could be your ticket out of that house." Kayla reasoned, thinking she was slick.

"No! And I don't plan on it. You think you got all the sense. I'm not like you, cars don't amaze me," I reasoned.

"Okay, well they amaze me. Give me the number and I'll put his money to good use. I need a new wardrobe." Kayla held her hand out.

"No problem the number is still in my purse," I pointed.

Kayla retrieved it and picked up her bedroom phone. She had no cut cards. I just sat back and smiled at her go get'em attitude.

"Girl what are you doing? It's almost two in the morning."

"Remember he said his phone was available 24 hours a day." Just as she finished her statement, someone picked up.

"Yeah?" It was him. I could hear that deep baritone voice through the phone, which immediately tingled my clit when I heard it.

"Hello, can I speak to Trey?" Kayla asked in a semi-seductive voice.

"This is him - who is this?" Trey replied

"This is Paris from earlier today." I jumped up and tried to snatch the phone, but it was too late. Kayla began to run around the bed as she continued to speak.

"So what do you have planned for tomorrow?" Trey asked, getting straight to the point.

"I got school tomorrow, but I get out at noon. I would love to see you." Kayla poured it on.

"Hold up, hold up. School? How old are you Paris?" Trey curiously asked.

"I'm 18. This is my last year at Banneker High School."

"Oh, so you're a baby then?"

"Maybe, but I'm more women than you think, I hope. I know your old ass not scared of me."

After I heard her say that, I tried once again to snatch the phone away, but to no avail.

"Where am I picking you up from?" Trey called Kayla's bluff. "I live in Twin Oaks Apartments on 14th and Randolph in Northwest." Kayla clearly spoke.

"I know where that is. What time is good?" Trey asked.

"You can pick me up from my job about 8:00P.M."

"And where's that?"

"I work at the BET sound stage next to the McDonald's that we met at."

"Aight I'll see you then. Oh and tell Paris that she didn't have to be scared to get on the phone, also tell her that I will be there so she can leave that scared shit at home." Trey revealed his hand.

"I'll tell her. Bye." Kayla hung up the phone.

"Kayla, I hate you. Why did you do that?" I fictitiously whined.

"Because you're my best friend and I refuse to let you be a dumb hoe. Now go to sleep. You have a big day tomorrow," Kayla replied as she eased back on her pillow and pulled up the covers.

"What did he say?" The deed was done now. I wanted to know what the hell got said.

"He's picking you up at 8:00 tomorrow night from work."

"Oh my God! What am I gonna wear?" My insides immediately gained butterflies. Kayla immediately sat up in her bed.

"I knew you liked him you undercover hoe," Kayla

34

pointed at me. I just blushed and then came clean.

"Okay maybe a little." I used my index finger and thumb for emphasis. We both laughed a little longer, and then fell asleep.

CHAPTER FOUR

PARIS

I couldn't sleep at all last night. Just thinking about going on a date with Trey had me so nervous. The thing was, I was really more nervous about myself and controlling my hormones than him. Let my body tell it, it was time for me to open the gates of heaven, but my mind was nowhere close to being on that level. I was in a battle for my cherry within.

Early in the morning I snuck into my house to take a shower and pick out something nice to wear for tonight. I wrapped my hair in a tight bun with a few straggling pieces falling over my face. When it came to my outfit, I kept it simple. I didn't want to entice him too much because I knew he'd surely try to entice me quite a bit. Because of that, I picked out a pair of sky-blue linen pants with a white halter top and a pair of white Prada boots I'd borrowed from Kayla. For myself and maybe just a little for Trey, I threw on a white thong just to be able to say as I looked into the mirror that I was a "Sexy Bitch." I was *killing them loudly* forget *softly*. But I will be honest, even though I may sound conceited, arrogant and cocky, I was actually really scared to death.

As far as my job, it went pretty good. The work wasn't

exhausting, and there wasn't a lot of drama going on - so to be honest, I was at peace the entire time. Now Kayla was a whole different story. That girl was trying to stick her nails in every suit and tie that came across her path. I just laughed. She will never change, I thought to myself.

Eight o'clock came around rather quickly, and I had butterflies flying all over my stomach. Once we got outside, it finally hit me.

"Where the hell was Kayla gonna be?" My question was answered when she walked straight passed Trey's BMW to a money green Navigator. I immediately stopped in my tracks. "KAAAAAYLAAAA!" I yelled after her. *This sneaky bitch thinks shes got all the sense*, I thought as she got out of the navigator and ran back to me to see what I wanted.

"What's wrong now Paris? Don't tell me you're getting cold feet. It ain't like you marrying the dude - just go and have fun," Kayla said. *Some real fucking words of encouragement*, I thought.

"You didn't say that you weren't going to be coming along with me," I whined, crossing my arms over my chest.

"This is why I didn't, because I knew your scary ass wouldn't go. Just go Paris for me please," Kayla begged. This bitch was really pouring it on.

"Okay, okay! If something happens to me, I swear I'll haunt your ass for the rest of your life. Here write his license plate number down," I dug in my purse for a pen.

"You one scary hoe, Paris." Kayla laughed then hugged and kissed me on the cheek. "Have fun," she reminded me, and then turned off to proceed with her date.

I looked at Trey and gave him the fakest smile that I could muster up. Taking a deep breath, I took the steps I needed to make this happen. As soon as I opened his car door, his scent hit me. *This nigga smelled good.*

"So where are we going tonight?" Trey asked as he put

his car in gear.

"I don't care as long as it's public, and you get me home before 12:30A.M. I don't know if I trust you yet," I said, hoping that wasn't too cold of a statement to make.

"Look, I'm not a rapist or no serial killer, so you don't have to be scared," Trey assured me.

"Who said that I was scared?" *Damn his smile's sexy, I* lusted.

"I'm not even going to answer that question," Trey laughed, seeing right through me.

That brought a smile to my face for the first time that night. He ended up taking me to the Baltimore Harbor where we ate dinner on a boat. Everything was so beautiful and relaxing. Lights were everywhere, especially bouncing off the water ripples. The scenery was so beautiful; I was finally able to relax around Trey.

"So where are your parents?" Trey asked, cutting his steak.

"I live with my mom. I never knew my dad. My mom never talks about him. All I know is that I look like him with my mom's features. She still harbors hate for him. I guess that might be part of the reason why she and I don't get along. I always have dreams about him though. I pray I get to meet him one day. What about you?" I looked up into his eyes.

"My mom and stepdad were murdered while I was a baby. I was told that it was done right in front of me, but I don't remember it. I just found out my real dad's name. I probably won't go look for him though. I think it would be too awkward and would open healed wounds. I'd rather leave that chapter of my life closed and unexplored. I live out in Congress Park. And just to get away from it all, I'm thinking about moving to Delaware or the Carolina's." Trey took a sip of his Moet.

"Do you work or are you just another drug dealer?" I boldly asked. No sense in biting my tongue. If this thing did work between us, I wanted the cards to be laid on the table right now. Besides, the Moet had me feeling good and free spirited like a motherfucker.

"I do what I gotta do to support myself. You call it drug dealing, I call it surviving. I've been doing for me since I was thirteen. So like it or leave it - it is what it is." Trey spoke with authority in that deep baritone voice and made my clit tingle.

"I choose to like it," I smiled bashfully as I rested my chin on my palm. "So how old are you?"

"Twenty-five, I'll be Twenty-six in May." Trey took another sip of his Moet. *Wow, just watching his Adam's apple move is turning me on. I think I better lay off the drink.*

"You're almost my grandfather's age. You have any kids?" I pushed for more information.

"You got jokes, huh? But, naw, no kids." *This nigga is too good to be true,* I thought smiling.

After dinner we walked along the water in Hains Point. I was in pure bliss and drunk as a skunk. Trey was a gentleman all night long. I really enjoyed myself. But all things must come to an end sometimes, someday, and ours was now. It was 2:30am. I was having so much fun that I completely disregarded my curfew. When we pulled up to my building, I looked at Trey and smiled.

"Thanks for tonight, Trey. I enjoyed every bit of it," I said, placing my hand atop his as the Moet had me feeling bold as hell.

"So I guess that means that I can see you again, I hope."

Trey interlocked his fingers into mine, slightly squeezing my palm. "Yeah, I'll call you as soon as I get in so you can have my number in your phone." *You can see me anytime you want to,* I thought to myself.

"What time do you get out of school? I'll be there to pick you up to take you to work." Trey took control.

"I get out at noon, but I don't have to be at work until 2:00 that afternoon," I replied.

"That's cool. So, I'll see you there," Trey smiled.

Now was the time that I dreaded so much. Trey leaned over and gave me the most intense and passionate kiss I'd ever experienced. His lips were so soft. He made things tingle inside my body that never tingled before. That one kiss made everything inside of me come alive. Before I knew it, we were roaming and searching each other bodies with aggression. Trey's touch was so intense that he brought me to the brink of ecstasy, and almost cause me to cum in my see-through white thongs. My mind was so gone that I had to fight to regain control of my hormones. Trey grabbed at my linen pants and that's when I knew if I didn't stop now, I wouldn't be able to.

" I can't do this Trey." I broke the embrace, catching my breath. "I'm sorry I led you on. Please don't be mad at me." I placed my hand on top of his, looking at him with pleading eyes. I prayed that I didn't just fuck up.
"I'm good Babygirl. It will happen when you're ready. Ain't no rush." Trey grabbed my chin and softly kissed me on the lips. With that, I was well on my way to falling and falling fast.
"Thank you Trey, I'll call you when I get in." I smiled and kissed him on the cheek before I stepped out of the car.

Once I got in the elevator I leaned against the wall and took a well needed breather. After coming off of cloud nine, I realized that it was now 3:00 o'clock in the morning. Man was I nervouse because I still had to make it in the house without waking anyone up. When I opened the door, I noticed all the house lights were off. I lightly closed the door, slipped off my heels and tip-toed to my room. I quietly closed the door and rested my back against it. I breathed a sigh of relief. *I made it*. I was safe.

****

PARIS

The next day I woke up full of energy. Like usual, I took a shower and got dressed. I knocked on Kayla's door, and as soon as it came open Kayla took me by the hand and pulled me to her room. I already knew what the urgency was.

"Girl if I didn't know any better, I'd say you got some dick last night, or is it just me?" Kayla put her hand on her hip.

"It's just you. If I didn't know better, I'd say you didn't get no dick last night, but I know better," I teased. I just knew Kayla got her rocks off last night.

"Bitch, stop playing and tell me the details." Kayla pinched me being overly anxious. "Ouch! Girl okay!" I replied, holding my arm.

"I'll tell you, but there is really nothing to tell. All he did was take me on a dinner boat in Baltimore, and then we walked along the water at Haines Point. That's it." I had to keep her in suspense. I couldn't tell her everything, but Kayla was no dummy and she knew I was holding back.

"What else Paris? You're not telling me the whole truth. You did fuck him didn't you?" Kayla assumed farther then she should have, hitting me again.

"Ouch." I laughed, as she pinched me. "Okay, okay I'll tell you. "Okay I didn't fuck him, but he had me about ready to."

"What else Paris?" Kayla held up her thumb and index finger threatening another pinch.

"Okay! I almost came on myself and never took my clothes off. There, you happy Matlock?" I sat on her bed.

"Yes. But how did it happen Hoe?" Kayla still pushed on.

"We were in a car, plus I had just met him. I'm not going to give my virginity up to someone I just met in a car." I couldn't believe Kayla. She was truly no holds bar.

"Bitch, stop faking. That strong motherfucker had your ass crawling the walls." Kayla laughed.

"Whatever Kayla. I don't get all giggly over every one-eyed monster that winks at me," I said because Kayla was really starting to get up under my skin.

"So are ya'll going to meet up again?" Kayla continued to pry.

"Yeah, he's picking me up after school today." I crossed my legs.

"Good. Now I can set me something up and get me a fix tonight." Kayla picked up her phone book.

"So what happened with you last night? Did you get some?" It was my turn to play Matlock.

"Girl that little dick motherfucker couldn't keep it in. It fell out on the first pump. For the first thirty minutes, I tried to ride him and that shit didn't work either. Eventually, I got tired and told pinky dick to take me home." Kayla held up her pinky.

"Kayla you are so wrong. You probably hurt his feelings." I honestly felt bad for him.

"Somebody needed to hurt his feelings. That's like bringing a knife to a gun fight. Then he tried to blame it on me, talking about - 'Oh your pussy's too wet.' Nigga please. Better get some Extenze." Kayla joked. I cracked up laughing. Kayla was a fool with her untamed tongue.

"Anyway, girl hurry up and get dressed I got a test today that I can't miss." I warned.

"Damn girl, it's the middle of your last year and you're still taking tests?" Kayla couldn't believe it, but I could. I took my schooling as serious as a heart attack.

"Yeah, I think that this one will be the last one." I replied. Then my thoughts shifted to Trey.

I couldn't believe that after just one date, I was so wide open. He even had me wondering if I should give him my virginity or not. Let my mind tell it, I was still planning to wait until I got married. I anticipated noon all day long. Soon as my last class let out, I rushed to the bathroom to reapply my makeup. While I was in the mirror, Kayla caught me red handed when she walked in.

"OHHHH look at Ms. Paris getting cute for her man." Kayla crossed her arms and leaned on the hand dryer.

"Stop it Kayla! He's not my man. We're only friends." I replied, trying my best to downplay it.

"Well since when do friends put hickies on friend's shoulder?" Kayla pointed.

"What! I didn't even know that was there." I turned to look in the mirror, trying to rub it off like it would actually go away.

"I wonder what else he was sucking on." Kayla laughed and answered her question for herself.

"Nothing, I got to go. I'll see you at work." I kissed Kayla on the cheek and ran out the bathroom.

"Whatever Hoe. Just do something that I would do."

"Never in a million years Nymphogirl," I yelled over my shoulder as I sped walked to the school exit.

Once outside, I immediately spotted Trey's BMW, and slowed my pace. I wasn't trying to look too anxious, although I truly was. Trey was all smiles when he saw me coming. It's funny because so was I. I opened the passenger door, and my breath was taken away when I saw twelve long stem roses sitting upright in the passenger seat.

"Oh my God! Trey these are so beautiful."

Trey was too much. My pussy stayed wet whenever I was around him. I'm going to have to start wearing a tampon to keep from messing up my thongs. Feeling comfortable I leaned over and gave Trey a kiss on the cheek.

"Did you give me that kiss because I bought you those roses or because you wanted to?" Trey asked, looking me in my eyes.

"Probably because you bought me the roses." I smiled,

teasing him just a little bit.

"In that case, I wonder what else I can pay for. Money ain't a thing." Trey licked his lips as he looked at my thighs.

"Not that, fast ass. But thank you for the roses. That was very sweet of you." I smelled the flowers again.

"I figured that you might like them. So are we going to dinner tonight?" Trey inquired as we pulled off into traffic.

"Sounds good to me. Where are we going?"

"How about Red Lobster out in Silver Springs." Trey suggested.

"Okay I'll get off work at 8:00P.M." I replied.

"Cool! I'll be there when you get off," Trey replied.

Before long, we were pulling up to my job and I could see Kayla walking towards the building. I reached over Trey to honk the horn, and then motioned for Kayla to come over to me. When Kayla walked back, I decided to officially introduce her to Trey.

"Kayla this is Trey; Trey this is my best-friend Kayla."

"So I guess this is who I need to be thanking for getting scaredy-cat here to see me then." Trey extended his hand through his car window.

"That would be me. Scary Smurf will run from her shadow if you let her," Kayla joked as she extended her hand as well.

"I will not." I tried to defend myself from Kayla's assessment.

"Anyway, Trey I got to go. I will see you tonight." I tried to step out of the car, but I was stopped.

"You ain't goin' nowhere till you give me some lip and tongue."

Trey got out of the car and approached me with lust in his eyes. Trey grabbed me by my wrist and explored my tongue with a vengeance. With that passionate kiss my pussy began to throb for a beating. When he pulled away, I pulled him back and gave him a peck on the lips. I guess you could call it marking my territory.

"I'll see you tonight." When I turned to walk off, Trey smacked me on the ass. All I could do was blush. Soon as Kayla and I were an ear shot out of Trey's view, Kayla couldn't wait to let me have it.

"Y'all two are going to be fucking before the year ends," Kayla predicted.

"We are not. I'm not having sex until I'm married." I turned my nose up playfully.

"Yeah, we'll see. That nigga got you wide open." Kayla would not let up.

"Whatever Kayla. I don't get strung out on men. They get strung out on me and never even smelled my kitty kat. Trey is no different." I lied with ease.

"You can tell that shit to someone else. That strong motherfucker's going to have you bent over before the year is out." Kayla stuck with her guns.

"Whatever Kayla." I tried my best not to look or sound gone, but Kayla was right. Trey did have me wide open. To be honest, if he kept doing the things that he was doing - my legs would be the same way. WIDE OPEN!

CHAPTER FIVE

MIDNIGHT

Free at last, Free at last, Thank GOD almighty I'm free at last. It had been thirteen long years since I was arrested. I got locked up when I was 20 years old. Once again, I too was a black man who fell victim to the system. Now I'm 31 years old and I was re-entering society. It had been seventeen years since I had been back in the Nation's Capital. The time was here, and I was now back.

I consider myself to be a hustler's hustler. You see, I got knocked for stealing German assault rifles from an overseas military base. I would smuggle between one hundred to two hundred of them on a daily basis, and I was making a killing. But like all criminally minded schemes, someone always turns state. I ended up having to plead guilty on three counts of distributing illegal firearms over restricted waters. That was a blessing because I had a 13-count indictment. I was also lucky that I didn't get time in a military brig. Instead, I was shipped back to the U.S. and given 16 years at Lewisburg Federal Penitentiary.

In the Feds I saw it all. From grown men getting raped to other inmates getting ice picks slammed in their neck. It seemed like every single day someone was getting stabbed or robbed. Something was always happening. While incarcerated though, I learned of a religion called Islam. I embraced it, and bore witness that there was only one God, and that Muhammad was the last prophet. This thing wasn't just a religion, it was a way of life that gave Muslim's morals and principles. But once I got released, I had one thing on my mind and that was money.

Thanks to my uncle, I walked out of the prison dressed to impress. Paper Denim jeans, Hugo sweater with a pair of soft bottoms. When I stepped out of the prison door, I saw my uncle leaned on his XJ4 Jaguar. As I made my approach, we hugged tight as if we were father and son. Uncle D was a known heroin pusher and had been doing it for the last 30 years.

"I see you're still doing it big Uncle D!" I pointed to the Jag.

"Same old shit nephew. It's good to have you home." Uncle D rubbed my shoulder.

"I ain't there yet, so let's go before these people change their mind," I laughed, walking around to the passenger side of the Jag.

As soon as I stepped in the street, a red Corvette speed balled passed us almost side swiping me. I was pissed at the driver's carelessness. I kept my cool and decided that I wouldn't press the issue. I was home and wouldn't let that dampen my mood.

"I hopped in the car and Uncle D pulled off. At the beginning of the ride, Uncle D was fairly quiet. I could tell he was in deep thought because he was sucking on his teeth out of habit. This was something he did when he felt bothered by something. Then he spoke directly about what was on his mind.

"So since you're home, what do you plan on doing for money? I got a spot for you in my organization if you want it? I'd love to have you with me Nephew," Uncle D briefly looked at me with serious unflinching eyes.

"I don't know yet. I'm playing everything by ear," I lied so I wouldn't seem too anxious. Besides, I haven't done anything with drugs since I was a kid.

"Boy, stop lying. I can see it in your eyes. I like that though. Never expose your true hand. That's how a lot of people ended up getting late by letting their left hand know what the right hand's doing. Never let anyone know your next move before you make it either," Uncle D preached. I laughed inside at how Uncle D saw right through me. Uncle D was doing about 110mph in 70mph zone. Before I could get the words out of my mouth, a state trooper pulled out the cut and began to accelerate behind us with lights flashing.

"Hey Unc, a Trooper just pulled on the road behind us. You might wanna slow down," I suggested.

"For what? I got two kits and two NOS tanks in this baby. Watch this." Uncle D flipped open the top of the gear shift and pressed a red button. The Jag jumped to 225 easy. I looked back, and the trooper turned his lights off and pulled over.

"You always got something up your sleeve Unc," I laughed. "Why wouldn't I? Oh yeah, I got a few gifts for you too. Sort of a welcome home, welcome to my organization type of thing."

Uncle D smiled at his own slyness. "You fuck with me, you're going to be a very rich man," Uncle D gave me a look of assurance that one would have no choice but to believe.

"You're truly determined to get me on your team ain't you?" One thing about my uncle, he was always persistent.

"Aight motherfucker, now come on so I can give you the first one." We pulled up to a beautiful two-story house on 16th street in northwest Washington. It looked like Uncle D was living the American dream of a black man.

"Damn Unc! This how you living huh?" I asked, looking up at the large house.

"Yeah something small. I just finished paying this thing off. It's all mines now. Come on, your gift over here." Uncle D waved me to follow him as he walked towards the garage. Uncle D removed a small remote from his pocket and automatically opened the door. Once it was open, there sat a brand new 2005 Cadillac DTS. Uncle D looked at me and tossed me the keys with a smile.

"I got it painted Candy Midnight black to match your complexion. Welcome home Nephew," Uncle D said in his regular old grungy voice.

"Uncle D you too much! I'm about to get back in a major way." I clinched the keys tight.

"Good. I hope it's safe to say, 'Welcome to the team.'" Uncle D extended his hand. At first I was reluctant and thought about it. Then I thought about myself owning a house and doing whatever I wanted. Then I realized that the only way this would happen was through my uncle, so I smiled and gave my Uncle D a firm handshake. It was show time.

****

PARIS

I was tired as hell from work today. At times it seemed like it would never end. The only thing that kept me motivated was the fact that I had plans with Trey tonight, and so Kayla also made some plans of her own. Kayla and I stepped off the elevator and noticed that her date was here early, and standing at the front desk, all in the face of the young ghetto girl. He was just a smiling, and so I just knew Kayla was about flip. Kayla walked up to her date, giving him a deep and passionate tongue kiss, and then looked at the girl.

"Don't get cut up Bitch." That caused the young receptionist to stand up.

"I ain't going to keep being too many more of your bitches. Bitch!" The young girl popped her neck.

"Bitch I'll ...." I stepped in and pulled Kayla away.

"Come on Kayla not here. This is our job." I tried to reason with her, but I already knew that Kayla was about to blow a fuse.

"No, Paris I'm tired of this bitch. I ain't never let nobody talk to me like I'm nothing. You got one more time to jump your ass out there and I'm going to bust your ass. Bitch!" As I pushed her out the door, Kayla was heated and yelling all kind of vulgar and obscene remarks at the girl.

"Why you keep tripping over that bitch?" I asked, getting fed up with the situation.

"Because she keeps provoking me. And why the hell was you up in her face Phil?" Kayla snapped at her date.

"Look, I just said hi to the girl. If I knew that it was going to be all this, I wouldn't have even spoken at all to her," Phil replied with his hands up and palms facing Kayla.

"And if I had known you were going to disrespect me by entertaining that bitch, I would have never called you. With that, you can take me home. I'm not going nowhere with you tonight." Damn Kayla dismissed Phil like a peon. I tried not to laugh.

"What! You getting mad at me for that?" Phil questioned. "Well fuck you then! Get home the best way you can," Phil stated, causing me to feel like I spoke to soon. Phil turned to walk off unaware of the fact that Kayla had picked up a brick.

Kayla launched the brick at Phil, catching him square in the back. Phil turned around with fire in his eyes. With the speed of lightning, he rushed Kayla, grabbing her by the neck. I tried to pull him off of her, but he was too strong. Suddenly, from out of nowhere, SMACK, SMACK. Trey smacked Phil twice with the butt of his nine and pulled him off of Kayla. He then picked Phil up and put him in the trunk of his own Acura. Trey jumped in the driver seat and pulled up to me and Kayla.

"Paris drive my car and sit in front of your building." Trey tossed me the keys and sped off.

****

MIDNIGHT

Figuring that it was time to get my money right, I called Uncle D and told him the time was now. I pulled up to his house and again my breath was taken away at the beauty of it. When I walked in I could hear Uncle D in the kitchen.

"Uncle D, where you at old man?" I yelled already knowing the answer.
"I'm in the kitchen. Hurry up and get in here, I got to tell you something."

Hearing the urgency in his voice, I put some pep in my step. I walked in the kitchen to Uncle D cooking some pancakes and eggs with a green apron on. The kitchen was immaculate with stainless pots hanging over a four-sided island grill, which was sitting in the middle of the floor. Black Onyx marble sat atop the counter. It was all fit for none other than a king.

"What's up Unc? I hope I got a plate," I joked.
"Sure, you can have a plate as long as you cook your own food," Uncle D laughed into a violent cough.
"See that's what happens when you be a smart ass." I laughed along with him as I grabbed a glass of orange juice from the refrigerator.
"But look Nephew, since you with me now, I need you to go pick up some money for me. There are a few people who've been owing me for quite some time now. I would have gotten it myself, but I'm old now Nephew. I don't have the fight in me like I used to. I never wanted to pay someone else to do it because with the type of money that's involved, they'd probably hit the road. You're home now, and I trust you with my life - so it's cash out time. Whatever you get you can have half." Uncle D put his hands on the table with a towel hanging over his

shoulder.

"Just give me the names and I'll get back with you." I took a sip of the orange juice.

"Good, they're right next to you and in case you need them, here's some twins for you. Uncle D pulled out twin Glock 17's and laid them on the table. "They're brand new and never been fired and here's two silencers for them as well. No noise, no unwanted attention. You follow me," Uncle D smiled.

"You got all the answers, don't you?" I returned the smile back at him.

"No, I'm just prepared, like you should be. It's four people on the list, at least two of them will give you some problems. Do what's necessary and not what's unnecessary. Most of all be careful." Uncle D made sure I heard that last part by grabbing my arm and looking me dead in my eyes.

"Come on Unc I'm Midnight-black as night and cold as ice. They shouldn't want any problems with me. Examples speak louder than words," I arrogantly replied.

"Good, just don't be the example. Oh - and here. If you need a hand, call this number. The guy's named is Trey. I want you to see what he's about. You know, see if he's about his work or not. I wanna see what kind of blood his heart pumps. He might be thoroughbred." Uncle D began cutting his pancakes up.

"I got you Unc. I'm about to get started on this right now." I stood up and finished the rest of my OJ.

"Be careful Nephew and don't forget to call the number." Uncle D reminded me.

"You call and tell them that." I smiled and tucked the twin Glocks on my waist. I then left the house to handle my business.

****

PARIS

By now, I was ultimately intrigued by Trey's whole thugged-out demeanor. I wanted to wait till I got married. But in reality, I knew that wouldn't happen with Trey playing his cards the way he was playing them. Kayla was right, Trey would probably have my cherry before the year was out. The bad thing was that it was already August. I was officially head over hills.

As instructed, Kayla and I were parked in the parking lot of my building waiting on Trey. It excited both of us the way Trey took charge. Now the only thing on our mind was did Trey kill him? We waited for about two hours before Trey finally showed up around 10:10 P.M. When Trey pulled up though, he wasn't in Phil's Acura. He was in a white Range Rover.

"Thanks for the ride Rocko, my car right over there." They pounded fists, and Trey got out.
"No problem Slim, just let me know when you re-up." That was Rocko. I learned that he was Trey's right-hand man. Trey told me that he took him in and got him on his game. Trey also told me that Rocko was the only male that he trusted.

"Aight Slim." Trey closed the door and turned to us. "Come on troublemakers," he yelled.
"Why you calling us troublemakers? You acting like we started the whole thing," Kayla said as if she were really innocent. I just looked at her like she couldn't be serious.
"Kayla you're the one who threw the brick and Paris you didn't stop her. That makes both of you troublemakers."
"Shut up Trey, niggas don't carry me like I'm nothing. I carry them!" Kayla popped her neck and rolled her eyes. She was seriously upset. I then decided to ask what's been bothering me the whole two hours.

"So what did you do with him Trey?" I wasn't even sure if I should ask this, especially in front of Kayla.

"Don't worry about it Paris, and Kayla take that niggas name out of your phone. Oh yeah, and Paris I got this for you today. "

Trey handed me a Nextel phone. I wasn't sure if I should be happy or what.

"So I take it this will be like a lease then right?" I held the phone with two fingers like it was contagious.

"If you want to call it that. The number is on the back. Now I can keep you in check easier. Y'all two troublemakers get in the car, we're going to Applebee's. I'm hungry." Trey instructed.

"Kayla don't turn down no food especially when it's free." Kayla hopped in first, and she was clearly overly excited.

"Three more years you're going to weigh 300lbs and have an inner tube around your waist," I laughed at my own joke.

"And you'll be ten years in your grave if you don't stop talking shit," Kayla playfully warned.

****

MIDNIGHT

I was riding along Georgia Ave. in my DTS with one of the Glocks sitting on my lap. I didn't have to, but I loved the adrenaline rush that it gave me, especially since I loved living on the edge. While driving, I was thinking of a good way to approach these names on the list. I knew the streets of D.C. housed some of the most ruthless criminals in the U.S. I also knew that I couldn't show any kind of weakness, or I would more than likely get taken for bad. Eventually, I came up with only one way and no choice; that was to approach things aggressively and nothing less.

First up on the list was a spot called, "The Turn Table". That was a spot located in northwest Washington on Georgia Ave. By the address, I figured this would be the hardest one. The spot was owned by Jamaicans who were known to be very ruthless and unforgiving. I parked with intentions of going in to see how many people were inside before I let it be known why I was there.

I tucked the Glock in my midsection and stepped inside with butterflies in my stomach. Immediately, I noticed about seven dreaded Jamaicans standing individually. I thought wisely and swallowed my pride concluding that seven was too many. After buying a drink and watching a little soccer, I was ready to go. As I stood to leave, a voice called out.

"Aye Junior, I need you to call Sylvia for me." I instinctively turned around to see a burly Jamaican in the corner with two beautiful women by his side. I was grateful for the man's outburst. Now I knew who my target was and what he looked like. I still saw that address as being a little too much to handle by myself, so I decided to call the number that Uncle D gave me.

"RING, RING, RING"
"Yeah," a deep voice answered.
"Name's Midnight, Uncle D told me to call you if I needed to." I had no time to waste, so I got straight to the point.
"Cool the name is Trey."

CHAPTER SIX

MIDNIGHT

After having a brief conversation with Trey, we decided to meet up at the Madness shop located on Georgia Ave. at 3:00 P.M. When I saw a burgundy MS pull up, I prayed that it wasn't Trey, but to my disappointment, it was. I cursed Uncle D for his match making skills. You see, the thing was I hated doing dirt with young dudes. Mainly because they were hot heads, and most of the time they acted before they thought. I preferred to deal with men my age because older guys were wiser with morals. Young guys today, when shit hit the fan, they fold under the slightest bit of pressure. I just did 13 years. If this dude showed the slightest bit of weakness, he was a dead man. I honked my horn and Trey came running over. It surprised me when he chose the backseat versus the front. He also carried a book bag causing me to wonder what was in it.

"What's up with this backseat thing?" I curiously asked, making eye contact with him over my shoulder.
"I never sit in the front because niggas get shot in the back," Trey arrogantly replied. I must say though that I did like his answer. It showed that he was at least a thinker; a quality that most young dudes lacked.
"What's up with the bookbag?" I wasted no time seeing exactly what this young dude was about.

"I thought you'd never ask." Trey unzipped his bag. "This a sawed-off Mac-90 with a seventy-five round clip guaranteed to knock flames out a nigga's ass."

Trey smiled as arrogantly as he could. The smile was slightly contagious because I smiled as well, thinking that this job might be easier than I thought. After thinking about it a little more I could remember hearing Uncle D's voice. *"Don't do nothing unnecessary."* With that, I decided to first try the subtle approach first. The change in plans was strictly because I valued my uncle's opinion on everything. I figured that he didn't last this long by making poor decisions.

We arrived back at the Turntable at around 3:00 P.M. I parked and we both had our guns set and ready to blast if need be. Trey had his book bag on both shoulders while I carried the Glocks on my waistline. I wore a long sleeve Dickie button up that I left open and untucked. That way concealing the Glocks would be of little effort and retrieving them would be of the same nature.

We stepped in the Turntable and were stabbed instantly by multiple slanted eyes through hazes of Marijuana smoke. Inside looked like early morning fog. I considered myself to be an old timer, so when their eyes locked on me, I immediately counted how many people there were and looked for a second exit. There were six Rastafarians, but only one exit and that was the one that we came in. Yep, one way in, one way out. Within seconds I located the target. The man who I'd come to know as Junior sat in the same spot he had been in during my earlier visit there this morning. He was also accompanied by the same females as well. As Trey and I approached him, both females stood and pulled 380. handguns from the small of their back.

"Hold up ladies, we come in peace." I held my palms up, facing them as a sign of no aggression."

"We don't take kindly to dem comin' round ear unannounced," Junior calmly spoke, pulling the girls guns down simultaneously.

"Look, we come in peace. We don't want no problems. My uncle sent me to collect an outstanding debt that you owe him." A smile crept across Junior's face.

"And what is that me! Junior, the baddest Jamaican Rastclad in D.C. owe dem?" Junior crossed his arms over his bare chest.

"According to him $65,000.00 dollars," I said, highly anticipating Junior's answer.

I was curious as to what he would say because his reply would let me know my next move. Trey played his position standing near attentively. By now all six Rasta's were paying very close attention to our conversation.

"Well den, tell pussy clad Uncle D I say fuck him, and I no pay him shit," Junior smiled again.

"Okay my man, I'll be sure to tell him that. Sorry to bother you." *I'm going to enjoy killing this cocky mother fucker,* I thought.

"No apology needed, but I appreciate it if you would leave me establishment," Junior pointed to the door and the girls laughed.

It took everything that I had not to at least attempt to peel Junior's shit back right there on the spot. I never let anyone talk to me like that in my life, even in jail. But with age comes wisdom. I knew better at this point than to show any sign of aggressiveness, so I tucked my tail and let him think I was cold bitch. I looked at the six men around us and bowed out gracefully. *Until we meet again,* I thought to myself.

Since that day, Trey and I both watched Junior's every move for about two weeks. As far as the other names on the list, all were on hold until Junior was stinking. Trey and I both realized that Junior was almost untouchable while he was inside the Turntable. So I did the next best thing and that was to sit on him and wait for him to forget all about me. Eventually, he did.

Junior traveled to many houses on a daily basis. It wasn't until about four days ago that I finally figured out which house was his. I was tired of laying on Junior and was ready to cancel his ass and move to the next address.

It was 11:30 P.M. on a Friday night. Trey and I were headed out to Georgetown. This section of D.C. held the more expensive houses. If you had money than most likely you'd live out there. The residents in the area included people like city politicians, political big wigs, and even a lot of pro athletes from the Washington Redskins, Capitals, Wizards, and Nationals.

We parked half a block away and walked the rest. Trey still carried the book bag with the Mac 90 in it. My Glocks were still on my waistline. Once we were upon the house, Trey scanned the windows and doors for trip mechanisms for the house alarm. It was just our luck that we found the back door that allowed us to breach the house with little effort.

"Watch the front while I search the house." I knew it might be a while before Junior arrived, so I figured I'd search the house to see what our friend was holding. I walked up the circular staircase with one of my Glocks leading the way. Reaching the top, I came to a door with two pad locks on it.

"No noise, no unwanted attention." I remembered Uncle D words, so I screwed on one of the silencers so I could shoot the locks off. I took a step back into a firing stance and took aim.

"TWIP, TWIP, TWIP, TWIP," four shots and the lock fell to the floor. After hearing the shots, Trey ran halfway up the stairs with his MAC 90 leading the way.

"What the fuck is you doing?" Trey asked me halfway

out of breath.

"I had to shoot some locks off. Go back and watch the door. I'll be done in a minute." Trey gritted his teeth, but complied. It was in his best interest that he complied with whatever I told him or he just might not make it out of the house. I stepped inside the room and was amazed at the sight of 75 exotic purple haze plants. All I could think was *"Jackpot"*. This nigga must be crazy having some shit like this in his house, but it was, and he did, and I was here to relieve him of it.

I continued the search, and before long I was upon what looked like the master bedroom. The room was by far the most elegant design I'd ever seen. There was a fish tank built into the wall that held about fifteen exotic fish and a Sony HD Plasma flat screen that was built into the bed. On the bed laid a comforter made out of chinchilla fur. All around the room sat strategically placed speakers, giving the room a theater sound. I walked to the closet with my mouth dropping to the floor at the sight of an 8 ft safe taking up the entire closet. To top it off, it was open. Before I could do anything my thought were drowned out by the sound of Trey's voice coming from downstairs.

"Aye Midnight they're here, get down here," Trey yelled, placing the strap of the Mac-90 over his shoulder. I whipped out my other Glock and placed the silencer on it as well. I hit the bottom of the steps ready for payment of my uncle's debt.

"Man, up nigga. It's crunch time." I looked over at Trey. We both strategically took up position on both sides of the door. Just as Junior walked through the door *smack, smack, smack, smack.* Junior and his two counterparts were smacked, dazed and temporarily neutralized by guns being put to their heads. The girls were quickly relieved of their guns. Suddenly, I kneeled down and aggressively grabbed Junior by the dreds.

"Remember me Rude Boy? You should have just paid the money. *Smack, smack.* I backhanded him twice, showing him the utmost disrespect for the lack of respect he showed me in the Turntable. "Give me the Mac and tie his ass up," I ordered.

Trey hesitated at first, but then complied. I could tell that he wasn't a fan of taking orders. To be honest I hoped he gave me a reason to kill him. Within fifteen minutes, the girls were tied up and crying their eyes out. Junior was being extremely tight lipped so I figured it would be my job to fix that. *WACK!* I smacked him again with the pistol. This time he almost went out.

"Wake your bitch ass up," I ordered, digging the silencer in his eye.

"Fuck you Batiy, me no tell you shit! The safe locked and built with a foot of Titanium steel. You never get in." Junior started laughing, thinking he was one step ahead of us. He was wrong. They say weed kills your short-term memory. Junior was a prime example.

"That's where you're wrong Coco bread. You left it open." With that, Junior was no longer smiling. "That means that you're no longer needed here." I walked around that back of Junior's chair and used my knee to support it, while I grabbed a handful of his dreads. With more then a slight tug, I pulled - forcing his chin to the ceiling. "Tell the devil you owed a bill and had to pay taxes, now open up."

With his chin to the sky and all the strength that I needed, I jammed the silenced Glock 17 down his throat to the trigger. Junior violently choked on every inch of the handgun.

"You should have just said *ahhh* fuck boy."

TWIP, TWIP, TWIP. I squeezed three shots down his throat. To my amazement either one or all exited through the solar plexus of his chest. His body instantly fell limp and gave its last twitch. I removed my gun from his mouth and used his shirt to wipe off all the blood and mucus. I looked over at Trey and slightly wondered why he hadn't killed the females, so I took the Glock by the silencer and handed him the handle.

"Is there a problem young boy? I'd like to get out of here as soon as possible." I nodded for him to take the gun from my hand and handle his business. If not, he'd see Junior again real fast.

"Naw ain't no problem at all."

Trey reached on his hip and retrieved an army hunting knife. With keen aggression, Trey followed Midnight's lead and used his knee to support the chair and pulled the first girl's hair to point her chin to the sky. On sight of the massive hunting knife the young girl tried to scream, but because of Trey that scream never got the chance to be heard. Trey slammed the knife deep within her throat, ripping it out. Finishing the job, he then slammed the knife dead in the center of her chest down to the hilt.

"Night, night bitch!" Trey then moved on and committed the same actions on the second female. I give credit when it's due, and I must say that I was truly impressed.

"Bravo, Young boy, Bravo. You didn't hesitate. I like that. Let's go to the kitchen and look for some trash bags. We got a lot of shit to bag upstairs."

"In this line of work I was taught that hesitating get you late." Trey replied.

He didn't understand how true his statement was, because if he would have hesitated, he'd be laying right next to Junior and those two bitches. Trey and I found a box of trash bags and headed upstairs. The task didn't take too long. Once we counted up everything, we had 15 bricks of cocaine, 75 purple haze plants of Marijuana, and $650,000 in cash. I gave

Trey $200,000, 50 plants, and five bricks. I think he got more than he expected. I'm glad he was satisfied. Now my focus is on number two on the list, which would take place tomorrow.

****

MIDNIGHT

After the move last night, I decided to call it quits as did Trey. I called Uncle D to let him know that I would be by his place in the morning with the first payment in full. I had to make sure that I called because he was never up before 9:00 A.M. When I gave him the news in detail, he was happy to hear it.

After a night like last I was feeling good. There was a cool breeze out, so I threw on some Ferragamo slacks with a white long sleeve t-shirt. I had a pair of Hugo shades, so I through them on as well. Once I got close to the house, I called and told him to meet me in the garage. When I pulled up, he was already there closing the door behind me. I popped the trunk and hopped out all smiles.

"One down, three to go," I stated as Uncle D searched through the trash bags.

"God damn Nephew, you hit the jackpot, didn't you?" Uncle D spoke with an unlit cigar in his mouth.

"Yeah Unc, that motherfucker was loaded. I'll probably hit the next one by tomorrow." I said with a smile.

"Cool. Take your half and do what you want with the bricks." Uncle D removed the cigar from his mouth.

"Aight I hope the rest of them caked up like he was," I said, thinking of the future.

"They should all be like that and maybe more. That $200,000 should put you all the way up on your feet," Uncle D spoke in his usual grungy old voice.

"Hell yeah, I'm about to get all the way on point. Ain't nothing going to hold me back now."

"All I have to say is keep your head Nephew and don't get blinded by the money. Stick to your game plan," Uncle D sincerely advised.

"It's only right." I replied once again taking heed to my uncle's wisdom.

"Good, now what's up with Trey? Did you call him?" I could hear the enthusiasm in his voice.

"Yeah, at first I seriously thought I was gonna have to leave his ass stinking, but then from out of nowhere he put that work in Unc. I give credit when it's due - and I can honestly say he's a prize piece," I said honestly.

"Good, good." I noticed that Uncle D instantly fell into a deep thought. Like usual he was sucking on his teeth.

****

MIDNIGHT

I would have started on number two today, but I needed to go back around my old neighborhood to see if I could find someone that meant the world to me, and possibly, still did. I knew that it was a long shot, but I wouldn't sleep right without at least trying to see if she was still there.

I pulled up on Park Rd. and when I saw a police cruiser with its lights flashing directly ahead of me I remembered the trash bags in my trunk. I almost turned around until I saw an ambulance and realized that there was some type of emergency in the same building that I was going to. I parked my DTS at the end of the block and walked the rest of the way. As I walked up the steps, I was forced to the side by the stretcher coming out. As it came out I recognized its occupant as someone that I truly and honestly hated with every ounce of

Eric Gardner

Midnight in Paris

blood in me as a child. I saw an elderly woman that looked oddly familiar standing on the side crying, so I approached her.

"Excuse me Ma'am, but where's that woman's next of kin or family?" I asked, pointing at the stretcher.
"I'm sorry baby but that woman's family left her a long time ago. That woman has been sick along time too. It's amazing she lived this long. She truly had a rough life. I'm glad to finally see her laid to rest." The elderly woman took a napkin and dried her face.
"Thank you Ma'am I appreciate your help." We shook hands and I descended the steps.
"No problem baby. You be safe in them streets."
"I will ma'am. You have a nice day," I replied with a wave. I thought to myself that old Miss Miles had aged well. She didn't even recognize me. I was crushed because the only woman that I'd ever loved was unable to be found. With that I did the only thing that I could do. I prayed to God and asked Him to bring her back into my life. Hopefully He would hear my pleas. I hopped back in my Caddy and sped off into a world of my own. Eventually, my mind got back on track and that was a bad thing for number two on the list.

****

OLIVIA

I had just gotten in from work and was dead tired. As soon as I took my shoes off and sunk into my couch, there was a knock at the door. I didn't feel like moving at all. My feet were killing me, so I did the next best thing, I called Ron.

"Ron can you get the door please," I yelled down the hall with my feet propped up.
"Woman you got to be crazy. You in the living room. You get it." Ron's grungy voice yelled back from the back room.

"You ain't shit - you fat motherfucker!" I yelled. "Get on my nerves," I mumbled as I reluctantly got up and answered the door without seeing who it was. When I opened it, I saw a face that I hadn't seen in years.

"Ms. Miles is that you?" I was shocked and looking for confirmation.

"Yes Baby and look at you. You've grown so much and you're so beautiful. How old is your daughter now?" Ms. Miles asked. I couldn't believe it, after all these years she remembered Paris and I.

"Oh she's 17 and grown as ever. Come and tell me why I owe you the pleasure of this visit. I know you're not just in the neighborhood," I stepped to the side giving her room to come in.

Ms. Miles took a seat along with a deep breath. I just knew this was something about Ms. Rita.

"Well Baby, I came to talk with you about your mother." Ms. Miles placed her soft and fragile hand atop of mine as I took a seat next to her.

"What about her? She doesn't want nothing to do with me or my child, so whatever it is, I could care less." I meant every word of it too.

"Baby your mother passed away this morning. That HIV she contracted years ago finally progressed into AIDS, and took her life. You may have every right to be upset with her Olivia, but she still was your mother. She brought you into this world."

"Not by choice." Ms. Miles tried to reason with me and I understood that but my hatred ran deep. "How did you find out where I live?" I asked. "Ms. Rita didn't even know that."

"Oh yes she did Baby. You see, your mom gave me a set of keys to keep just in case she lost hers. After they took her body this morning, I went over to find your address and phone number. Believe it or not and for what it's worth, your mom loved you very much and regretted letting you leave every day after you left. She'd used drugs for so long that it must have tainted her decision-making abilities even when she got clean," Ms. Miles continued to try to convince me.

"What's done is done. Don't take offense Ms. Miles, but if my mother never came looking for me when she was alive, I'm damn sure not going to shed a tear because she's dead. Secondly, she's done too much wrong for me to take your word on how you 'SAY' she felt about me," I replied, hoping I didn't hurt Ms. Miles feelings.

"No Offense taken, but if you don't believe me then maybe you'll feel differently after you read these."

Ms. Miles reached into her purse and retrieved an old diary with some old mail sticking out. Upon reading the return addresses, I saw that they were all from Derrick Brown in Germany as early as the second day after he left. Now I began to cry at the thought of Ms. Rita withholding Derrick's letters. It not only affected me, but Paris as well because now I knew it was Ms. Rita's fault that Paris grew up without her biological father figure.

While I cried, Ms. Miles consoled me by wrapping her arms around me. As she did, I began reading passages in the diary about how much Ms. Rita loved and missed me. That emotion was the complete opposite of how I felt about her at that point. Ms. Rita had yet again found a way to break my heart. Mentally I was scarred with a wound that only one person could heal, and that was my Puppydog, Derrick Brown. Ms. Miles walked towards the door and turned around.

"Oh and Olivia before I forget; this morning a man was asking where Ms. Rita's family or next of kin was. He looked very familiar. I don't know if it was Derrick or not, but his skin was dark as night just like his." I couldn't believe what I'd just heard.

"Was Derrick back?" I questioned. I could do nothing

but cry as I watched Ms. Miles exit my apartment.

CHAPTER SEVEN

MIDNIGHT

Again, I was extremely happy with the way things turned out with Junior. Although I had never killed as an adult, it still didn't bother me as it did with so many others. How I saw it, it was either kill or be killed. If it came down to me surviving and someone dying, then that someone was going to be stinking.

As far as Trey went, I enjoyed working with that young boy. It was as if we had some type of connection. Trey was a thinker and a person who would cease any bullshit before it happened. As for the list, I was on number two and hoped that I would be able to handle it by myself. The fewer people involved, meant more to split between me and my uncle.

Number two on the list was a restaurant called, "*The Southern Diner*" located on Georgia Ave. The owner of the place was a guy named Magny. Magny was a 65-year-old A-Rab that was fronted some money by Uncle D when Magny came home from River's Correctional Institution.

Before getting knocked, he was silently running the entire southwest with the best dope D.C. had seen in a while.

Its name was Black Gangster. One run-in with the DEA and he was a done deal. Magny got caught with three bricks of raw heroine and was forced to take a plea and pay a fine of $150,000. Subsequently, he was sentenced to ten years at River's Correctional Institution; and when he came home, due to disloyal friends and family - he was flat-broke. In turn he chose to deal with Uncle D and got fronted $50,000 with the promise of $75,000 to be returned in a month. Magny accepted the deal and got on his feet.

Soon after, he ended up serving a DEA agent. This time the only way he would get a deal was if he turned state on his cousin, Abdul Wali. The DEA had reason to believe that Abdul Wali was traveling back and forth from the U.S. to Iraq smuggling raw dope into the U.S. The reason Magny wasn't dealing with his cousin in the first place was because long ago he stole from him. That was how Magny initially got on his feet in the first place. For Magny's act, Abdul Wali beat his ass and told him that he could never get anything from him. Now it was time for Magny's dark to come into the light.

I pulled up to the restaurant and checked my lone Glock 17. Since I killed Junior with the other, I was forced to get rid of it. According to Uncle D this shouldn't involve any gun play to get the money. Like a lot of money getters, that's what they do, get money. The first sign of any danger they'd turn straight bitch. Magny was a prime example. When I walked in the restaurant, all eyes fell on me. As I got to the register, I noticed that the young girl was a Muslima (Muslim female). Although she was fully garbed, I thought her eyes were beautiful. Sensing and seeing the lust in my eyes she looked to the ground as I began to speak.

"I'm looking for Magny. Is he here Beautiful?" I flirted knowing I was dead wrong, but I could tell she was smiling.

"One second Sir, he's in the back. I'll go get him," she replied and walked off to a room nearby. About five minutes passed before Magny was standing in a doorway.

"I'm Magny Sir, how can I help you?" Magny spoke while removing his eyeglasses."

"Uncle D sent me here to see you. Can we talk in private?" I asked. You could see the nervousness wash over his face. I could tell that he was desperately trying to figure out my intentions. Unconsciously, he looked over towards the Muslima and replied.

"Yes," in a shaken voice. Magny showed me the way to his office. I stepped in and took a seat. I wasted no time getting to the business at hand.

"I'm told you owe a bill that needs to be taken care of. Uncle D is pretty upset that you've been avoiding him. Almost, as if you don't want to pay." I leaned back and crossed my legs.

"Look, tell Uncle D I aint got it, and when I do I'll call his ass." (SMACK) I slapped him

"Watch your mouth A-Rab. That's family you sassing. I tried to go about this the nice way, but you weren't trying to see that. So we're gonna do this the hard way. I reached on my waist and placed the Glock 17 on the table. Gradually, I leaned back and eyed a Chinese dagger style set on the wall.

"Now you dumbfuck, you tell me where your money is?" He growled as he stood from his seat. Magny really thought he had the upper hand. He even walked around the table and placed the gun to my temple. So gullible."

(SMACK) I opened hand smacked him. Magny's anger shot to the moon as he pulled the trigger to my face. (Click!) Nothing. I sent a crashing right hook across his jaw causing him to drop my Glock. I picked it up and extracted the empty clip to replace it with a full one. For emphasis I cocked it back so he could feel that I wasn't bullshitting with him.

"You dumb motherfucker. You thought I was gonna let you get a loaded gun on me?" Where the money at before I slaughter your soybean eating ass?" I placed the silencer to his forehead.

"Please don't kill me. It's under the rug." Magny begged, pointing at the rug I was standing on.

"Get the fuck over here and open it then. Move wrong and I'm gonna see you thinking." I held the glock pressed firmly to his ear. Magny crawled over to the safe and opened it. Soon as he did. (SMACK!) I smacked him with the pistol and pushed him out the way. Just as suspected, there was a nickle planted nine within reaching distance. I placed the nine on my waist.

"Bag all that shit up." I demanded. Magny quickly complied. After that was done, I push him back to his chair behind his desk."

"Just because you thought you were slick, I'm gonna show you what reaching get you." I grabbed the same hand of the same shoulder that was wounded and placed it flat on the table. Before Magny realized what I was preparing to do, I grabbed a knife from the Chinese dagger set and sent it crashing through his hand and into his desk.

"AGGGHHHHH!" Magny screamed out in pain. With all the noise he was making I knew that it was time for me to make my exit. Like déjà vu I walked out the office and all eyes were on me. I kept my stride and headed straight to the door. I quickly hopped in my DTS and sped off up Georgia Ave.

*****

PARIS

My life had been going so good. I recently got a raise, and was really saving money for my college tuition. My drive was impeccable. There was nothing that could deter me from being successful. Today was another workday for me and Kayla. I loved my job and was also falling in love with Trey.

My main way of saving money for school was Trey because basically he took care of my every need. I felt that he had to have developed strong feelings as well because of the way he treated me. I also knew our feelings were genuine, because we never had sex to cloud our judgment. I was at my desk finishing up some work for office supplies when Kayla brought her loud ghetto ass over.

"All your ass wanna do is work," Kayla leaned on my cubical.

"If I'm not mistaken Kayla that's what people do when they're at work. If you don't then you usually don't last that long at that job," I sarcastically replied with a smile.

"You can save the lecture. I get enough of that at my house. So where we going to eat for lunch?" Kayla changed the subject.

"You act like we got a car. We gonna eat at the same place that we been eating at MCDONALDS!" I replied, signing the last order form for the office supplies.

"You must didn't see what Ms. Kayla drove in today," said Kayla, holding up a pair of keys that went to a Benz.

"Girl them keys to a Benz. Who car you done stole?" I snatched the keys out of her hand. Kayla was a mess. I don't know how she did it, but I would bet my life that she could trick a man out the blood in his body.

"Stole! I'm offended. Girl please! I'm like a female Goldie. I pimp niggas like it's a religion!" Kayla snapped her fingers.

"Girl you stupid! So where we going Ms. Driver for a day? We only got an hour," I warned.

"Let's drive to Eddie Leonard's. I want some chicken and mambo sauce." Kayla said, licking her fingers as she visualized the carryout food.

"Kayla you are so ghetto. You need to stop eating that stuff." I stood up en route to drop the order forms with Kayla now.

"Well what you getting Ms. God Art Thou, Holier Than Almighty," Kayla teased.

"I'm getting a steak and cheese with French fries." I already knew that Kayla would say something smart about that.

"I rest my case Ms. Undercover Hoodrat," Kayla laughed as I passed the forms along.

We then walked back to my station, so I could prepare myself for our lunch break. To Kayla's surprise when we walked down to the lobby, she ran into one of her many acquaintances. His name was Twan. He stood about 6'2, and he was dark skinned with a full beard. He and Kayla met at one of Barry Farms basketball games. Although she met him in Southeast D.C., he was from Uptown in Northwest. Normally Kayla wouldn't care about any of her men. To her they were like drugs in jail, only there for the moment, and they changed with the weather. But Twan was different. Kayla actually cared about him. It could have been the money, or it could have been the thirst-quenching sex he gave her. Either way she was hooked.

"Twan what you doing here, I thought you had to go to North Carolina on business?" asked a surprised Kayla.

"I did, but I ended up having a last-minute change of plans. The police raided my people's house. Since I didn't leave, I came here to see my wifey." Kayla blushed as Twan wrapped his arms around her waist.

"Well we're about to go eat lunch. Why don't you come with us?" Kayla suggested with hope in her eyes.

"I'll meet ya'll there, I have to go over to the Social Security place. Where y'all going?" Twan asked.

"Nowhere far, just to Eddie Leonard's on Bladensburg Rd."

"Well soon as I finish I'll be over there," Twan replied

"Okay well hurry up, you know it won't take long for our food to be ready," Kayla slightly pouted as she rubbed on

Twan chest.

"Aight, I got you, now let me taste those lips," Twan demanded. Kayla blushed again but willingly complied.

Walking outside Kayla was so caught up in Twan that she forgot that she was walking to an $80,000-dollar car that Twan knew damn well she couldn't afford.

"This your car Kayla? You riding expensive ain't you?" said Twan immediately becoming suspicious. Kayla quickly came back down to earth realizing her mistake. She began to think as fast as she could.

"I wish! This is my friend's father car," Kayla gave me a look that said play along.

"And what your friend's name Kay?" Kayla loved when he called her that. Then she made the introduction.

"Paris this is the man of the hour, Twan - Twan this is my best friend Paris. Now go do what you have to do. My break is only an hour long. Come to the carryout when you're done."

Twan looked at her suspiciously, but let it go. Kayla kissed him on the cheek and hopped in the car. Once the doors were closed, she let out a sigh of relief.

"Damn that was close," said Kayla.

"Somebody's falling in love, somebody's falling in love," I sang teasing Kayla.

"Shut up Paris." Kayla hit me knowing that I was right.

Since Kayla couldn't let Twan see her driving the car, I had to drive and didn't mind one bit. I pulled out the parking lot and proceeded towards Eddie Leonard's. Once we arrived, we placed our orders and quickly received them. Twan was nowhere to be found and Kayla was mildly disappointed because just the sight of him only moments ago made her spirits rise and her panties wet. Pulling back up, Kayla noticed that Twan's truck was still parked in the same spot it was when we left. Kayla knew that Escalade EXT anywhere.

We parked the 500 hundred and proceeded toward the entrance. Walking in, Kayla immediately dropped her chicken and mambo sauce and was stuck watching Twan kissing the receptionist. I thought, *ain't this some shit! We waiting on this nigga and he sitting here.* Kayla was fuming and hell was surely about to boil over.

"Ah hell naw bitch, your hand called for this one." *PAP!* Kayla gave the girl a left hook that sent the girl crashing to the floor with a vengeance.

"Wait! Wait! Hold up Kayla!" Twan tried to reason and calm Kayla down, but it was to no avail. This was too much drama, so I stayed out of it.

"Fuck you, nigga! You in here sucking this bitch face while we waiting on your trifling ass!" Kayla yelled as the girl got up and swung a wild haymaker that Kayla easily weaved, giving herself enough time to get to her box cutter.

Kayla slid the razor out, sending it across the young girl's face, opening a huge gash along her cheek. As the blood shot out her face like a water gun, the young girl screamed out in pain. Kayla tried to advance on her but was grabbed by Twan.

"Get the fuck off me you dirty dick motherfucker!" Kayla yelled

"Bitch! Calm the fuck down!" Twan replied, holding her by the shoulders.

"Bitch! I got yo bitch!" Kayla wiggled free and swung the razor at Twan.

Trying to deflect the blow Twan put his wrist in the line of fire subsequently getting it sliced open. Seeing his own blood, Twan's eyes turned bloodshot. He then took his good hand and reached for his P-90. Kayla saw the gun and hauled ass out of the entrance door. Twan was right on her. *BOOM, BOOM, BOOM.* Twan let off three shots and missed terribly. Now seriously fearing for her life, Kayla hopped in the 500, threw it in reverse and smashed the gas. Twan was still trying to catch her, but Kayla hit the gas so hard that the car whipped out of its parking spot ultimately hitting Twan. Kayla didn't care one bit. She tossed it in drive and sped away. As she drove away, Twan raised his P-90 again but was too hurt to aim and fire. Kayla's heart was broken by the first man that she ever loved. With that, she vowed never to love again.

*****

MIDNIGHT

Money good, and money right. I had collected a nice bit of money for myself and Uncle D. Magny had $350,000, and was still trying to put my Uncle off; not to mention that it bothered the hell out of me that I was forced to let Magny live. It was bad enough that he would have to go to the hospital for his wounds. Had I killed him, the police would have been sniffing for me like a blood hound. I made a mental note to go back and finish that job. Hopefully, I'd still be alive and well to clean up the mess I left behind. Plans would be made and his life will be taken.

Next up in my quest for currency dominance was a Yankee ass Indian named Crazy E. Like the others, Crazy E was also caked up. Crazy E at one point had taken a fall from the top of the weed ladder from a federal investigation that to this day had him on the run. Unlike most people under federal investigation, Crazy E was running and lasting. Most would be caught within three to six months, Crazy E had been running for two years.

Having to go on the run, the Feds seized and froze all Crazy E's bank accounts, and pulled a quarter million out of his house. Crazy E was dead broke when he came to Uncle D. After Uncle D listened to Crazy E's sob story of his rise and fall from the top. Uncle D made some calls and got him one hundred pounds of hydroponically grown marijuana. Crazy E got back on in a major way and basically took Uncle D's kindness for weakness. He made the money to pay Uncle D back, but ultimately looked at Uncle D's old age and said, "FUCK HIM." Uncle D wasn't even charging him any interest on what he got, so clearly Crazy E was just a snake that truly needed his head cut off.

Saying fuck Uncle D would prove to be the worst mistake of Crazy E's frivolous life. Figuring that Uncle D wouldn't be crazy enough to come after him, Crazy E let his guard down as if the winds were calm. But little did he know that hurricane Midnight was quietly approaching. Thanks to a few of Uncle D connects, he found out that Crazy E was staying in a small house located on Varnum St. in northwest. It surprised Uncle D that Crazy E was still in Washington while still being on the run. That just showed how dumb he was and even dumber for crossing Uncle D.

*****

PARIS

Thanks to Kayla, Twan received four broken ribs and ten stitches. Kayla was lucky that Twan was a street dude to the fullest, and lived by the Omerta street code *"Death Before Dishonor."* The receptionist on the other hand needed 40 stitches to close her wound. Neither she nor Twan pressed charges. Kayla in turn was fired. Her dreams of becoming a gynecologist now seemed so far away, and I truly felt bad for my friend's dilemma.

It was about 8:15pm and as usual Trey was waiting out front to pick me up as he did every night since I'd met him. I was dead tired and couldn't wait to relax. I drug my feet until I finally made it to the M5. When I opened the door I was greeted by a big teddy bear holding twelve long stem white roses.

"Oh my God! Trey they're so beautiful." I smiled like a school girl then rushed to get in the car to kiss my man.

"Don't worry about it Baby girl, you know I got you." Trey gave off his trademark smile.

"You swear?" I licked my lips and made sure that Trey noticed my seductive tone and my come fuck me eyes.

"On everything I love, I do." Trey spoke with every ounce of truth in his body. I then let my heart lead me to his zipper.

"Well I got you too." I seductively replied while unzipping his pants. I could tell that Trey was taken off guard by my boldness. Finding the prize, I lowered my head and began to tease the head of his penis with my tongue. I had never done this before, but I would try with everything in my heart to please him. I eventually took in Trey's entire nine inches down my throat. I almost choked, but was still determined to please him. I knew that as strong as my feelings had grown for Trey it wouldn't be long before I finally gave my all to him. I was now settled on the fact that I loved Trey with all my heart. Maybe it was all the things that he showed me or maybe it was just as plainly the load he let loose in my mouth. I didn't say a word; I just opened the passenger door and spit it out. After wiping my mouth, I turned to Trey.

"Trey, I love you." I instantly got nervous because ever since day one of meeting Trey I always held my hand close to my chest. Now with my hand exposed I was unsure of what

Trey's response would be. Then I was put at ease when he expressed the same feelings for me that I felt for him.

Come to find out, Trey too was relieved that he finally told me how he felt about me. Love was an emotion that he never experienced, so he really didn't know how to go about it. Trey then pulled out of the soundstage parking lot with plans on his mind. Soon we were in Silver Springs, Maryland. Trey stopped and picked up some things to make the night go easier. Then we were pulling up to the Holiday Inn Hotel. From the order of things, I already knew this would be a night to remember.

Once we stepped into the room Trey went into the bathroom to run me a bubble bath with roses floating atop the bubbles. To help him out, I lit up some scented mango candles. The flames made Trey's shadow dance on the walls. I stepped on the balcony to take in the exquisite view of downtown Silver Spring. It was there that I silently thanked Kayla for not letting me let Trey get away.

*****

TREY

By the time I opened the bathroom door, I smiled when I saw the first true love of my life fast asleep on her stomach. Even so, I was still determined to make this a night to remember. I dug into my bag of tricks and pulled out some oil that heats up when it touches the skin. I sat on the edge of the bed slightly waking Paris, but not to full comprehension I found myself seriously having to control myself from ripping Paris' skirt off. I wanted Paris' body in a bad way. I took some oil and slowly massaged her calves, working my way up her thighs. As I reached her inner thigh, a slight moan escaped her lips. Methodically, I lifted her skirt around her waist and saw that she wore a pink thong. As unobtrusive as possible I slid it to the side exposing her moistened slit. I knew that Paris never had her pussy eaten, so I knew she was clueless as to what was happening to her when she began to feel all the sensation rushing through her body. I figured with all the pleasure that she was experiencing, she wouldn't dare stop me. I continued to massage her inner thighs, watching her pussy secrete more with each passing minute and every touch given.

"Oh Trey!" Paris moaned, letting me know I was doing something right.

Going for the kill, I remove Paris' thong down her legs and received no protest. Her juices were actually flowing out of her throbbing pussy. I then kissed her legs moving up to the back of her thighs. I could smell her sex and her womanhood was giving off this inviting scent. I spread her ass cheeks and began to lick around the rim of her rectum, causing her to moan even more.

"Oh God Trey, don't do this to me." My ears were deaf to her cries of ecstasy. Finally, I dug my tongue as deep into her pussy as I could. "Oh God Trey."

With the sudden penetration, Paris arched her back poking her ass in the air. I ate Paris' pussy with a vengeance, bringing her to climax three times. Paris was so gone that she never noticed me coming out of all my clothes.

I came up kissing on her back and neck while simultaneously rubbing my condom-covered penis up and down her cum-soaked pussy. I positioned myself and I applied pressure to her hymen.

"*AGGGHHH* no, no, wait. I'm not ready..... Please don't be mad at me." Paris sat up with her hands in her lap looking off nowhere in particular.

"It's alright baby. This night was all about you. We'll do

us when the time right. I'm not stressing it." I replied, placing my arm around her.

"Thank you, Trey. I love you so much." Paris leaned in and passionately kissed me

"I love you too scaredy-cat." I smiled and kissed her forehead.

*****

OLIVIA

I never in a thousand years thought that I would receive such devastating news from Ms. Miles. I'm not talking about Ms. Rita dying either! That was the least of my cares. I'm talking about the fact Derrick could possibly be back in the city.

Although I now had Ms. Rita's diary I had refused to read any of Derrick's letters to spare my own eyes from having to drop tears of agony. Today would be the first day that I would read one of Derrick's letters. I prayed that my fragile heart would be able to take it. It was now 2:00am in the morning. I pulled out what would have been Derrick's first letter. All it took was the sight of his handwriting and I broke down.

Hey Kitten,

You don't know how much I miss you. I fought my mom every step of the way, but it was useless. I can't see myself ever loving someone else as much as you. You're the center of my heart and my world.

One good thing that I have to tell you is that my mom and dad said that when I turn 18 that I can come back to the states. I plan on it, and will anticipate the day that I will see you again. I want to grow old together and then see our kids grow old. I won't make this letter long, but know that I love you Kitten.

P.S. I love you Kitten

Puppy dog

OLIVIA

At the end of the letter I was rushed with a whole new set of tears. With the words of that letter, I really didn't care that the part of me that tried to love Ms. Rita was no more. I really could care less that she was in her grave. What was really starting to bother me now was that I allowed my heart to hate Derrick unjustly. My tears were then interrupted by the front door opening. I could tell by the look on Paris' face that she was shocked to see me up and knew that she was in for it.

"What you doing walking in the house some two in the morning?" I was pissed off so Derrick would have to wait for a second.

"I, I, I was at my friend's house and fell asleep." Paris stuttered. I knew she was lying, especially when I saw a passion mark on her neck.

"You hot ass little tramp. What little dick motherfucker you been fucking Paris?" I was waiting on her to lie.

"I wasn't with no boy." Paris replied and tried to walk off, but I was not having that. *SMACK!* That's right I slapped the shit out of her.

"Don't lie to me you little bitch. What the fuck is that, if you weren't?" I pointed to the mark. Subconsciously, Paris grabbed her neck. She was caught and couldn't say one word. It definitely didn't help for Ron to add his two cents.

"I told you she fucking." Ron yelled from the back room.

"Shut the fuck up Ron you always got something to say." Paris yelled back in full blown tears. *SMACK!* I slapped her ass again.

"You better watch your mouth in my house Paris!" Paris grabbed her face and with her eyes shot daggers at me before storming off to her room. Once she got to her room, she turned back toward me.

"I hate you, Olivia." Then she slammed her door.

I could hear a lot of rumbling coming from her room and soon after she emerged carrying two suitcases and headed straight toward the door. I looked outside and saw her walking toward a Burgundy car. I immediately open the window.

"Since you leaving, let that nigga take care of your ass." I yelled.

"Kiss my ass Olivia!" Paris replied. Then from over my shoulder I heard Ron.

"I told you she fucking."

*****

MIDNIGHT

I'd been laying on Crazy E for a week now. I could tell that he was nervous every time he walked out of his house. The constant looking over his shoulder was a dead giveaway. It was on my mind exactly how I was going to get close to him. Crazy E was so paranoid that he might start shooting at the sight of me. Crazy E in my eyes was a predictable man. His routine hardly ever changed. Every morning he would go to three houses. My bet was that he was picking up and dropping off. Afterwards, he would return to his house, and I had his routine on smash.

Crazy E pulled up to his last house located on Fifth and

Delafield. Crazy E stepped out of his car and quickly assessed his surroundings. He was so paranoid that he would see someone there that he missed the obvious things. If he would have calmed down and thoroughly checked his surroundings, he would have seen me days ago. A scared man always makes mistakes and more importantly misses the obvious. Crazy E walked in the house and greeted his top worker.

"What's up Petey? What we do last night?"

"We sold three pounds. The money ready for you on the table," Petey pointed as he was busy cutting and bagging up cocaine. Crazy E collected the money and left him three more pounds.

"Aight I'll see y'all tomorrow." Crazy E hit the door and quickly walked back to his Tahoe. As usual he drove straight back home. After parking Crazy E began to feel comfortable because he was getting ready to enter his domain. Getting comfortable was yet another mistake on Crazy E's part.

Stepping out of his Tahoe, Crazy E saw nothing but a bum on the sidewalk. He looked in my direction and had me thinking that I was spotted. I clutched my Glock under my shirt when he began to walk in my direction. As he walked, he placed his hand inside his pocket probably clutching a small gun of some sort. Crazy E walked up on the car and knocked on the window.

"Who you around here looking for homes?" Crazy E asked.

"I came to pick my girl up. Who the fuck is you to be walking up on my shit?" the driver replied.

"My bad Slim, just next time double park in the street, and put your hazards on. We beefing out here. I don't think your trying to get aired out for nothing," Crazy E warned, smiled and walked off. Crazy E then smiled to himself at how paranoid he was. As he walked toward his house the bum spoke.

"You got any spare change youngster? I'll wash that

big, nice truck you got there," the bum begged with his hand out.

"Here you go. Go take a bath and don't touch my truck." Crazy E flipped him a quarter and kept on walking. "Pissy motherfucker," Crazy E mumbled to himself. Just as he opened his front door. *WACK!* The bum was standing over top of him clutching a Glock 17. As Crazy E turned over, I took the dirty blanket off my head.

"Didn't your mother ever tell you to respect your elders?" I asked. "Get your bitch ass in the house!" I kicked him in the ass as he struggled to regain full consciousness. I kneeled down and grabbed the collar of his leather jacket. I placed his nose on the tip of the barrel.

"Now you gonna make this hard or are you going to do the right thing?" I asked pulling the millennium nine out of his coat pocket. Crazy E was gritting his teeth clearly upset that he got caught slipping.

"Who sent you?" he managed.

"That's not important, but what is, is where the money at?" I dug the gun into his face a little harder for good emphasis.

"Upstairs in the safe behind the dresser. Please let me go man. I'm already on the run. The feds gonna find me anyway. You can have all the money just let me go," Crazy E begged.

"What's the combo?" I asked as if I heard nothing he'd just said; because truthfully, I didn't.

"One, two, three, four, five," Crazy E quickly relayed. I didn't trust him one bit so I smacked him with the pistol again and forced him up the stairs. After he opened the safe I laid him flat on his back. He immediately began crying and begging for his life.

"Please man! The Feds gonna find me anyway. You ain't gotta do this," Crazy E put his hands up as if they would block the bullets from destroying his face.

"You right the feds are going to find you .... "

TWIP, TWIP, TWIP. I shot him three times in the face without a sound being heard. I kissed the hot silencer, thinking to myself - *"Damn, I love these things".*

I bagged up the weed, the money and quickly left the house as if nothing ever happened. Just as I sat in my DTS, a fleet of black Crown Victoria's and squad car pulled onto the block and ran inside Crazy E's house. He was right I thought. The Feds were going to find him ...... STINKING.

*****
PARIS

Ring, Ring, Ring, Ring.

No answer again. It was one in the morning and Kayla still wasn't answering her phone. Kayla never stayed out this late unless she was with me, and she never broke her twelve thirty curfew. I was really beginning to worry about her. I hadn't even seen her at school. I checked with her teachers, and they said that whenever she did come to class that she would sleep the whole class session away. In fact, now that I think about it, I haven't really talked to her since the day she decided that she wanted to play Chef Boyar Kayla on Twan and that receptionist. I just prayed that she was safe.

As for me, life was grand. Since I left my mom's house I'd moved in with Trey. If there was any hardship that came my way, he'd make it his sole obligation to lift it off me. Now, instead of Trey having stop his business to pick me up from work and school, he bought me a new Camry. I was ecstatic. My own car.

After he gave me that car, I laid him back in the backseat of it and gave him the best head of his life. The next day I got my permit and was driving everywhere just to drive.

One place I made sure to go was Kayla's house. I parked my car and looked up at my mom's apartment and hoped that I didn't run into her. I got to Kayla's door and used my spare key that she'd given me a long time ago.

I stepped in and walked straight to her room. I turned the knob and just like I thought - Kayla was in there laid out. I looked over the room and saw all kinds of new hoeish clothes scattered about that I had never seen before. I paid them no mind and tried to wake Kayla by shaking her.

"Kayla."

"What! What! What! Damn, don't you see I'm sleep?" Kayla looked a mess and was cranky as hell. The first thing that I thought was drugs.

"Kayla, why you always sleeping? Girl are you on drugs now?" I pulled the covers off of her. She completely changed the subject.

"Paris, how did you get in my house?" Kayla sat straight up.

"I got a key that you gave me buckethead. Now why are you sleeping so much?" I got right back to the matter at hand.

"None of your business, damn! Why you sleeping so much? You ain't been worried about me, so why now?" By her statement I could tell that she had some ill feelings.

"Because you're my best friend and I don't want to see you hurt yourself, that's why," I replied in a manner to let her know that I still loved her like a sister.

"And how exactly am I supposed to do that by sleeping?" Kayla sat back up in her bed as sarcastic as she could.

"I don't know, why don't you tell me?"I crossed my arms over my chest and shifted my weight to one leg.

"Look Paris, you get to college your way, and I'll get there my way." Kayla was seriously avoiding my questions.

"What's that supposed to mean? Oh I get it, you're mad at me because you got yourself fired!" I was getting fed up with Kayla's bullshit.

"Whatever Paris! You need to get your head out of your ass." Kayla waived me off and laid back down.

"Head out my ass? You the one with all the hoe stroll clothes. You might need to ask yourself how many niggas got their head up your ass in one night." I pointed at all the clothes then regretted my words just as they left my mouth.

"Damn that was cold Paris. That's how you think of me huh? You think I'm a hoe?" Kayla looked up at me with tears in her eyes. I instantly felt bad.

"I'm sorry Kayla I didn't mean to say it that way. I'm just worried about you," I spoke as sincerely as I could.

"I'm glad that I finally see your true face Paris. I would appreciate it if you would leave the way you came please." Kayla looked to her lap letting the tears fall.

"Kayla I'm....." I never got the words out. Kayla wanted to hear no more.

"Get the fuck out of my house!" Kayla yelled pointing at the door causing me to jump. I then ran out the house. In all of our years as friends we've never kept secrets from each other. I really wondered what the hell Kayla was doing. I prayed that she wasn't selling her body. Although we had this argument I was still determined to be there for my friend.

*****

MIDNIGHT

I retrieved $350,000 and two silenced Desert Eagles from Crazy E's safe. Three down and one to go. I was now sitting in the newsroom watching the news anchor reporting from Varnum St.

"Hello my name is Tamisha Miller with Fox Five live. We're now in Northwest at a row house on Varnum St. Where police and Federal agents have ended a two-year manhunt for a man named Eric "Crazy E" Jamison. Two years ago a warrant was issued for Jamison's arrest after an ongoing investigation.

Jamison eluded authorities for over two years. Jamison was also named with 13 other co-defendants. Although authorities have ended a much-needed man hunt for Jamison, he will not be able to stand trial. After authorities received an anonymous tip from an undisclosed source, police and agents raided the house here behind me only to find Jamison with multiple gunshot wounds to the facial area. He was pronounced dead on arrival by authorities and the coroner. The police have no leads and will be asking the public for any kind of helpful information. You can call 202-842-8984.

Click - I turned the T.V. off and breathed out a sigh of relief, and thanked God for yet another successful hit.

"Damn Nephew, I wanna kiss you. That snake motherfucker ain't know what hit him!" Uncle D pounded his fist together and lit up a cigar in celebration.

"It ain't over yet Unc. Three down and one to go. Hopefully this will end with no bloodshed. I already know the chances for that are unrealistic." I grabbed a Budweiser from Uncle D's cooler.

"That's what I want, bloodshed. If I still had my youth, I would have been killed those bastards. You doing good Nephew. Go at them really calm, and then the moment they play pussy, I want you to fuck them real good; fuck'em all the way to their grave." Uncle D took a deep pull on his cigar.

"So what are we going to do after I collect from this last dude on the list?" I had to ask. Nothing had been discussed, so I was curious. Plus, I wanted to know why he let me keep all the drugs.

"Well Nephew, Uncle D had enough of the game. I been in the life for over 35 years. I gave you those addresses so you can get on your feet. I'm done. I'm leaving the whole operation to you. So do what you want with it. I'll have all my contacts with you by the time you finish with Guns." I couldn't believe this shit. He used me to clean up his plate so he could retire with no debts and no one owing him. I wasn't mad though because the benefits that I reaped were worth way more than the work.

"Done? Unc I just came home. We ain't even established nothing yet. At least help me get things moving," I tried to reason. "I mean damn, I wanted the operation to be us, not me."

"Moving! Hell Nephew you done did that already. I'm old and tired. I'm going to get out while I still can. I rather bow out on my feet than on my back." Uncle D pointed to his feet with his cigar hanging out of his mouth.

"Damn Unc after all these years, it's finally over now huh?" I look on in disbelief.

"Every dog has his day. Mines done came and went a long time ago. These days not like when I was coming up. Too much technology and too many snitches. I played a long time Nephew and refuse to be a victim of a snitch. You feel me Nephew?"

"Yeah, I hear you Unc go ahead and retire. I'll hold you down. Lay back in the shadows. We still gonna do this thing together. Blood thicker than money." I gave Uncle D a firm handshake and a manly hug.

"You just like your father Nephew determined as ever." Uncle D laughed.

"I gotta be. I won't get nowhere in life if I'm not." We shared a laugh.

"Just be careful Nephew the game ain't got no picks," Uncle D warned.

"I'm hip Unc that's why I carry one of these." I picked up one of Crazy E silenced Desert Eagles.

"You a nut Nephew! So how you like Trey?" I could hear the hope behind his voice. Then I wondered why he was asking me this question again.

"He's cool, doesn't like taking orders, but he cool why you asked me that again?"

"I forgot that I asked you. But that's good to hear. That boy got a good bloodline in him," Uncle D replied and began to suck on his teeth falling into deep thought.

*****

PARIS

I was extremely happy to be in the presence of Trey so much, but the hardest part of living with him was sleeping with him in the same bed. At times my panties would get so wet that I would have to change them in the middle of the night. My hormones would get so out of hand that it would literally become unbearable to keep them in check and my cherry intact. I would lay there with Trey's dick brushing up against my ass and would get heat flashes. It was to the point where I was seriously contemplated letting Trey take my mind and body to the next level.

I was in a deep sleep when I was awakened by the smells of Turkey bacon and pancakes. I hopped straight up to see what Trey was up to. All I had on were some French cut boy shorts like the ones Nia Long had on in the movie *Big Momma's House* and a tank top that showed my belly button. I knew I was playing with fire walking around Trey like this because he would be sure to snatch my ass up. I ran in the kitchen and was surprised at the feast Trey prepared.

"Since when you start cooking? I thought you only lived off of carry out?" I leaned on the wall with my hand on my hip.

My mouth watered at the strawberry covered pancakes, French Omelets, potatoes, turkey bacon, not to mention the fruit drink he made with the juicer.

"Just call me Chef Boyar Ghetto." Trey smiled. Then he immediately showed lust in his eyes as he took in every curve on my body. I almost felt embarrassed. "I see you trying to make me rape your little ass running around here in them shorts. You must be ready." Trey lusted unconsciously licking his lips.

"Maybe but I'm scared. You know I love you Trey and I want to give you every inch of me. It's just that I want to make sure that it's the right choice. But I have been thinking about us a lot lately." I wrapped my arms around his bare shoulders and kissed him softly on the lips.

"Baby you know I'm not going to rush you in the least bit. We have never had sex and you still keep me happy. But when you are ready, I promise you I'm going to knock a hole in your back."

"You promise?" I seductively replied and sucked on his chin. Trey grabbed me by the waist and explored my mouth with his strong and warm tongue. Through my boy shorts Trey rubbed my clit causing the juices to start flowing. He smoothly removed my tank top revealing my completely erect nipples. I loved every touch that Trey placed on me. I kinda got nervous when Trey went down and kissed my belly button. Slowly he made his way down to the spot that I cherished so much. Trey eased down my shorts making eye contact with my peeking clit. He then spread my legs throwing one over his shoulder as I stood against the wall. I was instantly pleased by Trey's long and wet tongue.

"On God Trey dddon't this to me." I was stuttering like Bobby Bouche, and couldn't get all my words out. Trey then took my other leg and like the other placed it on his other shoulder.

With ease Trey stood straight up with my pussy dead in the center of his mouth. My juices dripped from his chin down to his broad chest. "I'm about to cuuuuummmmm oh baby I'm cumming! Oh god baby I'm cumming! I then unleashed a heavy load of cum in Trey's mouth. Feeling satisfied that he pleased his women Trey carried me over to the chair at the table which held no utensils. As I wiped the cum off his chin and chest, he fed me by hand the entire meal he prepared for me. I was being spoiled by Trey and I was loving every minute of it. At times, I thought that I was dreaming because of how happy I was. I really couldn't remember a sad day since I met Trey. I was in heaven and didn't want to leave.

CHAPTER EIGHT

MIDNIGHT

Throughout my years under Uncle D I learned that when you do dirt you get dirt, and when you do dirt with people you should keep them close because you'll never know who has telling tendencies. Since pulling the move on Junior, I made it my sole obligation to get close to Trey. Being so, on a few occasions we'd hit the town together. We'd hit all the hot spots, such as Club Love, Skylark, Penthouse, Club U and since I was creeping on the come up of an old timer, The Chatoe. Trey didn't mind going either. He wasn't getting no pussy at home, so he didn't mind fucking a vet if he could and collecting a few dollars while he was at it. Let Trey tell it pussy didn't have a face. The only face he was concerned about was on green piece of paper.

On this particular night our club of choice would be the Skylark, a well-known strip club on New York Ave. This strip club had some of the baddest strippers in D.C. If you were from out of town and looking to have some fun this was the spot to be. We stepped inside the club like we owned it. Trey was wearing his street dude clothes, meaning a Solbiato sweat suit. I on the other hand, chose some Hugo jeans and a Prada sweater. While Trey grabbed us a table, I grabbed us a bottle of Moet and a bottle Remy Martin 1738. We were both struck at how quickly the strippers began to flock around our tables. It had to be the bottles because they both cost $120 a piece. Quickly a stripper with nothing but a white thong on approached.

"You want a lap dance handsome?" asked the stripper referring to me.

"Naw I'm cool babygirl but you can take this" I slid a hundred-dollar bill onto the mound of her pussy. Being thankful she kissed me on the cheek and strutted off.

"Damn Midnight, you tipped her a c-note. What the hell you been drinking?" We laughed.

"I'm cool she hustling just like we are. She might have a kid she trying to raise. That hundred-dollar bill was blood money, meaning free money. You gotta do good some time. That hundred-dollar bill might come back a hundred grand. You feel me young buck?" I smiled knowing that I just dropped a helleva jewel on him.

"Yeah, I feel you. Selling pussy's just like selling scramble; after a while the shit go bad." We both shared a laugh and popped opened the bottles.

"Trey you're one wild nigga if I ever saw one," I replied. Our convo was then broken up by the DJ on the mic.

"Ladies and gentlemen, I would like for ya'll to give a warm applause to one of our newer editions to the Skylark, she is as angelic as they come and goes by the name 'Angel'."

*****

TREY

My mouth dropped wide open when I saw Kayla walk out on the stage wearing angel wings and a white thong, and to top it off she had white stars over her nipples. I can honestly say that she took my breath away. She walked the stage like she owned it and looked damn good doing it. When she turned around, I was really turned on when I saw the angel wings tattooed on her ass.

Kayla was a sexy bitch and knew it. She calculated every twist and turn. I looked around seeing the patrons with lust in their eyes. All of us were all imagining all kinds of exotic things that we would love to do to her. By the middle of the first song Kayla had spotted me and it became as if she was directing every twist and turn towards me. My dick got rock hard when she bent over in front of us and touched her toes revealing her two-inch-long pussy lips that were open and dangling. She had me debating whether or not I should take her to the hotel. After thinking about it, I decided against it. There was no way that I would let a dumb mistake like that get back to Paris. When Kayla's set was over she approached the table.

"So I guess you're going to tell Paris you saw me dancing here tonight huh? " Kayla was trying to pick my brain for my intentions, but even if I were why would I tell her.

"Why would I do that? You your own woman. Where you work is your business," I replied taking a sip of Remy and looking off as if she wasn't there

"I'd appreciate it if you didn't. We had a fight the other night and ain't talking right now. I'm trying to save money for college," Kayla said to the men speaking in an angelic tone.

"You don't gotta worry about me saying nothing. Do what you gotta do to survive babygirl. Matter of fact, here take this money. I'm going to make your night a little easier for you tonight." I peeled off a hundred-dollar bill and handed it to her. "Thank you so much Trey. Would you like to go to the VIP with me?" She gotta be crazy if she thinks I'm about to fuck with her like that so she can go back and tell Paris.

"Naw, I'm cool. Just make sure you get to college and don't let this place break you from your goals."

"Yeah I will. Thanks again Trey." Kayla leaned down and gave me a kiss on the cheek before she walked off to the next patron of her night.

"Damn Trey you tipping c-notes and shit. What you been drinking. " I smiled, and Midnight leaned over to smell my drink as if I was drinking something different then he was. I then replied.

"She hustling just like we are," I smiled again.

"Yeah, I bet. I'm surprised you didn't go to that VIP with her." Midnight took a sip from his glass of Moet.

"Hell naw, that's my girl's best friend. That bitch won't tell on me." We both laughed at that.

*****

MIDNIGHT

After my night of fun, it was now time to get back down to business. I was now at the last name on the list. The name was a guy they called Gunz. Gunz used to run through an area called Potomac Gardens in the Southeast section of Washington, D.C. While I was in Lewisburg, Uncle D had Gunz doing all the extorting, collecting, and murdering. Basically saying, Gunz was what I am now- the Enforcer. Gunz was about six feet and 190lbs with a fairly dark complexion. Gunz and Uncle D parted ways on murdering terms two weeks before I came home.

Gunz had a serious gambling problem, especially when it came to dice and football games. Gunz came from the gutter, so he never had too much. In fact, he was only as rich as his reputation. The forefront of that consisted of extorting and murdering. The exact same things Uncle D hired him for. If Uncle D had known of Gunz's habits beforehand, he may have been able to prevent the unnecessary steps that Gunz took.

Since Gunz didn't have much, Uncle D set him up in his own apartment. He even lent Gunz his Lexus LS430 until he was able buy his own. As long as Gunz stayed loyal, Uncle D would have made sure that he was straight. After the action that Gunz took, Uncle D learned that Gunz's loyalty was nothing more than a fluke and worth nothing but a casket.

A week before Gunz's official departure from Uncle D's empire, Gunz was partaking in a huge crap game where the lowest bid was 10,000. The game pretty much consisted of Washington's heavy hitters. It was also a place where everybody's waist held plastic, or steel. At first Gunz was up a $175,000, but let his greed get the best of him. He ended up losing everything including Uncle D's Lexus. Gunz left the crap game and ducked Uncle D for a week. Seeing an opportunity to come up and hopefully get the Lexus back Gunz bet on a football game for $100,000 that he didn't have. The game was the Redskins versus 49ers. They both had a record of 8-0. The Redskins lost their quarterback and top receiver, so Gunz thought he had a sweet bet, but was wrong. The Redskins beat the 49ers 56-7 and Gunz didn't have the money to pay his debt.

Biting the hand that fed him, Gunz stole the money from Uncle D and laid low as possible. After finding out Gunz reason and the whole story, Uncle D was so heated that he put another $100,000 on Gunz's head. For the next few months Gunz moved around from house to house terrified to stay still long enough for someone to cash in on that money. Eventually, Gunz got on his feet and got himself an apartment, but it wasn't long before Uncle D found out about it.

Now that I was home a person who Uncle D trusted with his life. Gunz days were soon to be numbered. As I said before you do dirt you get dirt and Gunz was soon to be buried. Uncle D had found out that Gunz had obtained an apartment in the northeast section of Washington in a gated complex called Fort Chaplin apartments. The building had round the clock surveillance and security. That was without a doubt the reason why Gunz choose this building, hoping some rent-a-cop would save his life. Little did Gunz know, my hand went far beyond some bullshit security.

I did my homework on Gunz. Unlike the others Gunz was expecting someone to come on Uncle D's behalf. The money on his head let him know that someone coming was a strong possibility. I had to sit on Gunz for about three weeks. Whenever Gunz did come home I would already be there sitting in the parking lot watching the circling security guard, timing his reps. The difference from this and the other three men on the list was that this was a full-blown hit - no money, no torture, just cold-blooded murder.

This morning I made a stop by Sunny Surplus to get a fictitious badge. I needed to find out exactly which apartment Gunz resided in. There was no way of knowing and staying undercover but to go undercover, I threw on a blazer with some stone-washed jeans. I even threw on an ugly ass green tie. To the naked eye you'd swear that I looked just like a detective.

It was about 10:00am and the morning breeze felt good. Normally doing some shit like this I would be nervous, but Gunz disrespected my family, so instead of being nervous I was on a mission to disrespect his life. I stepped in the building easily finding the manager's office. There was a glass door that let me know it. Through it, I could see a petite white woman sitting at her desk. I lightly tapped on the door to get her attention. She looked up and gave a welcoming smile and motioned for me to come in. Opening the door, I was hit with the sweet smell of her perfume. She looked to be about forty years old with red hair and brown eyes. She looked like in her day she might have been a catch.

With age comes wisdom, so hopefully she wouldn't give me any problems with the information that I needed. We both made it to the front counter simultaneously.

"Welcome to Fort Chaplin Apartments. Are you interested in renting with us?" She shook my hand and gave me a huge smile.

"Actually, no. My name is Detective Maurice Jones with the Fifth district police station. I need some information on one of your tenants. Hopefully it won't be a problem," I sternly spoke as I showed her my Sunny Surplus badge. I retrieved it from my back pocket being sure to let the nine-millimeter on my hip in the holster be visible.

"Uh no Sir. That won't be a problem. Do you have a name or a picture?" She replied. This was easier than I thought it would be. I reached in my inside pocket and retrieved a picture of Gunz laying it flat on the counter.

"The person that I'm looking for is named Gregory Brown. This picture is from last year so he may have braids in his hair by now." I looked her in the eye to see her reaction to the picture in case she may know him and lie about it.

"Oh yes I know him quite well. Actually, he's on our list of tenants who will be receiving eviction notices." She slid the picture back to me.

"Could you tell me what apartment is his?" I tried to not have too much hope in my voice.

"Why yes, he's in apartment 412. Detective Jones I understand that you may not be able to disclose the case involving Mr. Brown, but could you tell me if you will be arresting him or not?" The lady interlocked her fingers on the counter.

"Oh no, I just wanted to ask him a few questions." I lied. Time was truly ticking down for him.

"Well if it will help you any, Mr. Brown will have thirty days to move before he will be forced out of here."

"Thanks for the tip and your help." I smiled and turned to leave. I thought that went perfect. No blood, no foul. I kinda thought that I might have to kill her too. Lucky for her, she was cooperative.

*****

UNCLE D

I must say that I was extremely proud and pleased at how my nephew was handling business in the streets. You see, Midnight was raised within a thorough bloodline that couldn't be tainted. I just wish that I had some youth to help back him up. Although Midnight was on top of his game, it still didn't sit well with me that he was adamant about handling the work solo. Out of all my years on earth I know that it was always best to handle dirt by yourself sometimes if not, all times. It was my love for my nephew that surpassed some street rule. I wanted someone to watch Midnight's ass, and for my personal reasons I wanted that someone to be Trey.

It was a Saturday night around 11:30pm. I sat in my living room with a cooler filled with Budweiser. While I drank myself into a coma I watched that old sitcom, *Sanford and Son*. Budweiser and T.V. was what kept my mind off of Midnight and his quest to murder my oppressors. While watching the show there was a knock at my door. I wondered who the hell was knocking on my door this late at night. I stood up slightly stumbling.

I realized that I was more drunk than I thought. I swung the door open but was greeted by no one. Just as I closed the door I heard my back door closing. With that I quickly sobered up. With my old instincts in overdrive I stumbled back into my living room to retrieve my pistol grip pump from under the love seat. I was paranoid as fuck. Could have been me or could have been the beer, but I could feel that I wasn't alone in my house. Hearing footsteps I cocked the pump. *CLICK, CLACK*. I let the pump lead the way as I scanned the premises of my home. Hearing movement to my right I turned and fired. BOOM! *CLICK, CLACK*. I hit nothing but the wall.

"Where you at motherfucker? Ya'll came for me, so let's do this like men," I yelled out of anger that they would bring this bullshit to my home. I stepped through my home with the look of a possessed killer. Faintly, a sound came from my kitchen closet. Anxious to get to the point, I approached the closet with the pump at its ready position. Again, I heard the same noise so by instinct I shot a spasm through my index finger causing the pump to react in a murderous way. *BOOM!* The buckshot exploded through the door catching my would-be assailant flush in the face, neck, and chest areas. His body then gave way and he fell out of the closet face first. Feeling relieved that it was over I kneeled down and removed his mask. The male had a long beard and I recognized him.

"Damn he had some heart after all." Suddenly the house phone rang. Startled, I turned the pump on the phone almost blowing it away. Calming my nerves, I picked it up and answered it. "Hello....hello.....hello." I got no answer. When I hung it up and turned around I was face to face with barrel of a silenced Desert Eagle. All oxygen escaped my body as I realized that it was finally over. My assailant wore no mask. Then he spoke.

"As-salaam Alaikum." (May peace be with you). *TWIP, TWIP, TWIP*. I was shot once in the face and twice in the chest. I was dead before I hit the floor and forced to take my assailant's identity to the grave with me.

*****

MIDNGHT

It was 8:00am and Gunz wasn't scheduled to leave for another hour. I was all the way into the part for the hit. I was now dressed as a janitor. I even pulled up in a van with shampooers in the back. I was determined to knock Gunz shit loose. I pulled into the gates with the security guards nodding their heads. As I parked, I noticed that the circling squad car was approaching. I immediately walked to the back of the van to begun unloading the vacuums and shampooers so the officer wouldn't get suspicious. As he passed, I waived to the officer doing the same as he continued on his way. Making it past security I went straight to room 412. While on the elevator I checked my pistols making sure that I was properly equipped for the task at hand. I knocked on the door and could hear movement inside. As I expected Gunz was home.

"Who is it?" Gunz yelled sounding groggy. "Maintenance," I said for lack of a better answer.
"I didn't call for maintenance." Gunz replied.
"The management called for it. We're spraying the whole building." I was trying to give his ass as little room as possible to not open the door.
"Aight hold up," Gunz replied. Just as he opened the door I kicked it in. The door swung open catching Gunz square in the face. Gunz fell to the floor holding his face as I stepped in the apartment closing the door behind me.
"You thought we wasn't going to find your thieving ass?" I said removing my silenced Desert Eagle from my jumper.
"Please don't kill me. I got Uncle D's money you can have that and some. Just please don't kill me," Gunz begged holding his bloody nose.
"Naw, nigga this ain't even about the money no more. You fucked up, so you gonna get it like you asked for it."
SMACK! SMACK! I brutally beat Gunz with the butt of my pistol opening huge gashes along his temple and forehead. Gunz was now only semi-conscious. By the time he came around he was gagged and hog-tied. Gunz smelled gasoline and realized that he was soaked in it. He looked up at me with pleading eyes.
"Tell the devil your clock struck Midnight you thieving motherfucker."

I struck a match and watched as the flames engulfed Gunz body. As Gunz body burned I made a silent prayer that

Allah let this be the last murder that I would have to commit. Now feeling that it was time that I make my exit I opened the door not realizing that I'd just released a thick cloud of black smoke into the hallway. Not to mention I was now standing face to face with the building manager who was attempting to place an eviction noticed on the door. Our eyes locked and asked a thousand questions. It was at that point that I realized that my prayers weren't answered.

"Mr. Jones is there something on fire?" The manager peeked her head in the apartment passed me.

"Nosey bitch!" I grabbed her by the back of the head slamming the silenced Desert Eagle down her throat.

"You in the wrong place at the wrong time bitch." *TWIP, TWIP, TWIP.* Her body hit the floor with a sickening thud. With the hall now filled with smoke I hauled ass out of the building. It was another job well done.

*****

MIDNIGHT

After handling my business with Gunz I was cool, calm, and collected. I couldn't wait to tell my uncle that the final one of his four oppressors was now laid to rest. I pulled the van to a disclosed area and drenched it too with gasoline." No evidence, no case," I stated right before I set the van ablaze. I hopped in my DTS and sped off towards Uncle D's house. Still I prayed that that would be my last murder, but if the moment arose then so be it. In a way I was also thinking of retiring right along with my uncle. All the murders were beginning to take a toll on me. With the money that I already had and all the drugs that I've accumulated I could lay back and let my life play out with what I already had.

I pulled up to Uncle D's house and for some reason I

was getting a bad vibe. I could feel that something wasn't right. I pulled into the driveway and could see the front door cracked open. I immediately grabbed my Desert Eagle as I approached the front porch. Uncle D hardly ever got up before 12:00pm. I knew something wasn't right. It was only 9:15am. Walking up the steps I notice on the front door there was note with a dagger lodged through it that said, "YOU'RE NEXT."

With my fingertips I slowly pushed the door open as I stepped inside the house with my D.E. leading the way. Before I made it through the living room, I smelled a smell that I prayed that I would never have to smell again, and that was the metallic smell of blood. Feeling that I was about to walk up on something that I couldn't handle I stepped back out of the house with no one to call but Trey.

Once Trey arrived, we both re-entered the house. We checked every room and came up with nothing. I could tell that Trey's attention was elsewhere. His eye caught a piece of mail on the dining room table addressed to Uncle D. With a flick of the wrist Trey snatched it up and placed it in his pocket. Just as he did, I yelled from the kitchen.

"Trey, I'm in the kitchen." Trey rushed to my side. When he reached the kitchen, I was down on my knees cradling my uncle's head in my arms. I let the tears fall freely. I stared blankly at the one man who taught me about survival, and loyalty. Trey knew that I was hurt so he said nothing. Instead, he decided to let me mourn my lost. By the minute pure revenge filled my heart and retiring my gun-toting ways was no longer a thought. Finding my uncle's killer would now be my sole obligation and anyone who got in my way would be slaughtered. I looked over to the other body and didn't recognize him at all. With him lying there let me know that my uncle went out fighting. I then swore by Allah that I would find my uncle's killers and force them to suffer the same fate that he did.

CHAPTER NINE

PARIS

I had been striving my whole life. The first step to my successful career was my graduation. I thought that I looked beautiful in my cap and gown, but there still were two things that caused me to cry on the inside and out, and that was Olivia not being here to watch me walk across the stage. Although we had our differences, she still was my mother and I loved her as such. I also cried for Kayla, who since being fired stopped coming to school altogether. I was scared for my friend and prayed every night that she got her life together.

Even though I didn't have the two most important people in my life there for support, I did have the love of my life standing by my side, Trey. For my graduation Trey rented a stretch white Hummer. He cheered for me one hundred percent. To me he was the most loving and supportive person that I knew and in my eyes could do no wrong. As I walked across the stage, I received a huge applause. Trey was hyping everybody up to get loud. After I received my diploma, I ran and gave Trey the biggest hug and kiss that I could.

"I love you so much Trey. Thank you for being here for me," I stated with my arms around his neck.

"We in this together babygirl, I'll always be there for you. I'm proud of you baby." Trey leaned down and kissed me softly on my lips. Then from out of nowhere I heard a familiar voice. I breathed in a sigh and quickly turned around.

"Yeah, I'm proud of you too." When I turned around, I was face to face with Kayla.

"Kayla what are you doing here?" I asked not really caring long as she was there.

"I couldn't let my best friend graduate without me being here." Kayla leaned in and gave me a hug.

"You should be here too Kayla. We both worked so hard for this day," I replied as we released the embrace.

"I still graduated. I just have to finish two more months of night school. Look Paris I'm sorry for lashing out at you." Kayla grabbed my hand.

"Kayla we've been friends since first grade. Ain't nothing going to come between us that small," I replied, looking Kayla directly in her eyes.

"I love you girl." said Kayla

"I love you too." We embraced again.

"So what are you going to do?" I asked referring to her future.

"To be honest with you Paris, I should have been honest with you that day at my house. I've been stripping at the Skylark. I'm about to move into my own apartment next week. I'll probably go to college next year. You know my mom presses the issue every chance that she gets." Kayla smiled. I could tell that it was hard for her to tell me about it, but I was glad that she did.

"That's your choice Kayla. I'm behind you one hundred percent and I won't judge you because of it. Just don't wait too long to go." I pointed my index finger at her as if I was a scolding mother. We both laughed at my gesture.

"I won't. I'm still striving to get my doctorate." Kayla replied.

"Why don't you come eat dinner with us tonight?" I offered. There was so much that I wanted to tell her, and I didn't want her to leave.

"Sorry Paris I can't. I have some things that I need to take care of before I have to be at work, so I'll have to take a rain check on that," Kayla declined

"Okay girl, I love your ass." I gave her another hug and we both parted ways. I was happy to see Kayla, and even more happy that she was still focused. She didn't know it but she gave me more juice to achieve.

*****

MIDNIGHT

I was now picking up the pieces from my shattered life. It was almost time to lay my uncle to rest so I was in real state of grief. The more I thought of who could have killed my uncle the more I became lost. Even so, I kept having the feeling that the answer was right there in front of me.

Uncle D was respected by many and feared because of his reach. There were few that would try him. The ones who did had no problems with him. I just prayed to Allah that He would shed some light on this thing. Wanting to relieve some of the pent-up stress I was having, I decided to go to a club called the Chateau. Once arriving I looked at the people and admired their smiles because from the outside looking in it looked as if they didn't have a care in the world and were living their life to the fullest while I was grieving over my lost. As I approached the bar I was approached by the bartender.

"By the look of that somber face it looks like you need a strong drink," said the bartender. I looked over and immediately thought that he looked just like Richard Pryor.

"You couldn't be more right. Let me have a double Remy with a little bit of ice," I said as I turn around completely to face the bar.

"Coming right up," the bartender began to speak as he made my drink.

"You know, I don't know what exactly you're going through but know this, that if God can get you to it, then he can get you through it." He handed me my drink. I liked his way of thinking as well. "Try living life with no worries, and leaving everything in God's hands. Just take a stab at it." He gave me a reassuring smile.

"You know what? You're right. How much do I owe you?" I said reaching into my pocket.

"Oh don't worry about it; it's on the house just stop stressing yourself out." He smiled and moved down the bar to the next customer. I eventually ordered another drink and by the end of that I was feeling nice and carefree. I then looked up and saw Trey, so I called him over.

"What's up young buck? What you doing in here searching for some old pussy?" We both laughed and shook hands.

"Very funny old head. But yeah, I came out and snagged me some veteran pussy," Trey laughed.

"These old women not fucking with your young ass," I laughed again.

"Let you tell it. I got a pretty red bone in the bathroom right now. She got grey eyes and everything." Trey boasted happily over his catch for the night.

"Oh yeah, how old is she." I wondered.

"She's like thirty something. I'm about to knock sparks out of her old ass tonight," Trey replied.

"I see you getting tired of waiting on your Virgin Mary," I laughed.

"Believe it or not, but the bitch I just bagged looked just like her," Trey replied.

"That young girl gonna put that knife in you Trey," I warned with a laughed.

"Bullshit, she so in love, she doesn't question nothing that I do." Trey spoke with extreme arrogance.

"You better hope so, but look I'm about to get out of here before I can't drive home." I stood up with a stretch.

"I'll call you tomorrow. Oh yeah slim, I'm sorry about your uncle." Trey showed sincere sympathy.

"It's cool, but when I find out who did it you already know what's going to happen," I spoke seriously.

"I'm already hip, you be safe blackman." Trey shook my hand.

"You too, and don't let that old broad pussy whip you," I joked as I walked off.

"Never that." Trey spoke to my back. I gave an absent-minded wave and kept it moving. Olivia then walked up behind Trey placing her arms around him.

"You ready Treyvon?" she asked calling Trey by his whole first name.

*****

PARIS
(ONE YEAR LATER)

I was still holding on to my virginity and Trey was still by my side. Although I had graduated I had still yet to enroll in college due to the fact that I was still saving money. With Trey by my side, I could have already gone with my full tuition paid, but I refused to allow him to help me. I wanted to do this myself with no help from anyone. Trey and I were deeply in love with each other and had now been together for close to two years. Believe it or not, I was now ready to let my cherry go. I wasn't going to tell Trey, but the next time that things got heated I wouldn't stop it.

I loved living with Trey, but I didn't like him staying out late. There were times that I would ask myself was Trey cheating on me or was he at the club or worst yet, both. I was scared to find out that he was so I never asked or pressed the issue. I guess I called myself giving him the benefit of the doubt.

My birthday was now here and I was turning 19 years old. My mom and I were even talking again. She still wouldn't talk about my dad, but I didn't press her either I was just happy that we were talking and not at each other's throats.

I even thought about moving back home. Don't get me wrong, I did love living with Trey, but I did miss my room, and in a way my mom too.

*****

TREY

I was now tired of playing cat and mouse with Paris' cherry and ready to take our relationship to the next level. I'd gone out and bought Paris a 3.0 karat diamond ring. Although we had only been together for the past year and a half I was ready to spend the rest of my life with her.

I planned an elegant evening for Paris and myself. I'd set up reservations at an Italian restaurant called   'That's Amore'. I even rented out a limo for the night. I wanted everything to be perfect.

Paris was dressed in an elegant dinner dress made by Baby Phat's grown and sexy line. I choose an all-white three-piece suit. Together we were killing them. Paris knew that I was up to something tonight but didn't have a clue as to what, and I wouldn't tell her. While in route to our first destination Paris continued to pick me for my intentions.

"Trey, please tell me where are we going? I'll make it worth your while." Paris tried the seductive approach by talking sexy and rubbing my inner thigh.

"Be patient baby you'll see. I want every aspect of tonight to be a surprise." I replied placing my arm around her. Seeing she wasn't going to find out no sooner than I   wanted her to. She cuddled up under my arm and pouted. I kissed her forehead and enjoyed the rest of the ride. Ten minutes later the limo stopped and we were in front of a huge boat. Paris stepped out of the limo with her eyes showing great amazement. She looked at the name of the boat and read the name aloud.

"The Spirit of Washington." Paris then looked up at me. I said nothing and pointed at the ushers dropping rose petals all the way up the ramp. Paris instantly began to cry as she hugged and gave me the most passionate kiss that she could. I was planning to spoil Paris the whole night. We cruised along the Potomac and listened to the sweet sounds of the water. I could tell Paris hadn't been this happy in a long time. I was trying to give her that happiness that she desired for the rest of her life. As soon as we got back home I was still trying to place things into motion. As we walked through the door I immediately wrapped my arms around her causing her to laugh.

"You know I love you, right?" I asked kissing her neck.

"Yeah I know. I love you too Trey. I don't ever want you to leave me." Paris turned wrapping her arms around my neck.

"That's not happening. Look, sit down and relax. I want to holler at you about something." I lead her to the couch and sat her down. She immediately became worried.

"What is it Trey and it bet not be no Jerry Springer shit." I laughed at Paris paranoia, and she smiled.

"Naw baby it ain't nothing like that. I just wanted you to sit while you listen to what I have to say." I was intentionally keeping her in suspense.

"What is it Trey? You're scaring me." Paris pouted crossing her arms over her breasts. I then disappeared into the back and returned with two glasses and a bottle of Rose' Moet. Trying to relax a little myself I took off my jacket shirt and vest, and only wore my tank top. I handed Paris a glass and sat down next to her.

"Paris from the first day that I met you I knew that I wanted to spend the rest of my life with you. You're the center of my life and the perimeter around my heart. My life without you would be mentally impossible. So to make sure that doesn't happen I want you to wear this ring and be my wife." At first Paris sat there with tears streaming out of her eyes. As I slid the ring on her finger she was at a loss for words. Then she jumped in my arms and squeezed me as tight as she could.

"I guess that's a yes?" I smiled at her reaction.

"Yes, yes, yes, yes! I'11 marry you. Trey I love you so much." Paris looked me in the eye.

"I love you too baby. I hope you never forget this birthday."

"Trust me baby I won't ever forget this birthday, and neither will you."

Paris whispered right before she slipped her tongue in mouth. By her intensity I could tell that she was ready to explore new levels, so I picked her up and carried her into the bedroom. As I walked with her in my arms she continued to kiss me with heated passion and unbearable hunger. Gently I laid her across the king-sized bed. Paris leaned back on her elbows as I maneuvered around the room to lighting the candles. I hit the remote bringing the stereo to life with the sounds of Anthony Hamilton. I walked over to the closet to retrieve a bag of pre-cut rose petals. I threw the bag in the air letting the petals fall freely over the top of Paris' body.

I took my fiancé' by the hand for her to stand. Our eyes locked never once breaking the glare. No words were spoken. I pulled her close reaching behind her back to unzip her dinner dress. As I came back around to the front I grazed her cheek with my fingertips as her dress seductively fell to the floor. Paris' body was blemish free and undoubtedly alluring under the dancing flames of the candles. I sat Paris down allowing her to once again lean back on her elbows with one of her knees bent. I kissed her body from her toes to her calves, then knees to her hip bone. Still we never broke our eye contact. Paris head tilted back as her eyes rolling up from the passion in my touch. I was giving her my undivided attention. Smelling Paris' aroma of her juices flowing, I gently pulled Paris' sky blue thong off one leg at a time. I grabbed the baby oil massaging every body part that I could think of. Soon we were both naked and feigning for more. I controlled my craving but Paris was tired of being teased.

"Oh stop teasing me Trey. I want you in me please," Paris begged.

"You've teased me for almost two years Paris. Now it's my turn," I whispered in her ear. I ran my finger from the entrance of her tunnel up to the clit of her slit and licked the juices off of it.

"Please don't tease me Trey," Paris begged some more. Paris' pussy was literally throbbing for more. I began to bite and pull at Paris' pussy lips and clit bringing her to climax back to back. Turning her over I used some more baby oil coating her entire body with it. From the small of her back up to her neck I planted soft kisses. Once reaching her neck I whispered in her ear, "Happy Birthday." I slid my manhood inside Paris' walls as far as it would go. Paris buried her face in the pillows as I worked my way through her virgin walls. After about fifteen minutes all the pain was gone and Paris was in heaven. I turned her over and re-entered her in the missionary position.

"Oh I love you so much Trey. Please don't hurt me," Paris moaned. It was at that moment that Paris released a whole new rush of tears and the biggest orgasm that she had ever experienced.

"*OH AGGGHHH* Trey I'm cumming. Oh God Trey I'm cumming Trey." Paris lower back lifted off the bed as she moaned and screamed. I continued to pump feeling my pressure center itself as it built up. I soon released a heavy load of cum deep within Paris' walls of passion. Out of breath we both laid there drenched in each other's sweat and baby oil. Paris lay atop my chest and cried herself to sleep. I laid there smoking on some purple haze thinking how lucky I was to have such a beautiful woman at my side. There was nothing that I wouldn't do for her.

*****

MIDNIGHT

I was dressed in all black with tears soaking my face as I laid my uncle to rest. I sent my uncle out in style. He went to the best funeral home in D.C., which was Thurgood Marshall's Funeral Home. Uncle D was decked in Versace from head to toe as he lay in his platinum colored casket. There were over ten thousand people in attendance to pay their last respects to Uncle D. Pimps, whores, dope dealers, you name it; the street life's elite were in attendance

"How you holding up son?" asked my dad who had flown in from Germany when he heard the news. He had the same things to say every time I talked to him. He reminded me all the time of James Earl Jones.

"You raised me to survive in any weather," I replied and already knew exactly what his next words would be.

"Well since you such a survivor, the army would love to have you son. Let the police handle Drew's murder. You keep running in these streets son they're going to swallow you. Get out while you still can." It was the same speech. I wouldn't hear it before. Now, with my uncle being dead I definitely wasn't trying to hear it, now.

"No offense Dad, but my uncle is dead and his killer is still out there. I'm not getting out until his assailant is no longer breathing. And, the Army is out of the question as well. You forget that it was the good old U.S of A that took thirteen years of my life. There's no way in hell I'd fight for a country that doesn't belong to me or my people. I hope you can understand that."

"You're a grown man son and going to make your own

decisions. Just be careful." He placed a hand on my shoulder.
"That's first and foremost, Pop." I gave him a hug. Just as the funeral ended, I stood up preparing to escort my mom and pop out. Just as I did so I was stopped by a man in a sky-blue suit with glasses. I could tell he was some type of lawyer or bill collector.

"Excuse me Sir, are you the head of this funeral?" He asked already opening up a brown leather briefcase as if he already knew who I was before I told him.

"Yes, I'm the deceased's nephew. How may I help you?" I replied wondering who the hell this guy was. I hope he wasn't no bill collector. I wasn't in the mood to discuss none of my uncle's assets. He then extended his hand.

"I think you can. My name is Marcus Hamilton. Your uncle had a will with you listed as the beneficiary. You see he left you the cars and the house. If you sign right here it will all be yours." He attempted to hand me the pen and the paperwork. He seemed a little anxious but so was I. I then thought of how Uncle D always thought of the next six moves ahead like a game of chess. Then I thought.

"Before I sign what happens to my uncle's bank accounts?" I asked not feeling totally at ease about the situation.

"Well, there is another beneficiary that will receive the monies in those accounts," he replied pushing his glasses back up on his nose.

"Whose name is listed other than mine?" I asked

"I'm not at liberty to say Sir, but if you sign right here everything will be yours." He pushed the papers back to me.

I then thought that if Uncle D wanted me to have the money, then he would have left it to me. I decided that I didn't care what happened to the money. I took the papers and signed them. Mr. Hamilton smiled gave me a copy and walked off.

I was glad that that part was over. I began to help my mother gather her things in preparation to leave. Just as we stepped out of the church a black Yukon Denali pulled up in front of the church with two men hanging out the window with assault rifles. Immediately, I saw that it was hit and yelled, "Everybody get down!" Just as the words left my mouth the rifles came to life. *BOC! BOC! BOC! KA! KA! KA! BOC! BOC!*

I pushed my mother down to the ground in an attempt to shield her with my own body praying not to catch a bullet to the back. Screams were everywhere. Some lay dead. Some lay wounded. Luckily neither I nor my parents were hurt. I looked at my mother who was visibly shaken by the incident. For my mother to have to go through such a horrifying ordeal made my hunger for revenge even stronger.

Finally, the police got there and came up with a body count of four dead and seven wounded. I thought back to the note on the door and came to the conclusion that this was a hit targeted at me. I was actually scared because I now knew for sure that there was someone trying to kill me and I had no clue as to who. I was now cautious of everyone around me, and trusting people would be the last thing that I did.

*****

PARIS

It had been eight long months since I last saw Kayla. I prayed that she was healthy and succeeding in life. I called Kayla house and Ms. Alice said that she doesn't live there anymore. Then I remembered Kayla telling me that she was getting ready to move that following week. Kayla's mother gave me her cell phone number so I   gave her a call.

RING. RING. RING.

"Hello," Kayla answered.
"Hey stranger, looks like you forgot all about your best

friend." I said in a somber tone.

"Paris?" Kayla yelled in a surprised tone looking for confirmation.

"Who else would it be Ms. Gynecologist? I see you got your own shit now." I injected.

"Yeah, I had to get out of there with my mom. So what's been up with you Ms. Virgin?" Kayla teased.

"I'm fine, but I'm no longer Ms. Virgin. Trey knocked sparks out my ass about two months ago," I revealed knowing that Kayla would act a fool.

"What! You lying. Your uppity ass finally got some meat?" That was the usual Kayla with her untamed tongue.

"Yeah, Trey put it on me. Now I see what I was missing. I should have been got my cherry popped. "

"Listen to you Ms. Hoe got a new vocabulary and all. Where you at I'm coming over?"

"Hell, me and Trey moved in together a while ago so I live at 1411 Good Hope Rd. in southeast."

"Okay don't go nowhere I'm on my way over," Kayla replied.

"Aight you want me to meet you at the bus stop?" I asked

"Bus stop! Girl please! I'm driving a cherry red BMW," Kayla boasted.

"Excuse me Ms. Money bags. Just hurry up and get here," I rushed.

"I will damn. Always rushing a bitch. Be patient." Kayla laughed.

"Whatever hoe, just hurry up. Oh, and Kayla!" I called out taking the excitement out of my voice.

"Huh?" she replied

"I love you girl. "I said truly missing my friend.

"I love you to Nymphogirl." Kayla hung up. I was excited as hell that I was going to see Kayla. I had been moving so fast that I never realized that so much time was passing by. By the time I got off the phone I got a craving for some pizza and butter pecan ice cream. Even though I was living the good life with Trey I did miss the fun times that me and Kayla used to have. It wasn't long before Kayla got there I looked out the window every five minutes until she did. One thing that I admired about Kayla was that she was a survivor and would be that through any weather. At about 2:30pm Kayla pulled up and jumped out the car screaming my name.

"Paaarrriiisss!" She ran and gave me a tight hug. We truly had a genuine love for each other.

"Look at you Ms. BMW. How much this thing cost?" I was being nosey.

"A little over $20,000. I bought it used and it barely had any miles on it," Kayla replied.

"Kayla I'm so glad that you have yourself together. You survive through any weather," I admired.

"I'm proud of you too Paris. How is your tuition coming along? You should almost be done," Kayla assumed.

"Okay, I guess. I got a little more to go and then I'm gone. Just thinking about leaving gives me chills." We walked in the house. Kayla eyes scanned every corner and stopped when they landed on my food.

"Girl I know your ass not in here eating no pizza and butter pecan ice cream," Kayla yelled with her mind spinning with ideas.

"Yeah, I've been having a lot of weird cravings lately. You want some." I asked flopping down onto the couch.

"Hell no, your ass is pregnant and need all the food you can get," Kayla replied pointing to my stomach.

"Shut up Kayla I'm not pregnant." Come to think of it I can't remember my last period. Oh no! I thought to myself.

"Well guess what? Lucky for you I always keep a spare test with me." Kayla dug in her purse and pulled out a brand-new pregnancy test.

"Kayla, I know you not walking around with a pregnancy test in your purse?" I couldn't believe Kayla.

"I sure am. I get my boat rocked too much for me not to. Now here go pee." Kayla handed me the test.

"I am not pregnant." I continued to defend myself.

"Okay then when was the last time that you had your period?" Kayla asked getting to the bottom of things.

"I don't remember like two or three months ago. But that don't mean I'm pregnant." I was in denial. Kayla said nothing else and just simply pointed to the bathroom. I got up pouting and whining as I stomped to the bathroom. Once following the directions on the box, I ran out of the bathroom.

"Where you running to? What it say?" Kayla asked with a mouth full of ice cream.

"I don't know. I'm scared to look. You go check it." I sat down with my knees to my chest.

"You's a scary hoe Paris. I'll go look but I bet your ass is pregnant." Kayla said as she walked to the bathroom.

"Shut up Kayla!" I yelled to her back knowing that she was right.

"Yep, I told you. You're going to be a hippo soon." Kayla walked back into the room with the test in her hand.

"That's not funny Kayla. Oh God what am I going to do? I can't go to college and raise a baby." I began to cry placing my hands over my face. That's when Kayla spotted my ring.

"What's this Paris?" Kayla grabbed my wedding finger.

"Oh yeah me and Trey are getting married soon," I said nonchalantly.

"Married! Then what the hell are you scared about being pregnant? That man is about to be your husband. Paris you didn't give that man no pussy for two years. I know he's gonna be happy about a baby. Besides you can get him to watch the baby while you're in school. He helped make it so he might as well man up, or I'll drive you down to the courthouse myself to put his ass on child support." Kayla sat next to me.

"Oh, Kayla I'm so scared. I'm not ready for no baby,"

121

I cried.

"Look at the bright side. Now he can shoot his cum all in you for the next nine months," Kayla joked holding up nine fingers.

"Shut up Kayla you get on my nerves," I laughed easing the tension I was feeling.

CHAPTER TEN

MIDNIGHT

I was laid back in Uncle D's house which was now mine sipping on Remy Martin trying to piece together all of the events that had transpired the last two weeks. I also wondered why someone would want me dead. I had done so much dirt across the city that it would be almost impossible to narrow it down to just one. I just prayed that I figured out who before the Grim Reaper came knocking on my door.

While I was thinking the murders that I'd committed were starting to weigh down on my mind. I couldn't wait for all this to be over so I could hang my gun up for good. Hopefully God would let that be possible. My train of thought was then broken up by a knock at the door. I jumped up and grabbed my Desert Eagle and cautiously approached the front door. When I got there and looked out I saw two white men standing there with cheap suits on that basically spelled the word pigs. I tucked my gun and answered the door.

"Can I help you gentlemen?" I asked in a no-nonsense tone.

"How are you Sir? My name is Agent Bright, and this is my partner Agent Simon. We're with the FBI. You mind if we come in and talk?" The white officer looked like Al Bundy. His teeth were stained from his day-to-day usage of coffee and

Newports. He tried to give me a re-assuring smile, but in my eyes a cop was a cop and couldn't be trusted.

"First you can tell me why you're here? From there where you stand." I pointed to the ground.

"Well first off we're asking the questions, so you can start off by telling us your name," Agent Bright replied. I'm very aware of the law, so he didn't know who he was fucking with.

"That's where you're wrong. If you don't have a warrant, then you can get off of my property. If I'm not under arrest and you don't want to leave, I can have you physically removed." Agent Bright's face turned bright red.

"That won't be a problem Sir you got that, but we will be seeing you again. I promise." Agent Bright then gave me that stained smile and place on his shades.

"I don't buy death," I replied.

"Pretty positive you don't Sir, or should I say Mr. Brown. You have a nice day." Agent Bright arrogantly smiled and stepped off.

I was completely on point when the pig said my name. Now I was even more paranoid. Mainly because this wasn't the MPD, DEA, or ATF even. I was an interest of the FBI. Now my next question would be why? For the agents to know my last name made me wonder what else they knew about me. Was it drugs, extortion, murder, or worst yet all of the above under the infamous RICO Act. I hadn't a clue, but from this point on I would walk light.

The rest of my day went pretty rough. Twice today I saw those same two agents in my rearview. They had me super paranoid. I need to relax and get my mind off things. So I decided to go to the Skylark for a few drinks. The agents had me tense, so I figured that I'd buy some pussy and relax for the rest of the evening.

It was about one in the morning when I pulled into the Skylark's parking lot. There were two girls out fighting. Hair and titties were everywhere. I decided to post up until one of the girls fell unconscious. Once that happened, I went inside. The police would be there soon, and I refused to be a witness or deal with anymore pigs for the rest of the night.

I stepped to the entrance and was carded and searched before I was granted entrance. I walked to the bar and ordered a double Remy. Once I received my drink I took a seat near the exit and was immediately approached by a familiar face. It was the girl from the last time I was here that I gave the hundred dollars to.

"Hey Mr. Big Spender. You came back to see me huh?" The young girl kissed me on the cheek. She wore nothing but silver tassels on her nipples with her pussy hair shaped up to the form of a heart.

"Yeah, I guess so. What's your name?" I asked.

"My stage name Strawberry, but you can call me Ebony," she replied.

"Okay Ebony you gonna give me that lap dance you owe me, or do I have to pay for it?" I asked. She better answer right because I wasn't up for the games tonight.

"Oh you gotta pay. That was then, this is now. I got bills to pay," she stated dead serious.

"Wrong answer you money hungry bitch. If you would have given me the lap dance, I would have taken your gold-digging ass to the hotel you dumb bitch. Now you ain't getting shit. Kick rocks bitch!" This bitch had me heated.

"Well fuck you then you little dick motherfucker and fuck that hundred dollars. I make ten times that in a night." Ebony stormed off into the crowd. It wasn't long before I was approached by another dancer. This one I wouldn't turn away.

"Hey Big Daddy. You want a dance? Hey, don't I know you?" Kayla asked looking into my face.

"Yeah, I was here a few months back with my man Trey." I could never forget her. She was a bad bitch all the way around.

"Oh yeah I remember you. So what's up? You looking for some fun tonight, or what?" Kayla asked making her ass clap as she talked.

"Depends on what type of fun you're talking about?" I replied letting her ass cheeks catch a dollar out of my hand. When they were clapping the angel wings on her ass made her look as if she was getting ready to fly away.

"Why don't we go over to the VIP for starters and see what we can come up with," Kayla replied turning back towards me.

"Hell, I got a better idea. Why don't you go and get dressed and meet me at the front door?" I wanted to cut straight through all the bullshit.

"Sounds good to me I'll be back in about ten minutes." Kayla kissed me on the cheek and strutted off to the dressing room with her wings flapping. While I was waiting, I was given a tap on the shoulder. I turned around and stood up. I was now face to face with Ebony and what looked to be her pimp. At that point with everything going on in my life I realized that I was bullshitting in a strip club without my pistol.

"What's up slim? You say something to this female right here?" The guy asked. He was dark-skinned with braids and minimal facial hair. I hoped that I didn't have to fuck this guy up.

"Yeah, I did. You got a problem with what I said to her?" I swelled up.

"Yeah, I do. This my hoe and I don't appreciate what you said to her. Personally, I think you owe her and apology." The guy brushed imaginary lint off of his shoulder.

"You bitch ass nigga! Who the fuck you think you is, Goldie? I'll leave your ass stinking in one of these alleys. You better find out who you fucking with." I felt disrespected by this clown. Then from out of nowhere *SMACK!* This fake ass pimp smacked me with his palm wide open. I immediately grabbed a patron's Remy Bottle and sent it crashing over top of his head. The bottle didn't break but he went out cold. I then dug in his pockets and retrieved all the money he had on him and tossed it into the crowd. As I got to the door Kayla was right there. I grabbed her hand and quickly left the club.

"Wait, what happened to Cornell?" Kayla asked as I pulled her along. I said nothing until we were pulling off.

"What the fuck happened back there? Why you in such a rush?" Kayla spoke in a tone that demanded an answer, so I gave her one.

"That fake ass pimp tried to swell up on me, so I knocked him out," I stated.

"You mean, Cornell, right?" Kayla began laughing hard. "Are you serious? He's the biggest punk in there. He tries to talk to all the dancers. He's a nobody." Kayla continued to laugh.

"That's even worst I got slapped by a nobody. Nigga better be lucky I didn't have my hammer on me." I was really pissed.

"Cornell smacked you?" Kayla repeated not believing her ears or controlling her laughter.

"Fuck that nigga! We going to the Holiday Inn. You with it?" I gave her a brief glance as I drove.

"I'm with anything if the price is right. I don't leave no disappointed customers. I make sure you get your money's worth." Kayla's voice sounded as if she was moaning as she grabbed my manhood causing me to smile.

"My money stay right. Don't chew off nothing that you can't handle," I warned her.

"Trust me chewing and swallowing won't be a problem for me." Kayla then stuck her two fingers in her mouth sucking them seductively.

"I like your attitude; you're cocky and confident. I'm gonna shut that up for tonight." I smiled.

"Sounds good. We gonna see who's biting off more than they can chew or better yet swallow, "Kayla replied with an arrogant smile.

I took Kayla out Silver Spring MD, to the Holiday Inn

with plans to obtain the presidential suite. When we stepped in the room our breath was taken away at how elegant the room was. It had a 65' plasma flat screen, King size bed and a Jacuzzi with under water jets. The paintings and rugs looked to be imported. Kayla walked to the balcony overlooking downtown Silver Spring. I walked up behind her wrapping my arms her waist nibbling on her neck. Kayla closed her eyes and let me have my way with her.

I slowly removed Kayla's loosely fitting halter top freeing her caramel breasts just big enough for a handful. I sucked on her nipples being sure to show each one equal attention. With the help of Kayla, I removed her halter top letting it fall to the floor right along with my own pants. I pulled my hard penis through the slit of my boxers and turned her around. Pulling her thong to the side I rubbed the head of my penis back and forth across her clit. Kayla willingly turned around spreading her legs apart. She slightly leaned over the rail with her ass arched as high as it could go. Kayla had the prettiest gap in between her legs. Nor her thighs, calves, or ass had a blemish on them. Just the sight of the angel wings on her ass turned me on even more. Slowly I entered her from behind. Kayla's pussy was so wet that her vaginal juices cascaded down her leg upon my entrance of her tunnel. With one good thrust I slid my manhood all the way in to the hilt of my shaft. Kayla dipped her back inhaling strongly from the huge intake. As I loosened her walls to adjust to my length, Kayla bit on her bottom lip.

"Ohh do it faster," Kayla moaned reaching back placing her palm on my cheek. The louder Kayla got the more excited I became.

Although we were on the balcony neither one of us cared who saw or heard us. We were only coherent to each other. The world didn't exist. It was only us and the orgasm that we both longed for. With everything that she had Kayla stopped and turned around looking me directly in the eyes. Slowly she walked back inside the room. I began to protest but was stopped by Kayla putting a finger to my lips. I read her eyes and realized that she wanted me to follow her inside. Like a dog in heat, I did just that.

Kayla sat me down and with one swift motion of her neck swallowed my whole ten inches. Kayla's head game was serious, and she was planning on taking me to the land of ecstasy. It wasn't long before Kayla's neck motion caused me to erupt in her mouth, and just as Kayla said before she had no problem swallowing nothing.

As my shaft pumped out its juices Kayla focused on sucking the tip being sure to get every drop down her throat. After my eruption I thought our little sexcapade was over, but I was wrong, and Kayla wasn't finished. She continued to work on my dick till I was back at full attention. Once doing so Kayla lubricated her asshole and slid my entire shaft deep within her ass hole. Kayla rode my dick backwards like no one I ever had before. With Kayla's ass being as tight as it was, I came again within minutes. Kayla was an animal, and her asshole was almost as wet as her pussy. She then took a rag and cleaned me up. Then once again she sucked me back to life. I turned her over placing both of her legs on my shoulders. I slid in and began to beat her pussy with no mercy. "AAGGGHHHH fuck me harder you black motherfucker. Beat it up harder. OOHH GOD your dick big." Kayla moaned relentlessly catching orgasm after orgasm. Kayla loved for her pussy to be beat up. Two nuts later we were both knocked out. I thought to myself that I really underestimated Kayla's abilities.

*****

PARIS

I was scared to death to have this baby. I was even more scared to tell Trey. What I really wanted was my mom. I was so confused that I didn't know what to do. Kayla tried to comfort me as much as she could, but I couldn't comprehend anything. All I could think of was being pregnant and not being able to pursue my lifelong dream to be a Respiratory Therapist.

I tried to call Trey but got no answer, so I paged him and put in the code 911 that he told me to use only in case of an emergency. After placing that code in he called right back, and I told him that I needed him to come home right away. He complied and said he was on his way. I was so scared to tell Trey but knew that I had to. I just prayed that he took it in a good way, and not turn his back on me. Trey got to the house within fifteen minutes. When he saw me crying he rushed to my side.

"What's up baby, what's wrong? Tell me what's up." Trey wrapped his arms around me.

"I'm so scared Trey. I don't know what to do. Please don't leave me." I sobbed and stuttered between my words.

"I'm not going to leave you. What's wrong baby, you got to talk to me. What happened?" I couldn't bring myself to speak the words, so I simply just pointed to the pregnancy test on the table. Trey looked and smiled like a kid in the candy shop.

"Baby your pregnant?" He looked up with his eyes shining like stars as he waited for my confirmation.

"Please don't leave me." I mumbled and looked off not wanting to look him in the eyes.

"Leave you? Baby this is great. I'm not going nowhere." *Fuck no this isn't great* was how I was thinking.

"Trey it's not great. I wanna go to college and be a doctor. I can't do that and raise a child."

"So you telling me that you want to have an abortion? You wanna kill my baby?" Trey's smile instantly disappeared.

"No Trey, yes Trey. Ohh I don't know what I want to do." I continued to cry.

"Paris look, I'm here for you every step of the way. I want this baby," Trey pleaded.

"I know Trey. I want this baby too, just not right now," I tried to reason.

"Baby I will take care of the baby and you can still go to school when you want to."

"And what about my job? They're gonna fire me," I whined.

"Fuck that job, Paris. I got you just trust me okay? Please." I looked up in Trey eyes and saw them began to water. I then realized that I was hurting Trey. Trey had been so good to me that hurting him was the last thing that I wanting to do. I decided to trust him.

"I love you Trey." I leaned my head on his chest as he cradled me in his arms.

"I love you to Paris just trust me alright?" He kissed me on the forehead.

"Yeah." And that was it, I was having a baby. Trey sat there and held me until I fell asleep in his arms.

*****

MIDNIGHT

Kayla put it on me in ways that I've never experienced. No women had ever worked me as Kayla did. I had planned to only give her $250, but after a night like last night I chalked up and gave her $500. If she wasn't a stripper I might try to handcuff and lock her down.

The next morning after I paid her I decided to take her to the International House of Pancakes for breakfast. We walked in and were seated in the back in the smoking area. After a while our waiter approached the table. He was a young white kid who gave a look that said he didn't need the job he was working.

"Hello welcome to IHOP my name is Josh, and I will be your waiter. Are you ready to order, or do you still need a minute?" the young guy asked. He was a little too jovial for my liking, almost grayish.

"I can order now. I would like the steak, egg and potato platter with a large orange juice." I folded my menu and handed it back to Josh.

"And I'll have the Belgium waffles with an iced tea," Kayla replied and also handed Josh her menu.

"Okay your food will be ready shortly," Josh smiled and skipped off into the back. Kayla and I engrossed ourselves in a lively conversation while we waited for our food to arrive. Kayla began to tell me all about her struggles to be a doctor. I thought that it was at least good that she striving for a better life with the money that she made, but me personally I thought the lowest degree of any stripper who sold her body to make money. Kayla was on a mission so I guess I could at least respect that much of her situation. After about twenty minutes of talk our food finally arrived, but it didn't arrive by Josh.

"Here is your food Sir. Will there be anything else?" the waiter asked.

"What happened to Josh?" I asked the brown skinned man with a white kufi on his head. Josh had an accident in the back. My name is Muhammad. I will finish up for him," Muhammad replied.

"That's cool." Muhammad then turned around and left us to enjoy our food. Kayla and I continued to converse as we ate our meal Kayla surprised me at how intelligent she truly was, yet she was stripping. That really made her lose points. Feeling the urge to relieve myself I excused myself and walked to the bathroom. When I returned the check was there with a note attached to it.

In the name of Allah, most gracious most merciful. By Allah I'm going to kill you like I did your uncle. I might start with your female friend.

As-salaam Alaikum

I instantly jumped up snatching my Desert Eagle from

my waist. I burst through the back in search of Muhammad. I searched every corner, nothing. I looked and saw the back door of the restaurant so I rushed to see if I could catch him. Again nothing. I looked to my right and saw Josh lying by the dumpster hog-tied with duct tape on his mouth and nothing on but his boxers. I knew that Muhammad was long gone. I then ran back to the table to get Kayla.

"It's time to go," I spoke to Kayla who was reading the note with a terrified look on her face.

"Let's go we gotta get out of here now," I demanded.

"Hell no! If somebody trying to kill you then that means that they'll kill me if I get caught with you. You on your own. I'll get a cab," Kayla replied not wanting me to touch her.

"Suit yourself you dumb bitch. You read the note. They might just kill you anyway." I tried to reason with her stupidity.

"I like my chances. They might be right outside waiting on you." Kayla stood her ground crossing her arms over her chest.

"Fuck it then. Suit yourself. I'm out." I wasn't about to sit there and try to convince this dumb bitch any longer that she would be safer with me than without me. Plus, I wasn't about to get cornered inside this restaurant. It was time to bounce and meet my fate head on. I grabbed my leather coat and proceeded to leave. I stepped outside with my D.E. in hand. In the parking lot, idling at the exit sat that same Yukon Denali from my uncle's funeral. From what I could see, all occupants wore kufis. Just as I raised my gun the passenger hung out the window clutching a Mac-90. Without regret or caution the man raised the rifle and began his murderous   assault. *BOC! BOC! BOC! BOC! BOC! BOC!* I jumped behind a parked SUV and returned fire. *BOOM! BOOM! BOOM!* I hit the back of the SUV as it sped off into the morning. Hearing sirens approaching I hopped in my DTS and sped off as well. I was extremely paranoid. In all my years I'd never been the prey. I'd always been the stalker. It was killing me not knowing who wanted me dead. By the note inside the IHOP I now felt not only was my life in danger but the people around me as well. The last thing that I wanted was for someone to lose their life because of how I was living mine.

CHAPTER ELEVEN

PARIS

It was 4:30 in the fucking morning and I had been waiting and stressing for Trey to come in. I called his two-way and his cell phone only to continually get his answering machine and got no return call. Not to mention, this pregnancy was causing me to have countless mood swings. I couldn't take Trey being in the streets all night not knowing if he was dead or alive, or even in someone else's bed. I was finding myself through many nights crying myself to sleep, and tonight was no different. I fell asleep eating chicken and grapes. Two in the afternoon the following day I was awakened by Trey who was just walking in the house. Seeing Trey, I jumped straight up.

"Motherfucker, you don't know how to call home and return my fucking calls?" I hit Trey on the chest. Trey immediately stood up and walked off.

"I'm not in the mood for your shit Paris," Trey replied over his shoulder. I ran and got right back in his face.

"My shit? Motherfucker I'm sitting here carrying your child and worried sick about your ass. I didn't know if you were dead or what. Then you gonna come in here and say you not in the mood for *MY* shit! Motherfucker I'm tired of YOUR shit!" I yelled hitting him in the chest again.

"You done yet?" Trey, easily not affected by my small

blows
"You motherfucking right I'm done. I'm done with your ass." I stormed off to the bedroom. Trey ran right behind me and grabbed my wrist to spin me around.

"Paris would you shut the fuck up so I can talk, damn? What the fuck you tripping for?" Trey shook me by the shoulders so I would listen.

"Motherfucker I'm tripping because you keep telling me you love me. If you did, you wouldn't be stressing me out like this. I don't know what the hell you doing out there!" I yelled wiggling free of Trey's grasp.

"What I'm doing out there?" I could tell Trey was heated now. "I'm out there keeping your ass in that fancy high price shit you like and feeding your hungry ass. That's what I'm doing out there. You need stop letting that pregnancy get to you!" Trey yelled.

"Well, you don't have to worry about that no more because I'm going back to my mother house. So fuck you!"

"Look Paris, just calm down. I know it's hard right now. Just give me a few more months and I'll have enough money to set us up for the rest of our lives. I got something in the making that's going to pay off big. Once I get this last pawn out of my way we can move to Jamaica or anywhere you want to. No more guns no more drugs, and no more running the streets. Everything gone and stopped. Just give me a few more months, Baby, please." Trey rubbed the side of my face while I listened with my arms folded across my chest. Trey sounded so convincing, and I wanted to believe him so bad. I really loved Trey and would do anything for us to work.

"You promise?" I replied allowing Trey to wrap me in his strong arms.

"Yeah, I promise. Then we can move wherever you want to. Now come here and let me kiss that fat belly you getting." Trey sat on the bed and lifted my shirt, kissing me all over my belly.

Trey then noticed that I didn't have on any panties.

"Shut up Trey! It's your fault I look like this." We both laughed then Trey worked his way down to the curl patch of hair atop of my pussy. Trey found my clit lightly flicking it with his tongue. My knees instantly became weak, and I'd forgot all about being mad at Trey. He then took me to levels that only he could. In seconds he brought me to my first orgasm.

"OHHH I'm about to cum baby." I started to grind my pussy into his face. I propped my leg up on the bed so he could have total access to my tunnel. As I came my other leg gave way, but Trey caught me lightly laying me on the bed. As he did so he continued to devour my pussy. "OOHHH god, Trey I love YOOOU." After he brought me to two more orgasms, he decided that he'd get some rest. Now drained, I decided to do the same and fell asleep with a smile on my face.

I ended up waking around 4:30pm to the sound of Trey cell phone going off in the living room. After a while I finally managed to get up and answer it. Reaching the living room, I grabbed the phone and read the name *Olivia* on the screen. My heart literally skipped a beat. My world had just come crashing down. It continued to ring as I held it in my hand. Finally, I gathered enough strength to answer it.

"Hello."

"Trey is that you?" Olivia asked.

"Who the fuck is this calling this phone?" *CLICK* The caller hung up the phone. I was pissed to no return. I ran in the kitchen to the utility door to get my weapon of choice. Now it was on.

When Trey opened his eyes, I was sitting on his knees with his dick in my left hand and a box cutter in my other. When he realized the position, he was in his eyes got big as hell.

"Paris what, what's up? What you doing?" Trey contended, scared shitless to make any sudden moves.

"I trusted you Trey. Why, why would you do this to

me?" I cried profusely still gripping on to his manhood tightly.
"Did what Paris? I didn't do shit, now please drop the blade." Trey pleaded to deaf ears. At that moment I was deaf and blind.

"Motherfucker who the fuck is Olivia then? Huh? Explain that you dirty dick motherfucker. I should cut this dirty little motherfucker clean off. I squeezed tighter.

"Paris, I don't know an Olivia. What are you talking about?" Trey calmly spoke holding both hands up in surrender.

"Lie again." I applied pressure with the blade to the bottom of his shaft. "The bitch been calling your phone all fucking day. I answered the phone Trey she said your name. Now lie again and I'm dismembering your ass," I warned and was dead serious. "Paris I don't know an ....."

"AGGGGHHHH!" I raised my arm getting ready to slice it clean off. Trey quickly sat up catching my arm as it came down. I wiggled free and ran to the kitchen phone to call Kayla to come and get me. Soon as I dialed her number and she answered, everything went black.

*****

MIDNIGHT

It was luck that I had survived yet another attempt made against my life. Could it be that I had a Rabbit's foot up my ass or could it be that it wasn't my time to go? Either way I was alive and grateful. Still, I wondered deeply who it could possibly be trying to kill me. The bartender's statement kept playing over and over in my head. *'Try living life with no worries. Just leave it in God's hands. Try it out. Just take a stab at it.'* I remember his every word but there was one part that kept playing over and over. *'Take a stab at it. Take a stab at it.'* I repeated these words in my head over and over. Then out of the corner of my eye I saw the dagger that was lodged in the front door when I found my uncle. I jumped up and went to the table to retrieve it. This was it. I remembered exactly where it came from. I wanted to go over there and shoot up everything breathing, but knew I'd land in D.C. jail quicker than Alpo would tell something.

I was far from stupid and definitely wouldn't go in the lion's den unarmed, nor did I want to end up outnumbered. Although I wasn't trying to trust anyone, I decided to go with Uncle D's choice, Trey. I flipped open my cell phone and called him.

"Yeah?" Trey answered.

"Aye youngbuck this Midnight."

"What's up Old timer?" Trey replied.

"I'm good, but we gotta talk as soon as possible," I informed.

"Aight, right now I'm at Washington Hospital Center with my girl. I'll call you when I leave," Trey replied.

"Naw this can't wait. We gotta talk now. I'm on my way." This couldn't wait. My uncle's killer had to die now.

"Aight we in the emergency room," Trey replied.

"Aight I'm on my way so stay there." *CLICK!* I hung up and was on my way out the door with my D.E. on my hip.

*****

TREY

After Midnight's and I had a conversation, I checked my pistol just in case he came on some bullshit. I would wait though and playthings by ear. Paris on the other hand with her being pregnant and all was under too much stress. She had called Kayla I guess to come get her and ended up passing out. When I put the receiver to my ear and heard Kayla's voice, I hung up on her and called the paramedics. I was fucked up at myself for being so careless to let Paris find out about Olivia. I already knew that was the cause of her blackout.

Paris sat in the emergency room with tubes up her nose and about three different machines hooked up to her body to help monitor the baby's progress. I never thought that my cheating ways would catch up to me in such a life altering manner. I never thought they would endanger Paris or my unborn child. Kayla knew that something was wrong, so she called back and I explained the situation vaguely to her. She found out the hospital we were at and got there as quickly as we did. When she saw me she gave me the third degree.

"Where the fuck she at Trey?" Kayla yelled at me.

"I ain't do nothing to her. She just passed out. Fuck you tripping on me for?" I replied.

"What room she in you lying motherfucker, and you bet not have hit her!" Kayla used her finger to push my head.

"The doctor said that we can't go in yet. I'm waiting for him to come and tell me what's wrong with her," I calmly explained hoping that my words would calm her down as well.

"You better hope she lives. Because if she doesn't, I swear to God I'm gonna cut your ass up!" Kayla threatened. I didn't know it, but she meant every word.

"Won't be the first time that someone threatened to cut me." I thought back to Paris and her box cutter. Just then the doctor entered the waiting area.

"Excuse me I'm looking for the family of Paris Clemons?" The doctor asked as he walked in.

"Yes, that's me how is she doing?" I stepped forward with eyes of hope.

"Okay my name is Doctor Gregory Ames. I've been Paris' doctor since she was little girl. I'm also the one who will be monitoring her pregnancy. What we have is a mild stroke. They normally happen to women Paris' age only when they're pregnant. It comes from too much stress. Paris is pregnant so stress in her body and mind will triple versus a woman who isn't pregnant. She'll be okay she just needs to be stress free and get a lot of rest."

"What about the baby she's carrying." I asked still worried about my child.

"The baby is fine. So like I said, she needs a lot of rest. If not, then she could very well lose the baby. I have another patient to tend to, so here are my numbers. You can call me if there are any more complications." He handed me his cards.

"Sure thing, Doc and thank you for everything." I shook his hand.

"No problem. You have a nice day." Doctor Ames smiled.

"Can we go in and see her?" Kayla cut in.

"Visiting hours are over for today but will start back up at 8:00 in the morning. Hopefully, she'll be up waiting on y'all."

Dr. Ames replied pushing his glasses up on his nose.

"Alright thanks again Mr. Ames." Kayla stated.

"Call me Greg, mister makes me sound too old. I'm only thirty-four." Dr. Ames winked at Kayla and gave her a smile, causing her to blush. As soon as Trey and Kayla walked out of the waiting room they ran straight into Midnight. Kayla looked as if she'd seen a ghost.

"Oh hell naw, you stay the hell away from me. I'm not getting killed for something that you did." Kayla blew straight pass Midnight without him saying one word to her. Letting Kayla be Kayla, Midnight focused on the situation at hand, and that was making Uncle D's killer meet his fate.

"What's up Midnight what's so important?" I asked watching his hands closely.

"The people who killed Uncle D are trying to kill me now. I also got an idea who they are too." Midnight revealed.

"Oh yeah, who?" I replied. Extremely interested in what he knew.

*****

PARIS

Finally, I opened my eyes. It felt like I was dreaming forever. I looked around my room and saw the most beautiful exotic flowers I'd ever seen in my life. At first I was overwhelmed, then reality sat in, and I remembered why I was in the hospital in the first place. More importantly, who was the cause of it. I could do nothing but sit there and cry. I swore that Trey could do no wrong so it hurt me even more to find out that he would deceive me the way that he did. The whole day I sat in a melancholy mood wondering what I did or didn't do to make Trey venture out into other waters. In a way I believed Trey's cheating was my fault.

At around 4:00pm I was greeted by my human survival kit, Kayla. One thing that I will always be able to say is that when I needed Kayla she was always there. In fact, half of the flowers and gifts were from her telling me to get well. I was still a little out of it from the medication, but was all smiles to see Kayla.

"What's up hoe. It's about time you woke up," Kayla smiled giving me a hug and a kiss.

"That medicine got me real tired and sleepy. Where all this stuff come from?" I asked.

"Most of it is from me and some from Trey." I didn't even want to hear Trey's name right then.

"Does my mother know that I'm in here?" I asked looking in Kayla face.

"No, I didn't call her because I didn't know whether or not you wanted her to know that you're pregnant."

"I'm glad that you didn't. I wanted to tell her myself." I replied.

"So are you going to tell me what happened and how exactly did you get in here?" Kayla lay on my feet.

"Girl it's a long story." I leaned my head back on the pillow.

"Well, I got all day and don't have to be at work until 12:00am, so spill it Nymphogirl." Kayla hopped in the bed and cuddled up next to me.

"Well, I remember calling Trey all day long, and he would never answer or call me back. Kay, I was so worried about him. When he finally came home the next day we argued and made up afterwards." Kayla cut me off.

"You mean make up sex?" Kayla smiled devilishly.

"Would you shut up and let me tell the story? Thank you. Anyway, we both went to sleep. Later I woke up because his cell phone ringing off the hook. I finally got up and answered it. When I looked at the screen it said some bitch named Olivia. I press talk and said hello. The bitch called Trey name and when I said something she hung up the phone. "

"Maybe it was your mom calling to check up on you." Kayla reasoned.

"No, it couldn't have been her because she and Trey never met before. But anyway, I went and grabbed my box cutter and woke his ass up with the blade to his dick. When I asked him who she was he swore that he didn't know her. I swung and tried to cut it off, but he caught my arm. I ran and tried to call you to come and get me but that's when everything went dark." By the time I finished telling the story Kayla was trying her best to hold in her laugh, but couldn't and burst out laughing.

"Girl you done went from Ms. Virgin to Ms. Bobbit." Kayla joked.

"Shut up Kayla it's not funny. I couldn't believe he would cheat on me. I did everything that he wanted. Why would he do this to me Kayla? Why?" I began to cry again.

"Stop crying Paris. Forget him. Men come and go. Plus, Greg said you can't be stressed out or you'll not only be putting yourself in danger but the baby as well. You can come live with me or can go to your mom's house. You're not going back to Trey's while you're pregnant," Kayla sternly said.

"I'll go to my mom's house. You work at night. I don't

want to stay at your house by myself," I whined and pouted.

"You are such a scaredy cat Paris," Kayla smiled then I looked up.

"Who's Greg Kayla?" I wondered.

"He's your doctor and he's cute and only 34." Kayla replied with lust in her voice. I could tell she was on the prowl.

"You mean Gregory Ames?" I couldn't believe Kayla.

"Yes, and he is fine and I mean that with every aspect of the word." Kayla tapped my hand.

"Eww, Kayla he's been my doctor since I was 13 don't your hormones ever stop?" I laughed.

"Nope. Especially when there is a doctor involved. He winked at me to. I think I can get him."

"And you call me Nymphogirl," I replied laughing.

CHAPTER TWELVE

MIDNIGHT

After filling Trey in on my assumptions and my reasons, Trey was all for going to see who Uncle D's possible assassinator was. We were both strapped up. Last night after leaving the hospital I made a few calls and obtained a few throw away guns equipped with silencers. I put my Desert Eagle up for two Hecklar and Koch ten millimeters. For Trey I copped him two nines. I made sure to tell Trey that once we inside that everything must die.

In a way I blamed myself for Uncle D's death because if I would have handled my business in the first place then my uncle would still be here. We pulled up to the Southern Dinner in the morning hours of the day. I planned on cleaning house, so I wanted the least amount of people to be there. We checked our pistols and quickly entered the restaurant with murderous thoughts. At the register was the same Muslima with the enchanting eyes. She looked up and smiled at Trey.

"Abdul Rahman. As-salaam Alaikum." She stated with a jovial voice.

"Wa Alaikum Salaam." Trey returned her salaam (greeting) as he whipped out one of his nines and took aim.

TWIP!

Trey sent a silenced bullet through the young girl forehead. She saw Allah before she hit the floor. Due to the slight ruckus the office door flew open revealing Magny's whereabouts. Once he saw me he tried to slam the door, but I was right on him. I whipped out both of my ten-millimeters kicking the door in. Inside Magny was frantically on the floor trying to open the safe. I sent the butt of my gun crashing down on his forehead.

"You soy bean eating motherfucker. You killed my uncle." *SMACK*! "Shot at my parents!" *SMACK*! "Tried to kill me twice." SMACK, SMACK!

SMACK! I repeatedly smacked him with butt of my pistol.

"Oh please don't, it was all........" SMACK! I hit him again dazing him.

"Shut the fuck up you lying motherfucker! This look familiar to you? It's the same dagger I used to stab you in the hand with." To my right hanging on the wall hung old Chinese daggers set with six slots and only five daggers. I placed the dagger in and it fit perfectly. I then took the dagger and stabbed Magny in the hand again all the way to the hilt.

"AGGGHHHHHH." Magny screamed out in agonizing pain. I got directly in Magny face.

"I hope my uncle tortures your hoe ass." I then placed my ten millimeter to his head. Just before I pulled the trigger he spoke.

"So this how it ends, huh Trey? I guess you ended up being the better man. Oh, and just so you know, I'm not the triggerman who killed your uncle. Although, I wish I had been. I would have hit that safe he got. But I didn't so fuck it, and fuck you too, and Uncle Flea. *TWIP, TWIP, TWIP*. I heard enough and seen more than I needed to. I refused to let this faggot disrespect the dead. The power of the ten-millimeter sent the knife through his hand and his body into the corner. Brain matter and blood owned Magny's desk and face. Although Magny last words had me confused I remained focus knowing that I had to get away. We both tucked our pistols and casually walked out the office. All praises were due because there wasn't a soul inside. Just as we took the first step to make our exit a Muslim couple stepped in wearing Muslim attire. I instantly looked at Trey as he gave each of us and Islamic greeting. We looked at each other and simultaneously whipped out *TWIP, TWIP, TWIP, TWIP*. The couple fell to the ground with their heads and faces full of holes. We kept it moving on outside and into our getaway car.

　　While driving I sat in deep thought about Magny's last words. At times Trey would try and make up conversation but I still sat quietly. Eventually, I gathered my thoughts and pulled into a secluded alley. Once the car stopped, I told Trey to get out. By the time he opened the door and stood up outside the car he was looking down the barrels of both my ten-millimeters. Trey almost shitted on himself.

　　"You even look like you wanna reach, you gonna make the news. Put your hands on the roof." I spoke with pure malice in my voice.

　　"What the fuck's up Midnight I thought we was on the same team?" Trey replied as he placed his hands on the roof in a trembling voice.

　　"Yeah, I thought so too. How the fuck Magny know you? I hit him by myself." I questioned.

　　"It's not what you think. I used to be a hit man for him. That's it I swear to you."

　　"Then how you meet Uncle D?"

　　"Magny referred me to him. Uncle D hired me for two jobs and afterwards we kept in contact," Trey replied.

　　"If that's the case then why didn't you do the list instead of me?" Something didn't smell right.

　　"I asked him the same thing. He said that too much money was involved and that you were coming home, and he wanted that money to put you on your feet," said Trey.

　　I thought about everything he was saying and, to be honest, it did sound like a move that Uncle D would make. One side of my mind said kill Trey, and ask questions later, then the other side said Trey was telling the truth. I then chose to go against my better judgment and lowered my guns. Trey breathed a sigh of relief.

"If I find out anything that you said was a lie I promise you that I will hunt you down and take your life accordingly." I felt that I had to warn him as sternly as I could.

"I'm all for the home team slim," Trey replied.

"You better be. Your life depends on it." We hopped back into the stolen car and continued the route back to our respective cars.

*****

PARIS

It had now been three days since I was admitted into Washington Hospital Center. My heart was still deeply wounded from Trey's betrayal. As far as my mom, I was puffed with pride just like she was so it took a lot just for me to call her and tell her that I wanted to come home. Right now my mind was on the life that I was carrying. Kayla, as usual, was right there to give me that extra push that I sometimes needed. I took a deep breath and picked up the receiver. The phone rang about three times before someone picked it up.

"Hello." Olivia answered.

"Ma, I'm in the hospital." I spoke softly.

"Paris?" Olivia asked looking for confirmation. I could hear it in her voice that she was shocked that I called her.

"Yes, Mom I want to come back home." I got straight to the point.

"Oh, Paris you could have always came back home. What are you in the hospital for?" Olivia actually sounded concerned.

"It's a long story ma." I twirled the phone cord around my finger.

"Well do you want me to come pick you up?" Olivia offered.

"No you don't have to. Kayla is here and has a car so she will bring me," I replied.

"Okay I'll be here waiting on you." I can't believe she said that.

"Okay thanks ma. I love you." I can't believe that I said that to her. It had been years since I'd said it to her.

"Oh, I love you too Paris I will see you when you get here." I could hear her smiling.

"Okay bye." I hung up. That was the hardest thing that I ever had to do. I was relieved nonetheless at how the conversation went. Although Olivia was my mother, I honestly thought that she would reject me. Seeing that Olivia welcomed me back with opened arms, I loved Kayla that much more for convincing me to call her. It goes to show that you really see who loves you when you're in need.

I hung up the phone all smiles. My smiles soon turned to frowns when Trey walked through the door and finally showed face. Almost instantly he could feel the tension coming from both me and Kayla. I wouldn't even look at him and guarded my tongue from saying anything to him. I already knew that Kayla on the other hand would be a big enough mouthpiece for the both of us.

"What time are they going to release you Paris so I can take you home?" Trey asked. Kayla used that as her cue.

"She's not going nowhere with you, you cheating motherfucker. You the reason she in here in the first place!" Kayla yelled. I couldn't have said it better.

"Shut the fuck up Kayla! You don't have shit to do with this." Trey pointed his finger in Kayla face.

"I got a lot to do with it. It's your bullshit that got her here. She at home carrying your baby and you out there sticking your dirty little dick in every slit with hair!" Kayla pointed to his mid-section.

"Kayla, I'm not going to tell you again. Mind your

fucking business! Paris, you going with me, or your hoodrat ass friend?" I could tell Trey was getting mad, but I still chose not to say anything.

"Hoodrat! You bitch ass nigga! You think because you killed Phil, I'm sc....." By the mention of Phil's name Trey advanced on Kayla with keen speed and agility. Trey then smacked and choked Kayla out.

"Bitch, don't you ever come out of your mouth like that again! Do it again and mention that nigga name and I promise that I'll put a hole in your head, and leave you where he at." Trey coldly spoke as he let Kayla's neck go. Kayla hunched over holding her neck and coughing air into her lungs. Unbeknownst to Trey I pressed the button for the nurses to come running in. When they came in they could feel the tension and could see Kayla gathering herself together. Then instantly they looked at Trey.

"Excuse me Sir, but I'm going to have to ask you to leave or I will be calling security," the nurse warned pointing towards the door. Trey was armed so he knew he couldn't afford any run in with the law, so he complied.

"Fuck it then, go with her, and don't call me when your mother beat your ass again. You better remember what I said Kayla, your life depends on it. Trey stormed out the room never taking another look at me. Kayla was then assisted by the nurse to stand. When she looked at me I saw a look on her face that I had never seen before. Kayla was scared. I then released my final tears that I would let fall over Treyvon Davis. Every tear drop that fell was an ounce of love that I held for Trey.

Finally, Kayla and I was en route to my childhood home. I was nervous but happy that my mother allowed me to come back home. I never thought that my mother loved me as much as she could, but I could honestly say that I was starting to see a different Olivia. The one thing that bothered me now was how Olivia would take me being pregnant. I knew how my grandma took it when she found out my mom was pregnant with me. I just prayed that Olivia didn't react the same way.

Today I made sure to wear a big shirt to hide my protruding belly until I could sit down and tell her the news.

When we pulled up, I saw my mom in the window. I looked up and took a deep breath as if to say, "Here we go." As we stepped off the elevator Olivia stood in the doorway. My head hung as I took the needed steps to reach my mother. It looked like Olivia couldn't take it anymore and rushed to my side with her arms stretched out.

"Come here baby, pick your head up. You're home now." Olivia wrapped her arms around me.

"He hurt me so bad ma. I thought he loved me." I cried hard into her shoulder. I guess my tears over Trey weren't over yet.

"It's okay Paris. Forget about him. It's his loss don't stress yourself out over him baby," she said rubbing my back softly like a loving mother.

"I love you, Ma, I squeezed her tight around her waist."

"Oh, Paris I love you too. Now come on in and get something to eat." Olivia then turned towards Kayla.

"Kayla, thank you for being there for Paris. I'll love you like my own for that," Olivia sincerely stated.

"It'll never be a problem Ms. Clemons. Paris is like a sister to me. Paris I'll be back I'm going to check on my mom. I'll come up later." Kayla stated as she walked to the stairwell.

"Thanks for everything Kayla." I began to dry my eyes.

"Don't worry about it girl we've been through too much." Kayla slightly laughed as she disappeared into the stairwell. My mom and I walked arm in arm to our apartment.

*****

MIDNIGHT

I was now at home seriously judging myself on the decision that I made not to kill Trey. I took his word for truth and let my kind heart lead the way. I hope I didn't make the wrong choice as I did with Magny. I leaned back in my uncle's favorite chair with my signature Double Remy as I thought about all the murders that I'd committed. I truly wanted all the bloodshed to stop. I came to learn that killing is just like lying. You kill one you then have to kill again. *INSHA ALLAH* (GOD WILLING) the murders will stop. By the end of the night, I came to the conclusion that Magny was my uncle's killer and Trey was as innocent as he said that he was.

Around 9:30am the next morning I received a visit by some unwanted visitors. Years ago, I became a Muslim bearing witness that there was no God but Allah, and Muhammad was his last messenger. Although a Muslim, I wasn't practicing to the best of my abilities. When I looked out my peephole, I saw two beautiful young women. Their beautiful skin and eyes instantly captivated me. Anxiously I opened the door.

"Hello ladies, can I help you?" I answered.

"Well hello Sir we're with the Jehovah's Witnesses. Are you saved?" The beautiful young lady asked. She didn't look to be no older than 25.

"I'm sorry ladies but I'm a Muslim. I do appreciate your visit though." I replied gracefully dismissing the ladies. I shut the door and laughed that a Jehovah's Witness would actually come and visit me. Before I could get back to my chair and have a seat there was another knock at the door. I laughed again thinking how persistent the girls were. I looked out and saw the same two girls. By the time I opened the door I was looking down the barbell of two twin 22. caliber handguns. Before I could say anything, I heard the words "As-salaam Alaikum" followed by a big flash.

BOOM, BOOM, BOOM, BOOM, BOOM. I was hit five times. I hit the floor staring off into space as an instant chill came over me. The two girls ran off. Just as they got to their getaway car they realized that the mailman saw the whole thing. Just as they raised their guns the mailman dropped his bags and tried to run but ended up catching a bullet to the ass. Hearing the sirens closing in they hopped in their car and sped off.

*****

MIDNIGHT

I felt like I was floating. There was a shining light up ahead. I knew better than to go that way. My pride wouldn't let me. I could feel hands all over my body as if they were pulling me. My head hurt and body stung. My mind was a complete blur. "What was happening? Where was I?" I asked to no one in particular. I got no answer. Then the light up ahead went dark. I couldn't see anything for a while. I tried to open my eyes and then there was light again. I looked around the room and realized that I was in a hospital. Soon, as I laid there unable to move a nurse walked in. She was beautiful. I thanked God for allowing me to see such beauty. I tried to speak but couldn't due to the large tube stuffed in my throat. I struggled and began to choke causing the nurse to rush to my side. She was beautiful. I eyed her name tag reading "Wiggins."

"Hold on Mr. Brown let me get that for you. Welcome back." She removed the tube and placed it in a metal pan. She then took a suction tube and cleaned the thickened and excess mucus in my mouth. The whole time she worked I stared into her beautiful brown eyes. She then caught me and smiled. I gathered all the strength that I could so I could speak.

"Damn you're beautiful," I said in almost a whisper.

"Look at you. You've been in a coma for four days and wake up thinking about the wrong thing already. You better worry about getting healthy Mr. Brown versus other things." She looked down to my midsection and pointed out my hard penis print that was clearly evident through the thin sheets. Realizing it I smiled bashfully.

"Okay Ms. Wiggins," again a soft whisper.

"Oh no baby. If you're going to call me then call me Tymia. Ms. Wiggins is my grandmother!" She touched my arm with that beautiful smile.

"How..... Did I get here?" I struggled trying to move unsuccessfully. Tymia rushed to keep me lying down.

"Mr. Brown you've been shot multiple times you can't try to get up yet or you will break your stitches and force your wound to start bleeding again." She informed with genuine concern.

"What? Who shot me?" Complete anger washed over my face.

"Just relax Mr. Brown. Wait until the medication wears off and then we'll talk." She fixed my pillows and set the call button by my side so I can call her if I needed to. Physically, I was fucked up. Due to the medication, I was on my brain was cloudy. With the damage that the bullets did and the meds they had me on, my brain was in a state of post shock. Subsequently, it was affecting my memory. The doctors eventually told me that I was shot five times; twice in the face, once in the neck, shoulder and chest. As far as the bullets that hit me in the face, one ricocheted off my tooth shattering it then exiting through my cheek. The other was lodged in my nasal cavity. I was truly lucky to be alive, but with my memory temporarily hit I could be a sitting duck for whoever was trying to kill me. God willing, I'll have my memory back by the time I leave this place. If not, then my life could end sooner than later.

*****

PARIS

I lay in the bed listening to the song by KC and Jojo called *All My Life*. It hurt to hear the words from it. This was the song that Trey and I decided on to represent the love that we shared. I couldn't lie and say that I didn't love Trey anymore because I did. I was just deeply scarred from his unfaithful ways. Before, I thought that he could do no wrong. Seeing differently, I now despised the ground that he walked on.

I was now five months into the pregnancy and could actually feel my baby moving around. I was told by Dr. Ames that in two weeks he would be able to tell me the gender of the child. As I lay on the bed, I decided to call Kayla. *RING, RING, RING.*

"Hello" Kayla answered the phone.

"Hey, Kayla," I said in a somber tone I could hear Ron walk out of the bedroom.

"Bitch what's wrong with you?" Kayla could tell that I was in a down mood.

"Nothing, I'm okay. What you doing?" I didn't want to tell her that I was thinking of Trey.

"Nothing my ass Paris. I'm already pulling in the parking lot, so unlock   the door.

Click. I was happy that Kayla was here.

Now I would have someone to talk to. It really got boring being cooped up in the house all day. I ran and unlocked the front door and ran back to my bed to jump under the covers. I turned my back to the door so I could act like I was sleep when Kayla came. My room door came open and by the strong smell of alcohol I could tell that it wasn't Kayla in my room. When I turned around Ron was in my doorway ass naked massaging his manhood.

"Hey Paris, how you doing? How about letting your old stepdad see what that pregnant pussy feels like?" Ron slurred as he stepped closer to me.

"Ron, get out of my room, or I'm going to scream! Please Ron you're going to make me lose my baby," I cried as Ron continued to stumble toward me.

"Oh no Ms. Paris you've been playing hard to get since you was a little girl. Play time is now over." Ron licked his lips. Just as I was about to scream Ron rushed me and placed his hand over my mouth. Ron had the back of my head pinned to his chest as his free hand fondled my breasts and stomach. Just as he reached in between my legs *CRACK!* Kayla shattered my radio over his head causing him to fall to his knees in agonizing pain. From the back Kayla kicked him in the nuts causing him to double over in even more pain.

"AGGGHHH you bitch!" Ron yelled in between breaths. Kayla reached in her purse and out came a chrome nine millimeter big enough to fit in the palm of your hand. *CLICK, CLACK.*

"Call me a bitch again and I'm going to shoot that little piece of skin you call a dick straight off." Kayla had the nine aimed at Ron's now black and purple dick. He made the right choice and stumbled out the door. As he did Kayla slammed and locked it behind him. I was now bald up in fetal position crying profusely. Kayla showed eyes of compassion and rushed to my side.

"Are you okay Paris? I'm glad I got here when I did."

"I hate that motherfucker Kayla. You should have shot him. Oh God, I hate him with a passion," I continued to cry.

"It's okay Paris you got to tell somebody. You can't keep letting him do this to you," Kayla advised.

"I did that Kayla. My mom doesn't believe me. Plus, last time she believed him and said that I tried to fuck him."

"Look Paris if you don't then, the next time there might not be no one here to save you!" Kayla reasoned.

"I know, I know I just don't know what to do," I cried. Then the next thing you know. *BANG, BANG, BANG* "Police open the door!" Kayla jumped up and yanked the door open. She was immediately snatched out and slammed to the ground. There, she was handcuffed and escorted out of the apartment. The police then snatched the gun off of the bed while another officer grabbed me attempting to put me in handcuffs.

"Motherfucker, get your hands off of me. I didn't do shit. Get the fuck off of me!" I kicked and screamed but easily overpowered and placed in handcuffs. When they walked me out of the room, I walked pass a fully clothed Ron who stood with a shit-eating grin on his face. I pulled up everything from my chest, nose, and throat and hog spit right in his face. He tried to get to me but was held by the officers. The whole ride to the precinct I screamed and yelled to no avail while Kayla stayed calm.

*****

MIDNIGHT

Tymia was nursing me back to full health with the quickness. I predicted that I would be back to a hundred percent in no time. Although my memory was still a tad bit damaged it was gradually coming back. The slightest thing would trigger a portion of my memory to come back. Tymia and I had even become good friends. Not a day went passed that I ate hospital food. Either Tymia would cook me a home cooked meal or I would have a feast of my choice. Tymia spoiled me as much as she could. One night after eating one of Tymia's gourmet meals I was greeted by two very unwelcomed visitors.

"Mr. Brown, I see you're getting back to your old self again. Mind if we talk?" Agent Bright asked standing at the foot of my bed. I was instantly annoyed by his presence.

"Look we had this discussion already. If you ain't got the paperwork then you can leave," I sternly spoke.

"You know I figured that you would say that. That's why I brought this with me. You see when you were shot, we pulled a Desert Eagle off of your waist which in the city of Washington it is illegal for felons to possess. Now, these are papers charging you with it. Now if you work with me, I'll make this go away. If you don't then you'll have a first-class ticket back to Lewisburg for a minimum mandatory five years. You'll be in court by the morning. I took the papers and read them over. They seemed legit to, but something told me that this white pig was bluffing.

"Tell me something Agent Bright. Both you and your partner are Federal Agents and are interested in me. One thing that I do know is that when the FBI gets involved in anything there is someone already under investigation. So I say that, to say this. Is it me who you're investigating?" I asked straight forwardly.

"Who we are investigating is none of your concern. We asked the questions and you're going to answer them. If not then you're going to be in Judge Rambert's court room by the morning. Now you can call my bluff or take heed to my words. It's your choice." Agent Bright finalized as I handed him back the papers.

"I call your bluff. If it is me who you are investigating and you being a federal agent leads me to believe that you want me for something bigger than a petty gun charge. If you do lock me up then so be it, but until then I don't hold extensive conversations with the law." I grabbed for my remote and called for the nurse to enter my room.

"Mr. Brown, are you okay?" Tymia asked as she entered the room.

"Actually, I'm not. These two gentlemen are all of a sudden causing me too much stress. Could you have them escorted out?" I spoke calmly as possible all the while never breaking eye contact with the Agent.

"Sure thing Mr. Brown, I'm going to have to ask you two gentlemen to leave or be escorted out by security." Tymia spoke in an angelic voice.

"That won't be necessary ma'am, we were just leaving. Good call Mr. Brown. We'll be seeing you again." Agent Bright smiled at Tymia and began to exit the room.

"I won't be looking forward to it," I replied letting my eyes follow them out the door.

*****

PARIS

Once arriving at the police station Kayla and I were charged with carrying a pistol without a license. They also charged me with simple assault for spitting on Ron. After seeing the judge, we were both released on our own personal recognizance. We were also instructed to appear in court at a later date. At first, I was worried about the gun charge, but then Kayla put me at ease when she told me that the gun was in her name and she was licensed to carry it.

I couldn't believe that Ron would call the police. Kayla kept trying to get me to tell the police of Ron's sexual advances, but I refused. If there was one thing that Trey did teach me, it was to keep the police out of your business at all cost. I decided that if Ron tried it again that I would sic Trey on him. Soon as I walked in the house my mom was all over me.

"Paris what the fuck happened? Ron said that you and Kayla jumped him. What the hell is going on?" Olivia stood with her hand on her hip.

"What! Ma that is not what happened in the least bit. Ron tried to rape me again and Kayla saved me. Plus, Kayla beat him up by herself. I never touched his trifling ass!" I yelled getting upset.

"If you didn't touch him then why the hell you get locked up?" Olivia popped her neck.

"Kayla had a gun ma, and the police charged both of us with it. They also gave me a simple assault charge for spitting in Ron face," I stated.

"Paris you're pregnant. What the hell are you doing fighting anyway?" Olivia words caught me completely off guard. I wondered how the hell she knew I was pregnant.

"You know, huh?" I looked to the ground, "How'd you find out?" I said in a small whisper.

"How I know? Paris you been eating up everything in sight since you got here. I was pregnant once upon a time. Now why the hell were you fighting?" Now she brought me back reality from being ashamed. I was seeing that Olivia wasn't seeing the bigger picture.

"Ma you're worried about me fighting, and your husband just tried to rape me for not the first, but the second time and you still allow him to stay here. What the hell are you waiting for Ma? For him to succeed?" I pleaded in a tone of desperation.

"Paris I'm so sorry please believe me. I'm sorry. I'll speak with him." Olivia tried to hug me, but I pushed her away.

"Speak with him? Ma, I want him out of here. Damn can't you see that I'm scared of him?" I yelled.

"Paris please, let me do this my way. He's my husband, so let me deal with him." Olivia pleaded.

"Ma wake the fuck up! He's no good. Leave him. Please he's no good. I'm begging you Ma, please!" I fell to her knees holding both her hands in mines. As I pleaded with her through my tears, Olivia even began to cry.

"I will Paris, just give me some time. I promise." Olivia then fell to her knees as we both cried in each other arms.

*****

MIDNIGHT

Agent Bright's words weighed heavy on my mind. I'd come to the conclusion that it was me who they were investigating. I knew that it was truly mandatory that I stay under the radar. I had been in the hospital for two weeks now and had gained a lot of my memory back. Being shot gave me a whole new outlook on life. I now cherished everything that the world had to offer and was beginning to cherish Tymia as well.

Today I was scheduled to be released. Tymia planned to stand firm by my side. She even made sure that she would be off on my release day so she could drive me home. Tymia was willing and ready to stand by me through any weather. I also felt the same. Soon I was given my discharge papers and escorted out by my beautiful companion. Tymia was a good woman and showed me time and time again that she was down for the struggle.

We pulled up to my domain around 3:00pm. I was still mildly recovering from my wounds, so Tymia ran around and helped me out. Arm in Arm we walked to the front door. I reached in my property bag to retrieve my house keys. Once I unlocked the door my blood began to boil. The whole house was ransacked. I stood there speechless. Tymia not knowing what was going on played her position and stood by me with her hand on my back. I gathered my strength and proceeded to the first safe in the guest room. I snatched off the mattress and bed spring and revealed an untouched safe. I looked over my shoulder at Tymia standing there.

"Mia, take that picture off the wall and read the numbers on the back to me," I instructed and Tymia complied.

"13, 65, 18, 20, 3," stated Tymia. After entering the combo, I opened the safe. I gave out a well needed sigh of relief as it was untouched. Every last brick and pound of weed was accounted for. I then closed up and moved to the basement where the next safe was located. I had to get Tymia to help me move an old 72"-inch big screen TV. Under it sat the second safe. This one was built three feet into the floor. I punched in the code on the digital keypad and it opened like clockwork. Once open the powerful and distinct smell of cocaine engulfed the room. I smiled because just like the other safe everything was accounted for. Tymia looked on in amazement at the neatly stacked bricks of cocaine. I then closed up and Tymia helped me back up the stairs.

CHAPTER THIRTEEN

MIDNIGHT

Tymia was nursing me back to health at a rapid pace. My memory was almost back but the best part was that no one had made any attempts on my life. I hadn't seen Trey in a while so I decided that I would pop up on him and surprise him.

I hopped in my brand-new Escalade EXT that I bought as a welcome home present to myself. I thought that with someone out there trying to kill me that it was time to step the game plan up and change the play. Since being shot I now never left the house without wearing a vest and carrying two guns on me at all times. I refused to be caught bullshitting. If someone did come to kill me, they'd have their hands full. I was even trying to sell Uncle D's house to change headquarters. If they tried once to kill me here who's to say that they wouldn't try again. A move was now very warranted.

I pulled around Congress Park at around 4:00pm. Bending the corner I could see Trey bent over in a crap game. I pulled up and honked the horn. *BEEP, BEEP*. When Trey looked up, he looked as if he'd seen a ghost. He looked me dead in the eye as he was trying to read my intentions. As he smiled and began his approach, I noticed that he let his right hand graze his hip. I pinned the move. He was secretly checking to see if his pistol was still there.

"Midnight, what's up slim? I thought you was dead." Trey injected.

"How you figure that? Nobody you know, know me," I replied. Trey gave off a look that said that he knew that he fucked up.

"Look you can stop all that suspicious bullshit. I told you I'm with the home team." He tried to clean up his mistake.

"Yeah, I hope so young buck. I see you over there getting your pockets cracked over there." I nodded towards the crap game. "Never that old timer." Trey pulled out a wad of money. *WHOOP, WHOOP.*

"Keep it moving Sir," The police yelled over his loudspeaker as he pulled behind me. I was instantly nervous as I thought about the two pistols on my hip.

"The "Federalies" is on your back slim. Go ahead and roll and call me tonight," Trey said.

"Aight young buck, be safe out here." I said as I placed my truck into drive preparing to pull off.

"Most definitely. I ain't never bullshitting out here." I pulled off with the feeling that Trey's last statement was more so a warning. I brushed it off with plans to address it later.

At first, I didn't think that Trey had anything to do with my uncle's murder. Now I wasn't so sure. What I did know was that I didn't trust Trey at all. I had reason not to. The most recent was him knowing I was shot and then checking for his pistol. After thinking, it scared me because I let him walk straight up on me. Then I thought if it was Trey who was trying to kill me. How many other chances did he have to finish the task?

*****

163

TREY

When Midnight pulled off and the police cleared the area, we got right back to our crap game. Although we did, my mind was still with Midnight and the nine lives that he seemed to have. I knew that I should have just handled my business instead of leaving it to the A-Rab's hands. I had to get this shit done as quickly as possible. Midnight was getting extremely cautious of me. I knew that if he learned any more than he already did that he would surely gun for me on sight.

After losing two bets and winning one. I looked over my shoulder to a bad ass brown skinned female walking up the street with cornrows in her head. She had on some pink Rocawear coochie cutters, with a matching pink and grey hoodie that showed off her belly button. As she got closer, I could see that she had a diamond studded navel ring that said "URS". Her lips were glossed up, and she walked with a confident stride as if the world was at her feet. I stood up and walked towards her also matching her stride of confidence.

"She is outta your league slim," Rocko said from behind me. I briefly turned towards him.

"If anything, she's out of her league fucking with a nigga like me." I smiled arrogantly then focused back on Ms. Rocawear.

"What's a pretty girl like you doing walking by yourself?" I flipped my toothpick around in my mouth.

"Sorry, you need a better pick up line than that. Try again." She rolled her eyes.

"Aight, aight that was corny. What's your name beautiful?"

"That's original, but my name is Precious. What's yours?"

"They call me Trey. Won't you let me drive you to where you're going?" I offered.

"I live all the way Uptown that might be too much gas

money for you." She joked I pulled out a wad of money.

"Money ain't a thing babygirl. What you doing in southeast anyway? You pretty far from home ain't you?" I asked

"Well, I was with this guy and he expected me to fuck him in his car in the alley. I'm not no hoodrat so I'm not going to let no one treat me like one. I said no, so he said get out, so I did." She folded her arms over her chest.

"You did right sweetheart you too pretty for that hoodrat shit. So you gonna let me take you home?" I offered yet again.

"Yeah, I guess you can." Trey hit his alarm and started his car from his key ring. When Precious saw it start up by itself a look of astonishment washed over her face.

*****

THE FBI

"Ladies and gentlemen, good morning. As most of you know I'm Agent Bright and this is my partner Agent Simon. We are the lead agents on the case. As you know we've been knee deep in an investigation for the past year. This investigation has been an emotional roller coaster for all of us, but we stuck with it non-stop. All of our hard work has finally paid off, or at least about to pay off. Ladies and gentlemen, agents of the Bureau, I'd like to introduce you to Federal Agent Kimberly Kniffin." The room erupted in applause as a brown skinned female with cornrows approached the podium with Agents Bright and Simon.

"Ladies and gentlemen Agent Kniffin has successfully infiltrated the subjects circle and has already began to collect valuable information. I estimate in about six months we will have enough information to make an arrest, and our subject and anyone with him will be put behind bars. We're putting everything at Agent Kniffin's disposal. If she comes to any of you for anything, please do not hesitate on giving her what she needs. She's being completely backed by all the higher ups. That would conclude this meeting, and thank you for your attendance.

*****

MIDNIGHT

Now I was back to my old self again. My memory was fully back, and like the gangsta bitch that she was Tymia was standing firm by my side like a loyal Pitbull. We saw eye to eye on everything. Tymia was truly a gift from heaven. When I was released from the hospital and made it back to my house, I experienced a little bit of mixed emotions. Although I was happy that the money was still there, the drugs were as well. I had to make the choice to sell them for dirt cheap, or risk the Feds running in here and finding them. I sold drugs before, but I was a kid then and wasn't having unannounced visits by the FBI. I made the choice along with some calls to follow through with it. I had some once and a lifetime offers. The first person that I called was my man named Ant.

Ant was pretty much into everything. If it would make him a dollar, then it made sense. His main hustle though was pushing coke on Robinson Pl. in SE. Nowadays dudes wasn't getting serious money selling coke, but Ant was a natural hustler. I used to joke with him by telling him that he could sell a hooker some pussy. I had it set up so that Ant would come to my house so we could discuss the price that he would pay. For a minute I was battling with myself whether or not I should let Tymia witness the transaction. Then I figured that I didn't want to hide anything from her. If she was going   to deal with me then she was going to ride or die to the finish, or she was going to die in the beginning.

Ant came over to the house around 3:00pm on a Saturday afternoon. Tymia was in the kitchen cooking curry lamb and rice. I looked out the window and saw Ant pulling up in a white Range Rover. I walked outside and met him in a driveway.

"What's up baby? I see you sitting good." I spoke of his Range Rover giving him a gangsta hug.

"Something small to a giant. The streets love me. What's up with you playboy? I see you wasn't lifting no weights in the pen." Ant laughed smacking me on the belly.

"Maybe not but my locker stayed on blast. Come on in I got my wifey in there cooking some curry lamb."

"Hell yeah, you know I don't turn down no food." Ant smiled as I escorted him into the house. I decided that we would have the meeting in a part of the house that Uncle D used to call the playroom. The room held two Plasma flatscreens PS3, XBOX360, a love seat that folded out to a bed, and a bar that held almost any liquor you could think of. Once we got into the room Tymia informed us that dinner was ready.

"Mia, fix us some glasses of Remy and then come sit down," I instructed. Tymia quickly returned with the drinks and took her seat next to me.

"So what's up Ant, you still dealing in coke ain't you?" I got straight to the point.

"All day I gotta eat. I'm going to keep driving until the wheels fall off." Ant took a sip of his Remy.

"Aight look, I got some coke so how much are you paying per square?" I asked knowing that he'd lie.

"Right now, I'm paying nineteen-five each. Can you do better?" He probably was paying twenty-two.

"Hell yeah, I'll give you ten for $150,000. That's 15,000 apiece. We got a deal?" I asked.

"If the shit good hell yeah ain't nobody in D.C. got prices like that." Ain't nobody in D.C. got bricks for nineteen-five either. I thought.

"Mia, go grab ten bricks." Tymia did as told without question.

"Look Ant I'm going to give you the bricks now, and get with you in a couple of days. Hopefully you'll be ready for me by then." I finished my glass in two gulps.

"Whenever you call, I'll be ready," Ant replied just as Tymia was returning with the bricks in a large book bag.

Once she handed it to me I unloaded it one by one onto the table. If Ant was a real coke pusher, then he should already know that it's good by the potent smell. Not to mention that the coke was almost pink. I then smiled as I looked up at Ant.

"Need I say more?" I extended my hand to seal the deal. With no hesitation Ant shook it. I then looked over to Tymia who sat there with her cell phone in hand taking one of her cornrows out. Once the business was conducted, we all ventured into the dining room to enjoy the meal that Tymia prepared.

CHAPTER FOURTEEN

TREY

I was surprised that my invitation to take the young girl home was accepted. Being the opportunist that I was I wasted no time in proposing my proposal. My car alone should have let her know that she wasn't fucking with no little fish in the pond. I was the flashy type so in time I would have showed and told Precious everything that she wanted to see and hear.

As I drove, I couldn't help but look at her juicy thighs. Her tight little shorts were hugging her pussy like a boxing glove. Let Precious tell it she didn't consider herself a dime. She was a foreign coin.

"So where your baby daddy at? If I was him, I would have been locked your ass up." I smiled.

"First off I don't deal with more than one dude at a time. If I had a baby daddy, I wouldn't have been with that anything ass nigga that I was with earlier, and I definitely wouldn't be here with you." Precious snapped.

"Damn babygirl my bad." I held my hands up in surrender with a smile.

"Since were getting personal then where is your baby momma at?" She redirected my question to me.

"She cooling. We not together no more though. We

169

weren't seeing eye-to-eye on things." Precious looked at me with a pair of unbelieving eyes. Before she could reply my phone rang.

"Yeah?" I answered it. "Aight I'm on my way uptown right now. I'll call you when I'm out front." *Click*

"Look babygirl we gotta make a pit stop, and then I'm going get you home. Is that cool?"

"Do you think it's cool?" Precious replied placing her hand between her thick thighs.

As I continued to drive we both continued to talk. Before long I pulled into an alley and turned the car off. I held the break and pressed the eject button. The dashboard rose up revealing two bricks sitting atop a MAC-90. I looked at Precious who now sat with a look of amazement on her face. I removed a brick and held the brake again, but this time pressed the rewind button on the console to close the stash spot.

"Here put that on the floor under your feet." I said placing the brick on her lap. Precious did as she was told.

"If you're trying to impress me that did," she honestly spoke.

"I'm not one of those perpetrating ass niggas out here. I live and breathe this street shit." I spoke seriously.

"Well, you made me a believer, now go do you so I can get this shit from under my feet." Precious smiled for the first time. I can honestly say that it was a memorable one.

"Aight scary smurf," I laughed. I could tell already that she was going to be around for a long time, so I decided to run down the list of things that I expected from a female who deals with me. It was music to my ears when she agreed to all my terms.

Precious was ready to be a hustler's wife to the fullest. As promised once I handled my business, I got her home. I gave her a kiss on the cheek and told her that I would call her later. Just as she got out the car my phone rang.

*****

PARIS

The whole ride home I smiled thinking of the life that was growing inside of me. Kayla had taken me to go see what the gender of the baby was today. It turned out that I'm having a baby girl. Just knowing that my daughter was growing inside of me took away every scared or nervous bone out my body. I was now anxious to be a mother. Meaning school would have to wait. My daughter would come before everything and everyone. Kayla and I pulled up to my building around 9:00pm. We hung out all day in celebration of the news. Kayla was already making plans for the baby shower, and claiming herself to be the godmother, which she rightfully would be. I don't know where I would be without Kayla and her unwavering support.

Kayla dropped me off so she could go get ready for her stressful night at the Skylark. I don't know how she did it every night, but I definitely wouldn't knock her for it. I walked in the house not sure if my mom was there or not so I just went straight to my room. I took another look at the sonogram and stuck it on my mirror, so I could always see her. Knowing that it was the right thing to do I got on the phone and called Trey. I guess I felt obligated to at least tell him the gender of his child. The phone rang four times. Just as he picked up my room door swung open.

"Finally, Paris we can be alone. Ever since you were a little girl, I wanted a piece of that ass. Something or someone always got in the way. Now I got you right where I want you." Ron smelled of alcohol. As he stood at my door, he once again was stroking himself, naked to the world. I completely forgot that I called Trey and dropped the phone.

"MMMAAAAAAA!!" I yelled praying to God that my

mother was there.

"Oh she can't hear you Paris. She's not here. She's pulling a double tonight. That means we got eight hours all to ourselves to play," Ron stated now walking closer to me.

"You stay the fuck away from me you sick motherfucker!" I grabbed the phone in a feeble attempt to call 911. Ron smacked it out my hand before I could hit any buttons. *PAP! PAP! SMACK! SMACK!* Ron closed fist hit me then backhanded me so hard that my head hit the wall knocking me into a semi-unconscious state. I had on some Apple Bottom jeans that Ron ripped off with the ease. He then grabbed both of my legs placing them on his shoulders. Ron spit on his palm to coat his penis. Once positioning himself he rammed his dick through my closed walls. I let out an ear-piercing scream as Ron began to mercilessly pump away. My cries fell on deaf ears.

"You like this dick don't you Paris?" I was in shock and speechless from this ordeal.

SMACK!

"Answer me bitch!" yelled Ron viciously slapping me again. Ron then pulled out and flipped me onto my pregnant belly. He then stuck three fingers into my bloody vagina and coated my asshole with my own blood and vaginal juices. Again, Ron positioned himself and rammed his blood coated shaft deep into my virgin rectum. Ron place his 285lbs putrid frame directly on my back as he pumped away pressing all of his weight directly on top of my baby.

With every thrust Ron pumped harder and harder. I tried to move but in turn was severely slapped again. With a blow that left my ears ringing. Ron took his massive hand and pinned my neck down to the bed as he fell into the zone. Quickly his orgasm built up and he exploded into my ass. He then released his grip on my neck. Once he gained his legs back, he stood up easily towering over me.

"You disappoint me, Paris. After all these years I thought the pussy and ass would have been better!" Ron then violently shoved my head with his barefoot as he exited my room. I was scarred physically and mentally. I just laid there barely conscious from all the pain. My entire body hurt. I laid there dreaming of a life full of bliss and no hardships whether it be physical or mental; a life that seemed so out of reach. I could hear the shower cut on so with every ounce of strength I had left over I slid to the phone. I remembered the last number that I called was Trey, so I hit redial Trey frantically picked up the phone.

"Paris ......Paris.......Paris where are you? Are you alright?" Again, I gathered strength from the bowels of my soul and managed to whisper.

"Trey…..help....me. Apartment 720."

*****

TREY

When Paris first called me, I answered and could hear a male voice in the background. I called Paris name repeatedly but received no reply. I eventually sat quietly and listen to the male voice talk. Once I heard Paris scream for her mother, I knew she was in trouble. I threw my BMW in drive and sped all the way to Paris' house. I was just dropping Precious off so luckily, I was still Uptown. In minutes I was pulling into the parking lot of Paris' building. I didn't know what apartment Paris lived in so I ask everyone I saw did they know her, but it was to no avail. No one would tell me anything. Then finally my phone rang again. Paris sounded barely conscious, but was still able to give me the apartment number. I ran up seven flights of stairs completely disregarding the elevator. Reaching her door, I yelled and banged.

"Paris, Paris open the door, Paris." Suddenly the door swung open by a shirtless male.

"Who the fuck is you banging on my door this late?" He looked me up and down.

173

"Where is Paris, she just called me from here?" I meant business. "She ain't here. You just missed her," the guy replied and looked me straight in the eye as if he was sizing me up. Just as he was attempting to close the door, I looked past him and saw Paris stumbling out of her room. Her legs were covered in blood. Paris fell to the floor now only semi-coherent. My blood instantly boiled over. I kicked the door back open smashing it in his face. The guy stumbled back giving me enough time to whip out my nine-millimeter. I charged Ron and commenced to pistol whipping the shit out of him. After I saw that he was almost unconscious I picked him up and walked him to the garbage shoot in the hallway. I forced his head through the slot then with my nine placed firmly to the back of his head.

"Checkmate, you sick motherfucker." *BOOM! BOOM!* I shot him twice in the back of the head his body tried to go limp, but I caught him and gave him the extra push he needed to slide down the chute. "Bitch ass nigga," I mumbled.

"AAGGGGHHHH" I heard Paris back in the house let out an ear-piercing scream. I ran back to the apartment to find Paris bald up in fetal position. As I moved closer, I noticed a half developed skeleton lying beside her. I then realized that it was my unborn child. "NNNOOOOOO," I moaned completely crushed. Paris had a miscarriage on her living room floor. I fell to my knees and dropped tears that I didn't know existed. Paris then moaned bringing me back to reality. I checked her pulse and found none. I tried to think quickly so I tilted her neck and began my version of CPR. I pushed and pushed and then finally GOD willed and breathed life back into her body. She blinked her eyes twice.

"Come on Paris you going to be okay. Stay with me." I cradled her head in my arms.

"Trey I'm cold." Paris struggled.

I gently placed her down and covered her up with a blanket. I ran to the house phone and dialed 911. Once they arrived, I went back to my car through the back steps and waited for them to bring her out. Once they did, I followed them to the hospital. I decided once arriving that I would wait in the waiting area until I was able to speak with Dr. Ames. While I waited two fourth district Police Detectives came in asking for Paris friends and family. I knew exactly who the two Detectives were. They were both two dirty cops who made cases stick on innocent people. I thought of Ron's body and knew that they had to have found him by now.

"Is there anyone here that's friends or family of Paris Clemons?" They asked again, but I said nothing. As soon as they left the room I was out of the hospital as quick as I came.

*****

FBI

The FBI field agent was amazed at how bold and flamboyant the subject was. The agent figured that if the subject kept exposing his hand the way he was doing that they would have enough information to make an arrest in less than six months as predicted by Agents Bright and Simon. Agent Kniffin was given orders to call into FBI headquarters every other day to check in. Although she was sought to be the best agent for the job, Agent Bright was also aware that she was also a female and had feelings. Feelings that he didn't want Agent Kniffin catching. Feelings that could and would get her killed. *RING, RING, RING.*

"FBI Headquarters."
"Hello this is Agent Kniffin, badge number 4,3,0,5. Calling to speak with Agent Bright."
"One second I will connect you to his office," replied the receptionist. Moments later the line came back alive.
"Agent Bright."
"Agent Bright this is special Agent Kimberly Kniffin

checking in as instructed," I stated professionally.

"Agent Kniffin I was just thinking about you. How's our boy doing? Agent Bright smiled as he leaned back in his swivel chair.

"Well Sir he's playing right into our hands. I emailed you a little something, so check your email. I'm pretty sure you will be pleased with it," I stated

"One second let me check. I'm online right now." Agent Bright was gone off the line for a quick second and then returned.

"Oh good Agent Kniffin. These are very good. Keep up the good work and keep me informed." He commended me.

"You know it's real sad because he would have made some young girl really happy."

"Agent I don't want to hear you talk like that. If you can't control your feelings and jack this case, I'm going to make sure that I have your badge on my desk. Are we clear?"

"But Sir I was just......"

"Are we clear Agent Kniffin?" Agent Bright spoke in a tone that finalized the conversation.

"Yes Sir." *Click.* He hung up.

*****

MIDNIGHT

I was truly surprised at how quickly Tymia adapted to my lifestyle. She was truly that ride or die bitch that all street dudes needed in their life. She kept me on point and corrected me when needed as well as comforted me. She pulled me up when I was slipping. To be honest I felt she loved me and would do anything for me. It was as if she was my backbone and without her I couldn't stand to be the man that I'd become since the shooting. Today would prove her ultimate loyalty.

"Tymia come here I need to holla at you." I yelled for

Tymia to come in the room that I was in. When she got there, I sat her down on my lap.

"What's up baby?" She wrapped her arms around my neck.

"Tymia I need you to do me a favor. I gotta go check on this new house, so I need you to drive your Lexus truck to the Wendy's on Georgia Ave. and deliver these bricks to Ric. I already talked to him so all you have to do is just give them to him. They are already paid for. You gotta be there by 3:00pm. Can you do it?" I explained as easily as I could.

"You need to start consulting with me first before you start making moves and decisions like that. I love you and will do anything for you, but you got to talk with me first before you jump to do something like that. Plus, how you know that I wanted drive my car to do something like that?" She truthfully replied and I will admit that she was right.

"First off I only asked if you could do it. If you can't then say so and I would like you to drive your car because if the police just so happen to pull you over the truck is in your name and all the paperwork is legit. You want me to talk with you first, well consider this that talk. Now I ask again can you do it?" I spoke with assurance.

"Where the coke at? Damn you get on my nerves." Tymia laughed and got up. I then smacked her on the ass.

"That's my baby. You always there when I need you. Here go some money for doing it." I gave her a thousand dollars and hugged her.

"I love you, black boy." Tymia melted in my arms as she lightly kissed my lips.

"I love you too and don't be driving crazy," I warned not wanting to distract her from her task.

"You sure got a lot of demands for someone who ain't riding dirty. You be acting like I'm new to this shit. Let me do me damn." Tymia snapped.

"You better take your slick mouth ass on before I lay this pipe to you." I laughed

"OHHHH you talking dirty now," Tymia replied grabbing my dick then walking away with a little extra switch in her hips.

*****

TREY

I was completely intrigued by Precious' whole demeanor. She held all the characteristics of a ride or die bitch. In fact, I never met a female who seemed more all for me then her. Not even Paris could match her open display of loyalty. Paris wouldn't touch any drug let alone let them be in the same house with her. Precious on the other hand was all for the cause. Even at this very moment Precious was holding six bricks of mine at her house. She was truly ride or die.

After the incident with Paris, I was mentally fucked up in the head from the way she was beaten and raped. I may have killed Ron, but mentally I was broken down. Paris was carrying my first and only child. When Paris miscarried my child a piece of me died right along with it. That made my mind even more devious and wicked and my heart colder than ever.

Now with Precious at my side I planned to use her to my full advantage. Anything I needed or wanted she did. She was at my mercy. As a treat for her loyalty, I rewarded her with a trip to Atlantic City. Plus, I needed the trip to get my mind off of things. Precious had a ball and even won $10,000 for herself. We got back home around 2:00am. Precious was knocked out from the long ride.

"Wake up sleepyhead." I gently tapped her to wake her up causing her to yawn.

"We here already?" She asked with a well needed stretch.

"Yeah, go ahead and get some rest. I'll come by tomorrow and get the bricks." I rubbed her cheek and kissed her forehead.

"Okay just call me and let me know when you're coming." Precious leaned in and gave me a kiss on the lips, and got out the car. As I pulled off she waved.

PRECIOUS

Soon as I put my key in the door my cell phone went off. I looked down at the screen and was instantly disgusted.

"Why are you calling me? I was supposed to check in with you," I said clearly annoyed by the phone call.

"You been gone the whole weekend with ole' boy. I figured that I would call and make sure that your feelings and your priorities still in check." The voice spoke with authority.

"Look I'm working as fast as I can. This thing isn't going to happen overnight," I scolded.

"Did you learn anything new about his operation?" The voice continued to press the issue.

"Like I said before I seen guns, and I have coke in my house as we speak. When I see the money or learn something new, I will let you know. Now do you mind if I go to sleep?" I tried to finalize the conversation.

"Yeah, go ahead and get some rest and don't be catching no feelings," he warned.

"Whatever." *CLICK* I hung up the phone clearly frustrated and tired.

*****

TYMIA

I couldn't believe that I was in MY Lexus in route to make a drop for Midnight's ass. I couldn't believe I let him talk me into doing this shit. Then again, being the position that I was in within Midnight's life I knew that I had a job to do and I would do that to the best of my ability. On the ride I thought of how long would Midnight and I arrangement would last. Would it be six months, a year or even the forbidden a lifetime? I hope. I looked over to the bookbag on my passenger seat and prayed to God that by fucking with Midnight that I didn't lose my life whether it be legally or physically.

I pulled in the parking lot and immediately spotted the car that was supposed to be Ric's. He drove a seven series 750IL BMW. As I drove pass the car I made sure to make visual contact and give a head nod. I parked, made a phone call and proceeded inside the restaurant.

I ordered a taco salad and took a seat. Before long, Ric walked in with the book bag on his shoulder. As he walked pass he spoke.

"Tell slim I said that I will see him again before the week is out." Ric kept it moving without making any more contact.

I gave him no response. I watched him to his car. Ric never made it out of the parking lot before he was swarmed by a fleet of all black Crown Victoria's. A swarm of FBI Agents surrounded him. I almost shit on myself when an officer came in the Wendy's and escorted me outside.

CHAPTER FIFTEEN

PARIS

I laid in the hospital bed in a coma. If it weren't for Trey's quick thinking, I may have died that night. Unfortunately, my child could not be saved, and breathed her last breath before she took it. Olivia arrived at the hospital about four hours ago, and couldn't stop crying. She knew that the loss of her grandchild and the pain and torment that I went through was completely her fault. Only if she would have listened to me, my baby would still be inside of me growing into a beautiful little girl.

Kayla and Olivia stood firm at my bedside. Olivia was crushed that her decision almost cost me my life. She would lean down and cry on my forehead. As she did a tear fell on my cheek causing me to open my eyes.

"Where am I? My body hurts," I mumbled still slightly groggy. Olivia immediately began sobbing and pleading.
"Why are you crying ma? What happened?" I asked again. Olivia sobbed some more then looked to the floor as she continued.
"Paris, Ron raped you, and you lost the baby. I'm so sorry Paris I should have listened to you. I should have kicked him out when you told me to!" Olivia continued to cry. Her words instantly refreshed my memory bringing the most

mentally and physically painful night back to the forefront of my memory. I unconsciously rubbed the spot where the love of my life once lived. Slowly, tears fell from my eyes. Kayla took a Kleenex and wiped the pain from my face. Blaming Olivia, I turned my head completely disgusted by the sight of her. I then looked at Kayla.

"Where's Ron?" I asked with as much anger and intensity as I could.

"Someone killed him, Paris. He's dead. He's in hell where he belongs. The police have been asking a lot of questions about who killed Ron but haven't come up with nothing. Do you know who killed him, Paris?" Kayla asked grabbing my hand.

"Hell no!" I lied. I remember clearly that Trey killed Ron somewhere in the hallway. There was no way in hell I would tell on the one person who gave Ron what he deserved. I was pretty much still being affected by the medication, so I ended up falling back to sleep. Later on, I learned just how messed up my body really was. I had to receive twelve stitches between the area of my rectum and vagina, a broken nose, and a closed eye. I felt worse than the common knowledge of the injuries. I thanked God over and over again for allowing Trey to kill Ron and saving my life. Honestly, I did still love Trey, but trust played a major role in any relationship that I chose to be in, I could never let myself trust him again, but for saving my life he will always be my friend.

*****

MIDNIGHT

I had just returned home from checking on a new house. The ordeal went smoothly. I saw some things that I liked and disliked. Things I liked within a bad neighborhood and vice versa. Only one thing was for certain and that was I was moving as soon as possible. They came here once for me, so I refused to be a sitting duck for them to come a second time. I couldn't live my life wondering if I was going to wake up or not. My life was getting on track, and I didn't want to lose that for reasons that were unknown to me. I stepped in the living room and cut the T.V. on. As I was taking off my shoes it immediately grabbed my attention.

"Hello, my name is Kathy Wells with Fox five news. I'm here at Wendy's restaurant on Georgia Ave. in northwest Washington where FBI Agents accompanied by Metropolitan Police officers have arrest known drug dealer by the name Ricardo Langdon. Police apprehended James along with two kilos of cocaine within his possession. Police have also arrested a female who police suspect was a part of a drug deal. Police have released her name to be a Ms. Tymia Wiggins. Both suspects will be taken to the fourth district police station where they both will be booked and processed for illegal trafficking of an illegal substance. More charges will also be pending.

My world was suddenly falling apart. Never in a thousand years would I have thought that my temporary dealings in narcotics would corrupt Tymia's life in such a way. I could now see Tymia and I plans falling apart, but what worried me the most at this point was if she was as gangsta as she portrayed herself to be or would she crack under the pressure and send the police at me. Trying to plan for the worst I ran to my safes and cleaned them out with plans of relocating all the drugs, guns, and the money. If she did turn state, then they wouldn't get shit.

*****

PARIS

It had been two weeks since Ron attacked me. Today I would be released. I really wondered why Trey hadn't come to see me while I was in the hospital. I figured that he might think that the police would be here waiting for him, so he was probably trying to stay out of the light. Only if he knew he had nothing to worry about. I would make sure of that. Olivia constantly begged for my forgiveness, but I blamed solely her for me losing my baby, and having to undergo such a life altering ordeal.

I was mostly healed up but mentally I was scarred for life. Ron may have died but he left a lasting impression on my life. I resented my mother for that. Thanks to Kayla, who was always there for me had me walking out of the hospital in style. Kayla bought me some black Manolo boots, Blue Seven jeans, and a leather Prada jacket. All courtesy of the Skylark. Olivia offered to drive me home, but I choose to ride with Kayla. At this point I wouldn't let Olivia drive me to heaven. Olivia was disappointed but I didn't give a fuck. She should have taken my word for gold.

We pulled up to my building, and Kayla helped me get my bags upstairs. Walking in my house I was stopped in my tracks when I spotted the spot where I miscarried. Olivia tried to clean it as best she could, but you could still see a brown spot on the plush white carpet. Both Olivia and Kayla rubbed my back as I fought back the tears that welled up behind my eyes.

I pulled myself together and proceeded to walk forward. I was careful to just walk pass and not step on it. Kayla stayed on my heels all the way to my room. Once I closed the door Olivia got the hint, and let us be. Maybe she would go and cook the three of us lunch or something. In the room Kayla played her position and stood by me.

"You okay Paris?" Kayla asked as she sat next to me on my bed.

"Yeah, I'm good. I'm just a little shaken up, but I'll be alright," I assured her.

"You know I'm here for you girl. You see I got you fresh." Kayla joked referring to my new clothes. She always knew how to lighten a mood.

"You did, you did, and I thank you, but when did you start getting Prada money big baller?"

"Stripping pays me real good. You see my car, don't you?" Kayla arrogantly smiled.

"So what are you going to do now?" Kayla asked.

"What do you mean?" I replied looking into her eyes.

"Are you going to get another job or are you going to apply for financial aid and go to school? I know you not discarding your dream?" Kayla asked in an unbelieving tone.

"I don't know my mind is so messed up right now. Plus, I still need another $15,000 dollars."

"Well, why don't you work with me at the Skylark?" Kayla slyly suggested thinking that she was slick.

"I would be too scared. I couldn't." The frightened look was already on my face.

"Paris I'm going to be right there with you. You'll get everything that you need for college in six months, and still have some spending money. It's easy Paris. Trust me. I got you, and I swear I won't let nothing happen to you."

Kayla pleaded. I just stayed quite as I thought of everything that she said. I couldn't think of nothing that was worth me putting off my future any longer. I then decide that now was the time to sacrifice and do something with my life. By any means necessary.

*****

MIDNIGHT

Within twenty minutes I had cleared out all the safes in the house and had their contents in a nearby Hotel on the Maryland side of the D.C. Maryland line. I called down to the Fourth District police station and found out that both Ric and Tymia were made co-defendants. That night I chose not to sleep at my house. I went back to the hotel and purchased another room aside from the one I bought to stash the gun, drugs, and money in. I did love Tymia, but my uncle taught me to be ready for all scenarios, so yeah, I loved her but wasn't going to let my heart get me a hundred years.

Tymia and Ric were scheduled to be in front of a judge in the well-known and feared district court. They'd be in front of the most feared judge in D.C. history. Judge Rambert was a no non-sense judge that didn't tolerate anything from anybody. Although a judge, he had the power of a politician or a congressman. He didn't care about your position or your money. He'd lean on judges, prosecutors, defense lawyers, and even the mayor. He had no picks. The only good thing about him was that   he gave you law no matter what the reason. The downside was that although he gave you law, if you lost a trial in front of him you would be guaranteed to get the maximum penalty for whatever the charge was.

Before long the clerk of the court called the court docket for Tymia Wiggins and Ricardo Langdon. There was no way that I was going to let her come to court and not be here I wanted to hear firsthand everything that got said in the hearing.

Tymia walked in cool, calm, and collected. I thought damn she was calm as shit for someone who never been locked up. When Tymia saw me standing in the back she rolled her eyes at me. That small gesture scared the shit out of me and made me wonder did she already turn state or not. I had a good notion to get the hell out of that courtroom. She then looked again and smiled with a wink. I then thought to myself that's my bitch. I returned the smile. The clerk called the case number, and the judge began to speak. I listened attentively as he spoke.

"Good morning, ladies and gentlemen, I guess I'll hear the government first."

This was my first-time seeing Judge Rambert I thought he had a striking resemblance to Jaba the Hut from *Star Wars*.

186

Judge Rambert was seriously overweight. Throughout my bid in Lewisburg, I would always hear stories of the guy. He was from Texas, and actually a member of the Albert Pike Society which was one of the founding societies of the KKK (KLU KLUX KLAN). He was the epitome of a racist and a prejudice motherfucker. If he could he'd hang every black man and woman that came in his courtroom. And get away, he would. Since he couldn't, he gave you law and waited for the verdict to come so he could legally sentence you to injection or to spend the rest of your life behind bars.

"Thank you, your honor, Debra Sines for the government. At approximately 3:00pm on September 25, 2007, police and Federal Agents conducted surveillance of a suspected drug lord that's recently been linked inside another ongoing investigation. He was apprehended and found to be carrying in a bookbag on his shoulder two-thousand grams of powder cocaine. The narcotics were field tested and returned with positive results for cocaine. Also on his waist was a Star Nine Millimeter with a full cartridge holding 17 live rounds of ammunition. Upon detaining Mr. Langdon's 750IL BMW color white, agents sent it to the FBI Auto unit where Mr. Langdon's car was found to have several secret compartments. Within the compartments authorities obtained a 50, Caliber Desert Eagle, one AK-47 assault rifle and a Glock 21 all guns were fully loaded and in ready positions. After tests were done all guns were deemed to be fully operable. The car was also in the Defendant's, Ricardo Langdon name. We the government have labeled Mr. Langdon a menace to society and asked that he be held without bond pending indictment. Ms. Sines stood straight up as she finalized her argument.

"Ms. Sines you are completely right about Mr. Langdon, yet I see a young woman here as well. What part does she play in all this madness?" The judge could have been reading my mind. The prosecutor said that Ric was a part of an ongoing investigation. I knew that if they said the same thing about Tymia that they would be coming for me as well.

"We will be making her a co-defendant of Mr. Langdon. Her name is Tymia Wiggins and we believe that she sold the drugs to Mr. Langdon. We would ask that the court also hold her without bail pending indictment.

"Is she also a part of an ongoing Investigation?" Judge Rambert looked down over top of his wire rim glasses.

"At this point, she is not, but that could change in the future pending a grand jury hearing."

"Well as of now she isn't. Counsel would you like to speak on behalf of your client?"

"I would like to your honor." Ric's lawyer tried to speak up.

"There is no need for you to say anything for your client counsel. There's no way in hell he's leaving custody. Now you can just wait there while I deal with Ms. Wiggins, the client of counsel who I was just referring to in the first place."

"Yes, Your Honor." Ric's lawyer tucked his tail with his face beet red. Judge Rambert then focused on Tymia and her lawyer.

"Counsel you may begin." Judge Rambert instructed as he leaned back in his swivel chair.

"Thank you, Your Honor. My client is completely innocent of all charges and accusations against her that was brought before the court. The only thing that she is guilty of is purchasing a hamburger from the wrong Wendy's. She is accused of selling the kilo's to Mr. Langdon. If that is true, your honor, then where is the money? There was none recovered. In fact, Ms. Wiggins only had $60.35 on her person at the time of arrest. She was never seen with Mr. James, nor caught on camera with him. The government mentioned no form of contact between the two at all. I asked that the charges be dropped, and she be released."

"FBI Agents think that they may have seen them conversing inside the Wendy's." The prosecutor spoke up.

"Ms. Sines you really don't have enough to hold this woman, but I will set a $100,000 bail with a 10% lease on it. Mr. Langdon will be held without bond until the probable cause hearing." The Judge made his ruling and that was it. It was a blessing from God that she got bail. The court was adjourned, and I slipped out. I had already made up my mind that I would pay Tymia's bail. If she was thinking about telling, I'd get her out before she made up her mind.

I left the court house and headed straight to the hotel to get the money. Ten thousand wasn't shit compared to my freedom.

*****

PARIS

"Paris, would you come on and stop being so damn scared. You act like you gonna die if somebody touch you!" Kayla yelled. I stood at the trunk of the car now having second thoughts and cold feet.

"Kayla I'm not used to anybody dick rubbing up against me." I whined.

"Ain't nobody dick gonna be on you. They don't pull it out. You know what, fuck it. If you ain't coming, I'm not going to let you make me late. Do you scary ass." Kayla was mad as she walked off. I was hoping that she would turn around, but she didn't. I definitely didn't want to be by myself.

"Okay Kayla wait!" I yelled as Kayla reached the entrance.

"I knew your scary ass wasn't going to stay out there. The boss of the place said that you're on after me." Kayla revealed. I knew that I heard her correctly, but I wanted confirmation on what exactly "ON" meant.

"I'm ON? What the fuck you mean I'm on?" I yelled.

"Paris, one thing about this place is that you have to dance on stage at least once every night." Kayla knew I wouldn't like that.

"Kayla I'm not ready for that." I tried to reason.

"Paris stop crying I seen you dance in the mirror and at the Go-Go. This ain't no different. Just don't look at the people and pretend they're not there. You gotta earn the money, so if you're not doing shit then you're going to be a broke bitch. Which means no college, and you gotta stay in Ron and Olivia's house." I jumped at the mention of Ron's name. Kayla noticed my reaction and hugged me.

"I'm sorry Paris, but I gotta get this money. I'll be watching you the whole time."

"You promise?" I pouted with my arm across my chest.

"Yeah, Scary hoe. Now come on and get dressed." Kayla pulled me into the dressing room. I finally said fuck it and used my determination to succeed in life as my motivation to show my goodies and stack that paper. I got dressed in a cute little costume. I was a little nervous, so I went to the bar to get a little something to drink to help me unwind.

"Excuse me can you make me two blue motherfuckers?" I yelled to the bartender.

"Coming right up Ms. Lady," he replied. I wasn't a drinker but knew that this drink would open me up real nice. I held my nose and down both of them. Five minutes later I was feeling mellow and ready to take on the world. I had been walking around with a robe on that barely covered my ass cheeks. Once that drink took affect that robe quickly met the floor. I now strutted with a tiger print thong and a long tail dragging behind. I even had Kayla paint some whiskers on my face. I was looking drop dead gorgeous. My ass accented the tail perfectly because the whole time that I walked around that tail sat in the crack of my ass. I definitely had the club's attention. Patrons constantly tried to get a lap dance, but I politely denied them all. I was open, but not that open.

After walking around the club for about thirty minutes, I had about $350 sitting in my thong and never sat on one-person lap. I could see eyes all over the club stalking me. My attention was then drawn to the DJ announcing the next dancer on the stage. Kayla walked out wearing a skintight Wizards Uniform. Kayla was a bad bitch and knew it. She walked the stage like she owned it. Kayla turned her back to the pole letting it idle between the crack of her ass. Kayla then pulled up her snow-white thong high above her waist causing it to dig in her pussy lips. I was surprised to see how my girl worked it on stage. By the next song Kayla was butt ass naked getting ready to attempt her patented trick to the blaring sounds of Young Buck's song *Ride Wit Me*. Kayla took a 16oz. water bottle and drank it with her pussy. Seconds later she sprayed the crowd with water and pussy juice. The crowd loved every bit of Kayla's assault. After watching that I ran to the bar and downed two more Blue Motherfuckers, and ran to the back to get ready to let go. Getting in the back I ran into Kayla.

"Damn girl you blew everybody away. Literally." I joked.

"Like I said it's nothing. You up next, so I hope you ready," Kayla warned.

"I'm straight just stand where I can see you." I was slurring like a motherfucker.

"Paris you drunk as a skunk. Since when you start drinking?" Kayla asked surprisingly noticing my slur.

"Just a little Blue Motherfucker. Nothing big. I needed something to loosen me up," I explained.

"Blue Motherfucker! Paris that's all-white liquor. You sure you can dance?" Kayla sounded worried.

"Ladies and gentlemen, I'd like to welcome our newest edition to the Skylark. It's her first night so let's not stare too hard. She goes by the name Ms. Nasty." The D.J announced. I then looked at Kayla.

"Just watch me. Ms. Nasty about to work." I smiled seductively and walked off leaving Kayla with her mouth hanging wide open. She stood there in a state of shock I retrieved my robe just as the sounds of Ciara's song *One Two Step* starting blaring through the speakers. "I want it, one two step." I danced on to the stage to the vibrations of the bass line. I then turned my back to the crowd letting the rob fall off of my shoulders as I two stepped back up the stage. Reaching the pole, the music died down and then switched over 'Trick Daddy and Trina's *You Don't Know Naa*. I let the robe fall to the small of my back and made each cheek of my ass jerk to the base line of the song. Every time that one of my ass cheeks would jump the robe would fall off more and more. Once it fell I bent over giving the crowd a full view of my goodies I licked my fingers and dug them deep into my pussy walls. I turned around as seductive and as nasty as I could. I sucked them clean. I got down on all fours making sure that my tail was daggling between my thighs as I crawled along the stage.

As I did so, I made my ass jump to the baseline of the song. Like stalking tigers, I locked my eyes on my unsuspecting prey sitting at the end of the stage. Once I reached him, I sat on my ass and spread my legs in his face. I took his hands so I could guide him into taking my thong off completely. As he slowly pulled on them, I whined like a Jamaican dance queen seductively wiggling out of it as he slowly tugged. Once the thong was completely off, I wrapped it around his neck and pulled his face into my pussy. Soon as I felt his tongue, I moaned out loud "OHHH GOD." That was for the extra effect. Before he could really get into it I aggressively pushed his head away and threw my thong in his face. I flipped over onto all fours and continued to bounce my ass in his face. The young guy stood up with a wad of ones and made it rain on my back. When the song ended my set was over, so I turned and gave him a kiss on the cheek. He tried to give me my thong, but I took them and put them on his head. I then kissed my finger and put them to his lips. We never spoke a word, but I could tell that I made his night. "You can keep the thong and thanks for the help." He smiled and I ran off the stage and right into Kayla.

"Paris you are such a hoe," Kayla laughed and hugged

me.

"You the one with the water gun pussy." I teased.

"I can't believe your scary ass just showed off like that. Now I don't feel bad calling you Nymphogirl. "

"Naw, don't call me Nymphogirl. You can call me Ms. Nasty." I pinched Kayla's nipple and strutted off with my tail over my shoulder. That night I made $1200. By the end of the night, I was drunk as a skunk, but felt liberated. I even ended up giving a million lap dances. I was then dead tired and couldn't wait to get in my bed.

*****

PRECIOUS

I was in a sports bar downtown in the northwest section of D.C. called the Clit. I sat there nursing a drink thinking if I didn't have a job to do, I could love Trey. I knew I wasn't supposed to catching feelings for him, but I was a woman in need, and I needed to be loved and not ordered around. I knew that came along with the career I chose, but I just needed more out of life on the personal side of it.

I sat around the bar thinking for over an hour and a half. So far, I had batted down four guys who had approached me. To all of them I would say that I was waiting on someone special. They took the hint and didn't hassle me any longer. I was the type of women that if you didn't stabilize me financially then you were useless to me, and I wouldn't deal with you. By the looks of the four guys, they didn't look like they could afford to buy me a Gucci purse.

I sat at the bar continuing to nurse my Long Island Iced Tea. The whole time that I sat I never knew that I was being watched vigorously on camera by a man with the utmost look of lust in his eyes. Unaware of his approach I was startled. He pulled up to my right sliding a hundred-dollar bill toward me.

"I hope this will cover what you've spent here tonight. Your money is no good. My name is London, and this is my establishment." London extended his hand. I accepted and thought to myself *Just who I've been waiting for.*

"My name is Precious, and you can keep your money. I'm more than capable of buying myself whatever it is that I want." I shook his hand and handed his money back to him. London stood about 5"9 brown skinned, with dreds freely hanging off of his head. He walked with the type of confidence that said he was a man of morals, stature, and principles. Although he had a smoothness about himself you could tell that he was still deadly in his own right.

"Is that right Ms. Precious? So you're independent huh?"

"If you wanna call it that. Money don't make my world turn like it do some females." I lied.

"Then tell me Ms. Precious, what does make your world turn?" London verbally stalked.

"That's like me asking you what your weakness is, some things are better kept to yourself. Do you think if Lex Luther didn't know that Superman would have told him that Kryptonite is the only thing that could kill him?" I took a sip of my drink. This man must be crazy if he thinks that I'm going to expose my hand so I can make myself vulnerable.

"You mean kept to yourself like secret lives and relationships?" He hit that right on the nose. That also made me smile.

"Maybe, that question sounds like you trying to get somewhere. Don't beat around the bush," I boldly stated.

"I see that you're very conclusive. Where is your man at?" London got straight to the point.

"At home why?" I played cat and mouse.

"Is he in my way in anyway?" He asked.

"He only has something to do with me when I'm in his presence. I don't see him here, so I guess what he doesn't know won't hurt him." I smiled seductively.

"So I guess secret lives are something that we both partake in." London smiled arrogantly as he removed a fallen piece of hair from my face. His gesture caused me to blush.

CHAPTER SIXTEEN

MIDNIGHT

It was 11:00am when I paid Tymia's bail. All day I sat on edge awaiting her return. I didn't bring the stuff back from the hotel yet, but I did have two Desert Eagle 50. Calibers for my own protection. I was extremely happy that Tymia was awarded a bail. I quickly dropped that money for her. What really gave me a breath of relief was when the Prosecutor said that she wasn't involved in the ongoing investigation. Tymia's only link to any drugs was through me. So how I saw it was that if she was under any type of investigation then that meant that I would be to, and vice versa.

Since being shot, anytime that I would hear a door open I would instantly get on point. Sometimes I would go as far as whipping out. Tymia made it home around 7:00pm. As the front door came open, I sat in the dark with 50. Calibers aimed at the door. Tymia looked up and jumped back when the large handguns winked at her.

"Boy put that shit away. Scary ass! Ain't nobody coming in here!" Tymia yelled.

"Better safe than sorry. What they say to you?" I got straight to the point.

"What, you deaf motherfucker? Weren't you there? You heard the same thing that I did!" Tymia snapped and walked off toward the Livingroom. I came up behind her and turned her around to embrace her.

"Damn Babygirl, I'm so sorry that I put you in that position. I didn't mean for this to happen. I had no idea that he was being watched." I pleaded and Tymia instantly broke into tears.

"Baby they touched all over me and made me strip. They treated me so bad." Tymia buried her face in my chest as she released her tears of pain and humiliation. I played my position and held her close. I then held her head up and licked her tears away. Softly I planted kisses on her face until I found her succulent lips. With no restraint Tymia matched my intensity. Our tongues intertwined gracefully together. I roamed her body like a lion in search of food. I carried her back to the living room with her arms around my neck and legs wrapped around my waist. Slowly I undressed her with a hint of aggression. Sliding her pants off I was greeted by a curly patch of pubic hair. I began to lick all over her thigh while inhaling the scent of her pussy. Her hands rested on the top of my head as she stood in front of me. I tried to taste every part of her body that I could. As I flicked my tongue across her swollen clit her legs began to shutter.

"Oh please don't hurt me Midnight. Bite it, baby." Tymia moaned.

I place her right foot on the couch to gain more access to her love tunnel. Licking and teasing I nibbled on her clit and sucked at the same time.

"Oh Midnight I'll kill you if you hurt me. Oh baby that feels so good." Tymia moaned again now finding it hard to stand on her own.

"Oh you're gonna, oh baby you're gonna make me cum. Midnight I'm cumming, baby I'm cumming." I then laid Tymia down without any of my clothes off; I pulled out my shaft and entered her in whole. Tymia's mouth hung wide open as her scream was caught in her throat. I took over her body. With every thrust I gave her I dominated her mind with control and concentrated passion. Constantly, I would feel her leg shaking on my biceps. Before long I felt my own pressure building up.

"AAAGGGHHHH oh yeah ARRGHH," I moaned. Five thrusts later I exploded within her walls. As I sat there catching my breath, Tymia continued to gyrate her hips in an attempt to milk every drop of nut that I had in my body. Eventually we rolled over onto the carpet wrapped in each other's arms.

*****

TREY

I was in James Creek with my right-hand man Rocko. As we smoked purple haze, I continued to think that I had a real gangsta bitch in Precious. I felt that she kept it 'all the way live' with me at all times. She would hold my guns and drugs without question. All-in-all she was a bad bitch that was all for me.

"Aye Trey whatever happened to that bad ass brown skinned female you bagged that day when we were shooting dice?" Rocko asked.

"As I recall you tapped me and then told me that she was "out of my league," being so and I still bagged her. That piece of pussy is none of your business Playboy." I inhaled the exotic smoke.

"And she still out of your league." Rocko laughed.

"Naw she's cool though. The bitch keeps it all the way real with me. She holds the work and everything." I boasted.

"You better hope she don't clip your dumbass." Rocko laughed.

"Naw, I ain't worried about that. Shawty ain't going nowhere. My old baby mother ain't fucking with me. I got to have a wifey. It's only right. I got plans for her too. Somebody gotta fall for somebody to come up ya dig?" I smiled wickedly holding my fist out for Rocko to give me a pound. I then passed him the smoke.

"Oh yeah when the hell she gonna drop that baby anyway. She's been pregnant for a minute." Rocko said.

"Man, slim, she had a miscarriage. Her fucking stepfather raped her and made her lose it." The thought instantly placed me in a solemn mood.

"Yeah, I know you crushed him for that shit?" Rocko pried.

I just looked at him without saying a word. He eventually caught my drift. You see, me and Rocko grew up together. If anyone knew Rocko it was me. The reason why I chose not to elaborate on what I did to Ron was because Rocko was the type of person that if he knew any dirt on you, he would eventually use it against you in some form. I knew that if he ever did that to me that I would kill him. I loved Rocko like a brother so to keep him out of the line of fire I just didn't tell him shit. I was helping him not make a life altering decision. Treachery would either get you death or get you rich, but even that don't last forever because payback is always a bitch.

*****

PARIS

By now it had been four months since I started working at the Skylark. I was all the way used to it now. I no longer needed Blue Motherfuckers to loosen me up. I would pull in close to a thousand dollars nightly, while being sober. I even got Kayla back focused about going to school. Although I did, I was starting to worry about her. Recently, Kayla had started taking ecstasy pills. It also looked as if she was starting to get addicted as well. Kayla had been there for me through so much that now it was my time to be there for her.

Tonight, the Skylark was jammed pack mainly because today was a Saturday. We'd been on the floor now for about two hours and had both accumulated 400 apiece. Although Kayla was high as a kite, I made sure to keep my eye on her at all times. I watched her go to the bar to get a drink and to towel down. I think the pills had her dehydrated and sweating like pig. As she received her drink she was tapped on the shoulder. When she turned around a look of terror washed across her face.

"Trey, what are you doing here?" Kayla stuttered completely terrified.

"Shit, just came by to have some fun. Hopefully with you." Trey smiled and tried to hug her. Kayla could smell the alcohol all over him.

"Stop Trey! Don't touch me. Get your hands off of me." Kayla pushed Trey off of her and took a step back.

"Fuck you mean stop bitch! You playing big now?" Trey slurred heavily.

"Trey you're a murderer, can't you see that I'm scared of you?" Kayla pleaded with tears welling up behind her eyes.

"What the fuck you just say?" Trey, with his massive hand gripped Kayla neck. "I told you about your mouth, didn't I?" Trey spoke in a murderous tone. I instantly ran over to help her out.

"Trey stop please don't hurt her," I begged grabbing Trey's arm. Trey looked over to my scantily clad body. My fishnet body suit caused a whole rush of anger to overtake him.

"So this your new profession now? You let this bitch talk you into stripping?" Trey yelled releasing his grip on Kayla's neck.

"Stop it Trey it's not like that. This is my choice. I needed money for college." I tried to explain.

"College? You know you could have asked me for it." Trey pointed to himself.

"Trey, I didn't want your money when we were

together, so why would I want it now? I'm independent and will get it myself."

"You should get the hint that she don't want your sorry ass," Kayla injected. Trey aggressively swung a wild backhand that just barely missed Kayla's face as she jumped back.

"Keep running your mouth I got something to shut you up," Trey stated with pure malice in the tone of his voice. Trey was going to hurt Kayla, so I knew that I had to get them apart from each other.

"Look Trey, come to VIP so we can talk." I pulled him along. Trey came but as he walked, he never took his eyes off of Kayla. As soon as we sat down Trey started.

"So you fucking for money now? What hap....." I cut him off stopping him mid-sentence.

"Hold up!" I put a hand up to stop him in his tracks.

"Trey don't you ever disrespect me like that. I wouldn't disrespect myself, so I won't sit here and let you do it." I had to check him for stereotyping me. "I don't fuck for money. I sell fantasies". His remark alone just reminded me of how much I hated his ass.

"All females that work here fucking for money, fucking for drugs or fucking because their pimp tell them to. You got to be doing one or the other." Trey was making me sick by the minute. I couldn't believe the shit that was coming out of his mouth.

"Trey I barely fucked you for free. So why would I fuck for money? Don't be stupid Trey." I scolded.

"Look Paris, if you're determined to do this and leave to pursue your dream then do it. Don't let this place suck you up and break you. You're too precious to be in here strung out on whatever it may be- money or drugs. Just get in and get out."

"I'm stronger than that Trey. You should know that."

"That's what I know, so I don't want to see you hurt yourself." Trey rubbed my cheek.

"Look I never got the chance to say thank you for

saving my life and ending Ron's. I just wish it would have happened sooner." I pulled his hand from my cheek.

"Oh you saw that huh?" Trey smiled and looked off.

"Partially, I was pretty much in and out. The police interrogated me about who killed him." My statement caused Trey to immediately look in my face.

"What you tell him?" He now spoke in a serious tone.

"Don't worry Trey. The one thing that you did teach me was that the police cannot help you. I told them that I was unconscious and didn't know. I just wanted to say thanks, and how can I ever repay you?" I touched his hand.

"We can start by us getting back together." Trey went out on a limb.

"Trey I'm going to be honest with you. I could never trust you again. Our relationship would be full of hate and arguments. I don't want to go through that." After hearing that Trey aggressively stood up.

"You ain't grateful." I tried to grab his arm but he snatched it away, and walked off leaving me sitting in VIP alone.

"Wait Trey don't be mad!" I yelled. Trey stopped at the VIP entrance and turned around.

"I should have let your ungrateful ass die." His words cut straight through me. He then stepped out. Seeing Trey coming Kayla moved closer to the bouncers. He then stopped and whispered in her ear.

"Your mouth wrote a bad check." He then spit in her ear and walked out of the club. Kayla stood there in shock.

*****

TREY

I tried to psych myself out that I didn't still love Paris. That quickly became a lost cause because I couldn't suppress the way I felt about her. Accepting reality, I told myself that I fucked up and lost the one woman who I could have spent the rest of my life with. I leaned my seat back and let my mind drift into the land of purple haze. As I relaxed in my high my cell phone went off.

"Yeah." I answered.
"Hey baby." Precious jovially stated.
"You in position?" I got straight to business.
"No not yet I'm working on it though. I wanted to see how you was doing," Precious replied in a childish voice.
"Fuck how I'm doing. Get on your job bitch! While you're worried about me you could be on your act. You dig? You wasting time so get the fucking job done!" I yelled holding my ground.
"I was just thinking about your ass DAMN."
"Think about what your ass supposed to be doing then call me." *CLICK* I hung up.

*****

PRECIOUS

I couldn't believe that I was actually sitting here thinking about his ass and he disrespected me like that. Then he's got the nerve to call me a bitch. I didn't do anything, and he treated me like that. I was really starting to not like Trey at all. I flipped my cell phone open so I could relieve some of this stress. London's phone rang about three times before he picked up.

"I've been expecting your call." London answered.
"How did you know that it was me?" I blushed through the phone.
"Technology is everything. So what is good with you?" London spoke smoothly.
"My significant other is acting like an ass," I replied.

"Well look I'm in the house so why don't you come see me." London more so demanded than asked.

"What's your address?" I grabbed a pen.

"4218 Call Pl. in Southeast. Can you make it or do you need me to come and get you?"

"I'm a big girl, I think I can manage. So I'll see you in a minute." I smiled thinking to myself damn that was easy.

"I hope so," London smoothly replied. Within an hour I was pulling up in front of London house in my pink Mercedes. When I pulled up, I thought to myself that it looked like a block party out here. Then I realized that it was just a bunch of crackheads. I knocked on the door and almost immediately it opened. London stood there with two wine glasses and a bottle of MOET. The lighting across his face made him look breathtakingly handsome.

"Damn MOET? You must be plotting on some kitty kat," I smiled seductively.

"Naw not really. I just knew that you had a rough day so figured I'd put you at ease," He smiled.

"And how do you plan on doing that?" I quizzed.

"It's only one way to find out." London seductively smiled and stepped to the side.

I gradually stepped in. On sight of how his house was set up my breath was taken away. The entire house was in candle lit form. On, each step sat a candle with its own flame that danced to the silence. The candles were also coupled with white rose petals strewn about. London closed the door and grabbed me with his lips, pressing me up against the wall as we kissed with unconceivable hunger for one another.

"SSSHHHHH." London pressed his index finger over my mouth, and led me to the stairs.

I stepped pass London never losing eye contact. Even as I took every step backwards, I continued to look deep into his hazelnut eyes, looking deep into his soul silently telling him that I needed him inside me. Once reaching the bedroom London stepped back to me again burying his tongue deep in my mouth. I suddenly pulled back touching his lips with my finger as I strutted off toward the bathroom.

I got a surprise for you. "I bit on my bottom lip as I closed the door. I placed my purse on the sink and took out a pack of LifeSavers Gummies and my cell phone. Fifteen minutes later I was ready. When I opened the door, I was wearing a sky-blue panty and bra set. London walked toward me. We were now standing face to face. He was still fully dressed. He picked me up gently lying me down on the bed. Softly he kissed my thighs. The whole time my pussy smelled of fruits and berries. The smell was driving London crazy. London took one of my feet and sucked on each of my toes individually. Slowly he slid his reptilian tongue down my calf and to the back of my thigh. I was going crazy over London's tease game. I could feel the juices in my body running freely. His hands moved to my hips sliding my panties off as he continued to kiss my thighs. Once my panties were off, he finally saw why my pussy smelled so edible.

As I spread my legs two gummy savers slid down the slit of my snatch. "Damn I'm going to enjoy this," London stated. London dove straight in with his tongue leading the way. With ease his tongue caught every delinquent gummy saver that slid out my soaking wet slit. London licked and sucked until he was greeted by my love cream.

"Oh damn, that feels good," I moaned as I came. I was making all kinds of fuck faces from his tongue at work on my pussy. After London licked all the cum off of me, he stood up and removed his clothes down to the bare back. I spread my legs wide as I could, as if I was silently telling him to beat it up. London chooses to stay in control and flipped me over onto my hands and knees with my ass cocked up in the air. Once my ass was spread London saw that some of my cum had escaped him and slid down the crack of my ass. From my asshole to my lower back London licked me clean being sure to pay extra attention to my rectum.

"London, I need the DICK! Stop teasing me," I cried out, but London ignored me. He then stood up without warning and rammed his dick in my pussy pumping as violently as he could. I loved every thrust that he gave.

"Yeah baby, beat it up. Fuck me harder nigga!" I spoke in the raunchiest voice that I could turning him on more and more. My antics made him work harder and harder with each outburst. Before long I could feel London dick swelling up inside me, so I contracted my pussy muscles like a vice grip around his dick sucking him deeper with every contraction. Just as he was getting ready to explode, he felt an all too familiar feeling of cold steel being pressed behind his ear, and the voice of death whispering.

"Didn't your mother ever tell you that unprotected sex will kill you?" Trey asked wrapping his forearm around London's neck, pressing the gun harder into his ear.

"Slim you ain't even gotta do it like this." London's dick instantly went soft, and he slid out of me

"Nigga shut the hell up before I let this hammer bust a nut in your ear." *SMACK* Trey smacked him with the 357. Magnum. I then hopped off the bed and kissed Trey on the lips.

"Hey baby." I greeted to let London know this was all my doing.

"Bitch you set me up?" London asked unbelievingly holding the gash that the 357. had left. Trey then kicked him in the face.

"Shut the fuck up nigga and tell me where the money at?" Trey spoke with malice behind his voice.

"In the closet just don't kill me please." London begged.
SMACK

"Get your bitch ass up," Trey demanded and London followed suit and did as told.

"Check the closet and get everything," Trey demanded from me. He then walked London down to the living room where he tied his hands and feet together behind his back like a pig. Just as he was placing the duct tape on his mouth, I was walking down the stairs fully dressed with two pillow cases of coke and money.

"You get everything babygirl?" Trey asked still holding he pistol to London head.

"Yeah, I got it come on let's go," I replied completely unaware of Trey's intentions. Trey turned to London and drug him to the fireplace. He then pulled out two coke bottles of gasoline and drenched London's body with it.

"Next time you should practice safe sex. You'll live longer." Trey then struck a match setting London's body ablaze. I couldn't believe how ruthless Trey was. Setting London on fire was a good piece of dick gone to waste. London tried to scream but his cries fell on deaf ears as Trey and I slide out of the back door.

CHAPTER SEVENTEEN

MIDNIGHT

After that night of passionate sex with Tymia I no longer felt that she was a threat to my freedom. After really thinking about it I could really say that I cared about her, maybe even loved her. I had good reason to. She nursed me back to health, handled work for me, and was all for the struggle. She could do no wrong.

I was driving my caddy truck up New York Ave. in route to see an old timer named Doc. I had twelve bricks left and five pounds of purple Haze. Doc was the last person that I could think of that I could sell anything to and not have to worry about the police coming to see me about it. Doc was highly efficient in getting money, but if you disrespected him, well you could imagine what would happen. Doc was the epitome of a street dude. A killer. Basically, saying a straight up Gangster.

Doc was also a highly respected Muslim throughout Washington. One thing about D.C. was that man respected man. Doc was a firm believer in this aspect of life. He was wise beyond his years. That's partly why I choose to deal with him. I pulled up to the light on New York and Bladensburg Rd. and took in what a beautiful day it was. Deciding to partake in it, I hit the sunroof. Just as it was open my neck popped. Someone had smashed into the back of me. I quickly snatched my pistol off my waist and hopped out. Stepping out I saw that it was a pink Mercedes with a woman in the driver's seat with both of her hands covering her mouth. Once she removed them, I saw that her beauty was uncharted. With that I became at ease and tucked my pistol.

"I hope you got some insurance beautiful," I stated with a smile as I approached her car.
"Oh my God, I can pay in cash. I am so sorry. I can't afford to have my insurance company get involved."

The young girl began to cry. I looked at the dent and summed it up to be minor and quickly thought of a resolution.

"Look baby girl you ain't gotta cry. I got a solution to all of our problems." I rubbed her back causing her to look up.
"What? Some pussy?" The young girl shot and continued to cry. But if she was willing, I definitely wouldn't mind though.
"Naw,' but if you let me take you out then we will call it even." I gave her a reassuring look. She then stopped crying and looked at me.
"Look I'm sorry I said that. I'm just so used to that being all men want from me. What's your name anyway?" she asked sincerely.
"They call me Midnight. What about you?" I replied.
"My name is Precious." She extended her hand, and I shook it.

*****

KAYLA

Paris and I continued to stack paper by shaking our ass at night. Paris was on a mission. The girl wouldn't spend a dime. Everything that she made was going straight into the bank. I didn't blame her either. She'd been through a lot. Happiness had to come for her sooner or later. I too, was also saving up. Not as quickly as Paris but I was moving along nicely, and would also make it to be a doctor.

Tonight Paris was kneeling in front of the toilet throwing up everything but her intestines. I figured that she might have come down with the flu or something. She was bald up and clearly in pain. Soon, she started dry heaving and nothing would come up.

"Paris, what the fuck is wrong with you?" I asked rubbing her back.

"I feel like someone is slicing my stomach with a razor. I think it's something that I ate," she replied.

"Can you dance tonight?"

"No, I'm going home. This shit hurts too bad. Call me a cab?" Paris asked. I immediately did just that. I waited with Paris out front until her cab pulled up.

Once it did, I wished her well and headed back inside. I went straight to the dressing room to pop a little pill called a sour apple. Now it was time to stack that paper I was high as a kite while slinging my hips to the beat like a seasoned pro. In two hours, I had $450 easy. All night while I walked, I made sure to make my ass clap in appreciation. I was then stopped by someone placing a C-note into my thong. I turned and smiled.

"Oh you want a lap dance huh big man?" I smiled while straddling him. The patron was a big light skinned guy with the pockets to match. He wore a Hugo Boss sweater that had to have been tailored to fit him because Hugo didn't make big sizes. He was a big dude but had a stride smoother than Courvoisier.

"Naw no lap dance, just a few minutes of your time.

That possible?" He palmed my ass grinding into him.

"I guess so, your money, your time. What you got to say?" I slightly slurred.

"Well first off how much is it going to cost me to taste that kitty kat?" Damn he got straight to the point.

"Hold up cowboy slow down. What's your name?"

"My fault babygirl. They call me Rome what about you?" He nodded.

"Well my stage name is Angel so you can call me that. Now tell me how much you willing to spend, and I'll take it from there." I took control and grinded my hips into his midsection rubbing the back of his neck.

"That's cool. How about two stacks for the whole night?" Rome threw the number like it was nothing.

"I'd say that I could suck the skin off of you and hope you can keep up with me," I whispered into his ear and licked his earlobe.

"You got a dirty mouth I like that. Go get dressed. I'll be out front in a black Hummer."

"I'll be ready in ten minutes." I stood up catching a slap on the ass as I turned to leave. In ten minutes, I was fully dressed and met Rome outside in his black Hummer. I was above almost every nigga's standards so Rome felt that his two grand was being spent wisely.

Rome was a big dope boy from around Savannah Terrace. He had three houses where he would either cut, bag, or whenever he just wanted to have some fun. Tonight, was a night for fun so he chose one randomly. The whole ride Rome played with my pussy while listening to the sounds of Young Jeezy blaring through the speakers.

"Since you already got your hands down there why don't you stick these in there?" I handed Rome two ecstasy pills.

Rome wasted no time complying with my wishes.

Before we could get out of the truck Rome was fired up and ready to knock sparks out of me. The huge truck wasn't even parked straight before he hopped out and instructed me to follow suit. We got up on the porch and Rome was so excited that he fumbled with the keys. When he finally opened the door, he allowed me to step in first. Stepping in *SMACK* I was instantly dazed and knocked to the floor. Trey stepped out the shadows clutching a 357. Magnum.

"Damn nigga you could have waited till I fucked her. That bitch just popped two pills in her pussy." Rome was upset about that. Trey being the snake that he was quickly turned on him.

SMACK, SMACK, SMACK. Trey viciously began pistol whipping Rome.

"Get your bitch ass over there and sit down. Cry baby ass nigga," Trey growled pointing with his 357. Showing which way, he wanted Rome to go in.

"So you gonna carry me like that Trey? She wouldn't even be here if it wasn't for me." Rome began to cry as he crawled to the corner.

WACK Trey kicked him in the mouth ultimately knocking three of his front teeth out.

"Shut the fuck up nigga. This is a dog eat dog world. Don't trust nobody you dumb motherfucker," Trey spat then looked my direction. By the sight of Trey, I instantly peed on myself as I felt my life span coming to a close.

"I didn't knock you out Kayla so I can tell you why you're going to die. I tried to be nice and stop that nigga Phil from slaughtering your dumbass, and now you want to call ME of all people, a murderer. That was an understatement BITCH! I'm a cold-blooded murderer. Trey smiled sadistically yet as arrogantly as he could.

"Please Trey I'm so sorry. I didn't do anything. Please don't kill me. I'll suck your dick and you can fuck me. Just please don't kill me." I cried and pleaded to the best of my ability, but Trey's mentality was far too evil to hear my cries.

"I've got a good idea. Take them thongs off." Trey ordered and squatted down as I complied with his wishes. I started to feel a little relieved until Trey placed the barrel of the gun in my face.

"Suck it like a dick," he ordered.

"What?" I wasn't sure exactly what he was asking. Trey then aggressively grabbed a hand full of my hair jamming the gun into my mouth to the trigger.

"I said suck it, BITCH!" Trey forcefully began fucking my mouth with the barbell ramming it in and out of my mouth as if it were actually a dick.

The heavy-handed gun would split the back of my throat with every thrust. I cried profusely. Soon the gun was covered in saliva and blood. Trey removed the gun and jammed it into my pussy to the trigger.

"AAAGGGHHH!" I screamed from the agonizing pain. Again, with the gun he fucked me with blunt aggression.

"When you get to hell make sure you tell the devil your pussy burning Bitch." Trey jammed the gun back to the trigger looking over at Rome with a smile. *BOC, BOC, BOC.* The bullets ripped through my insides with one of the bullets exiting through my eye.

*****

TREY

"Damn Rome you…." Trey looked at Kayla then back to Rome. "You wasn't going to fuck her was you?" Trey sarcastically smiled with a laugh.

"Please man why you got to kill me? I ain't never did nothing to you man." Rome literally cried.

"Look at you Rome. 6"5 300 lbs. balled up on the floor crying. You should be ashamed of yourself. You ain't nothing but a waste of time, money, and space." I raised the Magnum. *BOC, BOC, BOC!* I shot him three times in the head. I then bent down and used Rome's shirt to wipe Kayla's blood from the barrel of the gun. Casually as I could I walked out of the house.

CHAPTER EIGHTEEN

MIDNIGHT IN PARIS

PARIS

I was in pain the entire ride home. I wish that I could have driven myself, but since Trey and I split he took back the Camry he bought me. I wasn't mad though, that just gave me more of a reason to leave his ass alone. Once I got home, I drank some Nyquil and slept for the rest of the night. The next morning, I took a trip to go see my doctor, Dr. Ames.

Stepping in his office I saw that I had two people in front of me. Once he saw that I was there he said that he would see me right away. Two girls looked at me with daggers in their eyes. I didn't let it bother me though. I just kept it moving with my head held high. Dr. Ames closed the door and quickly examined me.

"Well Ms. Paris I'm sorry to say but you've got food poisoning. Do you remember what you ate?" He removed his glasses. Come to think of it Kayla was right, he was cute. I never noticed it.

"I did eat some carryout from Lucky House on Georgia Ave earlier that day. That might be what did it," I confessed.

"Well, I'm going to give you this shot and I'll write you a prescription. I don't think you should eat there anymore."

"I don't think I should eat there anymore either." I

laughed. Then Dr. Ames and I locked eyes for a brief moment. He then gave me the shot.

"UUMM let me go write that prescription." He replied nervously. He seemed embarrassed by the moment. He then left and quickly returned.

"Here you go Paris you must have an empty stomach when you take these. Take two first thing in the morning for three days, then you should be back to normal." He handed me the paper, then we locked eyes again.

"Paris? Will you have dinner with me sometime?" I couldn't believe he just asked me that.

"Dr. Ames are you asking me on a date?" I had to confirm his intentions.

"Well....Yes....I am. Will you join me?" He smiled assumingly like he knew that I would say yes.

"I'm sorry Dr. Ames I just got out of a bad relationship. Plus, with the miscarriage and all, I'm just not ready. Please don't feel bad. Under different circumstances I would love to. It's just that the timing isn't right. Please understand." I touched his hand.

"Oh believe me Paris I'm a big boy. I can handle rejection. My personal number is on that prescription. Please feel free to use it whenever you may need me. You have a nice day Ms. Clemons." He walked out of the room. I then thought to myself, damn I went from Ms. Paris to Ms. Clemons fast as hell. Oh well no sweat off of my forehead.

With the shot that Dr. Ames gave me, I felt a hundred times better, so I decided to call Kayla and tell her to come pick me up for work that night. I called and called but received no answer. I figured that she was probably on one of her many sexcapades and decided that I would catch a cab there. I knew I'd see her at work. Kayla wouldn't miss free money for anyone.

I pulled up to the Skylark around 11:30pm. I was happy to see that the place was crowded early. That meant a big money night. After getting inside I was dressed in a fishnet dress with nothing on underneath. I used silver lipstick and eyeliner to give myself an exotic look. I decided to go over to the bar for a drink to start the night off. While there I was approached by Cornell.

"What's up Ms. Nasty you got a minute for me?" He asked leaning his elbow on the bar.

"What for Cornell? I'm not fucking with you. All you want is some pussy that you ain't going to get." I tried to stop him in his tracks before he got started.

"Naw, Naw.....Well not me anyway. I was thinking that since you be having the customers here so sprung that maybe you need to start setting that kitty kat out. We can both get money." Cornell reasoned.

"So you trying to pimp me right?" I wanted him to clarify himself.

"Pimp is such a harsh word. I was thinking more along the lines of pussy managing."

SMACK. I cocked back and slapped the shit out of him. It felt good too. Cornell cocked back his hand like he was going to hit me back, but his attack was caught in mid-action.

"I don't think you want to do that slim." Cornell pulled away from the guys grip, and looked at him crazy.

"Nigga who the fuck is you?" Cornell was pissed.

SMACK The guy smacked him.

"That's for smacking me the last time.

SMACK and, that's for her." Cornell fell to the floor with ease.

"I'd advise you to leave before you can't." He warned swelling his body up. Cornell heard the seriousness in the guy's voice and got out of there before he got fucked up some more. He then turned to me.

"How much would you have made tonight?" Damn he was fine I thought.

"I don't think that's any of your business," I snidely replied.

"Look babygirl I'm not trying to rob you. Just give me a number." He smiled slowly placing me at ease. I finally answered.

"Fifteen hundred, there you satisfied?" I crossed my arms. He smiled at me and pulled out a wad of money. I watched him count off twenty-hundred-dollar bills. He then grabbed my hand placing the bills inside.

"That five hundred more than you would have made tonight. You with me the rest of the night." He spoke with a lot of confidence like I was supposed to jump.

"UMM, you must didn't hear me and Cornell's conversation. I don't fuck for money." I popped my neck.

"Who said anything about fucking I'm trying to get to know you." With that he really had me curious.

"And where are we supposed to be "ALL NIGHT"?

"Anywhere you want to be," he replied with a smile, leaving the night up to me.

"First off, what's your name?" I had to ask before he got me sidetracked.

"You can call me Midnight." There was that smile again. At that point I decided to follow my curiosity and see what this man was about. Since Trey, no man has ever sparked my interest as Midnight did. I could sense nothing but sincerity coming from him and that alone made me trust him enough to go with him.

*****

MIDNIGHT

I was completely intrigued by just the sight of Ms. Nasty. So much that I was just happy that she accepted my invitation and completely forgot about asking her real name, but then I figured that in due time that would come. She even reminded me of someone who I knew a long time ago.

When I saw her altercation with that fake ass pimp my body reacted before I could think. It was like something pulled me to protect her. If all is well, I may make her a permanent fixture in my life. Ms. Nasty quickly got dressed and met me at the bar.

"So are you going to tell me your name?" I wanted to know everything about her.

"I guess so, you can call me Paris."

"I drove to the RIO out Frederick MD where we sat and talked to sunrise. I was intrigued by her every word and more. I could tell by the origin of her conversation that she was no hood rat. Normally when a female says that she is stripping for college I'd take it lightly, but with Paris I took everything she said as gold. Paris was truly a diamond in the rough. I planned to allow her to shine as much as her potential would allow her to.

*****

MIDNIGHT

For the past few nights, I would stay out all night at the Skylark just to be near Paris. All throughout the night we would exchange glances and smile at one another. Cornell proved to be a straight coward. Every time he would see me enter the club he magically disappears for the night.

219

I laughed at myself because at times I would find myself actually getting jealous when Paris would dance for her customers. I guess that was naturally apart of being a man. The lion has always been known to be territorial. Because of our lengthy conversations I understood that I couldn't pay for her college tuition. I truly respected the fact that she was determined to accomplish that task on her own. I tried to figure out countless ways to get her to stop stripping, but Paris's mind was made up.

Since meeting Paris, I had all but neglected Tymia fully. In fact, I haven't had sex with her in about a week. Had I not been so caught up in Paris I would have realized that not having sex with her would draw immediate speculation. My mind was completely on Paris; ultimately making Tymia a runner-up. Tymia had now even sensed my infidelities and didn't like it one bit. Tonight, I drove Paris home from work. She wanted to catch a cab, but I wouldn't have it. We pulled up to her building and she began to collect her bags.

"Thanks for the ride home. I'll call you in the morning," Paris yawned.

"Ain't no thanks needed just make sure that you call me." Then without warning I leaned in and sucked on Paris' bottom lip catching her completely off guard.

"You must be trying to make me remember huh?" She smiled as she stepped out of the car.

Paris had my nose wide open. The whole ride home I was on cloud nine. Every time that I would see Paris, I would fall that way. She had an effect on me that only one other person in my entire life had. As soon as I walked into my house Tymia was sitting in the Lazyboy with the lights off. Startled I almost reached for my pistol.

"Why you in here sitting in the dark?" I asked sensing her anger.

"Did you get rid of all the drugs that you needed to?" Tymia asked flatly with a blank facial expression.

"Yeah, I did that a few days ago." By time I answered I then realized that her question was a set up, but it was too late. Tymia hopped out of the chair full of rage.

"Then why the fuck you ain't been coming home? Who the fuck you out there fucking?" Tymia yelled with her fist bald up.

"First off bitch, don't you ever question nothing that I do. This my house, I come home when the fuck I want to. So play your position bitch!" I stood directly in Tymia face.

"Bitch! I got your bitch you lying motherfucker!" Tymia ran to the couch and retrieved her Glock nine. Soon as I seen the gun in her hand I ducked off around the corner.

BOOM. BOOM. BOOM. Tymia let off three shots barely missing me. She then ran around the same corner in pursuit. Soon as she did, I was waiting on her.

PAP. PAP. I gave her a left hook followed by a left uppercut. Tymia was knocked out before she hit the floor. I kicked her gun away and slightly kicked her to wake her up.

"That's how you feel Mia? Huh? You was gonna shoot me? Get the fuck out my house bitch. Your time is up." Tymia immediately began pleading and sending her apologies.

"Please Midnight I believe and trust you. Please don't do this to us. Please Midnight I love you." I wasn't hearing anything she had to say. I grabbed her hair dragging her to the door.

"Love the door bitch before your family don't find you," I warned. I grabbed her leather jacket and tossed it to her as she continued to plead.

"Please don't do this to us Midnight?" Tymia cried.

I'd had enough of this shit. I whipped out my chrome D.E.

"I said get the fuck on bitch." Seeing the gun Tymia ran off to her car with her heart broken. Tymia truly loved Midnight. She was to the point where she wouldn't let anything come between them. Pulling away she stopped at the corner and cried her eyes out now feeling that she made a fool of herself. She now regretted every time that she pulled that trigger.

*****

PARIS

Midnight had my mind all the way open to the point where I was thinking of a possible relationship with him. Since Trey I thought that I'd never love again, but now with Midnight's persistence I was finding myself falling head over heels for him. Even when we would talk on the phone and said our goodbyes one of us would always call back. I would be dancing with a customer, but my mind would be solely on Midnight. If we miss a night without talking to each other we'd swear that something was wrong. Basically, we both had it bad.

It had now been two weeks since I had seen Kayla. Out of all of our years knowing each other this was totally out of the norm. I was beyond worried. I could feel it in my gut that something was wrong. Kayla was the type of girl that revolved her life around money. It gave her the energy that she needed to motivate her every day. For her not to come to work for such a long period of time I knew that something wasn't right, and I was determined to find out exactly what.

I decided that I would catch the bus over to Kayla's apartment. Luckily Kayla had given me a key so I wouldn't have any problems getting in. I unlocked the door to a horrid smell. I walked into the kitchen to find a pot of spoiled chitterlings. The apartment itself looked deserted. I walked to the answering machine seeing that Kayla had 45 new messages 15 of them were from me. At that point I concluded that Kayla was indeed missing. I tried to check the messages but couldn't because you needed a code to access it.

All kinds of ideas began to running through my head. The one I worried about the most was that Kayla left the club with a derange customer. I searched for Kayla's car keys, but they weren't in sight. I stepped outside to that parking lot to see if I could see her car, but that to was nowhere to be found.

Not wanting to but knowing that I had to, I hopped back on the bus this time in route to the Skylark. Since it was daytime, and the club was closed. I knew that the parking lot would be clear so if her car was there. I'd spot it right away.

The ride to the Skylark was for the most part a quiet one. I sat nervously as I thought of all the possible scenarios. All of my memories of Kayla ran through my head. At that point I felt obligated to say a short prayer for Kayla. Kayla had been there for me so much; I would just die if something happened to her. As the bus pulled up to the club a rush of emotions came over me. As bright as day Kayla's bright red BMW sat all alone in the back of the parking lot. I didn't know whether to be happy, thinking that maybe she was inside, or think that' this was confirmation that Kayla had suffered a horrible fate.

Nervously, I stepped off the bus dreading every step that I took towards her car. Reaching it I immediately knew that it was Kayla's by the picture she kept on the dashboard of the two of us. After confirming that it was indeed her car I ran to the entrance of the club. It was just like it was supposed to be. Closed. Even still, I banged and yelled.

"Kayla you in there?" I received no answer. I picked up my cell phone and called Kayla again as I walked back to her car. As I got closer to it I saw that her phone was sitting in the ashtray. I was at another dead end.

Eventually I made it home. Once arriving I did the one thing that I knew that I had to. I went to see Ms. Alice to inquire about Kayla. I knocked and Ms. Alice answered quickly. Instantly I could tell that she was crying. As I stepped in, I saw two white men wearing cheap suits and worn ties.

"Detectives, this is my daughter's best friend." Both of the detectives stood to make my acquaintance with a formal handshake.

"Hello ma'am. My name is Detective Peters, and this is my Partner Detective Rice. Could you tell us the last time that you saw Kayla?" He asked in a solemn tone.

"About two weeks ago at our job," I replied crossing my arms.

"And where might that be?" He probed deeper.

"At a strip club called the Skylark." Ms. Alice immediately cut in.

"A strip club? Kayla never told me that she worked at a strip club. She told me that she was an intern at Howard University." Ms. Alice began to cry harder already thinking the worst.

"No Ms. Alice she and I both worked there to save money for our college tuition next year." I clarified fully.

"Oh my God I just know that something has happened to my baby." Ms. Alice sat down continuing to cry. I then decided to help the detectives as much as I could.

"I really think that something happened to her. I went passed her apartment and everything looked to be untouched for a while. I couldn't find her car keys so I went outside to see if I could see her car, but it wasn't there. Then I went by the club and found her car in the parking lot."

"What kind of car does she drive?" Detective Rice asked.

"She drives a cherry red BMW." I replied.

"Do you know anything else ma' am. Anyone you think might want to hurt her for any reason?" asked Detective Peters. He was looking me dead in my eyes. I thought long and hard but know that I would be going against everything that Trey taught me. Kayla was my sister, and I wouldn't let her death be in vain if she was dead.

"Yes, I think a guy named Trey had something to do with it. His name is Treyvon Davis."

*****

MIDNIGHT

Once again, I was going to see old timer Doc. Only this time there was no drugs involved. I was going to see Doc about something that I would normally turn to Uncle D for. Advice. Doc was very wise, so I figured I would entrust my problems with him. Every conversation I had with him I always learned something. Hopefully that would be the outcome today as well. You see back in the day Doc put in big work. Even some with the infamous and most respected Wayne Perry. As far as institutions go, Doc has seen what he called Rocks to Diamonds.

Doc was what one would call a murderous money getter. Even while in the Lorton Correctional Facility he was grossing 15,000 a month. Lorton was what he called a diamond because of the money he drew from it. Then there were other places like Wala Wala and Beaumont United States penitentiary in Beaumont, Texas that he considered Rocks. Those were the places that tested his murder game and his mind because he never got caught. This is why I say that Doc didn't get this far by being stupid. Naturally I would trust his word.

Doc and I had met up at Lewisburg Pen back in "97". Back then you had a lot of compound basketball games. The two of us would always bet against each other; ultimately becoming friends. Once I went home and left him my numbers, we stayed in contact. I pulled up into the complex and parked. Like the norm I checked my guns before I stepped out of my truck. It was fairly cold out, so I grabbed my leather and pulled it on. The complex was flooded with kids, crackheads, dealers, and people sitting out just being nosey. I reached the building and walked up the steps that carried a smell of urine. The steps held multiple crack bags from where the junkies would gather and take their hits. I looked up at the green door that belonged to Doc, but before I could knock the door swung open.

"Midnight, As-Salaam Alaikum." Doc smiled with surprise.

"Wa Alaikum Salaam, what's up?" I shook his hand as firmly as possible.

"Age and this old vessel that I'm sitting in Nephew." Doc calling me nephew instantly reminded me of Uncle D. Doc escorted me inside as he patted me on the back.

"So what brings you to this neck of the woods? I know that it's not drugs because I bought the last of those off of you the last time you were here. So what's bothering you Nephew?" Doc was on point as usual when it came to reading me.

"You always were good at reading people," I laughed. "But the reason that I came over here is because I need some advice on some things. I got a lot of shit on the table right now, and in a tough position." I explained resting my elbows on my knees.

"Midnight you're like family to me. Your problems are mine." Doc leaned back crossing his legs simultaneously interlocking his fingers around his knee.

"Look, remember a while ago when my uncle got killed? Well, I thought I found his killer........" He cut me off.

"And now you're not sure that you did?" Doc finished my sentence.

"Right, in fact I don't think that the man that I killed was the trigger man at all. Why, because when I killed him there has been another attempt made on my life."

"So who do you think was the trigger man?" Doc questioned.

"It's this young dude named Trey. I'm strongly starting to believe that he had something to do with it. I pulled up on him out southwest while he was shooting dice. When he stood up he grazed his side with his arm."

"He was nervous and checking for his pistol." Doc replied on the money.

"That's the thing, when I first came home. My uncle gave me a list of a few people who he wanted me to knock off and referred me to him if I needed any help. I don't know if I should kill him or what."

"Nephew you're smarter than this. What does your gut tell you?" Doc asked.

"My gut tells me that he had something to do with it," I replied.

"Then the answer you're looking for is to kill him. What you're doing right now is the prime example of sleeping. I bet when you pulled up on him and he grazed his hip you let him walk straight up on you. You only get one life. He's in the game Nephew, just like you. Death comes with this shit. You either kill him or he's going to kill you. Even if he didn't have anything to do with his death he may try to kill you because he's scared you're trying to kill him. A scared man with a gun is more dangerous than the cold-blooded killer. So your answer to your problem is a very simple one. KILL HIM! That's it. That's all. You hear me Nephew?"

"Yeah, I hear you Doc He's through on sight," I replied.

"See you not listening Nephew. What if he see you first, and feeling the same way that you do? I suggest that you go get him. Then remember this. If you're always the stalker, when do you have time to be the prey? This ain't hard Nephew, and ain't no need to talk about this no more. Anything else?" Doc finalized.

"I also had this female living with me. I met her when I got shot. She nursed me back to health, handled work, for me and was about to take a charge for me. The other night I came home late, and she accused me of cheating......." Doc cut me off again.

"Were you?" Doc slightly chuckled.

"Yeah, but that's not important. The bitch let three shots off at me, and almost hit me. Make a long story short I knocked her out and took the gun."

"Where is she now?" Doc became a tad bit more serious.

"I kicked her out. I guess she's at her apartment," I replied unsure.

"How much does she know?"

"A life's sentence worth. She could bury me," I somberly replied.

"Then the answer is once again simple KILL HER! Listen Nephew you got three types of females with the potential to tell something. The first: Is a female to lose a loved one; second, a weak female who gets pressed by the feds and then, like her, a female with a broken heart. It's simple Midnight either you kill them both or you better pick out your casket or retain one helleva lawyer, because I got her telling something. Anything else?" Doc asked.

"Naw old man I'm cool. Thanks a lot." I stood in preparation to leave.

"Anytime Nephew just make sure you do me one favor." Doc stood as well. "Make sure you kill them properly." Doc smiled. He made it sound like he got his rocks off by just the thought of Murder. My type of Guy, I thought.

*****

TREY

By now Precious was getting on my last nerves because of the time that she was taking to handle her business. Every day that she took was a day that Midnight could come knocking. He was entirely too suspicious for my liking. I wanted him dead as soon as possible. Had it not been for that A-Rab, Midnight would have been dead. I made the mistake of waiting, and now it was kill or be killed. I was fortunate with Midnight and the last two encounters because he was still unsure.

I was riding down the street listening to B.G.'s *The Heart of the Streets*. I was so caught up in the music that I never noticed that I ran a red light. It took nothing for a squad car to get on my tail. I was a black man driving an

$80,000-dollar car, a M5 at that. The officer hit his lights instructing me to pull over.

WHOOP. WHOOP.

"Pull over to the side," the loud voice spoke over the loudspeaker.

"Shit!" I cursed aloud as I complied with the officer's wishes. I placed my sig saw nine under my thigh and got out my license and registration. I looked in my side view mirror and watched the officer make his approach.

"License and registration please?" the officer asked with his flashlight atop his shoulder.

"What you pulling me over for?" I asked like I didn't know. The officer said nothing and returned to his vehicle to run my information. I watched my rearview attentively as the officer ran my info. He sat for about ten minutes. Then he suddenly popped open his door reaching for his police issue Glock nine. Quickly I grabbed my nine and cocked it.

CLICK CLACK.

The officer cautiously approached my car with his gun in hand aimed to the ground at its ready position. I waited till he was just beginning try to raise it, and slung my arm out of the window *BOOM, BOOM, BOOM.* I caught the officer three times in the chest dropping him. I quickly jumped out my car to retrieve my license and registration. As I was coming back, I noticed that the officer had a vest on.

"Aw hell naw, not today babyboy." I stood over top of him shooting him once in the forehead. I then hopped back in my car and sped off up Alabama Ave. doing about 80mph. Now that I knew that I was wanted   for something it was time to get the game over with.

*****

PARIS

By now I was back to my old self again as far as my relationship with my mother went. In fact, we were actually starting to get closer with each passing day. Although I still worried about Kayla, I didn't let it slow me down on my quest for success.

It was the early morning, and I was just getting in from work. I was dead tired. To my surprise Olivia was up cooking breakfast at 3:00am. There were eggs, steak, and potatoes with hazelnut coffee. I may have been tired, but the smell of a black woman in the kitchen would wake anyone up.

"Ma what you in here doing?" I tossed my keys on the table.

"Oh this is all for you Paris. I know how hard you been working so I decided to give you a treat." Olivia hugged me. My mouth watered at the sight.

"MMMMMMMM everything smells so good. I'm about to get fat," I joked sitting down at the table.

"So do you need a ride to work later tonight?" Olivia offered while she fixed me a plate.

"No I'll be okay. I have a friend taking me," I replied, causing Olivia to turn around.

"Oh really, and who might this friend be?" Olivia inquired as she placed the plate in front of me.

"Nobody special but his name is Midnight," I smiled unconsciously.

"I see that saying his name put a smile on your face, so what kind of name is Midnight? He must be the color of charcoal." Olivia assumed.

"He is and sexy as ever," I fantasized.

"Just be careful Paris I don't want to see your heart

get broken," Olivia warned.

"Trust me Ma my heart is well protected," I assured her while looking her dead in the eyes. Suddenly the house phone rang breaking up our mother daughter moment. Olivia rushed to answer it.

"Hello.......Oh hey Ms. Alice......oh, oh my god....... Yes, she's right here one second." Olivia handed me the phone I could tell that something was wrong.

"Hello?"

"Oh Paris, she's gone, Paris! Someone killed her. Someone killed my baby." Ms. Alice was crying.

"Wait, wait Ms. Alice, who's gone?" I asked I needed full confirmation.

"Kayla, Paris, Kayla. The police tracked her car down and used a thing called GPS to locate the keys to the car from the automatic starter. Paris, Kayla was murdered." Ms. Alice cried harder.

"NOOOOO, NOOOOO KKAAAYYYLLLAAA!" I yelled. I was crushed. I dropped to my knees as Olivia came to console me. I let it all go. All my life I only had one true friend and that was Kayla. Now with her demise I felt alone and scared. I also felt it in my gut that her murder had Trey written all over it.

*****

MIDNIGHT

I was now back in my car after leaving Doc's. As I predicted, I learned something. Now all I had to do was devise a plan to do the dirty laundry and get away with it. I wouldn't let Trey ever get that close to me again. If he did have something to do with my uncle being murdered, then he's going to wish that he got me out of the way as quickly as he did my uncle.

Taking heed to Doc's words I drove straight over to Tymia's apartment and knocked on the door but received no answer. In turn I stepped back outside and climbed up on her balcony to look inside. What I saw surprised the hell out of me. The apartment was completely empty. I didn't know what to make of it but wasn't going to try to either. I went back to my car and hit the road again.

Feeling the need to please my craving I stopped at a gas station to get some Newport's. I set my guns under my seat and hopped out. After purchasing the Newport's I was so caught up in opening the wrapper that I never heard footsteps running up behind me. Precious jumped on my back wrapping her legs around my waist.

"I should kick your ass for not calling me," Precious yelled scaring the shit out of me.

"Girl, get your ass off of me," I playfully laughed. Precious let go and folded her arms.

"Why you didn't call me?" Precious pouted.

"I been busy lately. What's up with you? Ain't you out past your curfew?" I joked.

"I just came from a club. What you getting into tonight?" Precious stuffed her hands in her pockets.

"Nothing serious, where you tryna go?" I replied seeing the opportunity she was presenting along with the lust in her eyes. If I knew better, I'd say she was looking for a booty call.

"How about the Travel Lodge on New York Ave?" Oh yeah, I knew for sure now.

"No problem. Follow me. I hope you can keep up." I teased hopping in my truck.

"I'll be telling you that when we get there," Precious gave me the nastiest smiled that she could. I watched as she switched off and hopped back into her pink Mercedes.

*****

PRECIOUS

I was hoping that after this that Trey wouldn't ask me to set no one else up and I could get on with my primary objectives. I climb in my Benz and dialed his number. After a few rings he picked up.

"Yeah?" Trey answered.

"We're on our way to the Travel Lodge on New York Ave.," I smiled knowing that Trey would be pleased about it.

"Good babygirl leave the door unlocked, after we get him, we going to Jamaica," Trey replied.

"Okay I'll see you when you get there."

Click I hung up.

*****

MIDNIGHT

I did about 80 mph all the way there. It was late so there weren't many police out. Pulling up I held up a finger to her to tell her to hold up while I went inside to obtain a room. By the time I paid for it and stepped out, Precious was right there.

"Hold up baby let me grab, something out of my car." I kissed her forehead and walked passed her.

"Hurry up so you can scratch my kitty."

Precious pinched my ass as I walked passed her. I gave her a look letting her know that my ass was off limits. I grabbed my 50. cal Desert Eagles and placed it on my waist.

As I walked away, I hit my car alarm. We practically ran to the room ready to tear off into each other.

I opened the door and allowed Precious to walk in first. I followed behind her never noticing the Burgundy BMW pulling into the parking lot. I closed the door flipping both locks on. When I turned to Precious, she was already slowly removing her clothes.

I walked up on her and slammed my tongue in her mouth. I was in no mood for foreplay. I spontaneously spun her around with her back toward me and began to undress her myself. Quickly, she was completely nude while I was still fully dressed rubbing her nipples. On my touch they quickly stood at attention. I slid my middle finger between her pussy lips sliding it across her clit. Aggressively I bent her over onto the bed as I removed my pistol from my waist setting it on the small of her back. Her body shivered from the chill of the cold steel.

"So you's a gangsta, huh?" Precious mumbled as she looked back with eyes that said, "Beat it up." I then removed the muscle that all women cherish. Before penetrating I let my dick sit in the crack of her ass so she could feel the length of what she was about to be treated to. Precious pussy was soaked and waiting. I gradually positioned myself and slid straight in her pussy. Her walls were like a vice grip with plenty of juice flowing.

"Ohhh yeah fuck me harder. Oh yeah that's it." Precious moaned harder with each thrust. Easily I fell in the zone and began to beat her pussy up thoroughly. I pumped with a vengeance. My sexual escapade was soon short lived by the shaking doorknob to the room. I immediately got all the way on point, and grabbed my 50. cal off of Precious back aiming it at the door still lightly pumping in and out of Precious's walls. I then slapped her on the ass.

235

"Go, open the door," I instructed soon as she stood up.

BOC, BOC, BOC. The doorknob fell to the floor with it being kicked in. I was now face to face with Trey. For a brief second there was a pause as our eyes locked on one another. Trey then realized that he was staring down the barrel of my D.E. and quickly ducked off to the side.

BOOM, BOOM, BOOM. I let off three shots missing terribly. Trey slung his arm back around to unleash his own assault.

BOC, BOC, BOC, BOC.

"Agggghhh!" I yelled as I fell to the floor. I could feel warm blood sliding down my neck. I reached up and felt that my ear was gone. Precious screamed, grabbed her clothes, and hightailed out the door. With Trey seeing Precious run out he knew that the police would be there soon *BOC, BOC, BOC.* Trey let off three more shots to hold me off as he walked past   the door to follow Precious.

"I'll see you again slim!" Trey yelled as he ran past. The whole way he kept his eye on the room. My ear was bleeding profusely. Trey ran to his car and yelled for Precious to follow him. I made it to the door just in time to see Trey's BMW speeding out of the parking lot.

"Damn. I'm going to kill that nigga." I spoke out loud with a pillowcase to my ear. I then heard Doc's voice in my head. *'If you're always the stalker when do you have time to be the prey?'*

*****

TREY

I was heated as I drove. I wanted so badly to step across that threshold and air Midnight's ass out and be done with him. I thought for sure that I would be able to end this thing tonight. After thinking about it I blamed Precious for Midnight still being able to breathe. I looked in my rearview to make sure that Precious was still following me. Seeing that she was, I drove straight to her house. I was acrimoniously distraught. Not only had the attempt failed, but it caused me to reveal my hand and my true colors. Any speculations that Midnight had before were now solidified. I waited on the porch as Precious parked her car. At first, she was scared to get out because she knew that I was pissed.

"Get the fuck out here!" I yelled. She jumped and then complied. She walked past me slowly with her head down. As she got the door open, I gripped her neck and shoved her inside.

"Get the fuck in the house bitch." Precious fell to the floor.

"Please Trey......Please don't......" *SMACK* I smacked her.

"Shut the fuck up Bitch. You almost got me killed!" I yelled. *SMACK, SMACK* I continued my assault as Precious sat in a daze.

"It's not my fault, he locked the door. Please Trey. AGH!" I kicked that bitch straight in her mouth.

"Naw, it is your fault bitch. Now you gonna pay for it!" I yelled while taking off my belt.

"No Trey please, it won't happen again. Please." *WHAP* "AGGGGGHHHH." I gave her a head shot with the belt causing a purple whip to appear on her cheek.

"Please Trey." Precious begged holding her face.

"Shut up bitch."

WHAP, WHAP, WHAP. Precious laid there in deep pain curled up in fetal position. Once he was done, I walked up the stairs leaving Precious to tend to her wounds. By now it was almost daybreak and I had been up for two days. I took a shower, loaded my clip, cocked it, place it on safety on, got some shut eye.

CHAPTER NINETEEN

PARIS

Today was one of the hardest days of my life. I was an only child, but with Kayla around I never felt like it. Kayla looked so beautiful in her white dress. It was hard for me to view her body, but I knew that I had to in order for me to gain closure in her death, and at least say goodbye. I didn't go to the burial but instead said a heartfelt prayer before I went home to get me some rest.

By 12:00 am I struggled to get ready for work. Before I was ready, I called Midnight to come pick me up because I was already late for work. He agreed and told me that he'd be out front in ten minutes. I continued to get dressed and pack my carry-on. While at the funeral I decided that tonight would be the last night that I would ever step foot in the Skylark, let alone work there. I had a gut feeling that Trey was the one who killed Kayla. Even if he didn't, I still didn't want to fall victim to the life of a stripper. I finished getting dressed and just like Midnight said he was out front. I ran out and anxiously sucked on his bottom lip.

"Hey baby." I smiled.

"Damn girl, what was that for?" Midnight smiled touching his lips as if he were savoring the taste.

"Nothing I just missed you." I then noticed his bandaged ear.

"Baby what happened to your ear?" I turned his head to the side truly concerned.

"Ain't nothing big, just an out-of-control ear infection. I'm cool though. How was your friend's funeral?" I noticed that he changed the subject, but I let him slide on it for now.

"It was cool. I thought that I wouldn't be able to handle it, but I was cool. She looked real peaceful, and in a better place now."

"Yeah, she is. Do the police know who did it?" Midnight asked and flicked on his left signal.

"Yeah, and so do I. Before I met you, I was pregnant by this guy. My friend knew that he killed someone and called him a murderer. He would have hurt her twice before, but I stopped him. Now she ended up dead. I can feel it in my gut. I know he did it." My eyes began to water by just the thought.

"What's his name?" Midnight asked.

"Trey."

*****

TREY

Once I finally got to sleep, I was down for the count. I needed the rest to calm my nerves from me not being able to kill Midnight as I hoped. Three attempts and they all failed. I would stop at nothing to end Midnight. I had more than enough motivation to get the job done. Coming out of my sleep induced coma my antennas shot up from a conversation that I heard coming from the hallway. Precious was talking to someone.

"Which room is he in?" The male voice sounded so familiar.

"Right there. He's in there sleep." I then thought to myself that I know she didn't call the police.

"Good, let's get this money then. I'm tired of waiting," The male voice stated.

"Wait, Wait, I don't want to kill him in here" Precious stated meaning inside her house. By that I knew with whomever she was talking that it was do or die. I grabbed my nine off the nightstand and quietly switched the safety off. I placed it under my pillow and lay on my stomach as if I were sleep.

"Fuck you mean not in here? We wouldn't be here if you would have got him to his house like I told you. Now would we?" I couldn't believe that this bitch had been plotting on me the whole time, but I did respect it.

"What about when the police come?" Precious reasoned.

"We make him get dressed before we kill him. Then put this mask on him. We fuck up the back door, so it looks like he broke in. He already fucked you up so they're going to have no other choice but to buy it. Now get the fuck out of the way, its crunch time." Precious stepped to the side. I laid there thinking "That's a dirty bitch." just as the thought escaped my mind the door swung open.

"Wake up fuck boy." Rocko smiled aiming his pistol at me. I looked up to the one man I would have least expected to set me up for the kill. My right hand man.

"Rocko! So you stepping your game up huh?" I was now lying on my side with my hand under my pillow.

"It's like you said slim, somebody gotta fall for somebody to stand up."

"After all I did for you slim? We grew from the dirt together. Now you gonna turn on ME!" I yelled. "I fed your ass when you was dead broke and hungry nigga. I did that!" Yelling did exactly what it was supposed to do. Make Rocko lose focus giving me   just   enough   time. With uncharted speed I whipped the nine out BOC, BOC, BOC, BOC. I caught Rocko in the chest four times dropping him. Precious screamed and tried to run, but I was on her ass. Just as she made it to the stairs, I grabbed her by the back of her pony tail lifting her chin to the ceiling. Knowing that she was dead she spoke her last words.

"The Feds gonna get you Trey!" she yelled.

"Not before death get you, you snake bitch." I stuck the nine under her chin BOC, BOC. Just as her body fell limp, I pushed her down the steps watching her lifeless body tumble to the bottom. By the time her body hit the floor it swelled up like a pumpkin.

I ran back to the room and got dressed. If I knew better, I'd swear that Precious intentionally had that hotel room door locked. As far as Rocko, I blame myself for him, I always knew that he could be a fucked up and untrustworthy individual from the beginning. I had the choice a long time ago to kill him, befriend him, or cut him off. I felt we'd been through too much and he could be trusted enough not to turn on me. That was a mistake on my part. Thinking about one of me and Rocko's previous conversations; Rocko was wrong. Precious wasn't out of my league. She was just like me. A SNAKE!

Soon as I was done getting dressed, I realized that I had slept the whole day and that it was now two in the morning. I knew better than to go to my house and couldn't get a hotel because I would have to use my name, which could possibly lead the police to me. I gathered everything that Precious was holding for me, a box of bullets and left to go to the one place no one knew nothing about so I could lay low. I picked up my cell and used speed dial. After about six rings a woman with a groggy voice answered.

"Hello."

"Can I speak to Olivia?" I asked already knowing that it was her.

"This is she. Who is this calling my house two in the morning?" Olivia replied.

"It's Trey and I need a place to lay for the night." I got straight to the point.

"Why can't you get a hotel? It's two in the morning," she questioned.

"Look I can't talk on the phone. What's your apartment number?"

"Damn Treyvon its 720 and hurry up I'm tired as hell."

"Aight I'll be there in five minutes." CLICK I hung up and realized that 720 was Paris' apartment, then said to myself "Oh shit!"

*****

PARIS

I could honestly say that the life of a stripper had completely drained me. The money was more than good, but this was a life that I could never make a career. Over 18 months I had saved $60,000. So I was happy to leave. Tonight, I pulled in $1700. Before I left the club for the last time, I placed a single rose in the locker that used to belong to Kayla, and then recited a short prayer. Afterwards, I left the Skylark for good.

On the cab ride home, I decided that I would go to Howard University to register first thing in the morning. My will power to succeed was even stronger now than ever. I was now not only doing it for me, but for Kayla as well. To me, being able to leave the Skylark was a big accomplishment in itself. In my 18 months there, I'd seen so many young girls come into the life with hopes of college and a career, and to this day none had made it. They all fell victim to being either pimped, drugs, or just as plainly to money. The worst fate was that some of the girls contracted HIV. Then you had some who fell victim to them all. I was fortunate to be able to get out. Now that I had I would be as successful as I possibly could.

The cab pulled up to my apartment building. I gave the cabby a twenty-dollar bill and stepped out. I couldn't wait to hit my bed. I stepped into the apartment and could hear music coming from my mother's bedroom. I figured that she may have been drinking and left it on, so I decided I'd cut it off for her. I opened her door. What I saw caused all my hateful feeling and emotions to come rushing back all at once. Seeing Trey with my mother bent over ass naked crushed me.

"NOOOO, NOOOOOO. I hate you both!" I yelled to the top of my lungs. I dropped my purse and ran to the kitchen. Trey tried to run behind me.

"Wait Paris I didn't know." Trey tried to reason as he ran behind me. I made it to the kitchen well before he did. I grabbed a butcher knife and charged at Trey with a wild swing. Lucky for Trey he caught my wrist. I wiggled free cocked back and slapped the shit out of him. I then ran to my purse and locked myself in the bathroom. I searched my purse and retrieved a whole bottle of Tylenol three. I popped the lid and threw back 12 pills.

Trey and Olivia stood at the door begging me to open it. I would hear nothing of it. Thirty minutes later everything went black.

*****

MIDNIGHT

Finally, I was able to move. I hoped it wouldn't take so long, but the paperwork took a while. All-in-all no matter how long it took I was now moving into my own house. Since the split with Tymia I purchased an apartment to stash all the things that could get me a hundred years especially since I couldn't find her. I didn't trust Tymia's intentions, so until she was dead, I would calculate my every move. Even the new house that I bought was in a bogus name. This would allow me to sleep with my money at my house.

I had been packing for a while now and was pretty much done. All I had left to do was Uncle D's things. I hated going inside his office because his scent was the most dominate smell there, versus any other part in the house. In fact, since my uncle's death I had only been in this part of the house twice, and even that was for a short period of time. Thinking of Paris, I decided to call my wifey and see how she was doing. She always put a smile on my face and put me at ease when we talked. Paris phone rung about five times before someone picked up.

"Hello."
"What's up babygirl?" I greeted.
"Excuse me this is not Paris, so may I asked who's calling?" Olivia snidely asked.
"Excuse me Ms. My name is Midnight. May I speak with her?" I kindly asked.
"I'm sorry Midnight but Paris had an accident. We're at Washington Hospital Center. This is her mother," Olivia replied.
"Well does she need anything? Is there anything that I can do?" I was genuinely concerned.
"No, no sweetheart me and her old child's father can handle everything."
"When you're able please tell her that I will be by later to see her," I said.
"Okay I'll tell her."
"Thank you." CLICK. I hung up. I was already on point when she said that she and Paris' old child's father would handle everything. I knew that had to be Trey. At first, I figured that I wouldn't fuck with him until I got him in a less public place. Plus, it was daytime. Then the words of old timer Doc crept into my mind, *'If you're always the stalker when do you have time to be the prey?'* It was that exact thinking that had me sitting in a stolen SS Impala with two silenced Desert Eagles on my lap in the parking

lot of the hospital. Death was stalking its watch and Trey's heart stopping was the alarm. Time was against Trey.

*****

PARIS

I felt like my body was flying I could see a bright light up ahead and voices calling my name.

"Paris. Paris. Go back Paris." It was as if I was in no control over my own body as I ascended into the clouds.

"Who are you? Who's calling my name?" I spoke back, body still ascending.

"It's me Paris. It's Kayla. You gotta go back Paris. Get Trey. Trey killed me, you gotta get him," Kayla's voice pleaded.

"Come with me Kayla. Come with me." I was now crying.

"No Paris. My life is gone. I'm at peace now. Go make Trey pay for what he did to me Paris, you gotta make him pay," Kayla's voice was like a whisper.

"Okay Kayla I will. I love you Kayla," I continued to cry.

"I love you too Paris. Now go before it's too late," Kayla demanded. As if on cue I opened my eyes. I was having a little trouble breathing because of all the tubes in my nose. I smelled my hospital gown and could smell Kayla all over me. My dream felt so real. Now awake and smelling Kayla I knew that it was. I also would make good on my promise. About five minutes after I opened my eyes

Olivia and Trey walked in with the nurse who began to remove the tubes from my nose and mouth.

"Oh Paris I'm so glad that you're okay. What were you doing?" Olivia rubbed my head.

"I should be asking you that." I groggily replied.

"Ohhh I didn't know, and neither did Trey. We'd been dealing with each other since Ron was alive. I never met Trey through you so how could I know," Olivia explained.

"So this is the Olivia that I found in your phone huh Trey?" I asked with a cold voice.

"Look I can't change the past what's done is done," Trey nonchalantly replied.

"How can you say that; Trey you knew? When you killed Ron, you knew what apartment I lived in. If you been dealing with her since then you had to know." Olivia was shocked at my revelation.

"Paris we ain't together so what does it matter? Why you tripping? You said you don't give a fuck about me. "Trey made a feeble attempt to reason.

"Motherfucker you fucking my mother!" I yelled subsequently grabbing my stomach wincing in pain. Olivia rushed to my side then looked up at Trey.

"So you killed Ron, Trey?" Olivia wanted an answer.

"Hell yeah, and I'll do it again. That sick motherfucker is the reason that I don't have a child right now," Trey coldly spoke.

"Trey, you being here isn't healthy for Paris. I think its best that you leave," Olivia firmly spoke.

"You know what? Fuck both you bitches. I'm out." Trey spun on his heels and stepped out the door.

*****

TREY

I didn't like how quickly Olivia jumped on Paris's side, but then I thought that my mother would have done the same for me, had I ever gotten the chance to grow up with her. I stormed out the room and headed to my car. I will admit though that I did enjoy seeing the look on Paris' face when she saw me blowing her mother's back out. Payback is a bitch.

I stepped out of the hospital into the brisk air. It was fairly cold out this morning. I boldly took out a Backwood of Purple Haze and lit it as I walked across the parking lot. I puffed on the weed with a unique professionalism. Just as I got about four feet from my car a Black SS Impala pulled up next to me. I was attempting to take another lung collapsing pull when I noticed the chrome Desert Eagle being extended out of the window. I tried to reach but it was too late.

"Looks like I saw you first fuckboy." BOOM, BOOM, BOOM, BOOM, BOOM. Midnight let off five rounds shots all catching me in the upper body dropping me. Luckily a police cruiser pulled around the corner forcing Midnight to speed off. The cruiser neglected to follow Midnight, but instead stopped to tend to me.

Following procedure, the officer hopped out dropping to his knees to see how badly I was hurt. Kneeling down the first thing that I noticed was that badge.

"Sir don't move. You can't get up," the officer warned. I looked at him dead in his face.

249

"Naw. YOU! Can't get up." BOC, BOC, BOC. I shot him three times in the face and hopped in my BMW and sped off along the D.C. Reservoir. As I drove, I snatched off my vest swearing by Allah and the ground that I walked on that I was going to kill Midnight in cold blood.

*****

MIDNIGHT

Calmly I drove the SS Impala to a pre-planned spot where I could burn it. One thing that Uncle D taught me was that fire gets rid of or distorts all evidence. I knew Trey couldn't have survived that, or at least I prayed that he didn't. I pulled up in Rock Creek Park, a known D.C. body drop off. My car was already there. I pulled next to it and popped my trunk. I retrieved a milk jug filled with gasoline and emptied it inside that Impala. Lighting a Newport, and after taking a few lungs collapsing pulls I flicked it in to the car watching it burst into flames. I hopped into my Caddy truck and sped off.

*****

PARIS

It had now been three days since my attempted suicide. There were only two things on my mind; Midnight, and my encounter with Kayla. As far as I was concerned Trey being Kayla's murderer was now confirmed. If I ever got the chance to kill Trey, I would. I promised myself that I would undoubtedly pull the trigger not only for Kayla but also for the pain that Trey brought into my life.

Midnight was also a big part of my thoughts and what life would be like at his side. Although at one point I thought I loved Trey, but now with the love that I was experiencing with Midnight, I knew that what I now had was far greater than that with Trey. I'd made my mind up that I would love Midnight with everything that I had and beyond.

As far as my mother goes, I was completely disgusted with her. That was the reason why I made it so that she couldn't visit me while I was in the hospital. The same went for Trey. There wasn't an excuse that Olivia could give me to make me forgive her. The point was that it happened and that she'd already hurt me too much in the past. My thoughts were then broken by the phone ringing.

"Hello?" I answered.

"What's up babygirl?" It was Midnight, my knight in shining armor.

"You." I blushed.

"Oh yeah, so when you getting up out of there?" Midnight questioned.

"Maybe tomorrow, why haven't you been up here yet?" He'd better have a good reason.

"I would have come the first night you were there, but your mom said that she and your baby father was there with you. I chose not to come for fear I would have to do something to him. Who's there with you now?" Midnight explained. I felt it was a good enough reason.

"Nobody, they can't come see me here. I gated both of them from coming." I asserted hoping that he would say that he was coming.

"Aight I'm on my way."

"Okay I'm in room 4130," I replied with a smile. "And oh yeah Midnight," I called out before he could hang up.

"What's up babygirl?"

"I love you." I couldn't believe I just told him that.

"I love you too, Paris. I will see you when I get there." I could hear Midnight smiling through that phone.

"Okay." CLICK I couldn't believe that I told Midnight that I loved him. Since I did though I'm glad I'd done so and even more so that he expressed the same sentiments that I did. I decided to take a quick nap while I waited for Midnight to arrive. Even in my sleep he was on my mind. I'd bet money that I was smiling in my sleep. Before I knew it, I was awakened by a heart filled kiss.

"UUUMMMM. That's a nice way to wake up." I smiled as I opened my eyes.

"I'm trying to wake you up like that every morning." Midnight pushed aside a piece of hair out of my face.

"Trust me I wouldn't mind one bit," I replied now holding his hand.

"So when you getting out of here so we can go home?" He had to clarify that.

"Well first off maybe tomorrow and second where is home?"

"Well, I just bought a house that's too big for me, so I was hoping you'd come live with me?"

"Are you sure, that's a major step," I replied, but was really thinking hell yeah.

"I mean what I speak," Midnight confidently replied. I never got a chance to reply because Greg walked in.

"Oh I see someone finally woke up." Greg greeted me with a kiss on the forehead-completely unprofessional, but I opted not to say anything; for the sake of his feelings. Midnight on the other hand looked at him like he was crazy. He then faced Greg in defiance I guess trying to mark his territory. I decided to introduce them to keep things under the radar.

"Midnight this is Greg, my personal doctor. Greg this is......." Midnight cut me off.

"I'm Midnight, Paris' fiancé." Midnight extended his hand. I thought to myself, 'when the hell that happen?' I knew that Greg wouldn't like hearing that. Surely, he looked at me with an expression that asked me if it were true. I just looked off.

"Nice to meet you." Greg let Midnight's hand go sensing the hostility.

"When can I go home?" I cut in to break the ice.

"Well, I was going to release you tomorrow, but since you have a ride here now, I'll do it today. I brought you these pills. Your stomach lining was pretty scarred from the pills so if you have any pain just take one and stay away from spicy foods or your stomach will feel like it's on fire. I'll be back with your release papers." Greg nodded to Midnight and exited the room.

"I don't like him. He's a little too friendly," Midnight stated.

"Midnight don't start. He's been my doctor and friend for forever."

"So that entitles you to a first name basis?"

"Uhhh yeah. I would think so. Can we end this conversation?" Midnight was being a little too jealous.

"Yeah, well make sure you keep his ass in check or I'm gonna play doctor on his ass," Midnight warned. After about thirty minutes Dr. Ames returned with my discharge papers, and I was released. For some odd reason I felt like Greg was kicking me out of the hospital, but I left it alone. Midnight and I were now on the way to our new home- TOGETHER.

CHAPTER TWENTY

PARIS

I was astonished at the beauty of our new home. When we pulled up, I stepped out and inhaled the fresh air of Fort Washington, Maryland. Once seeing the level of living that I was gonna be living in it gave me more of a reason to keep Midnight around.

*****

MIDNIGHT

I was happy that Paris loved the house. I made a promise to myself that I would make her the happiest women on earth. By the look on her face, I could tell that I was doing just that. The only thing that worried me was explaining the situation to her about Trey. I prayed that it didn't scare her off as it did Kayla. Once we got in the house and unpacked, I decided I would try to tell her. Paris swore that she was all for me, but this would be that ultimate test.

"Aye Paris, come downstairs for a minute. I need to holla at you," I yelled from the bottom of the steps.

"Alright, I'm coming," she replied and eventually trotted down the stairs. When she walked up on me, she gave me the most passionate kiss I'd had in a long time.

"Damn baby you must be trying to get pregnant." I smiled with my arms around her waist.

"Maybe." Paris replied with a devilish look on her face as she squeezed my dick through my pants.

"Keep playing we gonna break this living room in." I playfully warned, squeezing her ass.

"You promise?" Paris replied as she continued to play her little game.

She then slid down my chest pressing me against the wall. She lifted my shirt kissing along the hairs around my navel. Paris was preparing to take me to a world that only she could. Finding the prize, she sought out she wasted no time taking me in whole down her throat. With long and deep strokes, she easily allowed me to escape into a world of bliss. Soon she found a rhythm and began to suck the life out of me. After about ten minutes of throat wrenching oral sex. I exploded a thick load of semen down her throat. Not missing a beat, she swallowed every bit of it.

Paris stood up slowly sucking on her index finger from its base to the tip. She gave me a nasty look and walked into the living room with an extra switch in her step. Reaching the couch, she placed her knees on it with her back still toward me. She pulled her coochie cutter shorts down around her luscious thighs revealing her white thong. She pulled it to the side and looked back at me.

"I got you out the street now come beat Ms. Nasty's pussy up." Paris gave her ass a slight wiggle while spreading her pussy lips. My dick almost immediately stood back up to attention. I stepped out of my pants and approached her with a look of hunger in my eyes. As I came closer Paris dug two fingers in her snatch coating them with her juices. She licked the tips and then fed the rest to me. I loved the way she took control. Slowly I entered my shaft into her pulsating walls. I stroked her slowly at first causing Paris to moan with extreme pleasure.

"Baby you feel so good. Fuck me harder." Paris begged. I complied with her wishes pounding her into orgasm after orgasm.

"Oh I'm....I'm.... CCCUUUUMMMING." I continued to beat a hole in her back. Feeling my pressure building up, I grabbed her waist pounding her pussy to oblivion.

"Oh baby I feel your dick swelling up inside me." Paris continued to moan. "Baby I want you to cum inside me." Paris' dirty mouth pushed me over the edge allowing me to shoot my second load deep within her walls. We both laid there drenched in each other's sweat and wrapped in each other's arms.

*****

PARIS

Love was an understatement when it came to how I felt about Midnight, and vice versa. At times we were inseparable. The sex had both us hooked on each other. Now that my love life was fulfilled, and I had enough money to pursue my dream to obtain my PhD from Howard University I felt it was now time to begin to place my ducks in order and get the ball rolling.

*****

TREY

I must admit that I was completely surprised that Midnight came at me the way that he did. Now that he did I wouldn't feel that bad about killing him. In fact, now I felt motivated. I was thinking about Paris' face when she saw me fucking her mother and figured that she had to still have some feelings for me. I have never been one to waste time so I seized the moment and called to try and rekindle our flame. The phone rang a few times before someone picked it up.

"Hello." It was Olivia.

"What's up Olivia?"

"Trey why are you still calling? I thought we agreed for Paris' sake that we wouldn't see each other anymore," said Olivia. This bitch was feeling herself. I wasn't calling for her.

"Yeah, we did. I'm totally cool with that. That's why I'm not calling for you. Is Paris around?" I knew that Olivia felt stupid.

"Oh....well Paris doesn't live here anymore." Olivia revealed.

"What? Well, where she live at then?" I was pissed.

"With some guy named Midnight that she's engaged to," Olivia said with joy.

"Midnight? What he look like?" This couldn't be that same Midnight I thought.

"I don't know. Paris isn't talking to me and doesn't want me in her life, so I could care less. She's happy now, so I don't care who she's with as long as she is alive and healthy. She's also progressing toward her dream too. She's finally enrolled at Howard University. She saved up thousands on her own so she could get her Doctorate. I commend her for that so Trey, please do us a favor and let us be. Please."

CLICK Olivia hung up.

I was beside myself, and the mention of Midnight's name didn't help at all. Never in a thousand years did I think that Midnight would go behind my back and snatch Paris from under my nose. I didn't care if we were on killing terms or not. Paris was mine and off limits to anyone else PERIOD!

The next morning, I was at Howard University bright and early. My plan was to get her schedule and see her face to face. If I was right about her hidden feelings she had for me, it wouldn't take much to win her over. I stepped in the building and just like I thought, the clerk was female.

"Hello, my name is David Clemons. My sister forgot to pick up her schedule and asked if I could pick it up for her so would that be possible?"

"I'm sorry Sir, but we aren't allowed to give out that information." The clerk replied. I expected this so I came prepared. I slid her an envelope containing $5,000.

"That's five stacks in there. It's yours if you get that information for me." I gave her a stern look. It only took the young girl seconds to retrieve the money.

"What's her name?" She smiled.

"Paris Clemons." I replied and within minutes the info was attained. I ran back to my BMW and was in route to Paris' first class. By the schedule it would be held at 10:00am. Just like I knew she would be, Paris was right on time. I watched as she got out the cab. By the sight of her beauty my hormones shot into overdrive. Paris was looking good. I then shook the thoughts out of my head and got back to the business at hand. I jumped out the car and yelled for her.

"Paris...Paris." She turned around. Once she saw who was calling her you could almost see the fire ignite in her eyes. I ran to catch up to her.

"I see you meeting new friends Paris." I stated.

"Trey, what the fuck are you talking about?" I could tell that she was already annoyed.

"Midnight Bitch! That's who I'm talking about." Now she had pissed me off by playing dumb.

"Trey we are not together. My pussy don't belong to you." Paris tried to walk off, but I grabbed her arm, and spun her back around.

"Bitch, you stupid, that nigga gonna get you killed," I tried to reason with her.

"Then so be it. Trey why won't you leave me alone and let me be happy. I don't love you no more. DAMN. Get off my clit!" Paris snapped. Her words cut like daggers and easily ignited my anger. *SMACK, SMACK.* Twice I slapped the shit out of her for her mouth. Paris fell to the ground holding the right side of her mouth in disbelief.

"Bitch, you better remember who the fuck you talking to. Ain't shit changed. I'm still Trey," I warned her.

"And you a murderer too you bitch ass nigga. Yeah, I said it. What! You gonna kill me like you did Kayla?" No the fuck this bitch didn't come out her mouth like that. She must think I won't kill her ass too.

"At first naw, but now your mouth gave me a reason to." Just as I began to reach for my nine *WHOOP, WHOOP.* The campus police pulled up to our altercation. He immediately looked at Paris.

"Everything alright ma'am?" I thought to myself that if this officer even thinks of getting out of his car he's dead.

"Yes, everything's okay. I just lost my grandmother that's all." I couldn't believe that Paris just lied on my behalf.

"I'm sorry to hear that ma'am and I apologize for the intrusion. You two have a nice day." The officer gave me an awkward look but still pulled off. I then looked at Paris.

"I don't know your reasons for lying just now, but you better be lucky that rent-a-cop just saved your ass you slut bitch. Tell Midnight I'll be seeing him soon." I held my hand like I was holding a pistol squeezing the trigger and aiming at Paris. I quickly walked off as Paris sat there unsure of what to make of the situation.

*****

PARIS

After the altercation with Trey, I was filled with mixed emotions. I was scared for not only my life but for Midnight's as well. Plus, I was angry that Midnight didn't tell me that he knew Trey. I felt a little confused as well because Trey said that Midnight was going to get me killed. My mind was so out of place that I couldn't concentrate on anything else but speaking with Midnight. I called him and told him to pick me up at the school immediately. He eventually got there within fifteen minutes. As soon as I sat in the car Midnight began looking me over but couldn't see the right side of my face.

"Baby what's the urgency? You sounded like you was about to die." Midnight slightly laughed. That made me snap.

"Trey happened, that's what!" I yelled now pointing to my swollen face.

"Why the fuck you didn't tell me that you knew him." I started to cry.

"Fuck! Midnight punched the steering wheel

realizing his mistake. Trey could have seriously hurt me.

"Answer me Midnight, why the fuck you didn't tell me?" I hit him on the shoulder.

"Look, I was going to tell you when you fully recovered. What did he say to you?"

"Fuck what he said I wanna know how the fuck you know him." I continued to yell to the top of my lungs.

"I think he killed my uncle. No, let me rephrase that- I know he killed my uncle. Do you remember hearing about the shooting in front of the hospital you was in?" Midnight asked.

"Yeah, what about it?" I replied.

"I pulled up on him and shot him a few times in the chest. I thought I killed him. I guess he had a vest on. Now answer my question, why did he hit you?" Midnight rubbed my swollen face.

"Why the fuck you think, cause I'm with you. Somehow, he found out we're together and showed up at my school." Hearing that caused Midnight to immediately look into his rearview. I looked to see what he was looking at and only saw a U-Haul truck in the distance.

"You better calm your ass the fuck down Paris. You not gonna keep raising your voice at me and I'm not gonna say it twice." Midnight warned but I wasn't trying to hear that.

"Fuck you Midnight, you the reason my face like this." I pointed for an extra reminder.

"If you say so, but you won't have to worry about Trey. I'll make sure I handle that. I promise you that." Midnight used his thumb to wipe away my tears. He kissed my forehead placing me at ease. I looked up in the rearview and saw nothing.

CHAPTER TWENTY-ONE

TREY

Had it not been for that cop I would have ended Paris' life right where she laid. In a way I was glad I didn't. In broad daylight on a college campus might have surely landed me in jail. I had just ditched the U-Haul truck that I stole from the campus and caught the bus back. I tried to follow Midnight and Paris to their house, but the bulky U-Haul truck couldn't keep up with Midnight's truck. I wasn't tripping though because as long as I had Paris' schedule her determination to succeed would always lead me to her. In time, she would show me everything I needed to see.

*****

MIDNIGHT

We pulled into our three-car garage. The neighborhood was fairly quiet this morning. As I stepped out of the car my blood began to boil over. My uncle's 500 Benz and Jag were destroyed with the windows burst out and the words "DON'T DROP THE SOAP CHEATER" keyed into the hood of both vehicles. I was on fire.

"When we stepped into the house, I was even more devastated seeing that everything was trashed. My brand-new white Italian leather sofa was ripped up, with red paint splashed on it. Once again on the plush white carpet spelled the words "DON'T DROP THE SOAP CHEATER." I couldn't believe my eyes.

"What the fuck happened?" Paris yelled visibly upset. While I stayed quiet to access the situation.

"Better yet, who the fuck you fucking?" Paris crossed her arms shifting her weight to one leg. I just looked at her with a look that said *Shut the fuck up!*

"I'm calling the police." Paris darted to the phone. I quickly stepped to her smacking the phone out of her hand. There was no way I was going to have my house flooded with police.

"Fuck you mean you calling the police? We don't do that in this house." I picked   the phone up off the floor and hung it up.

"Then what the fuck we gonna do then? All our shit is fucked up," Paris replied.

"Correction, all my stuff is fucked up. I paid for everything in here. You get half when the ring go on your finger. Until then let me worry about this." I firmly spoke placing Paris in her place.

"Midnight I swear to God if you cheating on me, I'm going to stab the shit out of you." I grabbed Paris into my arms as she cried.

"Come on crybaby. Come upstairs. I got something for you." I walked her up the stairs. Making it to the master bedroom, I walked to the safe and entered the digital code.

Paris patiently sat on the bed waiting for me to reveal my intentions. Inside the safe I retrieved a small silver box. I sat next to Paris and popped its locks. Inside sat a chrome baby 380. It was small enough to fit into her palm of her hand.

"Look I want you to keep this with you at all times. The nigga might try to get at you to get at me. That means if you see him, you light his ass up," I clearly instructed. Once I handed Paris the gun. As soon as she touched it she felt an immediate surge of power.

"How many does it hold?" Paris asked seriously eyeing the weapon.

"It holds ten shots and the safety on the side." I pointed. *CLICK, CLACK.* Paris cocked it.

"That motherfucker gonna wish he never put his hands on me," Paris replied while massaging the trigger.

*****

PARIS

The next morning, I woke up to an empty bed. Still a little bit sleep I stumbled to the bathroom. As I finished my business, I heard a door close. "Midnight is that you?" I yelled but received no reply. Instantly I got paranoid and grabbed my 380. off the dresser, and cocked it. *CLICK, CLACK.* Slowly I ran down the stairs already making my mind up that if it was Trey, I would empty the whole clip in him. I could hear movement in the kitchen, so I slowly crept to the entrance. After gaining enough courage I slung around the corner with gun aimed *BOOM!* Midnight ducked. It hit the cabinet flying passed his head. I stood there in shock realizing my mistake I made. Midnight turned around with fire in his eyes and rushed me.

"Bitch what the fuck is you doing?" Midnight yelled with his hand around my throat simultaneously snatching the pistol from my grasp.

"I'm sorry baby, I was calling you and you didn't answer. I thought you was Trey. I'm sorry." I began to cry hard thinking of what could have just happened.

"This nigga got your head that fucked up? What if you would have hit me?" Midnight yelled.

"Midnight I'm scared." I cried harder. "When Trey was at my school, he was about to kill me because I called him a murderer. That might be the reason why he killed Kayla. The only reason he didn't kill me was because a campus police pulled up and asked was everything alright." I looked to the ground.

"What did you tell them?" Midnight asked feeling my cries for help.

"I told them everything was fine, and they left. Midnight I don't want him to go to jail." I looked up into his eyes. "I want him to suffer the same fate that Kayla did." I cried heavily as Midnight held me allowing me to cry into his chest.

I was mentally scarred from the stress that Trey had brought into my life. He brought me so much pain and anguish that I was to the point where I would give my own life for him to lose his. Midnight felt my pain and was now even more determined to get Trey not only for me, but also for himself as well. Midnight knew that Trey would play for keeps. This is why he was taking precautions.

Midnight lifted my crying head off of his chest and told me to follow him. At first, I was a little skeptical but when he gave me that smile that I fell in love with I'd follow him to my demise as long as he was with me. Midnight walked me to the front door and placed his hands over my eyes as we walked outside. Walking down the steps I could tell we were in the driveway. When Midnight removed his hands, I was standing in front of a baby blue Mercedes CLK 230.

"Baby that's a Mercedes." I turned and said to Midnight like he didn't already know.

"I know what it is, but what it also is, is yours." I jumped on Midnight wrapping my legs around his waist.

"I love your black ass." I then gave Midnight the most passionate kiss that I could.

*****

PARIS

Today was the day that I was scheduled to take my test to decide whether or not I would get half my tuition money back or not. The night before I could hardly sleep from how nervous I was. I still got a fair amount of sleep. I made sure to eat a nice breakfast. Afterwards, I hopped in my new car and headed to school.

The whole ride there I felt uneasy as if I were being watched. Midnight had taught me to always memorize the cars behind me anytime I was out. I was extremely paranoid. Although I hadn't seen Trey since he almost killed me that day, I still knew that he was out there watching and waiting for his opportunity to succeed. This was the reason why I drove with the 380 on my lap. If Trey did decide to show his face he had better be armed.

By the time I pulled in the school parking lot I had placed the 380. in my purse and hopped out the Benz.

Cautiously I looked in all directions before beginning my stride. As I got halfway to the entrance of the building, I looked behind me to a Crown Victoria with tints. When it stopped, I immediately got defensive be placing my hand inside my purse to clutch the 380. The passenger door open and I squeezed the handle tighter. I was then able to breathe a sigh of relief when a white girl stood up. That made me laugh at how paranoid I was being. I released my grip and walked into the building.

*****

TREY

As Paris walked into the building the Crown Victoria pulled off. Paris was being watchful, but it wasn't the Crown Victoria that she had to worry about. I was in the Dodge Charger sitting behind it out of her view. I sat behind the wheel laughing at the look of fear on her face. I knew it was all my doing. I did some groundwork and found out Paris would be taking a test for two and a half hours. I planned to wait those two and a half hours. I was gonna make sure no hoe-ass rental cop wouldn't pop up and save her life this time.

Just like clockwork Paris was exiting the building two hours later. She still cautiously walked with her hand buried in her purse. If I didn't know any better, I'd swear she was packing. Paris was so paranoid that she walked right past me and never knew I was watching her every move.

*****

PARIS

I was dead tired from the test. Luckily because today was my test day, and all my other classes were cancelled. I knew that I passed, I was already making plans to invest my money and make it double the legal way. I knew Midnight was more than capable to take care of me for the rest of my life, but I was independent and planned to stay that way.

By time I got home I was no longer tired and decided I would go to the mall and treat myself and maybe see a movie, I was dressed in thirty minutes. I wore a Dolce and Gabbana belly shirt with some Donna Karan capri pants. I looked dead sexy. I was felling at ease and forgot all about Trey. I got back in my car and was off for a day of enjoyment.

*****

TREY

From Paris' bedroom window I watched her pull off only if she would have looked back, she would have realized just how close to death she truly was.

CHAPTER TWENTY-TWO

MIDNIGHT

Since moving I was going completely legit. I was already wealthy with a beautiful woman that I truly loved. I saw no reason to jeopardize that by selling drugs. There was only one thing that stood in my way and that was Trey. I'd recently started to dabble in real estate and started buying houses. I even owned an apartment building in Baltimore. Soon I had a proposal meeting for a fifty unit building in Philly. If I landed that deal, I'd be set for life.

It was 10:00pm and I was almost home after checking out some property in Baltimore. Since going legit it was rare that I stayed out late. If I did Paris would always call me. On this night she didn't, so I called her. She picked up on the first ring.

"Hey baby?" Paris answered already knowing that it was me.

"What's up babygirl? You in the house? " I stopped at

a light.

"No, but I'm in my car on my way there. I'm coming from the movies. "

"By yourself?" I questioned.

"Naw, with two midgets that ran a train on me during the credits," Paris sarcastically spoke.

"Don't get smart woman." I laughed.

"Don't ask questions that you don't have to. Anyway, are you in the house?" Paris redirected the question.

"Actually, I'm not. I'm in route also. I'm just getting back from Baltimore. I'm kinda hungry too. You got me?" I asked.

"Oh I always got something you can eat," Paris seductively replied.

"Yeah, I bet you do. I'll see you at home." I laughed and hung up the phone thinking how much I loved Paris. Ten minutes later I was pulling up to the house. I had made it there before Paris did. I figured she'd be here shortly. I hopped out my truck and set the alarm. There was a slight breeze blowing as I stepped up on the porch. I unlocked the front door and stepped into the dark house. I disabled the alarm and picked up the mail from the floor. As I looked over the mail, I blindly flicked on the living room light. *SMACK* Trey smacked me with the butt of his nine-millimeter then stepped over top of me. *SMACK* The second blow instantly dazed me. Trey reached down and snatched my D.E. from my waist. Now clutching my D.E. he tucked his nine in his pants. Trey kneeled down as he spoke.

"Looks like you're the one stepped in some shit Midnight. Huh?" Trey knocked on my forehead with the barrel of the gun.

"Fuck you!" I contended spitting on to the carpet.

"Look man, let's just make this easy. Just tell me where the safe and the money is, so I can still make sure that

Paris and I have a nice life. Either you can tell me, or I'll beat that bitch ass until she does. It's up to you, black man. "

"First, tell me why you killed my uncle."

"Oh that's all you want to know. I can give you two million reasons why." Trey tossed Midnight piece of mail. He took from Uncle D house

"You see black man. Flip to the last page," Trey instructed. I read the heading and realized that what I was looking at was the results of a paternity test. The results said that Andrew Brown was ninety-nine-point nine percent Trey's father making him my cousin.

"So now you know black man, or should I say cousin. Killing you will be worth it. Now I'll be able to fuck Paris in peace," Trey laughed.

"What about his will? Your name was nowhere on it," I asked seriously trying to stall.

"Come on black man you're being naive. You of all people should know that money will get you everything. You got the house and the cars, and the jewelry because I gave them to you. Remember the lawyer at Uncle D's funeral? His name was Marcus Hamilton. Well, he's on my payroll, so it was nothing to have that altered. Money talks, black man, and bullshit walk. Not to mention he killed my mother."

"You're one vicious snake. You find the money when you find it." I gathered all the blood in my mouth and spit it directly in Trey face. SPAT! Trey instantly became furious. Slowly, he wiped his face with his shirt.

"You gonna wish you never did that." Trey dug his knee deep in my chest and began brutally pistol whipping me with my own gun. SMACK, SMACK. I tried to deflect the blows as much as I could, but it still hurt badly. Trey stood up now aiming the D.E. directly at my forehead.

"Tell my Father I said I was born just like him.

Money ruled my life just like it did his."

"Naw, you tell him that," Paris stated standing behind Trey clutching her 380. Trey tried to fire at her, but it was too late. Paris closed her eyes *BOC, BOC, BOC, BOC, BOC.* Trey flew back losing the D.E. Trey began to laugh because he had a vest on.

"Damn bitch you shot me. You actually fucking shot me. I didn't think you had it in you." Trey continued to laugh. "OOHHH I'm going to kill the shit out of you bitch! Just like Kayla. I should have let your ass die when your step daddy took that pussy." Trey tried to reach for his nine on his waist but was too late. *BOC, BOC.* Paris shot Trey twice in the forehead. Paris literally peeled his shit back to the white meat. She then began crying heavily, yet still she clutched the smoking 380. She sat there in a daze. All was quiet and Paris felt Kayla's spirit rest eternally.

*****

JUST WHEN YOU THOUGHT IT WAS OVER

MIDNIGHT

I scanned the room. Trey was lying there with two bullets in his forehead. He stared off into space lying motionless. I looked to Paris who also stared off into space while still clutching the gun. Soon as I touched her, she came back to reality, and let her tears flow freely.

"I killed him Midnight, oh God I'm going to jail." Paris cried into my chest. I sat there and held her not ever thinking about calling the police. If I did, they would surely arrest her. With every ounce of strength that I had I rolled Trey up in the throw rug. Inch by Inch I got him to the truck.

Without telling Paris where I was going, I hopped on the interstate en route to the Maryland State Junkyard. Normally, I cautiously watched my mirrors and every car passing behind, but I was too hurt and distraught to focus on a thing, but getting rid of Trey's body. Once reaching the junkyard I doused Trey's body with gasoline and set him ablaze. As quick as I could I got back in my truck and sped off.

*****

TWO WEEKS LATER
MIDNIGHT

Trying to forget about Trey and the night that Paris killed him was all in a day's work for me, but for Paris it was a task; a completely tempestuous task for her to overcome. At night she would awaken with cold sweats from dreams of Trey coming back from the dead to kill her. Paris honestly believed that Trey's soul was torturing her from the grave. It was so bad that I had to buy her a new 380. So she would feel more comfortable.

It was about 9:30pm and I had a flight to catch for my property meeting in Philly. Paris hated that I had to leave her in the house by herself, but respected my career and position in her life so she never protested.

"Look baby I'm about to leave. I'll be back tomorrow around noon," I said to Paris lying under her covers.

"Okay, be safe baby," Paris replied.

"You got your 380. with you? I asked trying to touch all bases. Paris pulled back the covers showing the chrome handgun sitting atop her pussy." I smiled.

"Girl you something else. I'm gone." I kissed her

forehead and headed out. Paris had taken some Nyquil, so before long she was out cold.

*****

PARIS

The sound of broken glass caused me to open my eyes. At first, I thought I was tripping. Then I heard it again, coupled with the sound of a door closing. By instinct I reached under the covers for my 380 but felt nothing. I jumped up snatching the covers off. Still no 380. By now I could hear someone walking up the stairs. I saw no other way, but to call the police. I picked up the phone, but it was dead. I tried to run and close the bedroom door, but it was too late. The man kicked the door back open.

"Please don't hurt me." I begged with tears. Suddenly, his face came into the light as he pulled a butcher knife out.
"I'm going to cut your nipples off bitch!" Trey yelled. With all his might Trey swung the knife. I screamed. "NOOOOOOOOO."

I sat up in bed drenched in sweat. It was another one of my nightmares. The murder I committed had my life spinning out of control and going downhill at a rapid pace. I hadn't been to school in two weeks. I had to get my life together. Trey was dead and still torturing me. I turned to the one person to get me through the night, Doctor Gregory Ames.
I looked at the clock that sat on the nightstand. It was 1:30am. At first, I thought it was too late. Then I remembered him telling me to call him anytime that I needed

275

help. So that's what I did. The phone rang about seven times before he picked up.

"Hello." It was Greg I could tell that he was still half sleep.

"Hey Greg, it's me Paris." Hearing it was me, I could hear him sit up in bed.

"Paris what's wrong are you okay?" I hear the concern in his voice.

"Not really, I've been really stressed out lately and keep having these really bad dreams. The dreams scare me so bad that I can't sleep. I can't even function properly at school."

"I can bring you some pills to help you sleep if you like?"

"Thank you so much Greg, I really do appreciate it." I smiled thinking how considerate Greg was.

"Sure thing. I already have your new address from your file, so I'll be there shortly," he replied.

"Alright and thanks again Greg."

"No problem. House calls are in my resume." I laughed as he hung up.

"I felt that I was very fortunate to have such a loving doctor. Greg was always there for me. It didn't take long at all for him to reach the house. At the ringing of the doorbell, I ran down the stairs wearing one of Midnight's oversized Redskins jerseys and a thong. I figured the jersey was big enough to cover my goodies. I opened the door and thanked Greg again.

"Thanks again Greg. I really appreciate it." Soon as Greg saw me, I kind of regretted what I was wearing because of the lust in Greg eyes. He looked at me from head to toe with no restraint.

"Don't worry about it. Here are the pills. They're

called Seroquil. They're going to make you sleep. They're also very strong so only take one," he explained as I stepped to the side to allow him to enter.

"You can have a seat on the couch." I offered then went into the kitchen and took a pill.

After I returned Greg and I sat for about ten minutes talking about school. With him being a doctor himself he could relate to everything that I said. Within another minute or so I began to dose off, and unconsciously stretched out along the love seat. Greg was instantly enticed. My jersey rose up to the cuff of my ass. Greg stooped down to the side of the love seat and begun massaging my shoulders. With the mixture of the medicine and Greg's strong hands I slightly moaned. Greg hands methodically moved all over my body. Slowly he crept his way to my lower back inching up the jersey. He softly kissed my thighs and ass cheeks. I was so far gone I never felt him move my thong to the side nor spread my legs apart. Greg brought me back to reality when I felt him tasting my juices.

"Oh damn, Greg don't do this to me." I moaned truly enjoying the feeling.

"Paris let me make love to you?" Greg whispered digging his tongue deeper in my pussy. With all the strength that I had I jumped up.

"Greg, I'm sorry. I can't do this. I'm sorry if I led you on, but this isn't right." I straightened my underwear and Jersey.

"Paris, can't you see that I love you? I've loved you for a long time now. Please don't reject me." Greg was truly pleading to the point that it looked like he was about to cry.

"I'm sorry Greg, but I only love one person and he

lives here. Please leave Greg." I walked to the front door and opened it.

"We may not be together Paris, but I promise that I will be here for you no matter what." Greg didn't say another word. He kissed me on the cheek and left the house. Once Greg left the pills really took a hold of me where I could barely stand. I locked the front door and practically ran to the bedroom. I will admit that I wanted Greg to feel my insides, but it was my loyalty to Midnight that wouldn't allow me to do so. Once hitting the bed, I was dead to the world.

The next morning around 9:00am I shot out of bed to the bathroom. I threw up a few times back-to-back. I chalked it up to the medicine not agreeing with my stomach. I was sick as a dog. I crawled back in bed and in seconds I was sleep yet again.

*****

MIDNIGHT

I had landed my deal. The building was bought for $700,000 dollars I couldn't wait to tell Paris the news. I entered the house and yelled for her but received no reply. Hearing the phone ring I rushed to answer it. Before I got a chance to say hello Paris had picked it up from the upstairs phone.

******

PARIS

"Hello." I answered still half sleep.

"Hey sweetie, how did you like what I gave you last night?" asked Greg.

"Oh God Greg, one word, WONDERFUL." I absolutely loved the pill.

"What about the massage?" I wanted to hang up on his ass, but then I thought that he hung up on me.

"Hello." I said.

"Yes Paris, I'm here," replied Greg.

"Good, I wanted to tell you that you were completely out of line. I'm about to be a married woman. What you did was very disrespectful." Just as I finished my statement Midnight burst through the room full of rage.

"Bitch, you fucked him in my house?" *SMACK, SMACK.* Enraged Midnight smacked me twice. "I grabbed the 380. but forgot to take the safety off. I aimed it at his head yet ultimately had it taken from me."

MIDNIGHT

I began crashing the pistol on her skull. Accidently a bullet discharged striking her in the temple. Paris was dead instantly. Seeing that Paris was shot, I stood up and wiped the gun off. With my blood still boiling I could care less about her dying. She was disloyal and broke my heart and my trust. Suddenly, Dr. Ames came bursting in the room. Immediately he was sickened by the sight of Paris' bludgeoned face.

"She's all yours Doc." I tossed the gun to him. He caught it and rushed to Paris' side. I ran out the house and used my cell phone to call 911.

"911, what's your emergency?"

"I just heard gun shots coming from inside my house. I also think that I heard my fiancé scream."

"Alright Sir. Don't go in the house police are on the way." *CLICK* I hung up and quickly changed my clothes tossing the old ones in the neighbor's trash can. Once the police got there Dr. Ames was arrested and charged with first degree murder.

*****

REST IN PEACE
MIDNIGHT

I had committed the perfect murder. Although I gotten away with it, Paris' death was taking a toll on me mentally. Never in my life had I let my emotions take over my thinking and rationalization. This was a first and it cost me someone that I truly loved. Paris was a fixture in my life that couldn't be replaced.

I rented a stretch limo to ride to the funeral in. When I thought about it, I didn't know any of Paris' family members to call. All I knew was that Paris hated her mother and wouldn't talk about her. I liked it that way though because it meant that I had fewer questions to answer. The whole ride I drank 1738 from the bottle. I was twisted and going. I looked behind us to a black Crown Victoria. I paid it no mind. I was mourning my mistakes.

We arrived at a church called Rock Creek Baptist. By now I was drunk as a skunk. I stumbled out the limo and up the steps of the church. I was so drunk that I disregarded the fleet of FBI vehicles lining up behind me. I stepped in the church and immediately sought refuge. "In the name of Allah most gracious most merciful." As everyone paid their respects, I sat in the back row awaiting my time to have my moment alone with Paris. As the last person stepped off, I stood in preparation to see Paris one last time. I took a deep breath but just as I stepped into the aisle that breath was taken from me when I locked eyes with Olivia. I recognized her as the one name that I had long forgotten slipped through my lips.

"KITTEN!" Olivia looked at me with tears and mouthed the words. "PUPPYDOG!"I stepped toward her as she cried harder with each step that I took. I took my left hand and wiped the tears from her face.
      "What's up Kitten what you crying for?"
      "Derrick, I've hated and missed you for over 22 years." Olivia cried calling me by my first name I then placed my hands on her cheek.
      "Well now you're going to love me like you used to for 22 plus years. You hear me?" Olivia melted in my hands with a nod. It then struck me that she and Paris had the same eyes.
      "Stop crying baby what's wrong?" After all these years I still hated to see Olivia cry. She then looked up.
      "Derrick, why are you here? How do you know Paris?" Olivia pulled my hands from her face and held them in her hands.
      "She was my fiancée. Someone murdered her. Why?"
      "Oh no Derrick I feared that you would say that." Olivia could barely get the words out.
      "What's wrong Kitten?"
      "Derrick when you left, I found out I was six weeks pregnant and gave birth to a baby girl that I named Paris." Olivia took a deep breath gathering her strength. "Paris is a product of what Donny did to me when I was younger".
      "Wait, wait so you telling me that.... Hell Naw." Then in my mind I could see Donny's face, then Paris".
      "I'm sorry Derrick I thought she was yours, but when she was born she was the spitting image of him. I had no

way of telling you".

"What the fuck you mean you had no way of telling me. Bitch I sent you letters. You had my information!" I yelled drawing the attention of the entire service.

"No, no I didn't my mother held your letters from me. I never got them until four years ago when she died. I swear to you Derrick." She grabbed my hand.

"So you telling me that Paris is Donny's daughter?" I asked wanting complete confirmation.

"Yes Derrick." Olivia looked to her lap. My entire world was spinning. What hurt the most was that I was the reason that Paris was dead. As for Donny I feel no indifference, somebody should been killed him. Paris was the daughter of the first man I ever killed. I stood up and began to slowly walk down the aisle. I now had tears falling like cannon balls. Just when I thought my life couldn't get any worse, it did.

"Derrick Brown don't take another step. You're under arrest." I turned towards the familiar voice and locked eyes with Tymia. I couldn't believe this shit.

"Bitch you the police?" I questioned in disbelief.

"Special Agent Kimberly Kniffen. You're done Midnight. We got Trey's body and the bloody clothes you tried to hide in your neighbor's trash. That doctor didn't kill Paris, you did. Derrick you're going to jail for a long time. Don't drop the soap cheater." Tymia's last statement let me know that she was the one who fucked up my house and cars. I turned around and continued to walk down the aisle. Reaching the casket, I studied Paris' features and could now see Donny's essence all over her face.

"Damn she looks like me." I thought my whole world was crushed. I came to the reality that if Paris couldn't live and enjoy her life then I didn't deserve to live myself. I looked back at Tymia and decided that I definitely wasn't going back to jail. There was only one way. I whipped out my Desert Eagle and cocked it. CLICK, CLACK. The church erupted in terror. I then placed the gun under my chin and took one last look at Paris.

"I love you, Paris. I'm sorry." BOOM!

THE KEY TO IT ALL

With my eyes closed spinning unconscious thoughts, in a land where nothing is impossible - a time and place where if you die, you're still alive. Clocks don't exist and time isn't counted.   Dates are irrelevant. What am I?

*****

The answer is: A Dream!

LEWISBURG FEDERAL PENITENTARY
(DAY ONE)

DERRICK

"No!" I said a loud. I sat atop my bunk drenched in sweat. I took off my shirt and wiped my face dry. That was one helleva dream I thought. I looked over and saw Doc offering the Islamic Morning prayer. Not wanting to disturb him I climb off the bed as unobtrusive as possible. Gradually, I stepped to the sink in preparation to offer WUDU (self-cleansing). So I could also offer my morning prayer. Once I did so Doc was all over me.

"Nephew you must have had one helleva dream last night." Doc stood up.
"How you know?" I asked.
"Nephew you was talking all night and sweating like dog this morning. You alright?" Doc asked truly concerned.
"Yeah, I'm cool, dreams are just that; dreams. I'm getting released today, so I'm on top of the world. I'm not gonna let nothing or no one get in the way of that." I stood up unfolding my prayer rug.
"Don't be so sure about that Nephew. Remember the Prophet Muhammad was taken to the seven levels of heaven on the night of power through a dream. Don't downplay your thoughts because it could be Allah revealing something to you." Doc leaned back on his bed. Doc always had a way of putting things so I would accept them.
"Putting it like that I can see exactly what you mean.

Doc man, that dream was filled with treachery and deceit. When it was all said and done, I was forced not to live. My voice began to shake. I was truly disturbed.

"Don't tell me about it. Allah showed that to you. If Allah wanted me to know what you dreamed, then I would have dreamed it, and woke up in cold sweats as you did. Now did your people send your clothes for you to wear?" Doc dropped another jewel and quickly changed the subject.

"I don't know. They never let me know if they were here or not. My uncle is picking me up anyway." I replied while writing down all of my numbers on a piece of paper.

"Well, here I want you to have these." Doc handed me a pair of brand-new Air Force Ones.

"Come on Doc I'm going home, you still got twelve more months.

"You'll need them more then I will. Besides I was going to leave you all my things anyway," I replied declining the gesture.

"I don't need anything Nephew. People always worry about what they can get from a guy going home. I try not to be like everyone else. If you won't take the shoes, then at least take this." Doc handed me his Quran. "I hope this be the one thing in life that you would never deny." I smiled and accepted it with my right hand. Before I could reply there was a knock on the cell door.

"D. Brown," The officer yelled.

"Yeah, that's me." I stepped to the door.

"State your Reg. number." The officer listened while studying my bed book card.

"23192-048," I quickly recited. The officer unlocked my door.

"Aight Brown It's 4:45am. Your escort will be here at five to take you to R&D. When you're done getting ready, let me know."

"Alright officer," I replied, and the officer left. I then turned to Doc.

"Doc I will accept this Quran. If you won't take my things, then give them to the young brother down the hall who just took his Shahada (Became Muslim). Here are my numbers make sure that you used them." I handed them to him. As he reached, I placed the paper into the palm of his hand while I gave him a firm handshake. I then pulled him in and gave him a manly hug.

"Thanks for the jewels old man." I spoke over his shoulder.

"Thanks for accepting them, Nephew," Doc replied as we broke our embrace. I gathered my linen and exited the cell.

As I walked to the office, I took one final look at the unit and made my final exit. As the officer escorted me to R&D I constantly thought of my dream and why Allah would allow me to dream such drastic and devastating things. Shortly we made it to R&D, and I found out that my uncle came through. The officer handed me a box filled with my clothes to dress out in. I took the box into the holding cell to get dress. I opened the box and was shocked. Inside sat a pair of Paper denim jeans, a black Hugo sweater, and a pair of matching soft bottoms. The exact things that I dreamed of. Deja'Vu was clouding my mind so much that I sat there stuck struggling what to make of it.

"Hey, you alright in there?" yelled the officer seeing me staring off into space.

"Uh yeah, yeah I'm good. I'll be ready in a minute." I replied shaking lose the cobwebs. I jumped up and was ready in seconds. I returned my institutional clothes and signed my release papers. I was given $20.50. After signing I was given my papers and quickly escorted off the grounds. I reached the front door and took a deep breath before I stepped out. Finally, I took my first steps back into freedom. As I stepped out, I was instantly overwhelmed by Deja'vu again when I saw my Uncle leaning on a money-green Jaguar XJ4 just like in my dream. I walked toward him completely confused.

"Goddamn Nephew, it's good to see ya, especially free." We embraced with me giving a half hug.

"What's wrong Nephew. You look like you seen a ghost," Uncle D spoke in his regular grungy voice.

"Naw, I'm cool. I see you still doing it big Uncle D." I pointed to that Jag. I thought to myself that he would reply by saying "Same old shit Nephew. It's good to have you home." Uncle D did just that. I was seeing everything that I dreamed of for face value.

"I ain't there yet, let's go before these people decide to change their mind." I shook off my Deja'Vu and walked around to the passenger side of the jag. At the last minute I remembered the Red Corvette. Before I stepped into the street I looked just in time, and just like I knew it would the sports car zoomed past.

"This shit getting crazy." I thought to myself. I hopped in the Jag and Uncle D sped off. As he drove, I looked out the window digging deep down into the lower bowels of my mind to remember every aspect of my dream. Uncle D then got down to business.

"So what you plan on doing for money, ya know...." I cut him off.

"As far as I'm concern, I never left the team. It's us against the world. I'll get the list from you tomorrow." Uncle D looked at me like I was crazy. I just hope I didn't jump the gun and was actually sounding crazy.

"Nephew how the hell you know what I was going to say? More importantly how you know about that list?" Uncle D was dumbfounded.

"Let's just call it a Gangsta's intuition." I smiled at him and continued to stare out the window. Within two hours we were home. Now I was waiting for Uncle D to give me that Caddy. As we got out the car I began walking toward the garage. Uncle D pulled a remote out his pocket and automatically opened the door. Just like in my dream sat a black DTS Cadillac. I turned and said what he was going to say.

"You got it painted Midnight black like my complexion." I smiled.

"How you know that?" Uncle D took his cigar out of his mouth.

"Call it a Gangsta's intuition." I laughed and stepped inside the garage to the house door. As I walked in I thought about what Doc told me about dreams and thanked him for the jewel that he gave me. That night Uncle D and I hit the strip club and partied till the wee hours of the morning. He even bought me some stripper pussy and a hotel for the night. While I went for my night cap Uncle D decided he would call it a night and caught a cab home.

___(DAY TWO)
KARMA BEFORE IT GO AROUND

DERRICK

I had a wonderful welcome home night. The stripper Uncle D bought took me to levels that I'd forgotten existed. I was slowly but surely forgetting about my time in Lewisburg. While on the ride home I thought the DTS road like a champ. I took in the sights of Washington D.C. I hadn't seen these streets since I was 16 years old. The city was one you couldn't forget, and I never did. I pulled up to Uncle D home and parked in the driveway. As I got out, I saw that Uncle D had the sprinklers on. With the sun out I could see a faint rainbow within the spray of water. Today was a beautiful day.

If my dreams were correct, then today would be the day where I would obtain the list of people who were delinquent in their bills. I wanted to clean the list up as soon as possible. Thinking of the list also made me think of Trey. Just the thought of him would get my blood boiling. I used my key that Uncle D gave and stepped in the house to the smells of a gourmet meal.

"Uncle D, where you at old man?" I yelled already knowing he was in the kitchen.

"I'm in the kitchen. Hurry up, I got to tell you something," he replied. Hearing the urgency in his voice I put some pep in my step. I walked in the kitchen to Uncle D at the stove cooking pancakes and eggs with a green apron on. I took in the beauty of the kitchen and admired it.

"What's up Unc? I hope I get a plate." I stated knowing that he'd say no.

"Sure, you can have your own plate as long as you can cook your own food." He laughed into a violent cough.

"See what happen when you be a smart ass." I laughed with him, and grabbed a glass of orange juice. Uncle D then spoke the familiar words.

"But look Nephew since you're with me I need you to go pick up some money for me. These...." I cut him off.

"I don't need the speech Unc just give me the list we split everything fifty-fifty. I know what time it is, and I know how you work. Just give me the list and I'll get back with you."

"Alright smart ass. It's right next to you. And in case

you need them here go two twins for you as well." There they were the two twin Glock 17's with silencers.

"They're both brand new and never been fired. Them silencers a must nowadays. No noise, no unwanted attention. You follow me?" Uncle D asserted.

"More then you know." I replied.

"Oh and here, if you need some help call this number. The guy's name is Trey. I want you to see what he's about. You know, see if he about his work or not. I wanna see what type of blood his heart pumps. I think he might be a thoroughbred." Uncle D began cutting his pancakes up. I thought to myself, that I wanted to see what type of blood his heart pumped too "literally."

I remember checking the place out by myself but that wouldn't be needed this time. I was trusting in Allah that he wasn't leading me astray. I called the number, and it was answered on the second ring.

"Yeah." Trey answered.

"I'm looking for Trey."

"Who is this?" Trey asked I could almost hear the treachery in his voice.

"The name is Midnight. Uncle D told me to call you if I needed any help. "

"Well then you're talking to him," replied Trey with no emotion.

"Meet me in front of the Madness Shop uptown in thirty minutes and be manned up. I'll be in a black DTS."

"See you there."

CLICK Trey hung up. There was nothing else that needed to be said. Within thirty minutes I was sitting in front of the Madness Shop. Soon I saw Trey's Burgundy BMW pull up. Trey hopped out with his book bag. Once he spotted my car he ran over and hopped in the backseat. I knew his reason for sitting back there so I didn't bother to ask. Throughout the ride I was laconic. If it didn't need to be said, then it wasn't.

"We going into the lion's den so be on point. We strike tonight." That was it. Trey didn't respond and I said nothing else. Ten minutes later we pulled up to number one on the list. The Turntable. Trey pulled the Mac-90 out the bag and cocked it before replacing it back in the bag. I checked my twin Glocks placing them both on my waist. We exited the car and gradually walked inside. Upon entrance six pairs of slanted eyes stabbed us from different directions. Junior was the target and was sitting right where I knew he would be. Cautiously, I approached with Trey in tow. Once I got close Junior's two females pulled their weapons out.

"Hold up ladies, we come in peace." I held my palms in the air as a sign of no aggression.

"We don't take kindly to dem come unannounced." Junior calmly stated pulling the girls guns down.

"Look we come in peace. We don't want no problems. My Uncle D sent me to collect an outstanding debt you owe him." Junior smiled at the mention of my presence.

"And what is that ME! The baddest Jamaican rastclad in D.C.!" Junior crossed his arms over his bare chest. "Owe Uncle D?"

"According to him $65,000." Junior's answer would end or begin our dealings to the next level, Murder.

"Well den tell dem pussy clad Uncle D I say fuck him and I no pay shit." He smiled again as he comfortably leaned back in his chair.

"Alright I'll tell him that. Sorry to bother you." I got up not worrying about the goon's eye balling me and walked out the Turntable. In the car, I still said nothing to Trey. Instead, I dropped him to his car and told him to meet me back here at 11:30pm tonight.

Eleven thirty came rather quickly and just like I instructed Trey was back. He hopped in the car and again I said nothing to him. I could tell that not speaking to Trey was starting to worry him.

"What's up with the silent treatment slim?" he asked leaning forward from the backseat.
"Nothing to talk about. We here to take care of business not make friends." Trey leaned back and that was it. We made it out Potomac, Maryland in about thirty minutes. I led Trey to the back window that didn't have a trip sensor, and in seconds we were in the house. I went straight upstairs to check on the safe and the plants. I got to the door with the pad lock on it, so I whipped out my Glock with the silencer equipped. TWIP, TWIP, TWIP. The lock hit the floor with a loud thud. Trey ran up the stairs with his Mac-90 in hand.
"Man, what the fuck you doing?" Trey said out of breath from running up the stairs.
"I had to shoot the lock off. Go watch the door," I sternly spoke. Trey was fuming but complied. I peeked in the room and all the exotic plants were there. I then continued the search to the master bedroom. I headed straight to the closet and was blessed to find the safe wide open.
"Aye Midnight they're here." Trey yelled from the bottom of the steps. I whipped out both Glocks and took up one side of the door while Trey took up the other side. Just as Junior walked in the house SMACK, SMACK, SMACK, SMACK. Junior and his two females were struck in the head and knocked to the floor instantly dazed. The girls were relieved of their guns and temporarily neutralized by guns being put to their heads. I kneeled down grabbing a hand full

of Junior's dreads.

"You remember me rude boy. You should have just paid the money." SMACK I backhanded him to show him the utmost disrespect.

"Give me the Mac and tie his bitch ass up." Trey hesitated breathing fumes out his nose, but then complied. Once tied, Junior was still dazed, so I open hand smacked him.

"Wake your bitch ass up." I dug the silencer in his eye.

"Fuck you baty, I no tell you shit. The safe locked and built with one-foot titanium steel. You never get in pussy clad."

"I'm starting to understand that weed really does kill you short term memory. You see that's where you're wrong coco bread. You left it open, so I don't need to torture you. Your time's up." I grabbed the back of Junior's dreads forcing him to look to the ceiling.

"Now tell the devil you owed a bill and had to pay taxes." I jammed the Glock down his throat to the trigger. Junior choked on every inch of the silencer.

"Say ahhh fuck boy." TWIP, TWIP, TWIP. I let three shots off down his throat. The hole in his chest led me to believe that one of the bullets exited through his chest. Trey looked on in amazement as I still held on to his Mac-90 seizing the moment I removed the Glock from Junior's throat and aimed it directly at Trey's forehead.

"Hold up Midnight, we supposed to be together." Trey spoke in a shaken voice.

"Naw, we supposed to be family, but to you, your money is more important." I gripped my bottom lip as I clutched the Glock tighter. Hearing my statement Trey knew that he'd been figured out and gave in.

"So the results are in huh black man? Just tell me one

thing. How'd you know my intentions?" Trey asked.
"Just call it a Gangsta's intuition."

TWIP, TWIP, TWIP. I shot Trey three times in the face easily dropping him. Just for being a snake I stood over top of him and emptied the clip in his head. I wanted to make sure that he had a closed casket. I then placed the Mac to the back of each girl head giving them twin fates. I bagged up the money and coke and left the plants. I left the house feeling that it was a job well done.

By now it was 2:00am in the morning, so I decided to get a hotel for the night with plans to see Magny first thing in the morning. As I rode, I made a short prayer "Almighty Allah, Most Gracious, Most Merciful, I thank you for allowing me to see my fate before, and allowing me to change it. Through your graces I'm alive and healthy. I pray you continue to shield me with protection from all evil that come my way. In your name I pray Allah Hu Akbar Amen."

*****

(DAY THREE)

DERRICK

As I opened my eyes, I caught a glimpse of the drugs and money filled trash bags on the floor of my hotel room. I had 15 bricks and $650,000. No doubt in my mind that was Junior's whole stash. I thought to myself 'damn, I been home three days and killed three people. As I sat there staring off into space I wondered, was I really doing what Allah wanted me to do? Was my soul just as corrupt as a non-believer of Islam, or worst yet, was I just as corrupt as

Trey? Today I would move on to number two on the list, but before I made that I had to make a stop. This was something that I had to do. This is what gave me the motivation to put things in order as I'm doing now. I was going to a street from my past. A place where I left my heart 17 years ago. I was headed around Park Rd. to look for Olivia.

I pulled up, and just like I was expecting there was an ambulance and two police cars. I placed my Glock under the seat and approached the building. As I reached the steps the paramedics were exiting the building with the gurney. As it passed, I immediately recognized its occupant as Ms. Rita. I hated that woman for what she did to Olivia growing up. I wanted so badly to spit in her face, even if she was already dead. "Good riddance," I mumbled. I then looked up the steps to an old familiar face. It was Ms. Miles. She'd aged well. She held the door for the paramedics and soon made eye contact with me as I walked toward her.

"Ms. Miles you've aged well." I smiled and gave her a hug.

"I truly appreciate the compliment baby, but do I know you?" She broke the embrace and touched my cheek.

"Yes, you do, I'm Derrick, Mrs. Brown's son." I revealed and Ms. Miles added on.

"And the love of Ms. Olivia life." I smiled at her comment.

"Yes, and that to." I looked off to the ambulance. "I guess life finally caught up to her for her wrongs." I looked back to Ms. Miles.

"Yes child, she had a rough life. Ms. Rita and I used to sit and talk regularly. She had a lot of regrets bottled up that was killing her slowly. She admitted to me countless times of all the mistakes she made. She always said that her biggest regret was treating Olivia so badly."

"That sounded nothing like the woman that I remember. The woman that I remembered was selfish and abusive both mentally and physically not only to herself but her only child as well." I spoke my mind feeling my anger rise.

"People change young Derrick, and I can honestly say that she truly did. She was punished for her wrongs through that deadly disease that she carried for all of these years."

"What disease?" I didn't remember anything about Ms. Rita being sick.

"Around the time that you left she was diagnosed with HIV. She lived with it for 15 years before it progressed into AIDS. Now two years after the progression she finally succumbed to it and was brought home." Brought to hell was how I thought.

"Ms. Miles do you know where Olivia is right now?" I finally asked.

"Come inside young Derrick. I have a spare key to Ms. Rita's apartment. She always knew where Olivia went when she left. Ms. Rita was so afraid Olivia would reject her that she would never attempt to see her. Ms. Rita made her life more complicated then need be."

Ms. Miles and I reached on her neck to retrieve a small chain holding two keys. She opened the door and we stepped in. The first thing that I saw was a large picture on the wall of Olivia as a young girl. With that I thought that maybe it was possible that Ms. Rita did change. The house was even a lot cleaner than I remembered. Ms. Miles instructed me to have a seat as she disappeared into the back. When she returned, she held a small diary with a bunch of old mail.

"I take it that you're going to find Olivia?" She took a seat.

"Even with my last breath, I will," I sincerely replied.

"Well may this help you in your mission." Ms. Miles handed me Olivia's address first. I saw that it wasn't far from Park Rd.

"You may also need this to pursue her. You see when you left, Olivia cursed the ground that you walked on because she thought that you didn't write her, and forgot all about her." I cut her off.

"I did write her. I wrote letters for two years and never got a reply," I replied. Ms. Miles placed a hand on my knee to calm me.

"I know baby; all your letters are right here. Ms. Rita kept every letter that you ever wrote her. So you see young Derrick, she never received any of the letters that you wrote to her."

"Was I part of the reason that she ran away?" I asked for clarity.

"Well, I will say this. I don't think so, but there's more to the story that I will leave for Olivia to explain." She had to be talking about Paris. Olivia must have gotten put out or ran away because she got pregnant.

"When you find Olivia, I want you to give her this so she will always know exactly how her mother felt about her before she died. Derrick this is for Olivia, so promised me that you will let her read it before you do." Ms. Miles wrapped my fingers around it and pushed it toward me. I was at a loss for words after hearing everything, but I did promise her and stood to leave.

"Thank you, Ms. Miles you've been a great help."

"You're welcome Young Derrick. Just do me two favors?" she asked grabbing my hand.

"Don't let her get away this time. True love only

comes once in a lifetime. And two, please send me an invitation to the wedding." Ms. Miles smiled.

"I'll be sure to do that. Thank you again, Ms. Miles." I leaned down and gave her another hug and kiss. I then exited the apartment.

With everything that I'd heard I knew that Olivia would have mixed emotions about seeing me. I just hoped that with what Ms. Miles gave me that it would be enough to suppress any type of hatred that she may house for me. I sat in the DTS and stared at the address for a long time ultimately deciding that now was as good as anytime. I put the DTS in drive and in minutes was pulling up to Twin Oaks apartments. I parked, took a deep breath and proceeded. On the elevator, I found myself actually nervous. I stepped off and began to follow the numbers on the doors until I reached 720. I straightened my clothes took another deep breath and knocked. I kicked myself in the ass for leaving my Glock in the car. A deep baritone voice then sounded off.

"Who is it?"

"UUHH is Olivia home." I answered firmly. Hearing my voice Ron snatched the door open.

"Who the fuck is you?" Ron yelled looking me up and down. He stood there with a tank top and some slacks.

"I'm a friend of the family," I calmly replied with a smile.

"Well, I'm the head of the family and I never heard of or seen you before, so if you don't want no trouble, I'd advise you to get the hell away from my place of residence." Ron slammed the door in my face. I took that as being very disrespectful and made a mental note to make sure that I kill him.

I left the building with plans of returning. Ron had my blood boiling to the point that I decided to go see Magny now, verses later. I threw the Caddy in drive and sped off to The Southern Diner. Pulling up, I decided to park around the corner. Before exiting the car, I screwed on the silencer and tucked the Glock on my hip. I wore a Dickie shirt, so as I stepped out the Caddy it would easily be concealed. Stepping in the restaurant I was pleased to see that only one patron was eating breakfast. At the register sat the lovely Muslima. She smiled with a greeting.

"As Salaam Alaikum. Would you like a table?" She began to grab a menu.

"That won't be necessary. I came to see Magny." I gave her a reassuring smile.

"Okay one second while I go get him. That's my dad, I think he's in his office," the young girl replied and then knocked on a door a few yards away. Seconds later Magny appeared in the doorway.

"I'm Magny how may I help you?" Magny removed his glasses.

"The name is Midnight, Uncle D sent me. May we talk in your office?" I extended my hand. Magny reluctantly shook it. At the mention of Uncle D's name Magny instantly became fidgety realizing that this was no social call.

"Yes, certainly. This way." Magny allowed me to walk passed him into his office. Once inside I took a seat as did he.

"Well Mr. Midnight this is as private as it's going to get, so enlighten me why you're in my establishment." Magny interlocked his fingers as he leaned back in his seat. Not liking his arrogance, I got straight to the point.

"My uncle tells me that you owe him a bill, so I'm

here to make sure that bill gets paid," I firmly spoke.

"Tell Uncle D I ain't got it, and when I do get it I'll call his ass," Magny snidely replied. With the speed of lightening, I whipped my Glock out sending it crashing over his temple. Grabbing a fist full of his sweater I placed the Glock directly between his eyes.

"Watch your mouth A-Rab that's family you sassing. I tried to go about this in a nice way, but you wouldn't let me. Now I want you to get overhear on the floor and open this safe. I know there's a gun inside so if you try to reach for it, I'm gonna see what you thinking I promise." I pulled Magny around the desk forcing him to his knees. He quickly opened the safe and scooted back into the corner. I grabbed a small gym bag and cleaned the safe out. Magny sat quietly as he watched his life savings slowly slip out of his reach.

"Last time I left you alive my uncle ended up dead. I won't make that mistake twice." I aimed the Glock at Magny's forehead TWIP, TWIP. Two shots to the head sent Magny out for the season. I stepped out of the office to Magny's daughter ringing up the patron who was paying for his food. She never knew what hit her when I put the Glock behind her ear.

"Hear no evil, see no evil, and speak no evil." TWIP. The patron's mouth fell wide open as he backed away from the register. I aimed. TWIP, TWIP. The hollow point bullets dropped him easily. Quickly, I left the restaurant and gradually walked around the corner to my car. I headed back to the hotel to pick up the coke and money that I took from Junior and headed back to Uncle D's house so we could break it down.

*****

UNCLE D
11:30 AM

I had been anticipating this day for the past week and a half. Out of all my 65 years on this earth I never had any kids and quite frankly never planned to have any. This world was too corrupt, and I was into too much. No way did I ever want to bring a child into this world while I was still knee deep in the game. Even now with me thinking about retirement and all, I still wasn't up for the task it was just too late.

Now all that had changed. When Trey came and mentioned a woman named Tonya Long, the aspect of me having a child in my life became very probable. You see, out of all the females I dealt with Tonya was that bottom bitch that every gangsta needed. She counted money, cut dope, and was one helleva driver. If there was anyone ever capable of being pregnant by me, it was Tonya. I never used protection and would fuck her brains out anyway that I would see fit. I could honestly say that Tonya was that love of my life. That is until I caught her with her hand in my cookie jar. I'd just gotten two bricks of raw heroin; 75% per pure, from a woman named Lady Sadie on consignment. I owed $300,000. That type of money back then people didn't have like that. I was still up and coming. Tonya stole the two bricks and left me out to dry with Lady Sadie and her people. When I tried to explain her actions she would hear nothing of it and gave me thirty days to pay the bill or else. I had no way of getting the money, so I did what I had to. In thirty days, I robbed 12 banks for a total of $780,000 dollars. I paid my bill and bought two more bricks. I haven't looked back since.

As far as Tonya, she ended up falling in love with a pimp named Smooth. He was the guy who had the habit and put Tonya up to stealing from me. A whole year had passed before I saw Tonya. I just so happened to be around on the track trying to buy some pussy and that's where I saw her. She was a hoe on the stroll. While watching her I saw Smooth pick his four girls up and drive off. Not wanting to lose her I followed. Luckily, they were in route home. Once they walked in I waited thirty minutes then kicked the door in with two 44. caliber Smith and Wesson pistols. There were three girls in the front room but no Tonya. I took a knot of money out my pocket telling them to be quiet. I then tip toed to the back room. I could hear a lot of moaning and grunting. I kicked the door in to find Tonya trying to shoot up while Smooth was blowing her back out.

"Motherfucker is you crazy, sucker!?" Smooth pulled out of Tonya reaching for his 38 revolver. *BOOM, BOOM, BOOM.* I hit Smooth three times in the chest. He began coughing up blood then eventually laid still staring off into space. Tonya didn't care one bit that I was there, nor did she care that I had just killed Smooth. The only thing she worried about was finding a vein. I walked up to her and snatched the needle.
        "Please Drew, please let me have that back. I'm sick baby."
        "Tonya, you left me out to dry. I took care of you." I looked at her in shame. Then I noticed a baby started to cry that was lying next to her.
        "Drew please. I know you're not going to kill me. Just let me have the needle please. You can have my baby. Just give me the needle."
        "You want this bitch? That is what you want?" He turned Tonya head to the side and slammed the needle in her temple, shooting every drop of the heroine directly in her brain.

I took one last look at that baby, gathered my wits and got the fuck out of dodge. When Trey showed up on my doorstep, I was completely aware that there was a strong possibility that Trey was my son, and he was the infant that was crying that night I killed Tonya. I woke up this morning anxious for the mailman to come. Today should be the day that the test results arrive. To be honest I wasn't sure if I would be happy or sad about it. All I knew was that I needed to know if Trey was mines or not.

I retrieved the mail, and it was here, I immediately opened it completely disregarding the other articles of mail. As I read the results, I unconsciously released one tear. The test results said that I was ninety-nine-point nine percent Trey's father. I was crushed because here it was now Trey was 26 years old and knew nothing about me. Then I wondered if he knew that I killed his mother? Regardless, I planned to love him as my son as only a father should. Suddenly the tears rushed me, and I was the happiest man on earth. It was like Trey had just been born. I was a father and proud of it. I turned on the T.V. to watch the morning News. Before I could reach my Lazyboy the bulletin quickly caught my attention.

"Hello, I'm Nikkie Myers with Fox Five News. We're out here in Georgetown D.C. where apparently there has been a quadruple homicide. I'm standing in front of Jamaican Mafia Boss Junior Kadafi's mansion where apparently the mailman found the bodies of two men and two young women. Police have identified the males as Junior Kadafi, and Tryevon Davis. The women have yet to be identified. Police are saying that the murders were done execution style with one of the males, Treyvon Davis being shot multiple times in the face. Police have no leads and have labeled the case a robbery homicide. Police are asking the public for any information that they may have to assist in the investigation."

I could hear no more. In just that quick of an instance I'd gained and lost a son. I was filled with so many emotions that the room started spinning. Suddenly I felt a sharp pain in my chest. I grabbed my chest trying to stumble to the kitchen phone. The whole time I never let go of the paternity test. Just as I reached the phone my legs gave way. I realized that with all the chaos that I was having a heart attack I laid on the floor watching my life flash before my eyes. I thought of my regrets and realized that I was going out the one way that I didn't want to, on my back. Soon my heart completely stopped, and my life was gone all the while I still clutched the test.

*****

DERRICK
2:30 pm

I drove as cautiously as I could. In the trunk of the DTS I had over a half million in cash along with 15 bricks. If a cop pulled me over there was no way that I was stepping out of the car. Going back to jail wasn't a part of my plans. I drove along 16th street wondering what else would come from working with my Uncle after the list was done. Only time would tell. By the grace of God, I pulled up to Uncle D's house safe and sound. I popped the trunk and retrieved the bags hurrying to the front. I used my key and set the bags by the door.

"Aye Unc where you at?" I yelled out and received no answer. I figured he might be in the back so walked toward the kitchen. As soon as I walked through, I saw my Uncle lying flat on his back. Both his hands and face were pale and blue.

"Unc come on Unc, don't go out like this," I frantically spoke.

I began CPR but still received no response. His body was ice cold. I tried for thirty minutes to revive him, but it was too late. My Uncle D was gone. I sat next to him and cried for about fifteen minutes before I noticed he was clutching a piece of paper. I loosened his grip and obtained it. Once doing so I realized that it was the paternity test for Trey and Uncle D. I then thought that Uncle D had a heart attack when he found out that Trey was his son. Even though I killed Trey before he could strike, he was still the reason for his death. Even with the gift that Allah allowed me to have I now realized that some things are just meant to happen and there was no changing God's will.

I walked to the front door to retrieve the bags to place them in the safe before I called the paramedics. Doing so, once they arrived, they pronounced Uncle D dead on arrival. I sat in his lazy boy and lit up one of his favorite cigars for him. "Rest in peace old man." I mumbled out loud.

It was 11:00pm by time the house was clear of police and medical personnel. When they left, I decided that I would go and finish my quest. I didn't care how late it was, I was going to get my woman, and put a bullet in Ron's head.

During the ride to Olivia's, I loaded Magny's nine-millimeter. I constantly thought of Uncle D and if he was at peace or not. I noticed the list sticking out of the ashtray. I then bald it up and tossed it out of the window. After Ron there would be no more murders. I wanted to focus on Olivia and Paris and building a family with them. I pulled up to the building and again took a deep breath before stepping out of the Caddy. Again, I was nervous as hell. When I stepped off of the elevator, I could hear yelling and screaming. As I got closer, I realized that it was coming from Olivia's apartment.

I stood at the door and listened.

"Ron, please I don't know who he was." *SMACK.*
"Who the fuck is he Olivia?" It sounded like Ron smacked her. *SMACK.* "Ain't no wife of mine gonna have men visiting unannounced." *SMACK.*
"Oh Ron please I didn't know." Olivia pleaded.
"Leave her alone." Paris yelled *SMACK.*
"AGGHHH." I couldn't take it any longer, hearing another man beat on Olivia. Aggressively, I knocked on the door. *(KNOCK), (KNOCK), (KNOCK).*
"Who the hell is it?" Ron aggressively spoke. I said nothing instead I knocked harder.
"Whoever you are you gonna wish you never came here." Ron snatched the door open as he continued his tirade but ended up meeting the butt of my nine. *(SMACK)* I caught Ron right on his nose splitting it on impact. Ron fell back clutching his face.
"AGGGHH God fuck! You broke my nose!" Ron yelled out in pain. I stepped in closing the door behind me. I instantly locked eyes with Olivia. She slowly sat up holding her bruised face. Neither of us said a word but our eyes said a mouthful. I finally kneeled down to help her never breaking the lock. Olivia then released a whole new rush of tears.
"Derrick." Olivia mumbled, clearly shaken.
"It's me Kitten." I smiled wiping the tears from her face.
"Oh Derrick I've missed you so much." Olivia fell into my chest, wrapping her arms around me. I was so caught up in Olivia I forgot all about Ron.
"Get the fuck off my wife." Ron spun me around giving me a right hook that sent me crashing to the floor, simultaneously losing my gun.

"Don't you know any better then come into a man's house and palm his wife'?"

"AGGGHHH." Ron kicked me in the ribs.

"No stop, leave him alone." Olivia pleaded sending a glass ashtray crashing over his head. Quickly as I could I got to my feet and retrieved my gun. I turned on Ron and began brutally pistol whipping him. I then place the gun to his temple.

"You gonna wish you never laid hands on me."

"Come on man you ain't got to kill me. You can have the bitch I wanted her daughter anyway," Ron pleaded not knowing that his words infuriated me even more.

"Open your fucking mouth." I jammed the nine down his throat.

"No Derrick." Olivia yelled. I looked at her seeing whatever little compassion that she may have had for him and didn't like it at all.

"Olivia, you make your choice either me or him."

"Oh Derrick, I choose you a thousand time over, but I don't want to lose you again to jail or anything else."

"Paris make your choice." I looked at Paris.

"Midnight, I've dreamed about meeting you for 17 years. I would never choose that fat motherfucker over you." Paris cried. I was taken aback when she called me Midnight.

"Get your fat ass up." I pulled Ron to his feet and opened the door.

"Wait Derrick where are you going?" Olivia asked.

"To handle my business, and not get caught." I replied.

"Are you coming back?" The look in Olivia eyes pleaded for me to say yes.

"Only death will keep me from you, and even then, I'll always be with you. I walked Ron out the door.

*****

MIDNIGHT
GRADUATION

"Kayla Bell....Robyn Jackson....Paris Clemons." We erupted in applause as Paris walked across the stage. I thought back to all the hardships Paris endured in my dream and thought she deserved it, no matter if she was Donny's Paris looked so beautiful in her cap and gown. Although she held a different position in my dream, I couldn't and wouldn't see that as a reality. Nevertheless, we're best of friends.

Me and Olivia are planning to get married next year. She hated me for all those years but when she saw me all of those feelings went straight out of the window. Olivia's love for me surpassed anything else in this world and as did mine. She was even pregnant and three weeks along. My chips were finally falling in order.

As for Ron, well we'll just say he's out of sight out of mind. It's been six weeks and his body still hasn't been found. Hopefully it never will be. Paris received her diploma and ran to us to give us a hug.

"Midnight I want you to meet my best friend, Kayla."

"How are you?" I extended my hand immediately thinking of my dream.

"I'm fine it's nice to meet you," Kayla replied. "I'll be back Paris. I gotta go see my family."

"Okay," Paris replied.

"Paris, I'm proud of you." I hugged her. "I got one question though, how did you know that my nickname was Midnight?"

"Well let's just say dreams do come to true. In my dreams I was always saved by a man dark as night, and always called him Midnight. That man was you." I smiled at her statement.

"More truth than you know, but speaking of dreams I got you something that should significantly help you to obtain yours." I reached in my inside pocket and pulled out an envelope. "Some people have to struggle and strive to get where they want to be in life. Some even degrade themselves. You'll never have to do that. You've done your part by graduating. The next move is on me." Paris stopped and opened the envelope. Inside was a check for 250,000 dollars on the front I just wrote 'University.'

"With that you can choose what University that you want to go to."

"Oh thank you so much," Paris cried as she wrapped her arms around my neck. I was proud to be able to send her to college. Paris had the will and determination to succeed. So I would help her in any way that I could. Our embrace was then cut short by someone calling my name.

"Derrick Brown!" I looked up to a fairly short guy wearing a blue suit and glasses. Immediately I knew that he was some type of bill collector or lawyer.

"Yes, that's me can I help you?" I replied stepping forward.

"Yes, you can. Sir you're a hard person to catch up with. My name is Marcus Hamilton, Esq. Attorney at Law. What I have here are some papers that require your signature. The first is the will of a Mr. Andrew Brown, within his accounts he held two million dollars, he owned his house, and two cars, all have been left to you. If you sign here this envelope containing the deed and titles is yours." He handed me the paperwork and the pen. I signed as quickly as I could.

"The second order of business is that the deceased also had a life insurance policy with you listed as the beneficiary. If you sign here this is an envelope containing a cashier's check for two million dollars. If you sign here our business will be concluded."

"Thanks old man, rest in peace." I thought to myself as I signed. I returned Mr. Hamilton's pen and he was off.

"Damn big baller, your dreams about to really come true," said Paris snatching the check.

"Naw Paris, my dreams started coming true the moment I walked out of jail." I smiled.

"Well I'm dreaming of a pizza, so let's go Midnight I'm hungry," said Paris. I thought to myself, *How she say she know that name?*

I couldn't believe that she said those words. Maybe she was having the same dreams as me. Remembering Doc, I wouldn't pry. If Allah wanted me to see her dreams he would have shown them to me. I then looked to the sky and said "ALLAH HU AKBAR!" (Allah is the greatest.)

To be continued . . . .

Order Form

MAKE ALL MONEY ORDERS PAYABLE TO:

FLOYD JACKSON
Co/					INTREPID
PUBLICATIONS
P.O. Box 573
Glendale, MD 20769

Name:_____A
ddress:_____
City:_____		State:_____
Zip:_____

Amount		Book Title or Pen Pal Number	Price
		Midnight In Paris $15.00	
		Included for shipping for 1 book	**$4 U.S. / $9 Inter**

5 or more books will be sold for $7.00. Please allow 7-14 Days for shipping. We do accept BOP & DOC Payments. You may also send an e-mail request to **intrepidpublications38@gmail.com.** **Or cashapp request to: $38records. Be sure to include title.**

Coming Soon – This title will be sold on Smashword!

This book can also be purchased on:
AMAZON.COM/ BARNES&NOBLE.COM/

Questions from the Author

1. Do you think Olivia is justified for treating Paris the way
   she did?
2. Did Paris have a right to be mad once she caught Olivia and Trey together?
3. Do you think there should be a Part 2?
4. Was Midnight wrong for having a dream like he did?
5. Do you think Paris was having the same dream that Midnight was having?
6. Did you see the character development within the book?
7. What do you think could have made this book better?

Thank you for reading this Novel. I truly hope you enjoyed it.

For answers to the questions or any other inquires you may have.

Please write to:
Intrepid Publication LLC.
c/o Eric Gardner 31997-007
P.O. Box 573
Glendale, MD 20769

313

A WAY WHEN THERES NO WAY.......

INTREPIDPUBLICATIONS A way when There's no way…
Email: IntrepidPublications38@gmail.com
C/O Eric Gardner
P.O. BOX 573
Glendale, MD 20769

MIDNIGHT IN PARIS

(In Stores)
If you enjoyed this book then you're going to love the other's.
Please grab my sophomore novel,

AMBROSIA HOUSE

(In Stores)

Available on Amazon, Barnes and Noble online, Ebook, and
Smashwords for your digital devices.

ALSO COMING SOON,

CLOSE ENEMIES PART 1
CLOSE ENEMIES PART 2
CLOSE ENEMIES PART 3:
THE REFLECTION OF A KILLER
DISHONORABLE JUSTICE
When the Legends Return
NKOSI vs. WAYNE PERRY
STUBENVILLE

For residents residing on the outskirts of Steubenville, Ohio the Steubenville Curse was more than just a man made myth . Unbeknownst to the towns people, the man made myth was alive, and believed to be the sole reason being countless murders and abductions this town has suffered over the past 45 years.

Since the year 1949, town's people believed that the spirit of Mary Ambrosia was haunting this town, due to the torment she was forced to endure as a child.

Mary Ambrosia was one of five bodies found inside Mary's house. Those bodies consisted of her father, her son, and Abby and Annie Rose Bridgedale. Although every murdered victim was never explained, towns people attributed the murder's to a racial of demonstrator's called KLU KLUX KLAN. As a whole this wasn't true.

Eleven years ago, Special Agent Sonya Peter's left Steubenville because of her sister falling to the abductions side of the curse. With her growing up in Steubenville, one could imagine the memories one would have her sister. Memories that tormented her. So much so, that she was forced to leave, or have a nervous breakdown. Therefore, she left, and then joined the FBI. Now after 11 years, she has returned to re-open her sister investigation. On arrival, she's hit with two more abductions and an attempt made on her life. Meaning, someone wanted her out of Steubenville, and was willing to kill for it.

If Sonya wanted to say alive and find closure to her sister's abduction, then she would need to find out the true history of the Ambrosia House Massacre.

Close Enemies 2
Shane's Revenge
By: Eric Gardner

The saga continues as Ric learns that the men he thought responsible for the ultimate death of his mother, Jalil and Tae, finds out that they weren't the cause of it after all. Along with understanding, he gains an enemy just as calculating and deadly as he is. Couple with his personal imbroglios, he becomes the interest of a Cartel leader from Ric killing his son. Another enemy added to a list already steep.

Shane, after doing so much time in prison, finally buries the hachette between he and Jalil. Yet subsequently it was untimely and Shane gets abducted by Papa and order to finish the business deal that Jalil started. With Shane's family lives in limbo, he had no choice but to comply.

Ervin Bond after coming home from doing 26 years, he's catapulted into a war to save Ric from the grips of death that Mink, a formidable adversary carried with him. Doing so, a target is placed on his head as well. With the countless enemies piling up, Ric is forced to rebuild his team and prepare to take on Papa and his massive reach, and the countless enemies vying to cease Ric's breathing.

Come with me on this ride of lies, deceit, and mayhem as I prepare you for,

Close Enemies 3: When Legends Return

Intrepid Publications
A way when There's no way...✓

Reflection of a Killer
By: Eric Gardner

My name is Marcus. Marcus Tidwell to be exact. This is my story of how corrupted the D.C. Government is. When I was twelve years old I was arrested for killing a man that was beating and raping my mother and who tried to kill me. Self-defense all day. But the D.C. Government, the same people who supposed to be protecting my rights tricked me into signing a plea deal. Had me thinking I was going home and ended up getting me juvenile life. Just took seven years of me like I was nothing. That was only the half.

Right now I'm currently serving a six year life sentence for some shit I didn't even do. Not to mention, the government sitting back and watching me go down. They say I even killed my own mother, which is a bold face lie. They just keep fucking every which way they can. It's cool though, because payback is a bitch, and I would have my revenge on that Child Advocate, that Lawyer, and that heartless ass Prosecutor, Michelle Jackson. I swear I'm gonna get my revenge.

By any means necessary!

I hope you enjoy the read because this is the last time you'll ever hear from me. Why? Simple!

Because I don't trust the motherfucking Government!

Sincerely yours,

Marcus Fucking Tidwell

INTREPID PUBLICATIONS
...A way when there's no way...

CLose Enemies Part I
By: Eric Gardner

They say money is the root of all evil. That cup could not have held more truth for this tale of lies, deceit, murder, and mayhem. This a story of how money can sever relationships once thought unbreakable.

Jalil was a brain, and a straight up money getter that would kill in an instant. With his mentor turning up dead, he gains aspirations to take over where he died. Consequently, some people felt he was undeserving of it.

Ric on the other hand, Jalil's right hand man. Since a child had always had dreams of being drug dealer. Attaining that status, accented by Jalil's imbroglios gave Ric aspirations of his own. Aspirations on the contrary to Jalil's.

Close Enemies is a tale of how your best friend can be your worse enemy. Ask yourself, who you think your Close Enemy is.

Intrepid Publications ...A way when there's no way....
PO box 573
Glendale, MD 20769
Email: Intrepidpublications38@gmail.com

QTY	TITLE	PRICE	TOTAL
1	CLOSE ENEMIES PART I BY:ERIC GARDNER	$12.99/ea	
1	MIDNIGHT IN PARIS BY: ERIC GARDNER	$12.99/ea	
1	AMBROSIA HOUSE BY: ERIC GARDNER	$12.99/ea	
	BOOKS IN THE RANGE OF 5 PLUS $7.00 PER BOOK		
	TAX	$1.15/ea	PER BOOK
	SHIPPING AND HANDLING	$4.00	EVERY 4
	TOTAL	$18.14	

Money order's accepted! Please make your money order's payable to Floyd Jackson attached with our current mailing address. Please allow 7-14 days for delivery. For inmates who wish to purchase a book from their FBOP computer we do except money gram. To do so please make the money gram payable to Floyd Jackson under the legal name first and last name portion in the right hand corner of the screen along with our mailing address. Once your email address has been approved please send us an email for your wish to purchase which title and to notify us when there is a money gram to be picked up. we are also available on Amazon, EBOOK, Smashwords.

ABOUT THE AUTHOR

Eric Gardner is currently incarcerated at the Yazoo Federal Correctional Facility on a 40-year sentence. Although he vehemently claims his innocence, he uses the power of his pen to escape the perils of incarceration. Since 2005, Gardner has penned 8 titles with Midnight in Paris as his debut. He has seven more titles complete and ready for the world. So when you see his name, know you will get al your money's worth. My next novel is called *Ambrosia House: The Origin of Bloody Mary.* A must read; I promise!

Made in the USA
Columbia, SC
04 February 2023

11246058R00174